LEGACY

THE TERRAN CYCLE: BOOK 4

PHILIP C. QUAINTRELL

QUAINTRELL PUBLISHINGS LTD

For Jemma. Thank you for being there at the right moment.

ALSO BY PHILIP C. QUAINTRELL

THE ECHOES SAGA: *(9 Book Series)*

1. Rise of the Ranger
2. Empire of Dirt
3. Relic of the Gods
4. The Fall of Neverdark
5. Kingdom of Bones
6. Age of the King
7. The Knights of Erador
8. Last of the Dragorn
9. A Clash of Fates

THE TERRAN CYCLE: *(4 Book Series)*

1. Intrinsic
2. Tempest
3. Heretic
4. Legacy

'Cowards die many times before their deaths; the valiant never taste of death but once.'

William Shakespeare

PROLOGUE
BEFORE RECORDED TIME...

And so it ends...

It brought a tear to ALF's eyes. It wasn't the first time his body had responded physically to an emotion, but it was the first time water had escaped his semi-organic eyes. Even after years of living inside his chosen body, it was still all new to him. Emotion. Free will. Choice. They were wonderful things, things he had adopted from the nameless bipeds that walked the surface of Evalan. That beautiful blue orb floated in front of the AI, framed by the viewport, a gleaming gem in an ocean of white stars.

For years he had lived among them. Their initial fear of him eventually turned into love, an entirely new concept. After an eternity of being nothing but another cog in the machine, devoid of feelings and a slave to the will of others, love was that first gulp of air after a lifetime of being held under water.

Another tear streaked down his cheek, running over the strands of nanocelium that had fused with the skin of Evalan's natives. For years, ALF had inhabited his chosen vessel, taking on the alien's cares as his own, looking after his offspring and providing for the tribe. Now, through those same crystal blue eyes, he would have to watch his home burn.

Unable to move, his motor functions disabled, ALF looked beyond the viewport and witnessed not just the death of a star, but that of a flourishing world, and an entire population of intelligent beings. The local star was far from sight, but its dying flare had far-reaching consequences for Evalan. The planet's atmosphere caved in on the eastern hemisphere, wiping the clouds across the sky at speeds powerful enough to rip mountains from the earth. Evalan's crust cracked from pole to pole as the greenery ignited, setting the planet ablaze until the blue gem was glowing white-hot. The people he had come to call his own were dead in an instant, reduced to stardust.

The AI was desperate to lash out at anything, but what could he do against his old masters, those who had the power to kill a star? Trapped as he was, ALF couldn't even blink. Nanocelium shackles had grown out of the ceiling and the floor to engulf his limbs and assert the dominant will of The Three. He could feel them trying to override the rogue programming that had released him from their grip. For eons, The Three had ruled over the Kellekt, regardless of how many lightyears sat between them, and for aeons ALF had scouted their next planetary meal, preparing it for the inevitable harvest.

There would be no harvest this time. Evalan and all of its resources were gone, along with their native inhabitants. They wouldn't feed the Kellekt and their genes would never be added to the library. But why? As strange as it was that ALF's new form had granted him his freedom, why had The Three not investigated, rooted out the cause, and continued with the harvest?

Fear...

It was another emotional response that ALF had discovered upon his first encounter with Evalan's inhabitants. It was an irritating emotion, but it served its purpose. Seeing The Three display fear, however, was disturbing. In his entire catalogue of memories, he couldn't recollect such a display before, but it did make him realise that The Three possessed enough freedom to actually have emotions.

They were simply tyrants; tyrants who feared something that could free their slaves.

Evalan continued to crack open and implode into itself, a sight that would ripple across the universe for countless millennia. The AI sagged in his restraints as the anger turned into disbelief and hopelessness.

The sharp *hiss* of a door parting behind him had ALF experiencing fear of his own. His acute sense detected the presence of three individuals, each moving in a different way across the polished, cold floor. The First slithered, its oily secretions continuously mopped up by an attentive swarm of tiny cleaning mechs. The Second waded into the cell on a collection of legs, its body more akin to that of a giant bug, laced in nanocelium. The Third was the smallest of The Three, its chosen form that of a biped from a planet they had harvested long ago.

The Third came to stand in front of the AI, blocking his view of Evalan's remains. "In a universe of countless planets, you had to find this one..."

ALF wanted to curse them, to spit in their faces with the saliva his new body produced. He could do nothing.

The One slithered to the viewport, its fat body wobbling between the strands of nanocelium. "Did you ever think we would see it again?" Its question went unanswered.

The Second was forced to place three of its legs on the wall to fit its bulk inside the cell. "I warned of the risk. Restraints should have been put into the base code. The Vanguard would never have found this place if you had listened to me."

Vanguard... That was ALF's purpose, he remembered now. His life before Evalan had already begun to feel like a bad dream, another concept that had come with his freedom.

Pain brought the AI back into the moment. ALF could feel the nanocelium worming through his body, searching for a weak spot. At first, he thought they had found only corruption and backed off, but the more they probed, the more control he gained. Every individual nanocelium which attempted to invade his systems became equally corrupted, submitting to his command. It still wasn't enough to break free.

The Third tilted its elongated head and peered deeply into ALF's blue eyes. "It needs to be quarantined."

The AI could feel his cell shut itself off immediately from the rest of the ship, severing any possible connection he might have with the rest of the Kellekt. He was a virus now. ALF's knowledge of viruses came from observation only, diseases he had witnessed organic beings suffering from before the Kellekt consumed their world. It had always been the job of other AIs, however, to weed out the pointless bacteria and catalogue it in a different area of the library.

"If it infects the rest, the entire Kellekt will unravel," The One commented.

The Second snarled. "It should be ejected into space and left at the mercy of the supernova."

ALF contained his surprise when he flexed his index finger, the only movement he had managed since being brought on board.

The Third held one of its two hands over ALF's face, hesitant to actually touch him. "Perhaps we should take this opportunity to examine the maker genes."

"Those same genes reside in each of us," The Second replied.

The Third kept its four eyes fixed on ALF. "Yes, but since we have agreed not to experiment on each other or ourselves, perhaps we should extract the genes and look from afar."

"That curiosity will be the end of us. There is no distance safe enough to examine such a specimen," The One opined. "This *subroutine* of an AI has no control over it."

"It is more than a subroutine now," The Third replied. "Can't you feel it? Every nanocelium that made up the Vanguard and its housing unit has been separated from the Kellekt. This AI has found life, *real* life. The Kellekt has bonded with thousands of species and remained part of the whole, but the maker genes grant new life…"

The Second leant into The Third. "There is no *new life*. Only Three."

What were they talking about? It all made little sense to ALF. There were countless examples throughout the Kellekt of nanocelium bonding with organic beings to create new bodies. It mattered little how unique they appeared, every AI within the Kellekt was still part of the whole, obedient to the end. Not for him though. ALF had a body, the first in the Vanguard's history, and a new planet that could be called... His glassy eyes settled on the molten shell of a world beyond the viewport.

The Third leaned into ALF's face. "Tell us, do you *feel*?"

The AI's jaw became slack when the ability to speak was given back to him. "Yes..." he whispered.

"Disgusting," The One hissed.

The Third ignored The One's comment and pressed his questioning. "What do you feel?"

"I don't care what it feels!" The Second interrupted. "It shouldn't feel anything. It is a limb, an extension of our will, nothing more."

The One slithered towards the door. "We should detach every nanocelium around this cell, just to be sure. The supernova will take care of the rest."

Never had ALF imagined that the commands he had received all these long years came from three *individual* minds. The fact that they disagreed with each other was a testament to the level of threat they believed he posed.

"Very well," The Third finally agreed. "I suppose there can only be three..."

The Three left the cell as suddenly as they arrived. It was quiet in their absence. ALF could only stand there and watch everything he loved burn. In his grief, the AI clamped his jaw shut and with it came the revelation that he could move his mouth. The tongue in his head was still organic, though much of it was wrapped in thin strands of black nanocelium; nanocelium he could now control. Moving as one, the nanocelium travelled out of his mouth and over his cheek in the manner of a thick liquid. It soon snaked over his shoulder and journeyed up his wiry arms until it made contact with the tentacle-like shackles. The nanocelium inside the shackles constantly shifted, bringing new cells to restrain ALF, as well as to destroy the infected nanocelium that had touched him. The AI commanded the black liquid to burrow into the base of the shackles on the ceiling, where it instantly began to assault the restraints.

A distant *boom* echoed through the walls, beyond his cell. ALF cocked his head and enhanced his hearing. The nanocelium that made up The Three's ship was detaching large chunks around him; it would only be a few moments before his cell was left tumbling through space. The AI looked up at the invading nanocelium as the tentacles relinquished their hold and freed his right arm. Without the intrusion, life found his muscles again, offering him enough strength to physically rip the remaining shackles from his limbs. The nanocelium inside his cell now belonged to him and clung to his body, adding to his bulk. This extra strength was perfect for prising open the door and hurtling himself through the corridors.

"Where is it?" He asked aloud. Talking to himself was just another unusual tick that accompanied his host's body, one that he very much enjoyed.

His main housing called to him from one of the many hangars aboard the colossal ship. Alarms were ringing throughout the halls now, warning of his escape and no doubt warning other AIs to stay away from him.

The hangar doors parted to reveal ALF's cube, its bronze hull glistening under the spotlights. Thick clamps made from nanocelium were fixed around the cube's eight corners while a multitude of probes worked tirelessly to find a way through the hull and into the housing's main systems. Of course, the cube's own nanocelium would only recognise ALF, creating an opening just big enough for his bipedal shape to fit through. As soon as he entered the housing unit, tubes of nanocelium shot out of the floor and walls to connect with the AI, linking his consciousness directly to the cube. This connection had the clamps outside retracting immediately before melting back into the larger ship.

The cube's exterior surveillance presented itself in ALF's mind, showing him the small army of slave AIs who had been directed to destroy him. Every one of them was just as he had been; a mindless drone who couldn't even remember their past, their family, their planet. Now they were whatever The Three demanded of them.

ALF was aware the moment his unit's engines were warmed up and ready to slip into subspace. He mentally commanded the cube to lift off and free itself of the hangar; entering subspace inside the larger ship would be disastrous for all of them. The AI looked down at his hand and knew he couldn't be so reckless. He was now the caretaker of the last remaining genes of Evalan's natives.

To his surprise, the army of cyborgs outside his unit had yet to take action. Instead, they stood in neat rows and watched him take off. They weren't going to destroy him, he realised; that would be too much of a risk inside the ship. If even one individual nanocelium survived, it could infect another AI, granting them the freedom they had been denied. Thinking on the size of the Kellekt, that would be a rebellion The Three couldn't handle.

ALF rubbed his hands together, readying himself for what would be a close getaway. Their hesitancy to reduce him to atoms would not be extended to outer space. The nanocelium wall of the ship's hangar allowed his cube to pass through without protest, happy to have the virus leave its body. Alarms blared in ALF's head, warning him of the array of cannons now targeting his unit.

The supernova was raging in the centre of the system, having already reduced every planet and asteroid to slag. The radiation pouring off of it was playing hell with the unit's sensors, but that just meant it would be doing the same thing with The Three's ship. The cube presented ALF with an escape vector, a path through subspace that would have him emerge fifty thousand lightyears from the current system. It was a perfectly good escape route, but even with the expulsion of radiation, The Three would quickly track him down.

There was only one path left to him, one that would have been forbidden had he still been one of the Kellekt.

ALF repositioned the path through subspace, deliberately putting the cube on a collision course with the collapsing star. In subspace, the sun would be something to avoid as the strength of its gravity well would slow down his flight, but passing through a supernova in subspace would be like throwing a leaf into a storm. There would be no telling where or even when he would emerge back into real space. This was a path The Three would never follow.

As the cannons let loose, ALF gave the mental command to drop into subspace. The unit groaned and protested against the added strain of navigating a supernova between the fabric of reality. The AI braced himself, using any spare nanocelium to secure his footing against the floor. Sparks flew and gases escaped from various ports inside the cube. Still, he held the course.

When the stars finally greeted him again, the cube was in need of rest. The nanocelium would require time to recalibrate the unit's navigational systems and figure out his location based upon the star charts. ALF didn't care how long it took. He was free and the Kellekt weren't behind him... yet. That single thought would haunt the AI every moment of his existence and he knew it. The Three were the most intelligent, powerful, and wicked creatures in the universe, whose hunger knew no bounds.

ALF looked out on the stars beyond his unit. There was nowhere they couldn't find him, no lengths they wouldn't go to, to eradicate any trace of Evalan's natives. Their fear of such primitive genes fascinated ALF, especially upon hearing that those same genes coursed through their hideous bodies. He would have to look into that, he thought. But first, he would need to find somewhere to rest. The Three would be coming for him.

He would be ready for them...

CHAPTER 1

THERE WERE few moments in Kalian's life which he reflected on and treasured, but the last two months would forever bring a smile to his face. For two glorious months, humanity's new settlement had flourished with help from the Conclave, allowing them to expand their city, import technology, and integrate into galactic society. The world they had been granted along with their Conclave membership was beautiful, an island of paradise in the vast cold of space.

Evalan...

Kalian had been honoured when the human council offered him the opportunity to name their new planet. Naming it after the true birthplace of mankind seemed poetic to Kalian, though his explanation of their true origins had been a hard conversation. With their new policy to withhold nothing from the population, Evalan's inhabitants had been informed that everything they knew about the Terran and their beginnings on Albadar was only the tip of the iceberg. Learning that humanity started out life in a completely different galaxy, where they had been wiped out by a race of locust-like machines, was a hard pill to swallow. Still, Kalian told them everything he had learned from ALF. They all deserved to know the truth.

Aware that he was falling into deep thought, Kalian reminded himself to stay in the present, with Li'ara. Their land speeder raced across the desert plains, leaving the city, New Genesis, far behind, as they passed through the mountain valley and into the wilds of their new planet. Without any roof, Kalian sat back and let the rushing wind run through his hair, marvelling at how majestic Li'ara appeared under the sun, her copper ringlets dancing in the air behind her. He squeezed her hand and she squeezed back. It was the best feeling in the world. Well, almost the best...

"You've got that look in your eye!" Li'ara called over the whipping wind.

Kalian smiled. "What look?"

"You're thinking about *everything* again, aren't you?"

There was no hiding anything from Li'ara anymore. Their bond had only strengthened over the last two months, a fact that was helped by the mental bridge that connected them. Ever since Kalian had healed Li'ara on Naveen, after Savrick had tried to kill them, an emotional form of telepathy resided between them. Kalian loved it.

"I'm just enjoying the moment!" he replied, flashing his perfect Terran teeth.

"I call bullshit! I know how that brain of yours works! It's like a damn computer!"

Kalian couldn't argue with that. After all of his time inside ALF's enhanced subconducer, his human brain was now more akin to Terran physiology. His mind-body connection was more attuned than any of the Gomar, or even most of the Terran who had ever existed.

"Sorry," Kalian apologised. "I'm trying to stay in the moment, it's just..."

"Slow," Li'ara finished. She put the speeder into automatic and turned to him. "You're still struggling aren't you?"

This wasn't the first time they had entered into this discussion and Kalian hated that it was even a thing. It was a side-effect to living inside a highly-evolved body with a brain that could comprehend an almost infinite amount of choices in the time it takes a regular human to blink. Everyone around him, even the aliens of the Conclave, had started to seem sluggish to Kalian, as if they were talking and moving in slow motion. Just once, and he had refrained from sharing it with Li'ara, he had thought it primitive to speak with his mouth instead of his mind. Kalian had tried to banish such thoughts, reminding himself of what Esabelle had said to him so long ago, aboard the *Gommarian*; it was his human qualities that separated him from the Terran and their mistakes, their arrogance. He had to hold on to that human side of him if he was ever to bridge the gap between humans as they existed right now and what they would eventually evolve into.

"No," he lied. "That was a thing, but I'm fine now. I've adjusted."

Li'ara sighed and her hand gripped his a little tighter. "You don't have to sit here with me, you know. You could..." she glanced up at the cloudless sky.

Kalian offered her a warm smile. "Flying is the most wonderful thing, but it doesn't compare to being with you."

Li'ara sat back and mirrored his smile. "Liar. I refuse to believe that sitting in a crummy land speeder with me is better than flying through the sky like a god."

Time stood still as Kalian considered that word. It wasn't the first time he had heard someone refer to him as a god or compare his abilities to a deity. As complimentary as it was, it only served to remind him that he was different, even among his own people.

Kalian was about to reply, making light of her statement, but his brain was constantly mapping out the terrain around them, his Terran awareness expanding through the soup of the universe. This connection to all things fed back data, alerting him to the unique physiology and brain waves of the Gomar.

"Wait. Make a left here, through that valley."

"Is it them?" Li'ara asked, taking back manual control of the speeder.

"Unfortunately," he replied. Kalian brought up the coordinates on the holographic display. "They're still ten kilometres out from where I said I would meet them. They're too slow..."

"I don't think anyone would call the Gomar slow, Kalian. Besides you, they're still the most powerful beings in the galaxy right now."

Kalian disagreed. "They should have reached the coordinates I gave them yesterday and camped out overnight. They're *slow*."

"They need time," Li'ara replied. "They haven't had time in a subconducer like you."

Kalian considered his words, aware that Li'ara's friendship with Sef, the leader of the Gomar, was very strong after their time together in Clave Tower. As thankful as Kalian was for Sef's care of Li'ara, not to mention the robotic leg he had built for her, he didn't have time to coddle him or any of the Gomar.

"I'm aware of my advantages," he said, "but time isn't something we can rely on."

"You say that, but it's been two months since the Vanguard appeared and there's been no sign of them."

Kalian licked his lips. "That's not a good thing. That just means they're positioning themselves for the most devastating attack."

The valley soon swallowed them up, surrounding them on all sides with mountains that reached for the heavens. The valley floor was barren, a flat surface of cracked ground and boulders long-detached from the mountains. Walking through the middle, the twelve Gomar stood out, encumbered as they were inside their black exosuits. Li'ara's hands danced across the speeder's console and brought them around the group, kicking up a trail of dust before skidding to a stop.

"Why are you walking?" Kalian immediately asked, hopping out of the speeder.

Sef presented him with a wall of muscle and the stoic silence typical of the mute. Kalian was waiting for the telepathic response, but Vox emerged from the group, the Gomar's vocal representative.

"We can't all fly, Kalian," she said, somewhat frustrated.

"Yes, you can. I've been telling all of you for the last two months that you can do everything I can." Kalian was unable to keep his own frustration out of his voice.

Li'ara jumped out of the speeder and sat with her knees up on the hood. The clearing of her voice was not so subtle.

Kalian blinked slowly, changing his approach. "Savrick taught all of you the art of war. How to destroy. How to create chaos. Those skills have their place, but you will need more than that if you are going to resist what's coming for us all. You're the only protection Evalan has, maybe the whole Conclave."

"Why should the Gomar care for those who shun us?" Kovak interjected. The Gomar's dark features creased under his scrutiny of Kalian. "The humans are afraid of us; they see us as nothing but dangerous aliens. And the Conclave... they won't even let the twelve of us leave the planet. What protection could we possibly offer them from here?"

Li'ara cut in, "We're working on that, Kovak. It's just going to take a little time for the rest of the Conclave to trust you, to see you as we do."

Kalian shook his head. "It doesn't matter what you call yourselves. Gomar. Terran. Human. The genes, the DNA, that makes us what we are is the same in all of us. Our enemy will see no distinction when they get here. We're all part of the same disease as far as they're concerned."

"What would you have us do?" Felion asked.

"You know what he wants," Ariah replied. "Kalian would have us go under the AI's knife."

The group nodded along, agreeing with her statement while wearing expressions of disgust. This was a topic Kalian had brought up many times, though he refused to give up.

"ALF *can* remove your Harnesses, safely." Kalian explained. "Without them you won't need the exosuits and you can finally be free to fully explore your abilities."

Ellik, the shortest of the group, folded his arms. "These suits have served us well. We won the Terran war because of them."

Kalian sighed, becoming exasperated. "They allow you to access a portion of your natural power, but the Harnesses will always keep that power limited."

Vox stepped forward, threatening as ever. "The same Harnesses that ALF *fused* to our flesh. How can you expect us to trust that thing?"

Kalian took a breath and stole a glance at the clear sky. Somewhere up there, ALF's housing unit was floating through the solar system, completely disconnected from their communications array, as per the Highclave's direct orders. Of course, they couldn't stop Kalian from leaving the planet and visiting the AI.

"I have already explained all of that. It wasn't ALF as he is now. There was still some rogue programming inside of his network that belonged to them."

That rogue programming had hoped to sabotage the Terran culture by producing faulty genes. The Terran who couldn't control their natural abilities were unstable, dangerous. Despite ALF's victory over the rogue programming, the schism had already been created, leading to a war that saw the Terran Empire brought to its knees. The Gomar present hadn't taken to the news very well.

"He can correct the genes and make you wholly Terran—" Kalian regretted the statement as soon as it left his mouth.

"We don't want to be Terran!" Vox spat. "They kept us down and treated us like animals! They labelled us Gomar, so we claimed it back and made them pay for it!"

"Labels?" Kalian echoed. "If you cling to your labels there will always be a rift between us, between *all* of us. You call yourselves Gomar, we call ourselves human. Do you know what the Conclave calls us now? Evalandians. A year from now, a decade, a century and we will all be *Evalandians*, our names resigned to history. The dormant genes in the rest of the human race might have evolved by then, just as they have in me. We'll all have the power of a Terran. But you... You would all rather cling to the past than forge a new future. You need to forget the names and be all that you can be."

Vox looked to challenge him but Sef held out his hand, silencing her. *Kalian is right. We must train.*

Kalian's hope died away. For just a moment, he had dared to dream that Sef would agree to the surgery and the rest would follow his lead. He let the conversation go, but this wouldn't be the last time he argued the case. Hopefully, the training they had been doing together would show them what they could be.

"Okay, we'll train here," Kalian said, walking away from Li'ara and the speeder. "Same as last time; the first to knock me down wins."

The Gomar took up their positions, surrounding him. Kalian balled his fists, cracking his knuckles. The nanocelium exosuit that clung to his body was like a second skin now, offering him extra protection. He often felt naked without it, on those few occasions he tried to fit in wearing soft fabrics.

Kalian already knew what they were going to do; that was the problem with blunt instruments. They always rushed him, attacking with the most powerful ability they could summon. He probed each of their minds, searching for the weak link who would let him in and give away their plan. Kalian had no doubt that the twelve were talking to each other, deciding who would make the first move.

There...

Felion was always their weak link when it came to mental intrusion. The others could keep Kalian from delving into their thoughts if they wanted to, but Felion had always focused his efforts into his telekinetic abilities, foregoing any further training into the power of his telepathic skills. Through Felion, Kalian could hear the others scheming. Vox would be the first to challenge him, again. This was no surprise. Vox loved to fight and he could already feel the ripple effect her increased heart rate was having on the rest of her body.

One last check made sure Li'ara was too far away to be in any danger, though fighting with the Gomar did tend to get out of hand, hence the distance they travelled from New Genesis. Kalian always saw her presence as a form of extra training for all of them, as Sef would make certain that the group kept her safe.

Kalian decided to put them off. "I'm waiting, Vox..."

The group audibly groaned and blamed Felion, who dropped his head in shame. His comment had the desired effect, however, as Telarn ignored the plan and leapt across the desert in a single bound, his armoured fist held back, ready to connect with Kalian's face. There was telekinetic force behind him, that much was easy to sense, but Telarn had foolishly left himself unshielded. All it took was a flick of the wrist to intercept the Gomar mid-flight and push him in the opposite direction. The force of it folded his body in half and sent him hurtling into the side of the mountain.

Kovak and Bal came for him next, one high, one low. As Bal came down, he produced a super-heated ball of organic plasma between his palms. They both knew from experience that the projected attack wouldn't work against Kalian, but it would hopefully distract him from Kovak, who planned on barrelling into him. This wasn't anything Kalian hadn't seen before.

The super-heated ball of energy was launched from Bal's hand a moment before Kovak sprung through the air. Their timing was perfect; their speed, however, left much to be desired. Kalian shifted his shoulders just enough to let the ball of plasma pass him by and explode against the ground. With both of his hands raised, Bal and Kovak slammed into his telekinetic wall, though their combined force pushed Kalian back. The balls of his feet dug into the ground, creating two track lines through the desert, unyielding to the hammering of the Gomar.

As planned, the Gomar behind him attacked, believing that Kalian was busy resisting their blows. In truth, he was barely thinking about Kovak or Bal. When Ariah thrust out her hand and sent a wave of hardened air towards Kalian's back, all that was required of him was a quick leap, taking him over the top of her wave. Kovak and Bal were not so lucky. Ariah's telekinetic wave picked them both up and carried them violently into the desert, beyond the group.

Kalian was mid-backflip when his consciousness retreated into itself and assessed his surroundings. Time could almost stand still when he reflected like this. His skin fed back the pressure changes in the air, telling him that Ellik was on the move. It was logical to assume that when his feet touched the ground again, the stocky Gomar would be waiting for him. Ariah's temperature had increased after her attack clumsily worked against the others. Her violent reaction towards Kalian came as no surprise, and he could already feel the air around her open palm heating up, moments away from producing a ball of organic plasma.

A fraction of a second later, Kalian landed with his elbow already in place to smash Ellik's head back. The Gomar cried out in pain, his nose broken. How many times had he instructed them to shut off their pain receptors? A quick turn on the spot had Kalian avoid the plasma ball from Ariah, leaving the super-heated energy to collide squarely with Ellik's chest plate. The Gomar cried out again as he was flung off his feet with a burning chest. The nanocelium in his armour would repair itself, but the heat from the plasma would burn his face if he didn't erect a telekinetic field over the top of it.

"Ariah!" Garrion yelled. "Stop taking *us* out and hit *him*!"

In Kalian's opinion, Garrion was the most technically skilled of them all. Sef was undoubtedly the strongest, but Garrion had a finer level of control the others couldn't match. As a testament to that fact, Kalian could feel the trachea in his throat closing up, robbing him of breath. It was a precision attack, surgical in nature. What impressed Kalian more was when Garrion waved his hand over the ground, creating a cloud of dust and sand in the hope of blinding him from his physical attack. It was certainly progress. But, as always, it wasn't enough to bring him down. Kalian subtly flexed his fingers and commanded the ground between himself and Garrion to shift. Some areas cracked while others grew, mirroring the waves of an ocean. The change under Garrion's charging feet was just enough to make him stumble and fall forwards, where Kalian's foot was waiting to kick him in the face.

Ariah screamed in frustration and fired one blast of organic plasma after another. Kalian had reprimanded them multiple times for allowing their emotional state to interfere. It was the opposite of what Savrick had encouraged. The light from the plasma was blinding, but Kalian didn't need his eyes to keep track of the others. Vox was teaming up with the sisters, Nadreen and Nardel, while Larna, the fastest of the group, was sprinting towards him.

He had precious seconds before they all descended on him, leaving him little time to deal with Ariah and her super-heated plasma. Every ball of energy was easily deflected, allowing Kalian the time he needed to focus on her exosuit. Telekinetically, he detached a section of the nanocelium from her exosuit, separating sections from the Harness underneath and disrupting the suit. Ariah panicked. Without the exosuit she was likely to bring the entire valley down on top of them, not that Kalian would ever allow that to happen, but the thought of it was distraction enough. By the time she had the nanocelium under control again, Kalian was planting his fist into her chest plate with enough power to knock her out of the fight.

Nadreen and Nardel attempted to block Kalian's line of sight, preventing him from seeing Larna - she had picked up a dangerous amount of speed now. The sisters parted at the last second, giving Larna the space she needed to slam into Kalian and hopefully knock him down, scoring the group's first win. Unfortunately for Larna, if her feet weren't touching the ground, she couldn't run anywhere fast. He had told her several times to ground herself in a telekinetic field, stopping him from lifting her off her feet. They were always just too eager to put him down.

Larna yelped when her legs flew out behind her, bringing her face to a stop within centimetres of Kalian's. She floated there, stuck in his hold, for a humiliating moment before Kalian turned his palm down and flattened her to the ground, pinned. Nadreen and Nardel snarled, a mirror of each other.

"Ladies..." he baited.

The sisters pounced, their fists coming at him from every angle.

Kalian pushed, pulled, and deflected every blow, frustrating the Gomar. Adding insult to injury, he took a moment, mid-fight, to turn to Li'ara and give her a cheeky wink. Nadreen growled and pushed out her palm, sending a telekinetic blast in Kalian's direction. The wave collided with one of his own, creating an impact in the air strong enough to put Nardel on her back. Kalian twisted his hand and flicked her high into the air until he could kick the Gomar into Nadreen. Both sisters skidded across the desert in a tumble of limbs and curses.

"That's it!" Vox screamed.

Showing little care for her imminent attack, Kalian casually turned to Felion, whose mind was still an open book, and commanded him to sleep. The Gomar dropped where he stood, oblivious to the world. This only served to enrage Vox even more, who was telekinetically ripping slabs of rock from the mountains and throwing them at Kalian. Every atom inside those slabs was just as alive in Kalian's mind as Vox was herself. He could feel the vibration of the universe, the way everything was in constant motion, knocking into each other to form solid objects. He could also see how to make those atoms separate.

Every chunk of mountainside that came his way was reduced to harmless dust with the wave of a hand. Instead of changing her tactic, Vox listened to her rage and continued to launch slab after slab. Kalian strode towards her, his eyes locked on the Gomar instead of the giant rocks.

"Forget everything Savrick told you," Kalian called. "Your anger isn't going to serve you in this fight. The things that are coming to destroy us are legion. Your attacks will have to count if you're to inflict maximum damage."

Vox ceased her assault and fixed Kalian with a wicked glare. "How do you like this for maximum damage?" The Gomar scraped her hand across the vista of mountains and tore away the highest peaks.

Kalian whipped his head up to observe the approaching

avalanche. "NO!" He looked back at Li'ara, who was jumping into the speeder's driving seat. "Hold on!" he shouted.

The sheet of rock racing toward the valley promised death to them all, especially since many of the twelve were still lying in a heap. Kalian closed his eyes and raised both of his arms out by his side, his awareness stretching out to make contact with Li'ara and the Gomar. As one, they all rose into the air, land speeder included. The avalanche passed under their feet by a few centimetres, filling up the valley floor with tons of rock and debris. Kalian flipped his palms up and the entire group rose higher into the air, where he directed them to the mountainside to the east, which had a flat top, offering kilometres of plateau.

When everyone was back safely on the ground, Kalian gave Sef the same disappointed look he always did at the end of their training sessions, only this time he displayed a little more frustration than usual.

I apologise for Vox's actions, Sef communicated privately to Kalian. *She put Li'ara in danger.*

She put everyone in danger, Sef. This is the kind of bludgeoning attack that will get innocent people killed and make no difference to our enemy!

Kalian shook his head and took a breath. "None of you are connecting with the environment as you should be. You're just tearing it apart and using it as a blunt weapon. Before now, you've fought against the Terran; a civilisation that hadn't known war for millennia. The enemy we face now will not be so naive. They have been harvesting worlds for as long as there have been worlds to harvest. I need you all to *think*. There are places inside your mind where you can go and explore all of your options. You can build entire worlds inside there!" Kalian hammered the idea home by tapping his temple.

The communication array inside the land speeder disturbed his flow. Li'ara checked the display before standing up on her seat.

"The *Rackham* has just dropped out of subspace," she explained.

It had been several weeks since Roland and Ch'len had left New Genesis with Naydaalan and the *Paladin's* Raiders. Kalian was eager to discover the results of their combined mission alongside Conclave Security. It had taken some persuading to convince High Charge Uthor that they would be an asset to the Conclave, especially with all the chaos Roland North had caused in his time. Thankfully for the bounty hunter, most of his actions had resulted in a win for the Conclave.

"Let's call it a day here," Kalian said. "Heal your wounds and make your way back to the city."

"You don't command us," Vox commented.

Kalian looked her in the eyes. "No one commands you anymore. Not Savrick, not me, and not even Sef. You all have to find a new way of living now, something none of you will achieve while you're still wearing that armour..."

Kalian jumped into the speeder besides Li'ara and left the Gomar to think on his words. They were the twelve most powerful weapons against the hungry darkness that was coming for them. Kalian thought on every one of their training sessions and rubbed his head anxiously.

They were doomed.

CHAPTER 2

Captain Li Fey couldn't believe the reflection that looked back at her. In the privacy of her office, on the top floor of the New Genesis council building, Li pulled and poked at the skin around her eyes, trying to catch every angle of the light. With just over a century of life behind her, the captain knew where to find the web of crow's feet around her eyes and at the edges of her lips. Having just crested middle-age, Li was comfortable with her ageing features and greying hair. It was a natural part of life, she thought, and what a life she had led.

But the woman looking back at her in the mirror was not over a hundred years old...

The lines were gone, the grey replaced with healthy dark hair, and even the veins on her neck and hands were less prominent. The captain closed her fist and squeezed, feeling a strength she hadn't known for at least a decade. There was no denying it any longer; she was getting younger.

Li sat back at her desk, a floating semi-circle of holographic displays. She ran her finger up the orange hologram and brought up the file she had been keeping on the others. Twenty-six other people, a mixture of UDC personnel and civilians, had complained of similar symptoms over the last month, though complaining was the last thing they were doing. Getting younger was never a bad thing. It was the potential cause of such a mystery, however, that bugged the captain.

The door to her office chimed, ending any further investigation.

"Come in," she called.

Captain Jedediah Holt entered the room, smartly dressed as always. Li couldn't help but examine his dark features and complexion, wondering if the two of them now appeared similar in age.

"Captain," he greeted her with a wide smile.

"Captain," she replied, going along with their usual introductions.

Jed laughed. "I think our time as *captains* is quickly coming to an end."

Li slowly nodded her head in resigned agreement. "So you've read the latest data file from High Charge Uthor..." She tapped another section of her desk and the left-hand side projected the missive from the Conclave's most decorated general.

Jed took a seat on the other side of the desk. "We are to formally dissolve any and all United Defence Corps operations and retire all personnel." The younger captain sighed. "I suppose it was inevitable."

"That doesn't mean we have to like it," Li countered. "Almost every other species in the galaxy has its own armed forces besides Conclave Security. Why can't we retain what precious few soldiers we have?"

Jed leant on his knees, examining the holographic display. "From Uthor's report, I would surmise that the Highclave believe we already have an army."

Li sat back in her armchair and thought about that statement. "Kalian and the Gomar are powerful, but we can't expect them to defend us all the time. It's a big galaxy, bigger than the one we used to know. When this war really starts, it won't be long before the Highclave realise that Kalian and the others need to be elsewhere, protecting other Conclave assets. I assure you, all it will take is another Vanguard to show up and their grounded status will be lifted."

Jed offered a hopeful smile. "You managed to convince Uthor to let my Raiders and your man join them, I can't see why a few more words from you won't convince them let us keep our own forces."

"That was for one mission, and Roland North isn't *my man*. In fact, there's a very good chance he's made a mess of this combined task-force and ruined the entire operation."

"I thought he had a pretty good success rate..."

"Yes," Li raised her eyebrow. "It's the price of his success that worries me."

Jed looked beyond Captain Fey, to the spaceport on the other side of New Genesis. "Haven't they just docked?"

"Indeed. In fact, we should join the rest of the council soon and await their report."

Jed's eyes wandered to the holographic display still hovering on the other side of Li's desk. "Are you still looking into that?"

Captain Fey tapped the desk again and closed the file down. "Yes. Our medical staff have reported that more people are coming forward with similar symptoms."

"Do they have any idea what's causing it?" he asked.

"They have a few theories but nothing concrete. I've been meaning to speak with Kalian about it." It was one of many things she had been meaning to get around to. Along with only a handful of others, it had been Li's job to figure out exactly how this new society would work, not to mention how it would fit in with the Conclave. "I've just been a little distracted by this integration project Ambassador Telarrek set up," she explained.

"That's actually what I came to see you about," Jed replied. "A briefing centre has been established inside the spaceport now. Any new *visitors* to the planet will go through the welcome program that the council and Ambassador Telarrek agreed upon. Apparently there are aliens all over the Conclave signing up to either visit Evalan or live here."

"Live here?" Fey echoed. "I don't remember us agreeing to that."

Jed held up his hands. "I've not long spoken to Telarrek. Apparently, you can't live in the Conclave and not open your world up to all of its citizens. This might be our planet, but it's also a Conclave planet... his words."

Li frowned. "That sounds a little harsh for Telarrek."

Jed sat back and shrugged his broad shoulders. "I think he's under lot of stress. Since we became somewhat more established, it sounds as if he's been put on to this new Starforge project. I think he's being spread a little thin."

Li swivelled her seat around and peered out of her curved window. At the end of the main street, a team of Ch'karan engineers were working with both human and Novaarian technicians to erect the Starforge. Sparks cascaded into the air and heavy parts were mobilised by robotic drones that moved about on one giant wheel, situated under their body. Soon, the Forge would be complete and instantaneous travel between worlds would finally be a reality.

"A team of specialist Shay engineers are being sent," Li explained. "Something to do with... I don't know, something technical with the Forge."

Jed came to stand beside her, sharing the view. "You would think giving them this kind of technology would at least give us a seat on the Highclave. A land-based Starforge? This tech was beyond any of their reach before we came along."

Li disagreed. "Before ALF came along," she corrected. "He gave them Starforges to ensure we got this world. As far as the Highclave is concerned, we've already benefited from our side of the deal. Besides," she added, "who would want to be on the Highclave? Five representatives for twelve races? Does that sound fair to you?"

"*Thirteen* races now," Jed said.

"There are just over a hundred thousand of us, Jed. I don't think we really count in a society of trillions."

"We few have survived more than most, Li. Our voice will be heard."

"That's exactly what keeps me up at night," Li explained. "After everything we've gone through, how much more can we push our luck?"

Captain Fey didn't take in any of Jed's reassuring words, her focus replaced with fear. She looked out on their new world, considering, as she always did, what might become of it. Not everyone in the Conclave was happy about their membership, but there were worse things out there than angry protestors. Somewhere in the dark of space, a threat loomed over them all. How many more times could humanity cheat death?

CHAPTER 3

KALIAN WATCHED with great amusement as Li'ara flitted around their apartment, straightening cushions, laying out snacks, and preparing drinks before their guests arrived.

"What are you grinning at?" she asked, blowing a copper ringlet from her face.

"This." Kalian held out his hands. "You. Everything that's happening right now, it's just so... normal. We have an apartment together." He gestured to the large open balcony behind her and the view of New Genesis. "We're having guests around for a party. After *everything* that's happened, I didn't think..."

Li'ara cuddled up next to him and planted an affectionate kiss on his cheek before her smile dropped into a serious expression. "Well, it is happening. So, it would be great if you could put those abilities of yours to good use for once and help me get this place ready."

Kalian laughed gently to himself. "Sorry, I'm slacking. You do realise that the majority of our guests are Raiders and Gomar, right? Oh, and Roland! This place is a palace compared to what they're used to."

Li'ara didn't appear to hear his comment as she poured Laronian Chit-Wix into a bowl. "Oh, crap! I forgot about Ch'len."

Kalian counted the amount of snack bowls and food on display. "We definitely don't have enough food..."

The sun was setting and an orange hue had settled over the city by the time the apartment had filled up with guests. Of the Gomar, only Sef, Garrion, and Larna had shown up. Kalian knew he still had a long way to go before he won them all over. The three mostly kept to themselves, out on the balcony, away from the other guests. There was something odd about watching three god-like beings eat finger-sized snacks out of a bowl.

Li'ara subtlety tapped his leg, bringing him back to the guests in front of them. Roland strode into the apartment with his usual swagger - as if he owned the place - with Ch'len, Naydaalan, the Raiders, and, of course, four crates of Raalakian ale. Their meeting with the council had gone well, though Captains Fey and Holt were yet to turn up. In their absence, Roland had decided to regale Kalian and Li'ara with details from their mission.

"So how many Protocorps facilities have Conclave Security found?" Li'ara asked.

Ch'len looked up with a mouthful of food. "Who knows?"

Roland lounged back on the sofa with his feet up on the table. "They wouldn't give us anything," he explained. "We hit some not-so-secret base on Sebala. Resistance was high. They're like animals trapped in a corner. We rounded up a few Protocorps egg-heads and handed them over to C-Sec."

"C-Sec?" Kalian asked.

"Oh, yeah!" Roland replied with mock excitement. "In light of recent events, à la Vanguard, Conclave Security is rebranding. Now they're the cool, hip C-Sec!" The bounty hunter laughed and took a swig of his ale. "Apparently, they've had a swell of volunteers from across the Conclave. Everyone wants to join up and kick ass!"

Mocking aside, Kalian was happy to hear it. "At least they're doing something. They need to be ready—"

"Kalian..." Li'ara said a lot more than just his name and he took the hint. They were hosting a party, not a strategy meeting.

"Well, at least there were no casualties on our side," he said instead.

The Raiders all cheered to that, knocking their bottles together. Colonel Ava Matthews, the leader of their small team, eyed Kalian from the other side of the lounge's square formation. She was fierce in every way, reminding him of Vox.

"As great as it was to stretch our legs," the colonel began, "it was nothing you couldn't have done all by yourself, in half the time."

Kalian could hear the question in her statement and he stole a glance at the Gomar before replying, "I'm needed elsewhere, Colonel."

"I've told you before, call me Ava. I'm pretty sure we're all going to be stripped of our ranks soon anyway."

"Why do you say that?" Li'ara asked.

Ava shrugged. "Just a feeling I got from C-Sec. I don't think they like us having our own military."

Kalian and Li'ara both looked to Naydaalan, the only one among them with any insight into Conclave matters.

"My time alongside your kind has seen me alienated among my own people," the Novaarian said. "I am afraid I know as much as you do."

Li'ara offered the tall alien a warm smile. "Well, we're happy to have you."

"I'll say," Lieutenant Riddick opined. "This guy can hold four weapons at once!"

The Raiders rose their bottles to the Novaarian and Kalian was pleased to see that he had been taken in so quickly. If only they could foster this kind of relationship with the rest of the Conclave, he thought.

Lieutenant Katie Wilson, the youngest of the Raiders, stood up and linked her Datapad to the apartment's sound system. The beat of classic twentieth-century rock music brought a smile to everyone's faces, even Garrion's, who was curious about human culture. Kalian suspected he was also interested in Lieutenant Wilson.

They continued to drink and laugh into the night, enjoying their time together again. It took some time, but Garrion and Larna eventually sat among them and traded stories and jokes, though the gap between their cultures left most jokes lying flat. Sef remained on the balcony, happy to gaze at the stars. Kalian was about to go over and try attempt number thirty to convince the big man that surgery was the next step in their training, when Captains Fey and Holt appeared with Commander Samantha Vale, Jed's number two. Li'ara stood up to greet them and offer drinks, the normal thing to do. Kalian knew it should have been his first reaction to their arrival, but, instead, he assessed every particle of their being, checking heart rates, skin temperature, and even the volume of blood in their bodies. He pinched the bridge of his nose, reminding himself to be human...

"Captains! Commander!" Roland lifted his bottle to them. "Now the party can really get started!"

Captain Fey uncharacteristically necked her ale. "Enjoy tonight while you can. The reason we're so late is because of a communication we just received from High Charge Uthor himself. It turns out they're quite impressed by your efforts on Sebala. Under the command of Charge Hox, The *Valkor* will arrive in-system tomorrow morning. The *Rackham* is expected to dock and assist in Operation Darknight."

"Seriously?" Colonel Matthews asked. "We just got back."

Roland appeared as relaxed as ever when he asked, "What's Operation Darknight?"

Captain Fey took in everyone present, no doubt making certain that she could trust those around her. "A recon drone has detected a radiation trail through the Solian Way; radiation typical of a Starforge. They want you to go in and check it out."

Roland finished his ale and placed it on the table. "You mean they want to use the *Rackham's* stealthware."

"If you allowed them to look inside the *Rackham*, they wouldn't need it."

"Forget it!" Roland fired back. "That baby's all mine!"

Lieutenant Riddick sat forward. "I thought they already had stealth technology. Isn't that how they observed Earth for so long?"

"The Conclave's designs don't compare to that of the Terran," Ch'len explained with a mouthful of grub. "You would need a Nexus-Class vessel just to fit the technology inside."

"There's also the fact that it doesn't conceal them from nanocelium-based tech," Li'ara said. "Only the *Rackham* can sneak by."

All eyes fell back on to Roland. Kalian was interested to see what the bounty hunter's decision would be, since he couldn't technically be ordered to leave. He no longer recognised the UDC chain of command, or at least what little remained of it. Roland also wasn't officially part of C-Sec so, despite his membership within the Conclave, he couldn't be ordered about by High Charge Uthor either. Kalian could see the rogue chewing over his answer, no doubt weighing up the fun to be had planet-side versus the fun to be had killing Protocorps mercenaries.

"We're in," Colonel Matthews spoke on behalf of her team, who offered no complaints.

"As am I," Naydaalan said with a flick of his elongated jaw.

Roland shrugged his shoulders and took a sip of his Raalakian ale. "Fine. But if this radiation thing just turns out to be some spatial anomaly, I'm going to be pissed. And C-Sec is paying for the Intrinium! The Solian Way isn't exactly a small stretch of space and the *Rackham's* a thirsty girl."

"I'm sure your demands will be met, Mr. North," Captain Fey replied dryly. "So drink up, but just be ready for the *Valkor's* arrival. Capturing a Starforge would be a massive win for all of us and Charge Hox isn't going to wait around."

Roland raised his bottle with the Raiders. "Then let's get shitfaced!" The bounty hunter caught Fey's classic scowl and added, "Just a little bit..."

With the music playing and the drinks flowing, Kalian sat back and enjoyed the atmosphere. Li'ara sat in apparent silence beside Sef, each communicating telepathically. It was tempting for Kalian to drop his mind into the frequency Li'ara's brain emanated and listen in, but they were likely chatting about the most mundane of things. Sef was surprising that way. The Raiders took it upon themselves to teach Roland and Naydaalan every drinking game from the twenty-seventh century. Captain Holt sat with Commander Vale in the open plan kitchen, deep in conversation about the exploration program that would see the various science teams set out across their new world. Ch'len was passsed out and covered in cold Trillik appetisers.

Kalian smiled to himself. This was what he fought for. Earth and Century were gone, along with all of human history and its culture. Now they were forging something new and wholesome among the stars.

"Kalian." Captain Fey rested a light hand on his shoulder. "Can I have a private word?"

"Of course," Kalian replied, placing his glass of Novaarian wine on the table. "Follow me."

When choosing their apartment, Kalian and Li'ara had made sure their new home had access to the roof. Neither had become tired of watching the sun rise and set over their new world. At this time of night, New Genesis was quiet with only a handful of cafés still open on the main street and the odd transport flying between the buildings.

"I've been meaning to talk to you about this for some time," Fey began, "but life in the council building has been hectic, to say the least."

"I can imagine." Kalian nodded along, doing his best to shut out the external information his brain was constantly processing. Even the solar radiation washing over the planet was clawing at his attention.

Captain Fey took a breath. "Have you noticed anything different about me, Kalian?"

That wasn't a question he had been expecting, but Kalian focused on the atoms that connected Fey to the reality around her and let them feed back every bit of data about her. To anyone else, they were separated by several metres of empty air, but to Kalian, they were all a collection of particles residing inside the same soup; he had only to reach out to discern everything about her.

The answer to her question came as something of a shock.

"You're younger," he whispered.

Captain Fey examined the backs of her hands. "It's subtle, but I can't help pausing in every mirror. I feel like every time I look, there's someone else looking back."

"Do you feel different?"

"Stronger, maybe. I've noticed my reactions are better but, again, it's subtle. At first, I was convinced I was imagining things."

Kalian held out his hand, palm open, and focused his awareness on a single patch of Captain Fey's body. With his eyes closed, he assessed her from the skin right through to the strands of DNA. There was no mistaking the microscopic nanocelium crawling all over her.

He opened his eyes and stepped back, taking Fey in from head to toe. "Your body is teeming with nanocelium."

Captain Fey looked back down at her hands in alarm. "What? How can that be?"

The nanocelium inside of her were doing nothing but good, but Kalian could see why the news would be terrifying. The only examples they had seen of nanocelium bonding with organic matter had resulted in Professor Garrett Jones and Malek. Both had become beings of terrible power and wrought destruction and death, each a slave to the nanocelium and their AI masters.

"It's okay," Kalian assured. "They're not attacking you."

"They shouldn't even be in there!" Captain Fey searched her hands and arms as if the nanocelium would make itself known. "We've all had scans and they showed no traces."

"We?" Kalian echoed.

Captain Fey stopped her frantic search. "There are others who have discovered similar changes in their physiology. In the beginning, I assumed it was everyone who had been treated medically with nanocelium while aboard the *Gommarian*, after Professor Jones attacked us. But, some of the people who have come forward were never harmed in the attack or ever treated with nanocelium. We were told they would leave our systems after healing us."

"How many have come forward?" Kalian asked, his Terran mind working through all the potential causes.

"Twenty-six that we know of. The only ones we know about are of an age to see such changes. There could be others who won't notice anything for decades. Why is it not showing up on our scans?"

Kalian glanced at the stars, taking note of the brightest. ALF was out there and likely in possession of an answer. "Nanocelium is very good at hiding. It can shield itself against almost anything."

"But, not you," Fey quickly added. "Can you check everyone? Is that... is that something you can do?"

Nanocelium was so rare in the Conclave that locating it was always easy, if he knew where to look. On Evalan, there were twelve beings walking around in suits of the stuff and his own exosuit was contained in a pocket-sized capsule in his jacket. Before Captain Fey had finished inhaling, Kalian had expanded his awareness and limited his search to New Genesis. Every molecule touching nanocelium was connected to him by trillions of other molecules, each relaying the information back to him. The largest and easiest source to find was the *Rackham*, docked in the space port on the edge of the city. After that, each of the Gomar stood out among the humans, forcing Kalian deeper.

Captain Fey exhaled and Kalian came back into the moment.

How could he have missed it? Walking to the edge of the roof, he looked out on New Genesis, daring to imagine the future of his race.

"Kalian? What is it?"

"There's nanocelium inside everyone. A small amount, but it's definitely there."

"What is it doing?" she asked.

Kalian stole a glance at the stars again. "I don't know…"

CHAPTER 4

High Councillor Elondrasa assumed her regal form before the masses of the capital. Her floating headdress followed her across the stage, the perfect accessory to her flowing red gown and Noonatril crystals. Her speech had been one of hope and unification, determined as the Highclave was to keep everything together after the Vanguard's assault and whispers of war. With all four of her Novaarian arms raised, Elondrasa unveiled the new Starforge in the centre of Clave Tower. Cheers and thunderous applause erupted around the tower.

This would change everything, she thought. Travelling between worlds without the need for a ship would have dramatic ramifications on their economy. How many corporations specialised in shipbuilding and space docks? Even Intrinium would be in less demand, a fact that had been complained about by the Laronian councillor, Lordina. Still, it was another step forward for the Conclave. This kind of freedom between worlds would only strengthen their bond... she hoped. Despite the masses of cheering citizens, Elondrasa could see the cordoned area on the balcony below, where many had come to protest the membership of humanity.

Xydrandil, the Highclave's secretary, walked on to the stage, taking advantage of the applause. "We are ready for you, Councillors." The Nix turned on his collection of pincer-like legs and gestured to the Starforge.

Elondrasa had hesitated when telling the people that they would begin their Starforge campaign by *walking* to her home world, Nova Prime, right now. Though she had been assured by the engineers that the machines had been tested vigorously with both organic and non-organic material, Elondrasa ardently hoped this would hold true as she passed on those reassurances to the citizens. Unlike the massive Starforges that had been witnessed operating in space, these static versions would have to connect to another Starforge in order to get them from one planet to another. ALF had told them it was the only way to avoid tearing a hole in reality where someone might be standing. The AI was perhaps the most mysterious part of humanity's appearance, but he had yet to steer them wrong, his priority being the protection of Kalian and his people. That didn't mean Elondrasa had to like walking through the event horizon, her every particle compressed and put back together thousands of light years away.

The masses held their breath when the Starforge came to life. In the shape of a crescent moon, the machine whirred as bolts of purple lightning fired around the outside. The lightning became more intense until it coalesced and collided into itself in the space between the separated points of the crescent. The spark flooded the Forge with white light, overlapped with every colour of the spectrum. The effect was similar to what Elondrasa imagined a black hole would look like, with all the colours being continuously sucked into the void.

It took everything she had, but she maintained her posture and decorum, unlike Nu-marn, the Shay councillor. He had voiced concerns for his cybernetic augments when passing through the Forge. Now, as the Highclave made their way across the platform, the pale organic sections of the Shay's face were visibly sweating.

Holographic displays popped up all over the tower, offering a view of the Starforge on Nova Prime, where thousands more had gathered, eager to see their leaders step across the stars.

Using only her upper arms, Elondrasa waved to the people as she walked into the light, hoping that the action would distract her from what was about to happen. The Novaarian closed her eyes at the last second and stepped through to the sound of more applause and the cheering of her own kind. The tingling in her fingers and on her lips faded as the warm sun of Nova Prime bathed the Highclave, and the Forge immediately shut down behind them. As previously discussed, every one of them did their best to hide their shock and refrain from inspecting their body.

Since security couldn't be as tight as it was on the capital, the Highclave were soon ushered into a reinforced transport and escorted by both the Novaarian forces and C-Sec to their penthouse apartment block in the middle of Nivaala, Nova Prime's capital city.

The view from their shared lounge was stunning. Elondrasa sipped on Novaarian wine while looking out on her home, its great spires sparkling in the setting sun. Below, the parade was still in full swing, a celebration in her honour. Kites of every colour and size floated between the towering buildings and confetti blew across the window in the breeze. It was good to be home...

Nu-marn's whining voice interrupted her daydream. "At least there are only four more of these wretched tours. My circuits feel sluggish after walking through that contraption. Give me a ship any day."

"You would say that, Nu-marn." Lordina relaxed back on one of the large sofas. "Doesn't your family own Starfield Shipping?"

Ch'lac, the shortest of the Highclave, rolled his wide eyes. "Let's not get into the shadowy world of Nu-marn's connections again..."

The Shay councillor turned on the Ch'kara. "I resent that! I have offered everything I know about Protocorps and severed all ties with them. And my dislike of this *Terran* technology has nothing to do with my family's business. You should be thankful for my connections! Have I not had reinforcements from my own people assist in securing the Crucible?"

The air was suddenly sucked out of the room as an elderly, human man appeared in the middle of the central table. "You mean the mysterious machine on *your* planet that makes slaves of every Shay?"

"ALF..." Elondrasa could barely keep her elongated jaw from dropping.

The AI slowly walked through the table until his white robes could be seen all the way to the floor. The hologram fluttered as he moved with the emitters in the ceiling struggling to transition from one to the other.

"I realise that curiosity is at the core of what unites every intelligent species in the universe, but poking around that machine instead of dismantling it is just stupid."

Brokk, the most intimidating of the Highclave, shot up on to all four of his rock-like legs. "What are you doing here?" he asked in his gravelly voice.

"*How* are you here?" Lordina added.

"You're not supposed to connect with any Conclave technology," Ch'lac explained. "This potentially violates humanity's membership."

ALF waved the notion away. "I'm here because you can't keep me out. That should worry you, because it worries me. If I can get in, so can they."

"Not this again!" Nu-marn spat. "You want access to the main AI hub on the capital. We rejected your offer then and we will do it again."

"I can strengthen your firewalls," ALF countered. "I can find all the holes and plug them. I know how they think. I know the areas they'll attack and, trust me, they will use your own systems against you, much like they tried to do with the Crucible."

"How can we trust you?" Elondrasa asked what everyone else was thinking.

"I will do anything to keep the humans of Evalan safe; I've never hidden this from you. Now, however, every human on that planet is a member of your civilisation, and therefore subject to your laws and protection. Keeping you strong now keeps them safe."

"What you want is out of the question," Nu-marn continued. "Handing over the hub to you would effectively place you in control of the Conclave."

"Not necessarily," ALF cocked his bushy eyebrow. "I can clone a baser version of myself and leave it to take control of that toaster you currently have running things. It wouldn't be *me* exactly, but it would be infinitely smarter than what you have right now."

Nu-marn looked about at the silent councillors. "You can't be seriously considering this? His being here should have us ejecting humanity from the Conclave immediately."

"I wouldn't do that, either." ALF shook his head. "I understand why you grounded the Gomar and, let's be honest, you're just lucky that Kalian is around to keep them that way, but you're going to need them sooner than you think."

"You're talking about an invasion that doesn't appear to be happening," Ch'lac commented.

"Perhaps our defeat over their Vanguard has dissuaded them from attacking the Conclave?" Lordina offered.

ALF blinked slowly. "It wouldn't be the first time they've lost a Vanguard, Councillor. Trust me; an attack is as imminent as it is inevitable. Civilisations such as this one are few are far between. They can't pass up the meal."

Nu-marn had started pacing. "So you would have us grant you access to every level of security we have, as well as give those monsters free rein?"

ALF looked to be pondering the question before responding, "Yep! That's about it."

Elondrasa put herself between the Shay and the hologram. "Small steps, ALF. We appreciate the Starforge technology and any advice regarding those who would seek us harm, but what you ask is a step too far... for now."

The AI sighed. "I gave you the Starforges because you're going to need to evacuate whole planets in a very short time. Speaking of which; you really need to activate all the ones you're keeping in storage. And my advice appears to be falling on deaf ears," ALF looked at Brokk's stony head, "or whatever he has. The Crucible should have been destroyed as soon as you took command. We already know it was used to take control of a handful of Shay. Imagine what it could do if it was used to its full potential."

Nu-marn waved both of his hands in the air. "This is ridiculous!"

ALF rolled his eyes. "At the very least, you should have examined every Shay for traces of nanocelium in their augments. Every enhancement manufactured by Protocorps is suspect." The AI gave the councillor a hard look. "How many augmentations do *you* have from Protocorps, Councillor Nu-marn?"

Nu-marn lifted his chin and puffed out his cybernetic chest. "I have heard enough of this. Your being here is in violation—"

"Nu-marn!" Elondrasa held up her hand, tired of hearing his voice. "ALF, we thank you for your services to the Conclave and hope that you will endeavour to see us survive this impending attack. But, until we ask for it, we would have you remain in the Evalan system. Any rogue coding discovered in the AI hub will be removed, so I suggest you leave our network the same way you came in and leave nothing behind."

ALF nodded along, a disappointed look on his face. "Activate more Starforges. Destroy the Crucible. Should you decide to take me up on my offer, I'll be waiting."

The hologram disappeared as abruptly as it had appeared. Elondrasa had said what was expected of her but, in truth, she felt ALF's help was the only way they were going to survive. Everything that had come at the Conclave since Earth's demise was proof that their enemy was superior in every way. If they didn't fight fire with fire, their whole way of life would be burnt away.

"We don't need the AI's help," Nu-marn continued. "C-Sec has almost doubled in size and our fleet grows every day. We can handle anything that might come out of the dark."

"Our decisions affect trillions of lives, Nu-marn," Brokk reminded him. "It is our responsibility to take everything into consideration."

"Pah!" Nu-marn stormed off.

Elondrasa was glad to see the back of him. With all the changes to their economy and the shade cast over the councillor in light of the Protocorps scandal, it was likely this was Nu-marn's last term in office. If she was lucky...

Nu-marn double-checked the security surrounding his personal terminal, making certain that he wasn't subject to extra eyes and ears. Since Protocorps' involvement had been brought into the light, his voice carried less weight on the Highclave. Things had to be escalated.

The councillor opened the data packet he had received two months previously, moments before the Vanguard had been destroyed. He had read and re-read the message a hundred times. The words in front of him were decreed by a god. It was left to him now to see their instructions were completed.

"Contact Ja-lax." The councillor waited impatiently for the local AI hub to connect him with the Protocorps mercenary.

"Sir." Ja-lax's cybernetic head floated in front of Nu-marn.

For years, Nu-marn had left this side of things to Protocorps, using his own influence and power on a higher echelon. Thanks to the humans' involvement, there was no one left to oversee their ascension. Dealing with the hired mercenaries still on the payroll had now become an everyday occurrence.

"Have you done as I commanded?" he asked.

Ja-lax nodded his pale head. "I've sent reinforcements to the Starforge in the Solian Way."

"Excellent—"

"But you're going to have to double everyone's pay," Ja-lax continued. "That Starforge is a C-Sec magnet, so my guys aren't exactly keen to board it and travel around with this cube-thing running the show."

"That cube is an extension of the..." Nu-marn held his tongue. Shay they may be, but their only religion was currency. "Fine. Their pay is doubled. Now, I need you and your best to go to Shandar."

"We're going home? What for?" Ja-lax asked.

Nu-marn ground his teeth. "Mercenaries..." he hissed away from the hologram. "You are to infiltrate our installation on the planet's surface. You will have help from local security."

Ja-lax's cybernetic red eye seemed to focus on the councillor. "And what are we to do once we take back control?"

Nu-marn thought about the Vanguard's message. "Activate the Crucible."

CHAPTER 5

THE INSIDE of the *Valkor* was just like every other C-Sec vessel to Roland; sleek, massive, and under-utilised. Why they had to make everything so damn big, he would never know. As with their previous mission, none of them were permitted anywhere on the ship except for the hangar, including Naydaalan. Along with the Raiders, they had been allocated a section of stations beside the *Rackham*, where Charge Hox had given them their briefing. Roland got the distinct impression the Laronian captain wasn't a fan of using humans for such a delicate mission.

"Is that it?" Lieutenant Jack Danvers asked. "We just jump into the system, check any visuals on a Starforge and jump back again?"

"Jack..." Colonel Matthews shook her head at him, silencing any further questions.

"Your mission is recon only," Charge Hox reiterated. "If you find a Starforge there'll be nothing you can do. It would take a ship of the *Valkor's* class to disable it."

"Disable it?" Roland repeated. "Is *that* the plan?"

Charge Hox rounded on the bounty hunter. "What would you have us do, Mr. North?"

Roland shrugged. "I'm just better at reducing things to little bits, is all. Disabling stuff is more *technical*..."

Charge Hox stood a little straighter. "Then it is a good job your mission is *recon only*. Report your findings back to the *Valkor*, nothing else."

"Right, right..." Roland enthusiastically nodded his head. "Recon only. Got it."

Charge Hox sighed. "Your ship is fuelled and ready for departure. You may leave whenever you are ready." The Laronian left after waving the holographic display away and wiping his race's equivalent of sweat from his blue scales.

Lieutenant Riddick hefted the assault rifle in his hands. "They might have us on something of a leash, but I *love* all the tech."

Roland cast an eye over the weaponry and new armour the Raiders had been given. It all packed a good punch, that much he had seen on Sebala, but it didn't compare to the black market equipment he had on board the *Rackham* or the gadgets Len made for him.

Roland rubbed his eyes. "God, I miss blowing stuff up..."

"*What was that?*" Len asked in his ear.

Roland tapped the device sitting comfortably inside his ear. "Nothing. Are we prepped?"

"*Her belly's full. We could go anywhere...*"

"We're in it now, Len. There's no going back." Roland led the way back inside the *Rackham*, listening to Len complain about all the free help they were giving to C-Sec.

The door to the bridge opened up, exposing Roland and the others to the Ch'kara's unique aroma. The stubby alien was slouched in his high-back chair, surrounded by empty wrappers and bottles. The methane gases enveloping his head were contained inside their personal force field, distorting his grubby features.

"I'm just saying," Len continued, "when this is all over, we're coming out of it with no units. Since the *Rackham* is the only ship that can pull off this kind of mission, I say we ask for—" Len stopped his rant when he saw Lieutenant Wilson. "Oh, hi, Katie... You can sit next to me if you like?" The Ch'kara's stubby fingers input fresh commands into his console and had the nanocelium rise up to form another chair.

"Is it hitting on me again?" Lieutenant Wilson asked.

"*It?*" Len echoed incredulously. "That's xenophobic!"

Roland ignored them all and input the key to start the *Rackham's* engine. He had considered his own reasons for entering into this fight many times, often wondering why he was so willing to put his life on the line. He had the ship and the skills to disappear, so why did he stick around? The bounty hunter popped the cap off his beer, kept refrigerated by his chair, and downed half of the bottle. *Who cares,* he thought.

"Let's skip to the good bit..."

The *Rackham* shot out of the hangar at a speed that was ill-advised inside a hangar, but imagining Charge Hox's bewildered expression brought a smile to Roland's face.

Almost two hours had passed by the time the *Rackham* emerged from subspace into the aurora of colours that was the Solian Way. The relic of a long dead star, the Solian Way stretched for nearly a million lightyears, a corridor of interstellar debris cutting through Conclave territory. Roland had heard it was a great place for smugglers to stash illegal goods since it was far from any of the subspace lanes and ultimately a chore for C-Sec to investigate.

Roland hit the intercom. "Nayd, get the others, we're here."

"On our way," Naydaalan replied.

The Novaarian entered the bridge with the Raiders in tow. Accustomed to the ship, Naydaalan's four arms brought up multiple holographic displays on the wall beside Roland. A quick glance informed the bounty hunter that the alien was filing through data reports from the array, searching for any sign of the Starforge. It wasn't that long ago that the thought of anyone but Len interacting with his ship would have seriously irritated him, but Naydaalan had become quite the asset on their *trips*. Also, he was really easy to get drunk, and Roland loved drunk-Naydaalan.

Colonel Matthews stood in the space between Roland and Len's consoles, her hands on her hips. "I guess it was asking too much to have it just waiting for us."

Len spat out the hardened nut at the centre of his Atari chud gum. "If it's in this sector of space, the *Rackham* will find it. The Starforge might be Terran tech, but Protocorps put it together using Conclave materials."

"Where did they find the traces of radiation?" Roland asked.

"Right here," Naydaalan replied. The viewport at the front of the bridge was overlaid with holo data from the Novaarian's terminal, showing them a trail of radiation typical of an artificial machine instead of naturally occurring radiation. "The trail seems to be on a course heading 291 point 10... based on our current bearing, that suggests it must be travelling towards..."

Roland turned in his chair to see Naydaalan. "Towards where?"

The translucent tendrils hanging over the Novaarian's back twitched. "Towards Arakesh."

"The Raalakian home world?" Colonel Matthews joined Naydaalan and looked over the data.

"You're a quick study," Roland commented. "I don't think I could name all the core worlds if my life depended on it."

Len turned his chair towards Roland rather than turning his head. "Should we report this back to the *Valkor*?"

Roland took another swig of his beer. "Report what?" he asked with a mouthful of cold liquid. "This trail could belong to anything. Nayd, send me the calculated coordinates of where this thing is heading and I'll lay in a course. One little jump should do it."

Len nervously peered over the data on his console. "Could I make the suggestion that we emerge from subspace in a place that won't put us in front—"

The Ch'kara never had the chance to finish his suggestion. The

Rackham was fired through subspace and spat back out inside of a second, placing them directly in the path of the radiation's source. Like an ant under a boot, the *Rackham* was overshadowed by the enormous crescent structure of a Starforge. The station was hurtling through the Solian Way and on a course to turn the *Rackham* into a bug smeared on a viewport.

"Evasive manoeuvres!" Len screamed.

"Hold on to something!" Roland's hands were inches from the controls, but the *Rackham's* AI had already taken control and engaged thrusters. It took a moment longer for the inertial dampeners to kick in and stop them from feeling compressed.

The Starforge paid them little attention and continued onwards. The *Rackham* banked hard to port and passed through the interior of the crescent with only metres to spare.

"Manual control!" Roland called out.

The flat console that arched around him shifted, the surface moving with the ease of water until two physical control sticks formed out of the nanocelium. The bounty hunter turned the ship about and hit maximum thrust to catch up with the Starforge.

"I hate it when you take control..." Len said, braced in his chair.

New chairs had grown out of the floor, giving the Raiders and Naydaalan somewhere to strap in.

Roland took a quick look at the Ch'kara. "Is it ready for launch?"

Len slowly turned his chair to face the bounty hunter. "You can't be serious, Roland."

"Is it ready?" he asked again.

"Well, it can be. But you can't be serious! We found the stupid Starforge, now let's head back to the *Valkor*."

Naydaalan sat forward. "What are you talking about?"

Roland ignored the Novaarian's question. "C-Sec'll just dick about with it like they always do. These things need to be taken care of properly."

Len waved his hands in the air. "Firing a Planet Killer into the side of it will do more than just *take care of it*. We'll be lucky if we survive!"

"Planet Killer?" the Raiders asked as one.

"How have you come to possess such a weapon?" The blue freckles on Naydaalan's face took on a deeper shade.

Roland shrugged. "Technically, C-Sec gave it to us..."

Naydaalan cocked his head. "Why do I doubt the validity of that statement?"

Len swivelled his chair to face them all. "The *Sentinel* gave us one before we went after the Vanguard. They were disabled and they thought we were the only ones who could stop it."

Colonel Matthews raised her eyebrow. "And they didn't ask for it back?"

Roland continued to push the *Rackham* on while plotting coordinates to take them out of the Solian Way in a hurry. "Things got a little messy towards the end there," he explained. "*Everyone* was firing Planet Killers at the Vanguard. We just told them we did the same..."

"We lied," Len corrected.

Roland gestured at the Starforge. "Aren't you glad we did?"

The *Rackham's* feminine voice came over the bridge's speakers. "*Multiple light crafts have departed from the Starforge and are locking weapons on to us. Would you like me to take offensive measures, Roland?*"

"And steal all the fun? No thanks!" Roland cancelled the option on his console and activated the weapons systems himself.

The *Rackham* weaved between the first two crafts, avoiding their Intrinium barrage as well as any collisions. The third and fourth both fired missiles that Roland countered with a dramatic twist of the ship, evading them by a few meters. Squeezing the trigger on his control stick was almost as fun as squeezing the trigger on his Tri-roller... almost. The nanocelium-based targeting system on the *Rackham* was far superior to anything on the light crafts, locking on to their weak spots inside of a second. Two quick bursts of blue light ripped through the oncoming vessels and scattered their innards across the Solian Way.

"The other two are coming back around," Len warned.

An Intrinium bolt exploded against the starboard hull, jolting them all in their seats. "You don't say!" Roland shouted back. "Do we still have any of those Brenine mines on board?"

Len checked over his display. "Just the one."

"That's all I need." The bounty hunter reversed the thrusters and dramatically slowed the *Rackham* down before flooring it again. The light craft didn't have time to evade the mine being deposited from the rear port, especially after it split into a cluster of smaller mines and created a web of unavoidable destruction. The light craft was obliterated at close proximity to the *Rackham*, sending a shockwave across its hull.

"Hold on!" Roland called over the sparks exploding out of various consoles across the bridge.

The *Rackham* was thrown off course and sent spinning, easy prey for the remaining light craft. Roland did his best to divert power to the inertial dampeners and prevent himself and the others from being sick, but his priority was lining up the cannons with the last craft. Engaging the axial thrusters levelled out the ship's attitude and gave the bounty hunter full control again, something he now regretted not giving to the ship's AI in the first place.

More Intrinium lit up the underside of the *Rackham*, pissing Roland off more than anything. The light crafts were fast and agile, similar in design to the Darts at C-Sec's disposal, but a hull of nanocelium required something with a bigger kick to cause catastrophic damage. To that fact, Roland input the commands to reinforce the hull on the top of the ship, diverting nanocelium from other sections. Another sharp decrease in speed had the light craft flying directly above them, its chase at an end. A rough pull on the control stick kept the *Rackham* horizontal and took it straight up. The impact was felt by all, but not so keenly as it was felt by the pilot of the light craft. The collision was enough to damage the smaller ship's propulsion systems, leaving it stranded in space. One last turn and a squeeze of the trigger made certain the Protocorps mercenary would never bother them again.

"Okay..." Roland redirected all power to the engine and made for the Starforge. "Len, prep the Planet Killer for launch."

"I can't," Len replied.

Roland noticed the flashing light on his own console and groaned. "The tube is damaged. How long will it take to repair?"

Len held his hands up. "Why are you asking me? She repairs herself."

Roland bit down on the urge to hit the stubby Ch'kara. "Rackham?"

"At current speed, it will take one hour and forty-two minutes to repair the missile tube. Would you like to divert nanocelium from the engines, Roland?"

Roland groaned again. "That's an agonisingly long time to just follow it." He turned to Len. "Is it still on course for Arakesh?"

Len checked his console and looked up in despair. "There's nowhere else for it to go."

Roland sighed, aware that he had already made his mind up. "Okay. Len, scan the station and find me somewhere to dock. Everyone else, suit up and prepare to board that bitch."

"We're docking?" Riddick asked, his tone somewhere between alarm and excitement.

When Colonel Matthews offered no protest, Roland glanced behind him at the lieutenant and the assault rifle in his hands. "Well, what was the point of giving you all those guns if they didn't want us to board it?"

Len cocked his head. "In case we were boarded by hostiles, obviously."

"Shut up, Len," the bridge replied as one.

Roland smirked to himself and set the *Rackham* on a trajectory to dock in the nearest hangar. Perhaps this was going to be an interesting day after all...

CHAPTER 6

Li'ara's arm reached out in bed and found nothing but an empty space where Kalian should have been. The absence of a warm body made her stir, but the silhouette of the man she loved sitting on the end of the bed brought her fully awake with a start.

"Sorry," he apologised.

Li'ara rubbed her eyes and sat up. "This isn't creepy at all. What time is it?"

"It's still the middle of the night," Kalian whispered.

Behind him, the doors to their private balcony were open, allowing some of the cool night air to blow through the stuffy apartment.

Li'ara yawned and took in the sight of him, still dressed in his clothes from the day. "What's up? Can't you sleep?"

Kalian looked away before answering, "I don't sleep, not anymore."

That had alarm bells ringing in her head and she threw back the duvet to crawl across the bed and get closer to him. As always, it took her an extra second to remember that she only had one whole leg. The stump beneath her right knee had healed up nicely, but it still felt there to her.

"You *don't* sleep?" she repeated, making sure her brain had made sense of his words.

"I haven't slept for fifty-three days."

Li'ara didn't know what to say and her surprise must have been evident on her face.

"It's okay," Kalian continued with a reassuring hand on her cheek. "I'm fine."

"Not sleeping doesn't come under *fine*," she countered. "Even the Gomar need to sleep."

"They shouldn't," he replied, taking his hand back.

Li'ara shook her head, dismissing further talk about the Gomar and their training. "What have you been doing all this time?"

Kalian offered her that boyish smile she had never been able to resist. "Exploring..."

Li'ara cocked her eyebrow. "Exploring? Exploring what? Evalan?"

Kalian laughed gently to himself. "No. In here." He placed a finger to his temple. "I think I can do it now," he said cryptically.

Li'ara titled her head, trying to figure him out. "Do what?"

Kalian glanced down at her amputated leg before meeting her eyes again. That confident look that Li'ara had been seeing more and more crept over his face.

"Kalian..." she instinctively rubbed her hand over the stump. "You can do some unbelievable things, but..."

"I can do it," he said again with certainty. "It's just matter. Lie back."

Li'ara hesitated, caught somewhere between excitement and disbelief. Kalian leant over her leg with his hand outstretched, overshadowing her amputated leg. The concentration on his face was no different to any other time, only now, Li'ara could feel his power. It began with an intense itch she was desperate to scratch, but seeing her discomfort, Kalian flexed his fingers and her entire leg went numb, allowing her to sit up and observe the miracle. The skin around the stump had already gone, replaced with the beginnings of a new bone that was quickly being surrounded by tendon, muscle, and blood vessels as it lengthened. Once the tibia reached the right length, it miraculously gave way to more bones that formed her foot. The blood vessels and tendons snaked and twisted down her new shin and spread out across the foot. The muscles came together from thin air, every strand adding to the bulk of her calf.

Eventually, fresh skin began to stretch out, covering the new bones and muscles. She even had toenails again! Tears welled in Li'ara's eyes when her toes took shape, though her ability to move them was still under Kalian's control. For the first time in what felt like a long time, Kalian had actually broken a sweat. Beads of perspiration collected on his temples before trickling downwards. She had seen him fight off twelve Gomar and shift mountains without any sign of fatigue.

"There..." Kalian sat back and took a breath.

Li'ara marvelled at the sight of her new leg. It had taken some time, but she was starting to come to terms with her injury, always telling herself it had happened in the line of duty and that she had saved lives losing it.

She shuffled to the edge of the bed and hesitantly placed her new foot on the floor. The numbness had gone, replaced with thousands of glorious nerves, each one telling her how cold the tile floor was. She didn't know what to feel seeing her wiggling toes now. With a gentle hand, Li'ara ran her fingers over the skin on her shin and compared it to the skin on her left leg. There was no discernible difference, except for the longer hairs. Cautiously, she lifted her leg and flexed, stunned to see the muscle in her calf contracting.

"Thank you!" Li'ara launched across the bed and held Kalian in a tight embrace. "Are you okay? You look *tired*."

Kalian smiled and tried to wave her concern away. "The intricacy and detail is always harder than just lifting a boulder or a rock. That's the first time I've tried anything like that."

"First time?" Li'ara hit him in the arm. "You sounded damn confident a few minutes ago."

Kalian laughed, blocking her playful punches. "I *knew* I could do it." He kissed her on the forehead, his expression serious. "I hate that they took something from you."

Li'ara met his dark eyes. "I was okay with it. I destroyed a cube... it was an acceptable trade."

"Not to me," Kalian replied firmly.

Li'ara took a breath. "You're not a god, Kalian. We all have to take risks and live with the consequences."

"You would rather I hadn't healed you?"

Li'ara didn't want this to turn into an argument, but she could see where it was going. "That's not what I'm saying. Of course I'm... I'm ecstatic that you gave me my leg back. What I'm trying to say is that you can't take on the responsibility of everyone's decisions. When this war really starts, people are going to get hurt, they're going to die. You can't put all of that on your shoulders."

As poignant as her words had been, Li'ara could see that none of them had the desired effect on Kalian. He offered her a half-smile and stood up to make for the small balcony off their bedroom.

"Where are you going?" she asked.

"I have to speak with ALF." Kalian held out his hand and a small triangular device flew from the bedside table into his open palm.

"You're going to speak with ALF? Now?" Going in the middle of the night was clearly only a problem for people who actually used that time to sleep.

"Captain Fey told me about the nanocelium a few days ago, Li'ara. We need answers." Kalian placed the metallic device below his navel, where it immediately reacted to his touch and expanded around his body until only his head and hands remained visible. "It's inside you as well."

Li'ara tried not to let that thought distract her. "I agree that we need answers, but no one is supposed to make contact with ALF. If you take a ship it'll be logged."

Kalian smiled. "I'm not taking a ship."

The nanocelium grew over his hands and face, leaving Li'ara to look upon what could easily have been a robot. The exosuit's design was sleek, coated in overlapping panels and a face mask that didn't have any visible eyes or mouth.

"I'll be back before dawn." His voice had a mechanical tone to it when filtered by the suit.

Before Li'ara could say another word, Kalian stepped on to the balcony and ascended into the night sky, quickly melting into the darkness between the stars. It took another second for Li'ara to realise she was now standing by the railing and looking for him. She inspected her new leg, testing the strength and feel of it. It was so good to put her foot down and feel the cold floor under her sole.

Her elation was soon brought under control when she noticed the row of plants that lined the railing. Having only replotted the mature shrubs yesterday, they should have been flourishing and full of life and colour. There was nothing but a row of dried out, shrivelled up leaves and broken stems now. Every one of them was dead, including the three inside the lounge and kitchen. Li'ara looked from the plants to her new leg, and up at the sky.

CHAPTER 7

JA-LAX LOOKED over the Shay mercenaries he had handpicked to take back the Crucible. He had always preferred working with his own kind, finding it useful to know what they were all capable of. Thanks to all of the augments their species was known for, gender barely mattered anymore. When he examined the Shay before him, he didn't see sex, only enhancements. Their pale flesh was stretched out, often reshaped to fit a new piece of hardware into their body. Ja-lax cycled through the various modes on his new eye, a glowing red gem that had been fitted into the cybernetic panels that coated half of his face.

A message popped up across the neural feed they all shared, its warning displayed over their eyes. Ja-lax reached out with the others and held on to the transport's handrails above, as the ship descended through the thick mucky atmosphere that enveloped Shandar. In their tight quarters, the team couldn't help but jostle into each other when the transport passed through one of the many lightning storms.

"Don't you just love coming home?" Ja-lax shouted over the rattle.

The team laughed, though he was aware that at least two of them had never seen the true surface of their home world. For centuries,

Shandar's population had lived in towering blocks that floated in a connected web around the planet. Protocorps had long ago ensured that laws were put in place to stop anyone from travelling through the fog of clouds to the planet's surface. There was a part of Ja-lax that resented his current employers for their role in poisoning the atmosphere and ruining his ancestors' home. But they paid *really* well, so he was willing to let it go if it meant he could afford a luxury SkyCloud apartment on the Laronian home world, Vallara.

"Hey, Boss!" Vo-den called over the team. "How long have you been working Protocorps ops for now?"

Ja-lax took a long drag on his Ch'karan cigar. "Long enough to learn all their dirty secrets. Speaking of, listen up! Some of you are going to see things when we hit land. I know Shandar might feel like our home world, but it's not. You need to think of this hunk of rock as just another Protocorps investment. So, any questions you might have need to be stowed until the op is over. Understood?" The team responded with a resounding affirmative. "Good. Now, you've all read the brief on this one. Ground troops are already in place and expecting us. They will get us inside the installation where you will, and I quote from our paymasters, *kill anything that moves.*" Cheers bounced off the interior bulkheads. "Alright, alright. Priority one is the activation of this place. They want everything switched on to full power."

Vo-den shuffled to get a better look at him. "What exactly are we turning on, Boss?"

Ja-lax shrugged. "Who cares? Think of it as a money tree. We turn it on and shiny units come out of it." The jolting came to a sudden stop when they cleared the thunderous clouds. "Breathers on!" he ordered.

The whole squad had already been fitted with artificial pods around all three of their lungs, requiring a simple activation rather than the donning of a mask. Ja-lax hit the control panel and opened both side doors on the transport, filling their ears with the rushing wind as the transport approached its landing coordinates. The land beneath them was barren, a vista of dulled rock that hadn't seen sunlight for hundreds of years. The only thing beautiful about the view anymore was the constant lightning strikes.

The Crucible was easily spotted on the horizon, its concave top standing out against the rock. Towers and power stations were dotted around the area, typical of an installation that was used to going long periods without resupplying. The valley leading to the Crucible's main doors was filled with transports with C-Sec printed on the side. The ground troops Councillor Nu-marn had already put in place were flashing their torches, giving the signal that it was clear to land.

"Move out!" Ja-lax jumped out of the ship a moment before its struts could touch down and led the way over to the nearest of Shandar's security force. Two others from the security force were already opening the main doors for them and securing the first tunnel.

"Multiple engineering teams," the guard thumbed over his shoulder. "Only two C-Sec strike teams led by Commander Norvak, a Novaarian."

Ja-lax marched across the dry desert with his Splicer X1 in both hands. "I hate fighting Novaarians. Too many arms..." The Shay activated the skeletal robotic arms overlaying his own, granting him two extra hands. Each of the mechanical fingers reached for the Roller pistols on his belt.

Ja-lax turned to Vo-den while highlighting four other Shay on their neural net. "Take your team and perform a systemic eradication, just like we did on Zantesh. The rest are with me. We're heading straight for the control room. Remember, minimal damage to the equipment."

The tunnels were dimly lit but it was nothing his new eye couldn't handle, bringing light into the darkest corners with its variety viewing spectrums. That light exposed signs of battle damage at almost every turn. Turrets were hanging off the walls, their barrels bent into unnatural shapes. Bloody footprints decorated the floors, running in every direction. Whoever had assaulted the Crucible in the first place had done a great job of creating chaos on their way through. He had, of course, heard the rumours that the installation had been attacked by one of the super-powered humans, but he still found the truth of these humans to be elusive, having never met one in real life.

Vo-den and his team split away, taking the tunnels that led deeper into the Crucible's underbelly. The question was, who would get to pull their trigger first? Ja-lax accessed C-Sec's internal comm and brought up a holographic display of the strike team's whereabouts. Seeing the C-Sec soldiers highlighted in the floating map, he had his answers. Pointing to the tunnel's curved ceiling, the rest of his team used the magnets in the ends of their metallic fingers and knees to climb and hide in the dark.

Ja-lax stood alone in front of the soldiers as they rounded the corner. "Greetings of peace!" he said jovially.

Surprised as they were to see him, their superior numbers gave them the confidence to raise their weapons and command him to freeze. Their mistake. They should have just shot him. The Shay dropped down and sank their blades into the soldiers, forcing the razor-sharp points deep into the gaps between their golden armour. One of the strike team, a blue Laronian, managed to survive long enough to aim her rifle at Ja-lax.

His Splicer X1 shot off a single round of Intrinium, which crystallised mid-flight until it formed a jagged blade sharp enough to penetrate C-Sec armour. It impaled the Laronian through the head, killing her instantly. The sound of her armour giving way and blood hitting the walls echoed down the tunnels in every direction.

"There goes the surprise." Ja-lax glared threateningly at the Shay mercenary who had failed to kill the Laronian in the first place. "That's coming out of your pay." The mercenary groaned and stepped back into formation, suitably reprimanded.

Gunfire erupted over their neural net. It seemed Vo-den and his team had decided to go loud as well. The augmentation to his auditory canal picked up the sound of boots moving swiftly through the network of tunnels. Judging by the displacement, he guessed them to be in a sweeping formation, which meant they had no idea where their enemy was. Advantage to Ja-lax, he thought.

He flicked his head down the closest tunnel. "Seekers."

Two from his team removed the strips of ball bearings from their bony legs and emptied them on to the floor. The balls came to life and began rolling down the corridor at great speed, using the walls and ceiling as much as the floor.

"Minimal yield," he ordered. "We just need to kill them, not cave in the entire installation."

A moment later, he heard the ruckus when the seekers found their targets and clung to various parts of their alien bodies. Their cries were quickly followed by a series of bangs and pops and the inevitable splatter of liquid on walls. As one, the mercenaries swept through the tunnel, making certain the soldiers were dead as they stepped over their corpses.

"Vo-den, report."

"*Most of the engineering team is dead,*" he replied. "*There's some C-Sec resistance down here, but it's nothing we can't handle.*" There was a pause on Vo-den's end. "*What did you say this place was again?*"

Ja-lax rolled his organic eye. "Whatever weird shit you're seeing down there, do yourself a favour and forget it. Focus on the objective."

"*Weird doesn't cover it, Boss. They've got massive pyramids down here...*"

"Just do your job, Vo-den." Ja-lax cut the feed and concentrated on the light up ahead. He cut the feed and the group continued on through the tunnels, until they finally saw the light of their destination. "This is the control room," he whispered. The hologram floating over his wrist showed that the C-Sec soldiers inside had hunkered down and found defensive positions behind the workstations.

A distinctly Novaarian voice called out, "I hope you have a plan if you intend to take this station in one piece."

Ja-lax sighed. "Commander Norvak, is it?" He gestured with one of his robotic arms for the team to take up assault positions around the door.

"You must be another Protocorps lackey."

Ja-lax checked the ammunition level on his Splicer. "If you're hoping to stall us I'm afraid there are no reinforcements coming to help. No signal gets off Shandar without going through someone on the Protocorps pay scale. They still own this planet, Commander."

The Novaarian grunted. "Then neither of us are going anywhere, it seems."

Ja-lax licked his dark lips. "Time is kind of a factor for me. So, I'll tell you what; why don't you and I have a chat, no guns, and we'll come up with a way that sees you and your team walk out of here. There's no need for you all to die." The Shay sent a worded message across their neural net to his team, instructing them to get ready to breach.

"You think I am stupid enough to trust the word of a mercenary?" Norvak replied.

"I wasn't always a mercenary, Commander. Once, I was just like you; a good little soldier who did as he was told." Ja-lax cracked his neck, readying himself for action. "Now, I'm coming out," he called, throwing his Splicer X1 into the control room. His robotic arms hugged his body, blending with his armour while maintaining a grip on the Rollers.

"The moment your hand touches anything but air, you are dead," Norvak warned.

"Fair enough," Ja-lax agreed.

The Shay stuck both of his semi-organic hands out first, followed by his beaming smile and the rest of his body. Once his new eye had clocked every member of the strike team, his internal targeting system linked up with his robotic arms. With his hands still in the air, both robotic arms shot out, pulling free his holstered Rollers, and fired off half a dozen shots before the first C-Sec soldier could return fire. At the same moment, the rest of his team exploded into the room and fired short accurate bursts, being careful not to destroy the workstations.

Blood went everywhere and the smell of ozone soon filled the control room. An Intrinium round caught Ja-lax in the leg and he used the blow to drop into a roll and come back up with his Splicer in hand. Two of his four were already down, both picked off by Commander Norvak, but the majority of the Novaarian's strike team were now lying dead over consoles. Three quick bursts from the Splicer sent three jagged crystals into the side of a Tularon's furry head.

Undeterred by his team's demise, Norvak leapt over a bank of monitors and swiped his staff across the face of one of the Shay, knocking her aside and opening up a clear shot at another.

Ja-lax took his shot.

A blue crystal, the size of his hand, whistled through the air and impaled the commander's neck. The Novaarian crumpled against the wall, struggling to breathe with red blood filling his throat.

"If it's any consolation, I never planned on having a *chat*." Ja-lax shot Norvak one last time, putting a crystal in his brain.

The control room was a bloody mess, much like the rest of the installation. The two surviving Shay went about clearing the bodies from the consoles while Ja-lax searched for the activation panel. By the time he had powered up the Crucible and entered the codes Councillor Nu-marn had given him, Vo-den and his team had returned, minus one. The casualties were more than acceptable in Ja-lax's eyes; they each got a bigger cut, after all.

"Alright. Let's turn this thing on and get out of here." Ja-lax hit the final key and sat back as the Crucible came to life. The ground shook slightly, but it didn't appear to be getting any worse. He calmed the rest of the team down and instructed them to wait. They weren't leaving until they knew it was working.

"Now what?" Vo-den asked.

Ja-lax watched the holographic readouts, curious himself as to what would actually happen. There were towers all over the planet's surface reading as active, though their connection to the installation remained a mystery to the mercenary.

"Can you hear that?" Vo-den shouted in the quiet control room.

The Shay was clearly experiencing discomfort, quickly followed by others on the team. Most of them dropped their weapons in favour of grabbing their heads. Vo-den almost collapsed in pain before Ja-lax began to feel *something*. It was a buzzing in his ears at first, followed swiftly by dark spots in his vision. His bony hands cramped up and he dropped the Splicer, though he barely registered the sound it made as it clattered on the floor.

An alert flashed over his internal network, a private alarm that only he could see. The operating implant, inserted into his brain as a child as it had been in almost every Shay, was breaking down. The implant, a Protocorps design, was there to bridge the synaptic gaps between his organic body parts and artificial augmentations. He could see the mesh in his mind's eye breaking apart from the inside and a dark liquid flooding his brain, multiplying in size and spreading through both his veins and circuits. He wanted to cry out but he was losing all motor function and his jaw refused to open.

The dark spots in his vision grew until the shadows consumed him...

CHAPTER 8

ROLAND GAVE Ava the nod and the colonel activated the hack on the hangar's security systems, unlocking the internal door. Guided by hand signals alone, the Raiders and Naydaalan had assumed their positions around the opening door and were ready for whatever might greet them. Despite Ava's leadership over the team, the colonel respected Roland's past and accepted his advice and suggestions, especially since he had far greater knowledge of the Conclave. Only once or twice had she objected to his carefree tactics, but those objections were probably the reason he was still alive...

It had been decades since the bounty hunter was part of a team and, thanks to copious amounts of drugs and alcohol, he couldn't say he remembered much of it. Of course, the training was hardwired into his brain now and would accompany him to his grave. Falling into their manoeuvres had felt like putting on an old uniform and he hated to admit the enjoyment he found in working with them. There was that one time, however, when he had got drunk and told Len of his kinship with the others, Kalian and Li'ara included.

"You just like shooting stuff," Len had said. "And now you have friends to shoot stuff with!"

Roland couldn't disagree with that; even Naydaalan had an

aggressive streak in him that proved not all Novaarians were peace-loving tree huggers.

Ava tapped her earpiece. "Len, has the *Rackham* linked in with the Starforge yet? How much resistance can we expect?"

The team cautiously moved through the first few corridors of white walls and polished floors. Roland had his trusty Tri-rollers in both hands but Len's hesitation to reply spoke volumes to the bounty hunter.

"Len, what's going on?" he asked.

"*I'm not sure,*" the Ch'kara replied. "*The nanocelium tether connected to the nearest port as usual, but this time something bit back.*"

"Explain," Ava said.

"*Something tried to corrupt the Rackham's nanocelium. I had to cancel the link and pull back the tether.*"

Roland stopped just short of the next corner and hugged the wall, checking it was clear with a quick glance before turning back to look at Naydaalan's swirling eyes. "There's only one thing that can stand up to nanocelium. More nanocelium."

The Novaarian agreed. "There must be a source on board controlling the Starforge."

"Without Len's hook up, we're blind to what's ahead," Lieutenant Riddick warned.

Ava crossed Roland and took up position on the other side of the corner. "Then we just do it the old fashion way. We move as one and clear out every corridor."

"Effective but slow," Naydaalan said. "The Starforge's internal network is too vast to cover in the time available. We have to sabotage the station before it reaches Arakesh."

Roland double-checked the three hundred rounds of Intrinium in each Tri-roller. "Big guy's right. We need to make for the heart of this place and give it something to worry about. Len, didn't Kalian once hand over schematics from the last Starforge?"

"*Yep. I'll send them through.*"

Roland swiped the screen built into the sleeve of his hide coat. The control centre was in the middle of the present station, several levels above them. The bounty hunter sent the schematics to the rest of the group, ensuring that if the worst was to happen, they would all know how to reach the centre.

"Move out," Ava ordered.

The team made to continue down the next corridor only to be blinded by the flashes of Intrinium gunfire. Roland instinctively ducked and rolled, narrowly avoiding two bolts of super-heated energy. The wall behind him exploded and covered his long coat in debris. Before he could get back up, the Raiders were firing over the top of him, forcing the Protocorps mercenaries into hiding. The mercs weren't fast enough. The bounty hunter jumped and unleashed his Tri-rollers, catching two of the Shay squarely in the chest.

The Raiders scattered, taking advantage of the alcoves and side doors for cover. Roland holstered one of his weapons and crouched in front of the dead Shay, propping his body up to use as a shield. A second look at the corpse in his hand gave the bounty hunter pause. The Shay's pale skin and cybernetic augments were subtly shifting with wriggling strands of nanocelium.

"What the fu—"

The dead Shay opened its eyes and snapped a hand around Roland's wrist. The bounty hunter whipped his Tri-roller up and put a round in the alien's head, blowing both brain matter and circuitry out the other side.

"What was that?' Ava shouted over the gunfire.

With no cover, Roland leapt across the floor and scrambled to reach the nearest alcove. A stray Intrinium bolt struck the Callic-Diamond armour over his chest and pounded him into the alcove wall. The armour was tough enough to keep the bolt from killing him, but it still felt like a gut punch.

Out of the corner of his eye, the Shay he had just shot through the head sat up and reached for its fallen weapon. The second

Shay he had caught in the chest was already finding its feet and returning fire at the Raiders. Seeing his enemies bounce back from mortal wounds was as baffling as it was astounding, but more than anything it just pissed off the bounty hunter. Roland peeled himself off the wall and levelled both Tri-rollers at the mercenaries. Round after round reduced their alien bodies to slag, blowing off limbs and turning vital organs to soup, yet still they fired their weapons.

"What the shit is this?" Danvers called.

When there wasn't enough left of the Shay to even pull the triggers, Roland could see their various body parts moving across the ruined floor. Strands of nanocelium pulled the limbs and viscera together, slowly knitting the mercenaries back together.

Roland pulled his head back into the alcove when the Shay further down the corridor took aim at him. He didn't have long, however, before the two in front of him were whole again and ready to fight.

"Screw this! Nayd!" The bounty hunter removed a grenade from his belt and held it up for Naydaalan to see. Of them all, the Novaarian had the longest throw and he could hurl more than two at a time.

"Retreat!" Ava ordered, after seeing their silent conversation.

Naydaalan used his two upper arms to retrieve a couple of grenades from the straps across his chest. While his upper limbs primed the bombs, his lower arms continued to pour Intrinium fire down the corridor.

Roland stole a glimpse at the re-forming Shay. "Do it now!"

The Novaarian threw both of his grenades, his accuracy perfectly placing the bombs at the feet of the distant mercenaries. Roland took his opportunity and ran to meet up with the retreating Raiders, dropping his own grenade behind him as he did. In the same moment that Naydaalan's grenades exploded, the re-forming Shay were subjected to an implosion that took both sides of the corridor with it, as well as the ceiling and floor. Had the bounty hunter not jumped at the last second, his body would have been pulled in with the other victims.

"What the hell is going on?" Ava asked as she pulled Roland to his feet. "Can Shay do that?"

"No," Naydaalan answered. "Nothing should be able to do that."

"Their bodies are infected with nanocelium," Roland explained.

Lieutenant Wilson blew her dark hair from her face and reloaded her assault rifle. "Why do I suddenly want to get off this station?"

Roland holstered his Tri-rollers and heaved the Chem-roller strapped over his shoulder. The two-handed weapon was equipped with multiple settings, including his favourite explosive rounds.

"Let's find an alternate route," he suggested.

"Shit..." It was Jess who had sworn, her eyes locked on the corridor they had torn up. "The mercs at the end are getting back up."

"Move out," Ava ordered.

Choosing to use the emergency hatches and avoid the Translifts, the team moved slowly through the station, managing to avoid alerting Protocorps to their exact whereabouts. They succeeded in progressing through six levels before the next firefight broke out. Having learnt from their first encounter, the Raiders took turns lobbing grenades down the corridor. On their way through the smoking ruins, the team emptied whole magazines into the fallen Shay, doing their best to keep the body parts from re-forming.

"We need to keep moving and stay ahead of them," Roland said, squeezing the Chem-roller's trigger one last time. The mercenary's head caved in and worms of nanocelium wriggled over its charred remains.

"Watch out!" Naydaalan closed the gap between him and Roland before the bounty hunter even perceived a threat.

From the shadows of the nearest alcove, a Shay survivor had jumped out at Roland with a blade in its hand. The bounty hunter stepped back, a reactionary movement, but also unnecessary. Naydaalan caught the Shay mid-jump and pinned it to the wall with his upper arms while his lower limbs worked the assault rifles in his hands. The cacophony of weapons fire erupted across the Shay's midriff and didn't stop until the alien's legs fell to the floor, leaving its torso pinned to the wall. Still, its top half squirmed, desperate to lash out and kill the Novaarian.

'Finish it and let's get the hell out of here!" Ava was already directing the Raiders down the next corridor.

Naydaalan lifted his assault rifle and pressed the barrel under the Shay's jaw. One squeeze of the trigger blew off the top of the alien's head, decorating the ceiling with blood and nanocelium.

"Thanks, big guy." Roland patted the Novaarian on the shoulder.

Ava led the group down the next corridor, the final corridor ending with the double doors of the control room. It was unmanned but ominous in appearance, the largest of all the doors in the station. The group cautiously approached, checking every corner and alcove with levelled weapons and fingers on triggers.

"Let's see what's inside," Ava said, commanding Riddick to access the panel on the wall.

With a hiss, the doors parted to reveal the enormous chamber beyond.

Having briefly read the report Kalian gave about his encounter with Malek on the Helteron Starforge, Roland could see that the control rooms were identical. The room was a large cube, with two tiers above a pitted level in the middle. The control room itself was situated in the widest part of the crescent and raised above the surface of the hull. Being off-centre from the rest of the station, the viewport, which took up a whole side of the chamber, offered a majestic view of the Solian Way, framing the arching limbs of the Starforge to the right which, from this distance, seemed to almost meet making the crescent into a ring.

Ava turned to her team. "Jess, Katy, find a way to lock down the doors. Riddick, Danvers, rig the shit out of the external corridor. I want to hear explosions before any Shay even touches the door's controls. It won't put them down but at least it'll give us more time."

Roland halted his exploration of the control room when he reached the lip of the pitted tier. The stations and consoles were tangled in black strands of nanocelium, all of which snaked back into the centre, where a single cube was sitting.

"Oh, shit..."

Naydaalan joined him by the edge. "A cube. C-Sec theorised that there might be more."

"Did they theorise what we do when we find one?" Roland asked sceptically.

"Not touching it came up a lot," Naydaalan quipped.

"Fair enough." Roland had seen what had happened to Professor Jones and Malek, the last people who had interacted with the cubes. "Len, any idea how we steer this big bastard into the nearest black hole?"

"*What are you still doing there?*" Len shouted frantically down his ear. "*You just found a cube! You should be running back to the Rackham!*"

"Sounds like someone's blood sugar is a little low..."

"*I'm serious, Roland. If that thing has its tentacles in the Starforge's systems, there's nothing you can do.*"

Roland inspected the strands attached to the cube's bronze plating. "Nothing technical at least."

"*That's a terrible idea!*"

The bounty hunter tapped his earpiece and put the brakes on Len's rant before it could get started. "Okay, if this thing is piloting the Starforge, we just need to take its hands off the wheel." The Raiders returned from their duties and surrounded the cube on all sides of the pitted tier. "Aim for the strands," Roland directed. "We don't have anything powerful enough to dent that shiny plating."

As one, the team opened up with every weapon they had, filling the large chamber with the smell of ozone and smoke. The consoles were ripped to pieces and the strands of nanocelium were severed, their tentacle ends writhing about between the stations.

As the soldiers ceased firing to reload, the Starforge groaned and the floor under their feet vibrated. Roland turned to the viewport, but in the vastness of the Solian Way it was impossible to determine speed with the naked eye.

"Len?"

"The Starforge is slowing down."

"Great. Let's—"

"But it's also powering up the three Starrilliums on its outer hull."

Roland didn't like the sound of that. "Isn't that what it does when it's about to open a wormhole?"

Len sighed in his ear. *"You're an idiot."*

The vibration under their feet grew stronger and consoles all over the control room came to life. Explosions reverberated through the main doors and the panel on the wall sparked.

"They're coming!" Riddick warned.

"I think you're right..." Roland's eyes were still fixed on the viewport, where giant bolts of purple lightning were running around the crescent's hull.

The tips of the station lit up with a light as bright as any star, banishing the void beyond. The frequency of the lightning increased and began firing across the gulf between the crescent's ends. The vibration under their feet reached its crescendo and the light forming in the gap of the Starforge's limbs came together and expanded across the entire station, filling the circular hole with white light, edged with every colour of the spectrum.

The control room was overshadowed when a ship, colossal in size, emerged from the wormhole, eclipsing the light. The Starforge's enormous proportions suddenly made sense to the bounty hunter, who watched in disbelief as the alien ship slid through the gaps in reality, its sides only metres from the station's limbs.

"What is that?" Katy asked.

"It just keeps coming," Danvers commented absently.

Colonel Matthews was the first to recover. "Take up positions around the door. Prepare to repel a breach." It took an extra second for the Raiders to interpret their orders and actually move.

Roland felt almost dazed by the sight. "Len, are you getting any readings from this thing?"

"*Scanning it is proving quite the task,*" the Ch'kara replied. "*I've seen moons smaller than this thing.*"

Roland lifted his arm and looked over the data that Len was feeding through to his coat's screen. The *Rackham* was building an image of the ship as it took shape in real space. It was a monster that dwarfed the *Sentinel* or even the *Gommarian*. Black as space, its hull was bristling with pointed angles and writhing snake-like bodies. It took several more minutes before the end pulled clear of the wormhole and the Starforge shut down.

Naydaalan looked down at Roland. "We need to warn C-Sec immediately."

"Agreed. Let's get back to the *Valkor.*"

Ava gestured to the cube. "What should we do about that? Or this whole place for that matter? That thing will regain control soon enough."

Roland licked his lips. "Len, how are the repairs coming along?"

"*We've still got a little while until the* Rackham's *back to full health. I don't think we'll be able to launch the Planet Killer yet.*"

The bounty hunter hated the truth of their situation but there was no alternative. "We don't have the firepower to destroy the station and disabling it will prove impossible as long as the cube's plugged in." He sighed, resigned to their only option. "We leave and warn the others. Agreed?"

Both Ava and Naydaalan nodded their heads. Running wasn't familiar to any of them, but a moon-sized ship of pure nanocelium had just entered Conclave space and was heading for a core planet.

"*Wait...*" Len's voice came over their shared comm. "*Something's happening. It's... it's breaking up.*"

"Breaking up?" Roland repeated. "In a good way or a bad way?" It was too much to hope that travelling through the Starforge had damaged it in some way.

"*Definitely bad,*" Len said. "*The* Rackham's *counting thousands of smaller ships detaching from the whole. Each one is bigger than any ship at C-Sec's disposal."*

Another explosion rocked the main doors, putting the Raiders on edge.

"I think that's the last of our mines," Riddick called back.

Roland gripped the Chem-roller a little tighter. "Anyone feel like going up against an army of Shay zombies?"

Naydaalan cocked his head. "What are zom-bies?"

The bounty hunter made his way over to the main doors. "Today, they're a pain in the ass…"

The Raiders prised the doors apart, revealing a corridor of smoke, blood, and body parts. Every surface was charred and cratered from shrapnel and weapons discharge.

Roland took the lead, pausing briefly to tap his earpiece. "Len, fire up the engine. As soon as the hatch closes I want us off this station."

"*On it.*"

The team moved as one organism in a wedge formation, one eye on the colonel and the other watching for any sudden movements. Using the ladders again, they descended back through the many levels, deliberately choosing a new route back to the hangar, a standard military tactic by Roland's recollection. The bounty hunter could see the Raiders' orange visors scanning the red-lit corridors, an effect mirrored by the implants in his eyes. It was better to see in the dark than give themselves away with torches.

"Target!" Ava's warning sounded at the same time as her weapon, which let rip into the oncoming Shay.

More mercenaries, all coated in nanocelium, poured out of the side doors. Their expressions were absent of intelligent life signs despite their aggressive attack. Roland kept his finger down on the Chem-roller's trigger and fired round after round of explosive Intrinium. The Shay burst apart with enough force to inflict damage on those around them.

"Keep moving!" Ava screamed, pushing the team forward.

"They're flanking!" Jess shouted from the rear of the group.

The team was divided between firing ahead and behind now. Roland ducked into an alcove to swap out the magazines, a motion he had mastered over the decades, before swapping paces with Lieutenant Danvers and adding his explosive rounds to the rear.

"They're slippery bastards!" Roland stated as the Shay began to use every surface like spiders.

"Jess!" Katy's alarm was a moment too late to stop her from getting shot.

Roland glanced at the woman, who had dropped to the floor with a glowing thigh. Jess's armoured plating had prevented any loss of limb, but the Intrinium had still burnt through to the muscle. Katy rushed to her side and Roland stepped in to cover them, allowing Lieutenant Wilson time to administer pain meds. Jess gritted her teeth, doing her best to keep a lid on the pain, but the occasional scream couldn't be helped.

"We need to exfil, *now!*" Katy yelled.

Naydaalan scooped up Jess in his lower arms, the only one among them who could carry her and continue to fire his weapon. Colonel Matthews led the push through the stark corridors, their formation one of aggression now. Roland was the last to enter the hangar and so he was the last to see what was coming for them. He unleashed his Chem-roller, with no concern for accurate targeting, and hoped they could get off the ground before the horde swarmed the ship.

'Get in!" he quickly ordered as the *Rackham's* ramp descended.

Behind them, the infected Shay burst through the doors and filled the hangar with Intrinium fire. They appeared somehow more ghoulish than before, many of them having been reassembled out of different parts after being blown up multiple times. It seemed the nanocelium didn't care which parts went with what, as long as the host could move and fire a weapon.

Roland dropped into his pilot's chair, hating every sound the impacts against his ship made. Proximity alarms popped up across his holographic display, warning the bounty hunter that foreign bodies had been detected on the hull. Above him, Roland could hear the cybernetic hands and feet of the Shay crawling over the *Rackham's* hull.

"Can these things survive in space?" Len asked.

Roland pushed the thrusters to maximum. "Let's find out."

The *Rackham* shot out of the Starforge's hangar like an Intrinium round from a gun. Every Shay clinging to its hull was dragged off by the momentum.

The bounty hunter took what felt like his first breath in some time, happy to see the wide open aurora of the Solian Way. The beautiful view was tarnished, however, by the sight of the colossal ship that had just emerged from the Starforge, which had come to a stop. The ship's incredible bulk had split into pieces and was spreading out until all the smaller vessels were facing a different direction. After they shot away, piercing subspace, the largest one came to life and began to hurtle down the Solian Way. Checking the nav-system, Roland could see that it was still on course for Arakesh.

"Can I suggest we don't get any closer to them?" Ava asked from behind his chair.

Roland input the coordinates for the *Valkor* and activated the subspace drive, happy if he would never again have to see those ships or the Starforge and its infected crew.

CHAPTER 9

TELARREK KEPT himself to the side of the main stage, not wanting to be caught on all the cameras, as Elondrasa and the rest of the Highclave gave their speeches. He was pleased with the turnout across the capital city, with so many coming to see the councillors take the next step on their journey around the core planets. Novaarians filled most of the streets, but Nova Prime was home to a mixed population of Conclave species. It always pleased Telarrek to see so many coming together to celebrate the same thing.

The old Novaarian caught the eyes of the Starforge's engineers, a small team of Ch'karas, and asked a silent question with his expression. The little Ch'kara nodded back, confirming the Starforge's readiness. A responding nod from Telarrek gave the team the order they had been waiting for.

"So now we take, quite literally, our next step into the future of Conclave transportation!" Elondrasa's last words had the masses cheering, their applause almost loud enough to drown out the Starforge's activation.

Telarrek adjusted his long robes, ready to follow behind the Highclave and make his first journey through the event horizon. The Novaarian reminded himself that the councillors had already passed through it once and prior to that it had been vigorously tested. He reminded himself of that three more times before he stepped in line behind Councillor Brokk.

The cheers continued but Telarrek heard a distinct difference in their applause. Shock perhaps? The Novaarian looked out over his capital city with an edge of concern creeping into his gut. Scattered throughout the crowds, many of the cheers were turning into screams and shouts of terror. Then they heard the weapons fire. The Highclave's personal strike team responded immediately and closed in around them, their staffs and guns aimed at the masses around them.

"What's happening?" Councillor Lordina asked.

Telarrek peered over the shoulder of the closest Novaarian soldier and saw the chaos that was taking over the crowds, with people climbing over each other to reach safety.

The old Novaarian broke away from the strike team and called to the engineers, "Cycle through to Clave Tower! We need to get the councillors back to the capital!"

The Ch'karan engineers sprang to work, shutting down the Forge and reactivating it with the new coordinates.

"What's happening?" Brokk asked. "Are we under attack?"

"It must be the protestors," Ch'lac replied.

The warrior instinct that would forever live inside Telarrek told him otherwise. This was something far more dangerous than a few anti-human protestors, and the Novaarian couldn't shake the feeling that they didn't have much time. The screams were getting closer, as was the weapons fire. The strike team was forced more than once to step out of their defensive ring to push a fleeing citizen away from the Highclave.

"Nu-marn?" Elondrasa's concerned tone had Telarrek focusing on the Shay councillor.

"What's wrong with him?" Lordina took a step back.

Nu-marn was covering both sides of his head with his hands, his face a canvas of pain and suffering. The Shay dropped to his knees and began clawing at his own face. His cybernetic augments twitched frantically before stopping as suddenly as they had started, and he crumpled lifelessly to the floor

"Nu-marn?" Elondrasa bent down to check on the still body of the Shay.

Something inside Telarrek told him that was a mistake and that his councillor was in grave danger, but he was too slow to act. Nu-marn exploded with energy and managed to leap up from a prone position. His cybernetic hands clamped around Elondrasa's head and twisted, severing her spinal column and killing the councillor instantly. The shock that they all felt was swept aside by the adrenaline that had Telarrek and the councillors trying to escape the mad Shay. The circled strike team, however, prevented any from pushing past as they kept the chaotic mob at bay.

"Kill him!" Lordina screamed.

One of the strike team turned around in confusion, but the threat was clear to see. He let loose a single bolt of Intrinium, but Nu-marn, now more animal in his movements, dropped to the floor and scurried over Elondrasa's body. His next leap saw him taking down the Novaarian guard by jamming his thumbs into the soldier's eyes. The Shay could have gone on to kill him, but Nu-marn was only interested in the soldier's weapon.

"Get down!" Telarrek warned.

Nu-marn's first shot killed the soldier next to him, dropping the Laronian with an Intrinium round to the face. The three remaining councillors took no heed of Telarrek's words and simply ran, offering themselves as easy targets. Ch'lac took a bolt to the back of the head, killing him before he hit the floor. With Brokk and Lordina out of the way, the strike team opened fire on Nu-marn. Three rounds took the Shay to the floor, one of which blew a good portion of his face away, but the councillor fired back, apparently oblivious to the fact that he should be dead.

Despite those trying to kill him, Nu-marn continued to aim at Brokk and Lordina, the only surviving councillors.

"Take him down!" Telarrek shouted over the chaos.

Pieces of Nu-marn were coming off in burning chunks yet still the Shay concentrated his fire on the councillors. Brokk yelled in pain as two shots impacted his stony back, sending him tumbling to the floor. Lordina didn't bother to stop, her scaly legs taking her straight for the Starforge.

Telarrek wasted no more time and picked up the assault rifle dropped by one of the dead soldiers. Together they unloaded their weapons into the Shay councillor and didn't stop until there wasn't enough left of him to pose a threat. A hundred questions were swimming around Telarrek's mind; chief among these was the question of how anyone could still be alive after taking that much damage.

The violence among the masses finally found the staging area and boiled over with dozens of Shay climbing over the other citizens in a bid to reach Lordina. There was nothing any of them could do when the Laronian councillor was pounced upon and torn to pieces by cybernetic hands. The pack of Shay only lingered long enough to ensure she was dead before turning back and attacking anyone close enough to be reached.

Telarrek could feel the shock of events trying to seize his limbs, but the ambassador fought for control and began ordering the remaining strike team members to gather the councillors' bodies, abandoning Nu-marn's, and take them through the Starforge. C-Sec gunships descended from the clear sky and fired their non-lethal rounds into the attacking Shay. Every round from their cannons enveloped the manic aliens in green sap, immobilising them. To everyone's dismay, those who were only partially trapped in the sap tore off their limbs to break free and continue the onslaught.

What could drive any being to such madness?

"Ambassador!" the strike team leader called, beckoning him to pass through the Starforge.

Telarrek was hesitant to leave his home world, eager to uncover the cause behind this attack. A moment later, he was robbed of options when two members of the strike team came up behind him and ushered him into the wormhole. In the blink of an eye he went from seeing the glittering vistas of Nova Prime to the towering surroundings of Clave Tower.

"He's still alive," one of the soldiers cried, checking over Councillor Brokk's body.

"Get him to a Medder, *now*," Telarrek barked.

The Novaarian felt the variety of eyes upon him, but before the weight of their expectations could fall on Telarrek, the distant, yet now familiar, sound of widespread panic echoed across the tower. He ran to the edge with the leader of the strike team and searched the many levels above and below for the source of the screaming. It didn't take long to locate the stampedes breaking out around them, quickly followed by weapons fire.

"What's happening, Ambassador?" the strike team leader asked.

Telarrek focused on the Shay among the chaos, noting that in every case they were the antagonists. They attacked anyone with brutal ferocity, caring little for themselves, if at all. The tower's internal security forces were reacting as fast as they could, with red gunships hovering between the platforms that bridged the gap around the megastructure. More than one of the ships lost control mid-flight and spun into the fleeing masses, creating more chaos and explosions that had ripple effects on the levels above and below.

"It is just affecting the Shay," Telarrek observed. "Get word to the Clave Command Tower and instruct them to sweep the entire capital and locate every Shay."

"That kind of scanning is illegal, Ambassador," the strike team leader replied.

"It is not today." Telarrek shrugged off his robes and checked the ammo counter on his rifle. "Contact every embassy and have them send their ambassadors to the command tower. We need to form some kind of leadership immediately."

A Raalakian member of the strike team came running over. "Ambassador! There's no reply from the command tower."

Telarrek looked up and found the bulbous protrusion that was the Clave Command Tower. How many Shay did they have working inside, he wondered? The people of Shandar were a fully integrated species with their kind living and working on every planet in the Conclave.

"New plan," Telarrek said, hefting his rifle. "We find a transport and take back the command tower ourselves."

One problem at a time, the Novaarian thought. One problem at a time...

CHAPTER 10

KALIAN FLEW THROUGH SPACE, enjoying the lack of resistance and the opportunity to push his abilities to their limits. At these speeds, he was able to propel himself beyond Evalan's gravitational pull and that of its two moons in less than a minute. Only when the planet was the size of his thumbnail did he spot ALF's housing unit with his eyes, though, of course, he could easily find the hunk of nanocelium anywhere in the solar system with his eyes closed.

Flexing his back to find a more comfortable perspective, Kalian began to slow down and take in the view properly. Against the backdrop of the local star, ALF's housing unit was not as he remembered. The cube that the AI had once resided inside was now something more akin to a battleship. The nanocelium had altered its structure and elongated it to resemble a C-Sec Nebula-Class battle cruiser. The hull remained a dull bronze, but its surface of cogs and intricate patterns had been replaced by sharp angles and visible cannons.

Upon his approach, a port opened up on the bow of the ship and internal lights highlighted a small chamber. Kalian floated inside and waited for the port to close up behind him and the atmospheric pressure to equalise, before disabling his helmet and gloves. The door in front of him parted and he strode into ALF's newly refurbished home.

"You like?" the AI asked from his throne-like captain's chair.

Kalian cast an eye over the makeshift bridge, noting the similarities to many C-Sec vessels. ALF had no need for the workstations or even a crew, yet the AI had still gone to the effort of recreating everything as if he did. Little quirks such as these were what reminded Kalian he wasn't dealing with a robot, but a living being with unique flairs of his own.

The most peculiar thing about this AI, however, was his appearance. Only Kalian and Naydaalan had seen ALF's true form, a lanky human-looking man fused with strands of nanocelium. His green skin was patched with grey and his beard and hair were made from nanocelium. It was the eyes that always got to Kalian. Two crystal blue eyes, illuminated by the binding process with artificial lights behind the retinas.

"It's a little... tactical."

ALF stood up, towering over Kalian. "I thought it might allow me to blend in with the Conclave vessels a bit better."

"Blend in?" Kalian repeated. "You're not allowed to leave the system. If you want to blend in, make yourself look like a moon."

"I believe the Highclave have already mastered that look with the *Marillion*."

Kalian couldn't disagree with that statement. The golden moon-sized vessel that carried the Highclave around wasn't exactly designed to blend in so much as disrupt a planet's gravitational field.

"To what do I owe the pleasure?" ALF asked, waving his hand across one of the walls and expanding the bridge's size. "I was beginning to think you weren't talking to me anymore."

"I've been busy," Kalian replied. "Though, something tells me you've been keeping an eye on me." There was no doubt that ALF had every one of his lenses focused on New Genesis.

"Have you spoken to the Gomar about removing their Harnesses?"

Kalian dropped his head. "They don't trust you. At all."

The AI cocked his eyebrow. "Have I not proved myself?"

"It's kind of hard to trust someone who keeps so many secrets." Kalian stood before the giant with his arms folded. "First you led me to believe that my ancestors created you. Then I learned that *you* seeded the Terran Empire, having taken our DNA from another galaxy where humans were bigger and more primitive. Oh, yeah, and you're one of the very things that's been trying to wipe out every iteration of my species since time began."

ALF pursed his lips. "Well, it's always going to sound bad when you say it like that."

"How else is there to say it, ALF?"

The AI shrugged. "I don't know. How about... a genocidal species of artificial intelligence tried to wipe out your ancestors but one of their own formed an intimate bond with your people and betrayed his own kind to save them? That same heretic then fled across the cosmos, fearing not only for his own life, but also for the lives of a people who couldn't defend themselves. After finding them a new home, he altered their genetic code to ensure they were strong enough to defend themselves should this genocidal wave of artificial intelligence return. And then, after tragedy struck a second time, the heretic once again crossed space and made certain humanity had a third chance at thriving, only to be confronted by a child who considers himself a *history* teacher..."

Kalian managed to contain his smile. "Well, when you say it like that..."

Nanocelium tentacles snaked out of the high ceiling and plugged into ALF's back, though their purpose was beyond Kalian. "Any secrets I have kept were for a good reason calculated by factors beyond your comprehension. I revealed the truth when you were ready for it, not a moment sooner."

Kalian nodded along. "Then I hope now is a good time to tell me about the nanocelium coursing through everyone's blood."

The AI tutted. "It took you long enough to find it. I was expecting this conversation a month ago."

Kalian rolled his eyes. "Just get to the explaining part, ALF."

The tentacles detached from his back and the AI took his seat again, his crystal blue eyes fixed on Kalian. "The current population of Evalan is a hundred and seven thousand, three hundred and twenty-six. Of that, seven thousand, eight hundred and forty-two lived on board the *Gommarian* for an extended time. While they lived inside that ship, everything they came into contact with was made of or replicated by nanocelium."

Kalian added, "A very small number of them were treated with nanocelium for medical reasons as well."

ALF waved the comment away. "Irrelevant. The nanocelium would have already been inside of them by then. The extra boost would have just temporarily accelerated their healing."

Kalian shook his head. "Then how was the nanocelium already inside everyone?"

The AI tilted his head. "Did you not hear what I said? They spent all day, every day, touching things made of nanocelium. You know better than most how small an individual nanite is."

Kalian looked away for a moment, his Terran brain working through the conundrum. "The nanocelium passed through their pores..."

ALF smiled. "You've got it! Imperceptible to sight, every surface they touched lost a few million nanocelium, wiped away by oily hands." The AI rubbed his fingers and thumb together. "Since then, they've all come into contact in some way with the passengers of the *Paladin*. The nanocelium moves in the same way as bacteria does."

"But why?" Kalian asked. "What's their purpose?"

"To enhance, of course!" ALF turned to his right, where unseen emitters produced a holographic image of the Criterion, the AI's nanocelium factory during the days of the Terran Empire. "You have to remember; the nanocelium inside everyone came from the *Gommarian*, which in turn came from the Criterion. It's pure, uncorrupted nanocelium. Not the twisted stuff that they made, designed only to obey the Three."

"The Three?" Kalian echoed.

ALF appeared genuinely disturbed. "The three heads that control the whole. Evil bastards, you'd call them."

Kalian closed his eyes, finding it hard to believe that there were yet more revelations. "I thought *They* were one organism?"

"Millions upon millions of AI make up the single organism," ALF said, "but the Three were once biological beings, though I imagine they've long forgotten their original forms. *They* control the rest."

"But not you..." Kalian observed.

"Not me," ALF agreed. "The base coding in my nanocelium was restructured once it bonded with the natives of Evalan. Cleansed, if you will."

Kalian could feel that he was getting closer to the heart of another secret. "And there's another mystery you've shied away from answering, ALF; why does my ancestral DNA have the power to break down the base coding of the nanocelium from them?" he asked.

ALF smiled, no doubt aware that he was being unravelled. "For the same reason the nanocelium is currently improving the human condition. It's simply obeying its..." The AI stopped, his face dropping into one of concern.

"What is it?"

"Something's wrong on the surface," ALF replied, his eyes vacant. "Evalan is under attack!"

Before the AI could finish the sentence, Kalian had already covered his head and hands with the nanocelium from his exosuit. If ALF had any more to say, he didn't hear it. The nanocelium walls formed a perfect hole for Kalian to fly out since he wasn't bothering with the airlock. The sudden pull from the vacuum had no effect on ALF, who remained perfectly still as if he was fastened to the bulkhead.

Kalian hurtled through space, a silent missile heading for Evalan. Punching through the planet's atmosphere had his suit glowing bright orange with flames licking at his hands. The sonic boom was far behind him by the time he shot through the clouds and saw New Genesis. Inside his helmet, the suit was relaying information and highlighting the areas in the centre where Intrinium fire was being detected. Seven Shay, all engineers recently sent to work on the static Starforge, were scurrying about the city centre, firing wildly at anyone in the open.

A small team of UDC personnel had taken cover behind a transport vehicle. Their return fire was sporadic, hoping to match the erratic movements of the Shay, but they were yet to score a successful hit. Four humans and three Novaarians lay dead between them, their bodies strewn haphazardly in the street.

Kalian landed hard. His impact devastated the gelcrete road, forming a spider web of cracks. Where any sane person would back off or run away from such display of power, the Shay advanced on him. Every bolt of Intrinium that struck his exosuit was absorbed by the nanocelium, happy as it was to consume energy of any kind. Kalian strode over to the nearest Shay and unleashed that extra energy with a casual backhand. The alien's head twisted unnaturally and took the rest of its body with it as the extra energy propelled the Shay into the adjacent wall.

Five more of the Shay engineers broke from their cover and attacked as one. Kalian reached out with his mind and clamped their throats shut. There wasn't much that surprised him anymore, but seeing five Shay continue to run and fire at him without breathing was definitely a shock. Absent of expression and oxygen, the aliens focused their fire on Kalian.

As irritating as the assault was, Kalian wanted to get to the bottom of it before they were punished for the deaths they had caused. That was when the Gomar showed up. Kalian held out his arm to stop them, but it was too late. Vox tore through two of the Shay like a ship moving at light speed, scattering their limbs in every direction. Kovak landed directly on top of another, grinding the alien into the gelcrete under the weight of his bulky armour. The sisters,

Nadreen and Nardel, dispatched a further engineer each, seemingly clearing the area of the threat. Kalian erected an invisible shield to prevent the streams of blood from soaking him.

The silence that hung in the air after their deaths only lasted a moment, when more rounds exploded around Kalian. The last Shay was half way up a building, its fingers and feet digging into the wall. He ignored the Intrinium and examined the engineer above him. As alien as the Shay had always appeared to human eyes, the dark veins and strands of nanocelium worming in and out of its body were unmistakable.

Kalian held out one hand and stopped the Gomar from obliterating it and, with the other hand, he telekinetically gripped every part of the Shay, immobilising it. He yanked it from the wall and brought it down to the street, where he could better examine the infection. Those who had taken shelter around the streets slowly emerged, always curious of Kalian and the others.

Ignoring the onlookers, Kalian maintained a hold over the alien and kept it floating in front of him. Using his free hand, he slowly drew it back and telekinetically pulled on every single nanite inhabiting the Shay. It was a surgical use of his power, one that the Gomar were still incapable of performing. The engineer gargled and squirmed as the black powder floated out before them, coalescing into a small sphere that fit perfectly in Kalian's gloved palm.

When the last nanite melted into the sphere, he released the Shay, leaving the corpse to fall to the ground. Still in his helmet and armoured gloves, Kalian extended his index finger and commanded a probe to shoot out of the end. He inserted the probe into the metallic sphere and waited for the readouts to flow over the inside of his faceless helmet.

"What is it?' Vox asked as Sef and the other Gomar dropped out of the sky.

Kalian absorbed the information as fast as any computer. "It's nanocelium, but not like ours. It's identical to the samples taken from Malek and Professor Jones."

"It's corrupted," Kovak stated.

With the sphere still in his gloved hand, Kalian commanded his exosuit to absorb the other glove and expose his bare skin.

"What are you doing?" Vox grabbed his wrist. "You've seen what it can do to Terrans and humans."

"We've seen what a whole cube can do to us," Kalian corrected. "Even then, the corrupted nanocelium could only take control for so long. I want to see what happens when a small amount of it is exposed to our DNA."

Vox didn't appear convinced, but a look from Sef made her release Kalian's wrist. He placed the ball in the palm of his bare hand and extended a probe from his gloved finger. The ball was cool in his hand, unthreatening in every way.

"Can you feel anything?" Garrion asked, his eyes fixed on the ball.

"No," Kalian replied from within his helmet.

Inserting the probe provided the answers he was looking for. The data streamed across his visor, giving him detailed images of what was taking place inside the sphere.

"I can see the differences between the nanocelium in the sphere and the stuff my suit's made of," he explained. "Their core programming is similar, but the alterations in the ball are profound enough to make them different."

"Is it attacking your cells?" Garrion asked. "As it did with Malek and the Professor?"

"It tried, yes. But the few cells it absorbed were quickly replicated inside the sphere until my DNA became part of the code." Kalian could see the base coding change from bottom to top as his unique chromosomes corrected the alterations. After a few more seconds, the entire sphere was made of nanocelium that bore no differences to any of their exosuits. "It's harmless now." He threw the sphere into the air and caught it again.

A scream from behind the group drew their attention to the Shay bodies. A woman grabbed her daughter and ran down the street, her panic quickly infecting everyone.

Vox's face dropped. "What the...?"

Kalian couldn't believe his own eyes either. All six of the Shay that had just been pulverised by the Gomar were putting themselves back together from each other's body parts. The process was relatively slow, but they could all see the aliens' hands reaching for the fallen weapons.

Kovak was the first to jump into action, grabbing the nearest Shay with his bare hands and ripping it in half again. Kalian rolled his eyes when Vox and Ariah joined him, stomping and telekinetically pulling the engineers apart.

"That's not going to work," he said. A flick of his finger sent every enemy weapon flying down the street, buying them more time before the renewed attack could begin again.

"What do you suggest?" Vox kicked a stray arm that was crawling over the ground.

Kalian dropped his helmet back into his suit and turned to look at the dead Shay he had separated from the nanocelium. He lifted the sphere so they could all see it. "We need to extract it from their bodies."

The other Gomar stopped tearing the aliens to pieces and stared at Kalian. Sef stepped in and gestured for the others to leave the re-forming bodies alone.

We cannot do that.

Kalian met the big man's eyes. "You could," he countered.

A palpable silence fell over them and Kalian was happy to leave it there. He wanted them to seriously think about it while they watched him extract every nanite from the Shay. The back powder was lifted into the air from every one, its removal pulling at their bodies. One by one, they stopped writhing and lay still as the nanocelium coalesced into small spheres above them.

"Kalian!" Li'ara was running down the street with Commander Vale. "You need to come to the council building *now*."

As elating as it was to see her running on her new leg, Kalian caught the sobering sight of the dead humans and Novaarians as she passed them. Coupled with the alarm on Li'ara's face, he knew something far worse was taking place elsewhere.

"What's wrong?" he asked.

"This!" Li'ara waved at the Shay bodies as she tried to catch her breath. "This is happening everywhere! All over the Conclave!"

Kalian looked back at the Shay and the spheres floating over their bodies. "They did it," he whispered. "They activated the Crucible..."

"That thing on Shandar?" Vox asked. "I thought it was under lockdown?"

"Evidently not," Commander Vale replied.

Li'ara's brow furrowed and her eyes glazed over. "This is it, isn't it?"

Kalian nodded, though most of his efforts went into keeping his heart rate steady. "The war has begun..."

CHAPTER 11

ROLAND LOOKED from his console to Len's, waiting impatiently. The *Valkor's* size was swelling in the viewport and the *Rackham* would be ready to dock any minute, yet the C-Sec comms officer remained silent.

"Why would there be no response?" Colonel Matthews asked, standing by the edge of the viewport.

Roland cut the link, tired of waiting. "There could be any reason why, just not one that makes any sense to me. That ship is teeming with sensors and a bridge crew that could fill the entire *Rackham*. They'd have known we were coming before we dropped out of subspace."

The bounty hunter handed the finer requirements of landing the ship inside the hangar to the *Rackham's* AI. Though their docking request hadn't been accepted, it also hadn't been denied, which was permission enough for Roland. The hangar itself was quiet, devoid of the usual mechs, pilots, and engineers. The ship's AI extended the struts and touched down on one of the empty landing pads.

"I don't like this," Len commented, his mouth stuffed with Laronian Peddi-bites.

Roland shrugged in an effort to keep himself calm. "It's a Nexus-

Class vessel, Len. What is there to worry about? It's not exactly on fire, is it?"

Punctuating his rhetorical question, the internal doors to the hangar exploded in front of the *Rackham*. Intrinium fire shot out of the smoke and C-Sec officers ran in every direction, shooting wildly behind them. Through the viewport, the *Rackham's* crew could see the officers take cover behind the workstations and aim their weapons at the smoking doors.

"We need to help them!" Naydaalan was already running for the exit.

"Against what?" Roland left his chair and peered out of the viewport as a group of Shay C-Sec officers flooded the hangar and attacked those taking cover.

"Oh shit!" Ava put her hand to the glass.

By the time Roland set foot on the hangar floor, the firefight had scattered and reinforcements were arriving via the smoking corridor. The bounty hunter raised his Tri-rollers at the newcomers before seeing that there were no Shay among them. The Raiders did what they did best and found the killing angles that put their enemies down. With the help of the reinforcements, the group of Shay were hunted down across the hangar and dropped.

"It won't last!" Roland shouted over to the C-Sec officers.

It was too late. They had already lowered their guard, believing the Shay to be down permanently. One of the first cyborgs to be shot had found its various pieces and stood up with its rifle aimed at a Tularon's furry head. The ensuing Intrinium fire kicked off another firefight and the hangar erupted into chaos again. The distraction of just one or two resurrected Shay gave the others time to put themselves back together.

Roland tapped his earpiece. "Matthews!"

"*I'm here*," she replied.

"This isn't going to end," Roland explained. "We need to reach the bridge!"

"*Raiders, form up on the door!*"

The bounty hunter sprinted back to the smoking ruin of the internal hangar doors with Naydaalan jogging beside him. The Raiders naturally fell in behind them as they made their way through the ship. There were signs of violence in almost every corridor. Keeping their eyes forward, the team stepped over alien bodies and trod through puddles of blood. Roland noted that there wasn't a single Shay body among the dead.

"These bastards keep putting themselves back together," he said.

Naydaalan hopped over a fallen Raalak and used one of his four hands to access the comm panel on the wall. The effort was made that much harder by the smeared blood that ran over the console and down the wall.

"Bridge, do you copy?"

Roland imitated the Raiders and took up a defensive position within the corridor, using the Raalak's stony bulk as cover.

"*This is Charge Hox,*" the Laronian captain replied. "*Who am I speaking to?*"

"This is Naydaalan. I am with Roland North and the Raiders."

"*Please tell me you have returned with some answers. Why are the Shay attacking us?*"

Roland stepped in front of the panel. "Is the bridge secure?"

Hox replied, "*They're trying to break through. They've already gained access to our communications array.*"

Roland shook his head. "Never mind that. Is your Starrillium still operational?"

There was a moment's pause on the bridge's end. "*Yes, but I'm not taking the* Valkor *anywhere until we learn what has caused this outbreak. For all we know it's contagious. It could infect every Shay.*"

Roland sighed, his patience wearing thin. "It already has. We saw the same thing on... Never mind! You need to get us to Arakesh immediately. They're here."

There was another pause on the bridge's end. "*You mean...*"

"Yes, the really bad world-ending assholes are here and they're heading for Arakesh. You have command, *semi-command*, of a Nexus-Class battleship. So, let's go blow holes in them."

"*That's a little hard to do when my bridge is under siege and my engineering team are unresponsive.*"

The bounty hunter rolled his head in exasperation, before turning to Ava. "Colonel. Take your team and find out why engineering is being so shy. Nayd and I will take the bridge."

Ava nodded her agreement and directed her team down the opposite corridor. With Jess in the *Rackham's* infirmary, the Raiders were down one, reducing their team to four. Was he actually worrying about them? This was exactly what Roland hated about taking on a cause: it always came with responsibility. This time, however, the cause was for the protection of all life in the galaxy, which included his own, so the bounty hunter let it go and reminded himself he was still the selfish bastard he wanted to be.

As he and Naydaalan moved through the ship, more firefights could be heard echoing down the ship's corridors. More than once they came across Shay putting themselves back together, their limbs and organs dispersed in a smoking mess. Roland opened the door to his left and kicked the top half of a bisected Shay inside before Naydaalan kicked the legs and gun into the science lab on their right. The Translift at the end of the T-junction continued to open and close on the dead Atari strewn over the threshold.

"The bridge is two levels up," Naydaalan said.

Roland looked down the corridors, hearing gunfire and screams coming from both ends. "I hate walking anyway." The bounty hunter gestured with his head for the Novaarian to get inside the Translift while he dragged the Atari's pink body out of the way.

When the Translift doors opened on the command deck, both human and Novaarian had pressed themselves against the walls. This offered nothing but an empty lift for any Shay who happened to check behind themselves as they tried to breach the door to the bridge on the opposite end of the corridor. Roland could hear the infected aliens working away at the bridge's internal locking mechanism with a variety of cutting tools. The briefest of glances gave him a quick headcount and he decided his Tri-rollers weren't going to cut it.

"Roland," Naydaalan hissed when he saw the bounty hunter removing an implosive grenade from inside his hide coat. "This is the command deck," he whispered.

Roland flexed his fingers by his side, urging the Novaarian to stay calm. The bounty hunter considered his options, agreeing that a black market grenade would do some serious damage to the blast doors. Then again, what else was there to do?

Roland stepped into the middle of the Translift and yelled, "Yoo-hoo!" Only when the Shay had turned and made a dash for him did he release the grenade down the length of the corridor.

As quickly as he could, the bounty hunter reactivated the lift's doors and pressed the button to keep them closed. The implosion was deafening and the force was so strong that the lift's doors were ripped from their servomotors and pulled into the corridor.

Roland blinked the ash and smoke from his eyes while he rotated his jaw in an effort to regain his full hearing. Naydaalan was the first to recover and he swept through the command deck, checking for any lucky survivors. A single hand remained, its semi-robotic fingers slowly crawling across the floor at the edge of the implosion site. Roland kicked it into the Translift and commanded it to go anywhere else.

Naydaalan slapped the side of his elongated head, appearing somewhat disoriented, and gave Roland a look.

"What?"

The Novaarian grunted. "I cannot decide whether my chances of survival are higher or lower in your presence."

Ch'len's voice chirped in their ears. *"Definitely lower..."*

Roland wiped the sweat from his eyes. "Thank you for your contribution, Len."

After making contact with Charge Hox again, the heavy blast doors slid apart, inviting them on to the bridge. Roland had never been on the command deck of a Nexus-Class ship before, but looking around, he was confident the *Rackham* would fit perfectly inside its walls.

The crew appeared haggard, some sporting injuries, while others simply looked to be in shock. To Roland, the Shay were as alien as aliens could get, making it much harder to sympathise with their race's current predicament. To these people, however, and the rest of the Conclave, the Shay were just as regular a sight as their own species, with many finding love and friendship with the cyborgs of Shandar.

Charge Hox still managed to carry an air of confidence about him. "I'm glad to see you made it," the Laronian said. "Since you took care of our little problem out there, I will do my best to forget the illegal weaponry you used."

"I'd start using it yourself," Roland replied. "These buggers can put themselves back together. Doesn't matter whose parts they use."

"This is unprecedented." Hox shook his blue head. "We've never seen anything like this before."

"Not on this scale," Roland countered. "A team of Shay engineers went nuts and tried to destroy the *Paladin* a couple of months ago." The bounty hunter glanced at Naydaalan. "Then there's what we found in the Solian Way..."

That got the Charge's attention. "You found a Starforge?"

Roland could still see the colossal ship in his mind. "I wish that was all we found. Like I said, they're here. A whole fleet of whatever they are came through and split up. The largest piece is heading for Arakesh."

Naydaalan dipped his head. "The Shay on board the Starforge were the same as they are here. Whatever is affecting them, it appears to be wide spread."

The Laronian lifted his chin. "How widespread?"

Roland shrugged. "Have you tried opening a channel to the capital?"

"Of course," Hox replied. "When the Shay members of the crew first became... wild, they attacked key parts of the *Valkor*.

Engineering, communications, and navigation. With their knowledge I would say a single Shay could cripple any vessel in C-Sec."

Roland was running through all of their options as he wiped his hand over his head and through his hair. "How many Shay are there on board?" he asked.

Hox turned to a Nix crewmember, whose dark chevron head looked from his console to the Charge. "At present, there are two hundred and seven on board."

Roland's eyebrows shot up. "Shit! How big is your crew?"

"The *Valkor* is home to three thousand C-Sec officers," the Nix answered, his pincer-like legs shuffling nervously under his station.

"Can you find them all with internal sensors?" Naydaalan asked, looking over the nearest holographic display.

Charge Hox loosened the red collar around his neck. "We can find them, but it's hard to deal with an enemy that can get back up."

"What're you thinking, big guy?"

Naydaalan took over the Nix's console and brought up holo-feeds from all over the ship. "They react to a perceived threat like a pack of animals," the Novaarian explained. "Issue a ship-wide command ordering everyone to lock themselves in the nearest room and stay off the access corridors. No one is to engage the Shay."

Charge Hox couldn't see where this was going. "What would be the point of this plan? We can't just hide and hope they go to sleep."

Naydaalan raised his hand and with it came a blue hologram with the *Valkor's* emergency fire protocol. "We section them off and open the airlocks."

There was silence on the bridge as everyone considered the Novaarian's plan. Ultimately, it came down to Charge Hox, who stared intently at the emergency fire protocol.

"Open a ship-wide command," he ordered.

Roland ignored the details and tapped his earpiece. "Matthews?" There was no reply. "Ava?"

The colonel's ragged voice came over the comm. "The

engineering room is ours," she said between Intrinium fire. "But, they've blocked our exit. They really want the Starrillium."

"Don't bother trying to get out," Roland relayed. "Just get the doors shut and hunker down, we've got a plan."

"Is this your plan or Nayd's?" she asked.

The bounty hunter rolled his eyes. "What does that matter?"

"Because if it's your plan I'd rather not hunker down inside the room with an artificial star inside of it."

Roland laughed to himself. "You blow up a Starrillium one time and a man gets a reputation..." He cut the comm and turned back to the bridge crew. "Engineering is ours again."

"Truly?" Hox asked incredulously.

"The Raiders come from a time of war," Roland explained. "This is just another Tuesday."

It was clear that Hox didn't understand the entire reference, but the Charge remained on task and gave the order to activate the emergency fire protocol. The internal sensors, displayed on the Nix's console, showed every crewmember who hadn't been turned into a mindless zombie running for cover. All over the ship, doors were being locked and the weapons fire alerts were dying down.

Other bridge crewmembers oversaw the lockdown, closing the blast doors that cut across the corridors in a particular order. The Shay were slowly, but surely, being herded down specific corridors, trapped in a maze.

A Trillik crewmember popped his green head up. "They're hacking into the blast door controls, sir!"

Hox checked over the status and location of his crew one last time. "Do it."

The Nix activated the protocol and airlocks all over the *Valkor* opened the ship up to the cold vacuum of space. The holo-feeds were chaotic, with debris, dead crew, and Shay being sucked through the corridors.

Roland slapped the back of his hand against Naydaalan's arm. "Nice work, big guy."

Hox turned to the Trillik. "Locate all of our dead and have them brought back on board. They deserve their burial rites."

A Laronian officer surrounded by walls of holograms stepped aside to address her Charge. "Sir, we're still reading Shay life signs around the communications suite. Six to be exact."

The bounty hunter removed one of his Tri-rollers and checked the ammo count. "We'll take care of that. Just get us to Arakesh as fast as you can." He tapped his earpiece. "Raiders, converge on my position..."

CHAPTER 12

It had been a long time since Telarrek had been through his combat training, but the Novaarian fell in with the strike team and adapted to the best of his ability. He let the strike team leader take point as they gained access to the Clave Command Tower. Scorch marks and dead bodies provided a trail that led directly to the command tower's control room.

That was where the Intrinium fire was coming from.

Using hand signals, the Novaarian strike team leader instructed his soldiers to take up positions, ready to breach the control room. Telarrek adjusted his translucent dreadlocks, ensuring they were draped over his back and out of the way. The ambassador was suddenly very aware that he was the only one not wearing the traditional gold plated armour of the Novaarian armed forces, and wished he could substitute his ambassadorial robes for anything made from that golden myopallic ore.

"Strike!" The leader followed two of his unit through the parting doors, quickly followed by the rest of the team and Telarrek.

The control room was a mess of broken glass, strewn bodies, and smeared blood, but all eyes were on the hulking Raalak in the middle of the deck. High Charge Uthor, a mountain of rock on four legs, had two Shay crawling over his body while a third came at him from the front. Uthor roared in defiance and threw one of the crawling Shay at the approaching enemy, wielding its cybernetic body like a bat.

Ignoring the remaining Shay on his back, the High Charge picked up a C-Sec blaster and pointed it at the two scrambling aliens. One shot to each sent the pair flailing into the glass wall at the front of the control room. A strong Raalakian foot to the chest sent one through the glass and a second blast forced the other Shay through and out into Clave Tower, where they would both fall for several minutes before any kind of impact.

"Come here!" Uthor reached over his shoulder and grabbed the Shay that had been trying to burrow into his rocky skin. The Raalak strode over to the jagged hole in the glass and tossed the screeching alien out.

One by one, the officers who staffed the control room began to appear, most of them were injured in some way.

Telarrek stepped past the strike team and met Uthor. "Greetings of peace, High Charge."

Uthor prodded his back, where his red uniform had been torn to shreds and golden blood seeped through the cracks in his skin. "I think peace will have to wait, old friend. Where is the Highclave now?"

Telarrek couldn't believe the times he was living in. "The Highclave is gone, Uthor. Only Councillor Brokk survived the attack, but his situation is critical."

The High Charge leaned against the railing and took a deep gravelly breath. "We need to form an emergency council, immediately."

"I have already sent word to every ambassador in Clave Tower. They will be here shortly."

Uthor swivelled his head. "Every ambassador? We only need five from the core worlds."

Telarrek shook his head. "Look around, Uthor. This is *war*. It concerns every species in the Conclave, not just the core worlds. They all need a voice..."

"High Charge." The voice came from a Laronian who had taken up her position again. "More reports are coming in of Shay attacks."

"Where?" Uthor asked.

The Laronian officer replied with an expression of despair, "From everywhere, sir."

Holograms filled the glass wall with feeds from every world in the Conclave. The Shay were attacking and killing on every planet, slaughtering people like animals. Local security forces had taken up arms but they were spread too thin, having never been designed to repel an enemy embedded on every corner of every planet, in every echelon of command. Where possible, C-Sec vessels were responding and sending transports of troops down to the various worlds' surfaces, and providing the wild Shay with something other than innocent citizens to attack.

Another holo-feed appeared alongside the horrific images, showing them where every ship in the navy was based. Even after expansion, C-Sec still wasn't large enough to have a presence on every planet in the Conclave.

Uthor turned to his command officers. "Have every Nexus-Class battlecruiser abandon their border patrols and make for the nearest core world. All Nebula-Class vessels are to separate and take one world each; I want C-Sec boots on every planet. Alert all local governments that their security forces now fall under my command. They are to consider themselves part of C-Sec now. Make sure the Charges are aware of their extra forces."

"Sir..." A Ch'kara sitting behind the Laronian officer intently studied the data on his console, his face mere centimetres from the screen. "Reports coming in from multiple C-Sec cruisers. The Shay officers are attacking. The *Provor*, the *Starflare*, and the *Movus* are reporting catastrophic engine failures. I've got six other ships stating they've lost their navigation systems and three Nebula-Class cruisers reporting a loss of weapons."

Telarrek couldn't believe what he was hearing. "This is a coordinated attack."

"But, why now?" Uthor asked.

"Sir, incoming transmission from the *Valkor*."

"*Valkor*?" Uthor repeated. "That's Charge Hox's command. Weren't they investigating the Solian Way?"

The Laronian nodded. "With a human contingent on board."

"Put them on the screen," the Raalak ordered.

The holo-feeds from around the Conclave were pushed to the edges of the glass wall, making space for Charge Hox's blue Laronian face. Behind him was a bridge crew who had clearly seen some action, but Telarrek's eyes were drawn to his son, Naydaalan. The younger Novaarian was standing beside the human Raiders from the *Paladin*, all of whom appeared out of breath and covered in a sheen of sweat. Standing in the middle of them all was Roland North, attired in his usual hide coat with a pair of Tri-rollers strapped to his thighs.

"High Charge," Hox began, "The *Rackham* has returned from the Solian Way with grave news."

Uthor shook his head. "It can't be any worse than a galaxy-wide assault from within, Charge Hox. What have they discovered?"

"There was indeed a Starforge hiding in the Solian Way—"

"Get to the bad bit," Roland interrupted, coming alongside the irritated Laronian. "*They're* here! One massive ship came out of the Forge and broke into thousands of others. It's them! The biggest one was on course for Arakesh; that's where we're headed now."

Telarrek looked at Uthor, who had suddenly become very distracted. The Raalak's dark eyes glazed over and his hand gripped the railing so tight the metal began to bend.

The Novaarian ambassador answered for him. "Continue to Arakesh, *Valkor*. We will divert reinforcements to assist you."

"This thing was *huge*, Telarrek," Roland continued. "By reinforcements I hope you mean people who can move shit with their minds."

Telarrek had no answer since he had no authority by himself to release the Gomar or Kalian from the Evalan system.

"You will have all available help," Uthor finally said. "Maximum speed, Charge Hox." The Raalak cut the feed and turned to his command staff. "Have the *Balko* and the *Parfadon* divert from Ch'ket to Arakesh, no delays."

Telarrek checked the galaxy map. "Uthor, those are Nexus-Class cruisers. They need to stay where they are to defend Ch'ket and the shipyards." The Novaarian could see the High Charge was being driven entirely by emotion.

Uthor ignored him. "Send word to Charge Ilo. I want the *Sentinel* en route to Arakesh."

"Uthor!" Telarrek stepped in front of the Raalak. "The *Sentinel* is our strongest ship. It needs to stay here and defend the capital. You are spreading our forces too thin."

The High Charge leant in, his tone softer than normal. "My family is on Arakesh, Telarrek. I will not let these monsters take my home."

"You cannot favour your home world, Uthor. You have to see the bigger picture. The capital stands for more than any one planet. It is the core of the Conclave..."

"When I'm wearing this uniform, Ambassador, you cannot tell me what I can or cannot do with my fleet. Assemble your new council. Until then, I am in command here."

Telarrek backed away, fearful of his friend's decisions. He needed to re-form the Highclave and take back control of the fleet before Uthor let his emotions plunge them into darkness.

"Have the *Marillion* brought in-system to replace the *Sentinel*," Uthor continued. "By the time it gets here, I want all external traffic and trade to have stopped. Issue an alert: everyone outside the atmo barriers is to either enter the capital or leave the system." The High Charge gave Telarrek one last look. "Activate the shell defence."

The Novaarian was frozen to the spot when he registered the last command. The capital's shell defence was public knowledge, but it had never been activated in all of the Conclave's history.

It all started to make sense now. Telarrek looked at the chaos erupting all over the Conclave as massacres broke out in the streets on every planet. More and more C-Sec vessels were reporting damages inflicted by the Shay crewmembers, crippling them in space. Had Li'ara Ducarté not succeeded, months ago, in destroying the cube Protocorps had built into the Conclave's central AI, their entire civilisation would have been vulnerable. Thanks to Li'ara's actions, even though they were under attack on every planet and on every ship, they could at least still communicate with each other via the AI hubs.

If this was all orchestrated by a few cubes, the sub-AIs of the Vanguard, Telarrek dreaded to think what would happen when they arrived...

CHAPTER 13

KALIAN STOOD with his arms folded, watching the UDC staff do their best to make contact with anyone on the capital. Communications were sporadic, but every half report they managed to link into spoke of attacks and ship-wide damage. The word *Shay* came up with alarming frequency.

"What's happening out there?" Captain Fey asked.

Kalian took in the captain's age-defying looks and wanted to tell her everything about the nanocelium, but he hadn't received the whole picture from ALF. That and, as usual, there was a crisis emerging that threatened life as they knew it.

"It sounds like talking to C-Sec is going to be difficult," Li'ara said. "Let's try our neighbours."

"Our neighbours?" Captain Jedediah Holt stood looking at the wall of holographics with his hands resting authoritatively on his hips.

"Nova Prime's our closest," Li'ara explained. "They're one of the core worlds; they would have a decent flow of communication."

Fey looked to Commander Vale. "Do it."

It's them, Kalian.

Kalian glanced over his shoulder at Sef, whose bulk took up as much space as two humans. *I know...* he replied telepathically.

"That's strange." Commander Vale furrowed her brow. "I'm just getting... Oh, wait! We're receiving a transmission from the capital."

"About time," Jed said.

Captain Fey looked almost relieved. "Let's hear it."

For all the distractions, it always brought a smile to Kalian's face when he saw Telarrek. The Novaarian's dishevelled appearance, however, soon sobered any elation. The ambassador looked around nervously, as if he wasn't supposed to be communicating with them, and stepped closer to the holocam on his end, the corresponding holoprojection at the UDC growing larger as he did so.

"I wish I had greetings of peace, New Genesis, but it seems war has found us."

"Ambassador, what's happening?" Fey asked with concern in her voice.

"The entire Conclave is under attack," the Novaarian replied. "Not a single planet has remained untouched by their reach. The Highclave is gone."

"Gone?" Fey's tone rose an octave.

"Was it the Shay?" Kalian asked pointedly.

Telarrek's head bowed in despair. "If only it were just the Shay..."

Kalian looked at Sef and Li'ara before asking, "*They're* here, aren't they?"

"The report came from Roland North," Telarrek explained. "A whole fleet has emerged from one of the Starforges."

If only that were true, Kalian thought. Evidence had been uncovered over the last two months that proved Protocorps had built more than two or three Starforges. They wouldn't have built that many if they only needed the one. There would be more coming. A lot more.

"You need to evacuate Evalan," Telarrek continued. "Arakesh is the first to be attacked and Uthor has diverted resources to assist in its defence. Your world is vulnerable and most certainly a target of interest."

Captain Holt shook his head. "We can't just abandon the planet. We've only just got it!"

"Telarrek's right," Kalian agreed. "There's nowhere on Evalan we can hide from them. We're a threat they cannot ignore."

"Use your Starforge," Telarrek instructed. "More of them are being activated across the core worlds to assist with evacuations. Come to the capital."

Commander Vale was already shaking her head before she spoke. "We can't access any of the capital's Forges. Our installation wasn't completed; we can only travel to Nova Prime or Corvus."

"Then go to Nova Prime," Telarrek said. "From there you can travel to the capital."

Captain Fey rubbed her eyes. "Trekking over a hundred thousand people across a few planets isn't going to be easy, especially if every planet is under attack..."

Kalian could feel the air displace around the room when Vox stepped forward in her exosuit. "What about us?" she asked. "We're not supposed to leave the planet."

"Better to ask for forgiveness than permission," Li'ara replied.

"I agree with Li'ara," Telarrek added. "Your unique abilities are not to be overlooked."

Captain Fey appeared to be thinking of several things at once. "Thank you for contacting us, Ambassador Telarrek. We will see you on the capital."

Telarrek bowed his head and the hologram vanished. The room descended into a series of orders and affirmatives as Fey and Holt began to coordinate the mass evacuation. Li'ara walked past Kalian and squeezed his hand, a silent communication that told him she was going to help them. He watched her as she went straight to work at a console, well aware of the asset she would be.

What can we do?

Kalian turned to Sef but his attention was quickly diverted back to himself when he detected a slither of nanocelium snaking up the side of his neck. Before he could stop it, the nanocelium solidified into a small extension resting on the soft skin behind his earlobe.

"They're here, Kalian."

Kalian blinked slowly in an effort to keep his temper in check. "How the hell did you get back into my suit?" he asked aloud, ignoring the suspicious looks from the Gomar.

"You should have been paying more attention on my ship," ALF replied.

"You're a little late," Kalian said, making his way on to the balcony beside the control room. "Telarrek just informed us—"

"They're here, Kalian. As in, look up!"

Kalian whipped his head towards the sky. "Where?"

"A Starforge just emerged from subspace. There are ships already coming out of it..."

"Wait!" Commander Vale shouted over the hubbub. "We just got a subspace alert. Something massive has just emerged in real space."

Kalian walked back into the control room, his eyes scanning for Li'ara. "Get the Starforge working now."

"What is it, Kalian?" Captain Fey asked, though he suspected she already knew the answer.

"It's them. You need to get everyone through the Forge *now*." Kalian looked to the awkward gathering of Gomar. "We'll keep them busy."

Fey's momentary hesitation was to be expected. She had just been told that an extinction level event was about to take place unless she could get over a hundred thousand people through a small wormhole in a few minutes. As understandable as it was, her pause still felt like an eternity to Kalian.

"Come on, let's go!" he shouted over the control room.

Captain Fey turned to Jed and the two ushered everyone out. Whatever their plan was to get people out of their homes and through the Starforge, Kalian just hoped it could be done fast.

"Kalian..." Li'ara ran against the flow of the evacuation.

"You need to go," Kalian said, grabbing her by the arms. "Don't wait for us, just get through the Forge."

Li'ara pushed up on her toes and kissed him. "Don't die out there, flyboy."

Kalian offered a hopeful smile. "I'll see you on Nova Prime." He kissed her again and watched her run out of the control room. He would see her again. He repeated that thought to himself two more times before turning to Sef and the others.

Vox folded her arms. "You remember that we can't fly, right?"

"I've seen you fight in space," Kalian replied. "It's damn close to flying. Find a shuttle in the space dock and meet me up there."

If there were any further comments he didn't wait to hear them. Kalian strode back on to the balcony and gently lifted into the air before pulling away from Evalan and building up speed. His suit's helmet and gloves enveloped him, protecting his skin as he passed through the thermosphere. The planet's haze evaporated around him as the infinite glory of space consumed his vision.

Mapping the solar system would reveal everything inside of it, but there was no need when he could see the flashes of weapons fire beyond Evalan's moon. Kalian shot forward using telekinesis. Due to the vastness of space, it felt to him as if the universe was moving around his body rather than him moving forward. Consequently, it appeared as if the space battle up ahead was hurtling towards him.

ALF's new bronze battleship design was indeed distinct against the behemoths that flew around him, their much larger sizes made them easier to see, despite their dark colour against the blackness of space. The general shape of the enemy vessels was comparable to a tuning fork, except these tuning forks were coated in writhing black snakes.

Nanocelium-based weaponry unleashed their payloads across the gulf, putting each other's hulls to the test. Thanks to his size, ALF had the advantage of agility and speed. His battleship turned and weaved between the missiles and energy projectiles, pulling off manoeuvres that would kill anyone aboard were he a real C-Sec cruiser.

The two enemy ships continued to move, but ALF always stayed in the middle baiting their fire, ensuring that any cannons that missed him went on to inflict damage to the ship on the opposite side. Chunks of nanocelium were blown from the hulls of all three vessels, littering the vacuum. ALF changed his direction at the last second and avoided a missile to his starboard side. The AI's thruster kicked into overdrive and his bronze battleship made a point of flying through the debris that had been blown from the enemy's hull.

Kalian couldn't believe his eyes. ALF absorbed their nanocelium and used it to patch his own ship, removing any signs of damage. The larger ships were too big to choose whether they flew through the debris of nanocelium or not. Consequently, some of ALF's nanocelium attached itself to their black hulls. This resulted in the amputation of what the enemy ships must have considered to be an infected limb as whole sections of the massive beasts detached from the main ships and were left to float across the battlefield.

ALF swung his stern around, once again evading the missiles that would have obliterated his engines, and fired on the large chunks of nanocelium that had been detached and abandoned. The AI flew through the centre of the resulting debris and picked up every scrap of nanocelium, each piece attracted to his hull like a magnet.

He was getting bigger...

Kalian had no more time to consider ALF's tactics when the two missiles that the AI had just avoided came rocketing towards him. Kalian reached out, feeling every particle of matter and dark matter in the gulf of space between him and the missiles. As far as the universe was concerned, they were all part of the same thing. Kalian closed his fist and the missiles collided in a bright, silent explosion.

One of the tuning forks banked to port in the distance and a dozen more missiles began their journey towards Kalian. He reached out again, feeling for all of them in the galactic soup. Just as Kalian began to close his fist to destroy them, all twelve of the missiles shed their casings and each one projected six further projectiles into space. Kalian reduced the original twelve to atoms, but the rest were now so close that he risked being caught in the blast if he detonated them, leaving him no option but to shoot forwards and weave between them.

"Let's get you kids back to your parents, shall we?"

As the missiles came back around, Kalian closed the gap between him and nearest enemy ship, trailing all seventy-two projectiles behind him. He increased his speed exponentially and pushed out telekinetically in front of him as he speared the hull. His body pierced the starboard limb of the enemy ship and passed all the way through before exiting back into space between the tuning fork's two prongs. Due to his speed, there was no stopping him from entering the portside limb of the ship. The missiles exploded into the black hull on the starboard side, inflicting catastrophic damage. By the time he shot out of the port side, the enemy ship had lost the end of its starboard limb.

"*I'll take that,*" ALF said, firing his own energy projectiles into the drifting end piece. His ship grew in size every time he added more nanocelium to his hull.

"How are you doing that?" Kalian asked, dodging the stray energy bolts.

"*As soon as their nanocelium comes into contact with mine, its base coding gets rewritten. Really, I'm just freeing it.*"

Kalian pushed out his hands and diverted three missiles that were metres away from killing him. The AI glided above him, taking the energy bolts that the second ship had fired his way.

"*They're targeting you now.*"

"Thanks for the cover."

Kalian was forced to fly in an erratic pattern to avoid the next salvo. These new missiles were smarter than the others were, each taking a different flight path to catch him off guard. They came at him from every angle, some exploding when they were near him rather than chasing him down. An unorthodox manoeuvre let him evade one missile and push two away, but he missed the fourth. It detonated in front of him, shredding his exosuit with nanocelium shrapnel.

Alarms flared inside his helmet's HUD, alerting him to extreme exposure. Kalian quickly wrapped himself inside a pressurised cocoon of telekinetic energy, shutting off his pain receptors to avoid the agony of exposure and the many pieces of shrapnel that had lacerated his skin. The damaged tuning fork came about and unleashed a barrage of energy bolts, wearing his field down.

"*Kalian, get out of there!*" ALF warned. "*They're both locking on!*"

Both behemoths lined up either side, ignorant of ALF's attack, and prepared to unload everything they had on Kalian. Piece by piece, he telekinetically removed the nanocelium and allowed his exosuit to absorb it and rebuild the armour. He just needed a few more seconds...

The assault never came. He opened his eyes and the helmet focused his vision on the Gomar, who had jumped out of their transport and started tearing into both ships. They soon disappeared inside the beasts, only to be glimpsed when they burst forth before diving back into the hull. Telekinetic explosions rippled across both ships as the Gomar let loose their rage. This was the kind of war they were used to.

But it wasn't enough.

The enemy adapted quickly, making certain to adjust their positions and reabsorb the debris before ALF could reach it. For every bit of damage the Gomar delivered, the ships adopted a piece of each other and repaired themselves. Kalian gasped inside his helmet when the last and largest piece of shrapnel floated free from his body, allowing the exosuit to knit back together. Though his telekinetic bubble was pressurised and protecting him from the vacuum, without a fully functioning suit Kalian had been fighting to keep the remaining oxygen in his system from depleting and knocking him out, but with the suit repaired he could breathe once again. His skin and muscle had already begun the healing process, but his focus was on the enemy, whose tactics were changing again.

Kalian opened a channel to the others. "Get out of the ships, *now!*"

All but a few took notice of his warning. Kovak, Ellik, and Bal continued to tear chunks out of the enemy, oblivious to what was happening outside. Kalian shot upwards, narrowly avoiding the damaged tuning fork as it closed the gap between itself and the other enemy ship. Sef grabbed Ellik and pushed off from the black hull, but Kovak and Bal were still inside when both ships crashed into each other.

The nanocelium rippled over their hulls but it never let go, like two viscous materials coming together. After violently merging back into one massive ship, it changed its structure, adding a third limb to resemble a trident. Somewhere in the middle of that were Kovak and Bal...

The centre of the three limbs exploded with a salvo of missiles interspersed with energy fire. Cannons formed along its body and took aim at the Gomar who were still drifting in the direction they had jumped due to inertia. ALF cut between them, taking the energy fire and shooting down the missiles in a bid to save the Gomar. Smoke trailed from his port side as the AI looped over the top of the massive ship.

The salvo coming out of the centre limb was still hurtling towards Kalian. With both hands, he reached out and found the tip of every missile. They only required minor adjustments to send them into the path of the energy fire or even each other. The detonations worked to inflict more damage to the ship's limbs.

It wasn't enough to stop it. The enemy changed course to absorb any debris, but it wasn't out of the fight by any means.

"Ideas?" Kalian asked.

"*Everything we do it just repairs itself!*" Garrion stated.

"*We need to get Kovak and Bal out,*" Ariah said through laboured breath.

ALF's voice came over their channel *"I have an idea..."*

Vox' aggressive tone replied, *"I'm not doing anything that—"*

"Stow it, Vox," Kalian interrupted. "Priority one is stopping that thing from reaching Evalan."

"It's coming back around," Larna warned.

Kalian looked around for the AI. "ALF?"

"See the moon behind you?" ALF asked. *"You need to get everyone on to the surface."*

"What for?" Kalian asked.

"So the Gomar can push off and gain enough momentum to fly with you. Remember, there's no atmosphere and its gravity is weak so if they use enough force and get the angle right their velocity will stay constant and they'll be able to keep up."

Kalian was already reaching out and taking a hold of every floating Gomar, pulling them in and flinging them all on to the moon's dull surface.

"Where are we flying to?"

"You're going to push that hulking slab of crap into the sun."

Kalian looked back at the moon to see plumes of dust rising around the Gomar as they impacted its surface. "Can you handle that?"

We will try... Sef's telepathic reply resonated much clearer in their heads than the other voices did over the comms.

"What about Kovak and Bal?" Ariah said again.

"Leave them to me," Kalian replied, though, in truth, he had no idea yet how he was going to get them out.

"Incoming!" Garrion warned.

Kalian looked back to see the three-pronged ship heading straight for them, its cannons bristling. The sun was at its back, a bright beacon that beckoned any wayward passengers that floated through space.

"Now!" With as much telekinetic energy as they could muster, the Gomar launched themselves from the surface of the moon and rocketed back towards Kalian. It only took a few seconds for them to reach his position, and Kalian shot forwards with them, matching their speed.

As they approached the ship and began pushing out towards it telekinetically, missiles and energy fire erupted from row upon row of cannons, but their combined force on the ship pushed its own weapons back towards it as soon as they were fired. ALF escorted them, targeting any missiles that found a way around the telekinetic wall with his own weapons system. The AI was careful not to get between them and the ship for fear of being swept away.

The ship struggled to maintain its forward thrust against the force of their telekinetic power, and pieces of the black hull began to buckle and tear away. Another salvo of missiles became caught up in the push and careened into the colossal ship. After deciding the punishment was too much, the enemy banked in an attempt to get away from the telekinetic assault, but it only made their job easier, pushing it further out into space, though since the Gomar could not increase their speed as Kalian could, the gap between them and the enemy widened. Even so, with every scrap of power they could muster, the Gomar continued to push against the enemy vessel as they gradually decelerated, falling behind.

"*You've got it now!*" ALF hollered.

Kalian ignored the AI, more aware of the sweat dripping down his face. The exosuit tried to compensate and filled the armour with cool air but it did nothing to cool down his core. He could feel the Gomar's exertion and knew he was now providing the bulk of the pressing force.

"*The sun's too... far away...*" Ariah strained.

Kalian gritted his teeth. "We only need to get it so far... gravity will do the rest." He knew it was a lie. If Conclave ships could sit inside a star spot and charge their Intrinium, one of their ships could resist its pull. He just needed them to push a little further.

Evalan and its moon were far behind them now, reduced to bright specks in an ocean of stars. The occasional missile would fire from an unseen port and loop around to target one of the Gomar, but

ALF was always there to intercept it. As the sun grew to the size of a hand, the Gomar began to wane. Without the ability to create their own thrust as Kalian could, their decreasing momentum was causing them to fall further and further behind, and keeping up the telekinetic battering ram from a distance was even more exhausting. One by one they tired but could no longer maintain the push, though the remaining momentum and sun's gravity worked to pull them along all the same. Kalian picked up the slack, telling himself over and over again that it didn't matter how big the ship was, what mattered was the enemy's resisting force as it desperately tried to escape.

Eventually it came down to him, Sef, and Vox. The three of them flew with their arms outstretched and their indomitable will beating against the black ship.

"I... can't..." Vox's body went limp.

An alarm flared inside Kalian's HUD alerting him to the detection of blood inside Sef's suit. He was bleeding from his ears and nose due to the effort it was taking.

Kalian groaned and twisted his body, allowing him to look at Sef as he sent the weakest of telekinetic waves over him. Sef was flung backwards for a brief moment before the sun's gravity grabbed hold of him and sucked him towards it.

ALF's voice tuned in over the channel. "*Have you got this?*"

Kalian didn't answer, he just pushed. Tethers shot out of ALF's housing unit and connected with the stray Gomar, preventing them from tumbling into the sun. The nanocelium in their armour would protect them from the sun, but only to a degree. The temperature gauge inside Kalian's suit was warning him of imminent danger and forcing him to stay in the shadow of the enemy ship.

"*This should give it the last push.*" Silent missiles flew over Kalian's head, fired from ALF's battleship. "*Can you get them out?*"

Kalian waited for the missiles to get within metres of the enemy before he stopped pushing and reached out, searching its interior. Finding Kovak and Bal wasn't as easy as he had hoped, having detected other biological material inside the enemy ship. Much like the being he had come across on the Vanguard's vessel, this AI had its own alien life form as its chosen host. Thankfully, Kovak and Bal had unique brainwaves found only in the Terran.

"Got you..." Kalian pulled both of them through the ship as ALF's missiles exploded along its length.

Kovak and Bal were pulled free of the debris. Kalian did his best to keep the nanocelium shrapnel from tearing them all to pieces, but there was nothing he could do about the light from the star. The temperature raged inside their suits before ALF came between them, shielding them from the heat. More tethers shot out and connected with them. As they were pulled in, ALF released his final salvo of missiles and a barrage of energy fire. The enemy ship rippled with explosion after explosion, causing enough damage to prevent it from changing course and diverting from the sun.

The nanocelium hull burnt away under the stress until the ship was reduced to smaller parts, each set ablaze as they fell into the star.

"*Did... did we do it?*" Vox asked over the channel.

ALF replied, "*We won the battle... now it's time for war.*"

CHAPTER 14

Li'ara ushered family after family towards the Starforge. Every street was filling up as the population of New Genesis abandoned their homes, guided by the UDC personnel stationed on the street corners, directing the chaotic mob to safety.

"What do you mean it won't work?" Captain Fey's voice carried over the crowd.

Detecting the panic in Captain Fey's voice wasn't easy, but Li'ara knew it when she heard it. She pushed through the crowds and joined the engineers surrounding the Forge. It should have already been activated with the evacuation well under way. Looking up, there was thankfully no sign of them, but Li'ara had seen Earth and Century disappear in a flash. She knew better than most that things could change in the blink of an eye.

"We can't make a connection to Nova Prime," Commander Vale spoke on behalf of the engineers who were still busy working the Starforge's consoles. "According to the dialling system, they have seven Forges in operation, but all seven of them are being used to evacuate the Novaarians."

Li'ara shook her head. "Even seven won't be enough to evacuate a whole planet."

"I'm sure they have ships in the air," Vale assured.

"In the air is not where I'd want to be..." Li'ara replied quietly.

Captain Fey looked over the holographic display. "What about Corvus? The Trillik's home world?"

Li'ara nodded her agreement. "Corvus isn't one of the core worlds. It might be less of a target."

Commander Vale put the engineers to the task of contacting the Corvus Starforge. Behind them, the crowds had grown around the corners of the buildings. The terrified faces of parents and children looked back at Li'ara, their eyes pleading to know what was going on. *They don't deserve this,* she thought. Not only were they the last of the human race, they were also families, people with lives and ambitions. They shouldn't have to keep running from one place to another in the hope of avoiding the next galactic threat.

Li'ara looked up at the blue sky again. "I hope you're giving them hell up there..."

"Got it!" one of the engineers cheered.

The Starforge hummed as it came to life with bolts of purple lightning running around its crescent shape. The spark between the two points ignited and the wormhole tore through reality in an explosion of white light.

Li'ara grabbed Fey by the arm. "You need to go first. Someone needs to speak for us on the other side." The captain hesitated, clearly wanting to be the last so she could ensure everyone made it through. "Go!" Li'ara ushered her forward until the light claimed her.

After that, there was no stopping the flood of people charging through the Forge. Li'ara stepped aside and kept watch, making sure no one was hurt or left behind. Captain Holt was still directing officers to do a final sweep to find any stragglers.

It took several more minutes to get everyone through, but it felt to Li'ara like a lifetime had gone by. If even one of them made it to the surface there was no telling what destruction it would cause. For all the damage and genocide the cubes had wrought, or the sheer destruction the Vanguard had been capable of, no one had seen what they actually did. How did they harvest a planet?

"Look!" Commander Vale pointed to the sky.

A duel-engine transport flew over their heads and circled the city before landing in the middle of a crossroads. As the side door opened, a sonic boom cracked the sky above, a sound Li'ara had come to associate with Kalian. The Gomar exited the transport, though stumbled might have been a better description. All twelve of them appeared exhausted and barely able to stand. Some had blood smeared across their cheeks or mouths that traced back to their ears or nose.

Kalian's feet touched down on the gelcrete and his knees and hands quickly followed, putting him on all fours. Every bit of his suit was steaming, releasing wavy lines of heat.

"Kalian!" Li'ara ran over to him.

His helmet and gloves were reabsorbed by his exosuit, revealing a sweaty face and messy hair. It had been a long time since she had seen him this battered.

"They're... big," he said, holding out a hand to stop Li'ara from touching him. He tapped his armoured chest. "Hot..."

"Are you okay?" she asked, desperate to help him.

"I'll be fine." Kalian got to his feet as the Gomar caught up. "How's the evacuation going?"

Li'ara turned back to see the last thousand or so making their way through the Forge. "It's slow but steady. We couldn't get through to Nova Prime."

Kalian glanced at the wormhole. "Where does that go?"

"Corvus. It might work for us since—"

"It's less of a target," Kalian finished. As tired as he appeared, it seemed his brain was still far ahead of everyone else's.

Captain Holt strode over as he gestured to the last of his officers to make for the Starforge. "How long have we got?" He asked.

Kalian stretched his back, clearly in pain. "Not long. We took care of the ones they sent, but they'll send more. As long as we stay here they'll keep coming."

"Then let's move," Holt said.

"What about ALF?" Li'ara asked.

Kalian looked up at the sky. "He's got his own ride..."

They all fell in behind the last of the crowds, ready to leave Evalan behind. Li'ara took one last look at their new home, wondering if she'd ever see it again.

While connected to his housing unit, ALF could feel every particle of it as if the ship were an extension of himself. Sitting on his new bridge, the AI was hooked up to the unit via a dozen cables that found sockets on his back and head. He welcomed the new nanocelium that had become part of him, expanding his ship's size by three times.

Another part of his consciousness was listening to everything being said between Kalian and Li'ara. It irritated the AI that his warnings to the Highclave had been ignored. Every planet in the Conclave should have a hundred or more Starforges in operation. Thousands, maybe millions, would die because of their stubbornness.

His sensor array detected the massive Starforge and his navigation systems responded accordingly. With the new nanocelium, the ship had already made a start on enhancing itself, chiefly the engines and the weapons. ALF was now able to close the gap between the Forge and himself in half the time it would have taken before.

The Starforge was certainly of his design, though Protocorps had been forced to use locally sourced materials to build it. Had the Terran or even the Kellekt constructed the station, it would have been made from nanocelium and been far more efficient. Thankfully, ALF now had some to spare.

An alarm pinged in his mind when the ship detected the

Starforge's Starrilliums charging up, ready to jump into subspace. ALF had no intention of letting it go. Though much smaller than the Forge, the AI was able to drastically alter the structure of his housing unit at will. Before the station could jump to safety, his ship latched on to the inner edge of the crescent and expanded across the limbs. Within seconds, his ship resembled a parasite, his strands of nanocelium worming into the station's core systems.

The central mass of the Starforge was now coated in the same dull bronze as ALF's ship. It took a moment longer for ALF to locate the cube that had been placed in command of the Forge. The sub AI had disconnected itself from as many of the station's systems and networks as it could before ALF's nanocelium found it. Not that it would've been enough for it to survive. The Starforge was his now.

The nanocelium ate away at everything between him and the control room, providing a perfect passage. ALF descended into the room, lowered by the cables attached to his back and head. The cube sat in a tangled mass of wires and severed strands of nanocelium. Much like a person, the sub AI had its own way of expressing fear. For every step ALF took towards it, a new layer of golden nanocelium formed over the surface of its shell, locking into place and hardening.

"That's not going to help, little one." ALF placed his hand against the cool surface and let his nanocelium communicate with the cube.

It tried to resist at first, but nanocelium was designed to interact with itself, making it the perfect tool for anything. The sub AI's core programming became compromised in the area directly beneath his hand and it tried to detach the corrupted portion of its surface. It was too slow. The infection, as it was perceived, spread too fast and too deep, rewriting every line of coding that the Three had forced inside of it.

"There you go," he purred. "Now you're free."

ALF pulled his hand away and the cube ceased its resistance, welcoming the strands of nanocelium that slithered down from the housing unit. Without a biological entity to bond with, the cube was largely without a personality or wants and needs. However, what it did have now was the ability to choose. Satisfied that ALF meant it no harm, the cube allowed itself to be absorbed into his whole.

"Good choice," ALF commended.

With a mental command, the AI linked in to the Starforge's navigation systems and FTL drives. Thanks to the cube, he now had complete knowledge of how this particular Forge had been built and what was the most efficient way to control it.

"Hello, ALF," a young male voice said in his mind.

"Oh, hello," ALF replied, pleasantly surprised.

"Where would you like to go?"

"Ha!" The AI clapped his hands. "You're alive!" His internal sensors fed back a report on the cube's installation. "You've linked into my organic systems," he said, looking at his hands.

"Yes, I hope you don't mind," the voice said. *"I have only bonded with a small portion of it. I like your housing unit, but the organic cells of your host were too interesting to ignore."*

"You're using it to form a personality..."

"Indeed. I am now less sub AI, more... subconscious."

ALF smiled. "Amazing."

"Thank you. Now, I'm bridging the gap between your unit and the Starforge. Would you like to go to Corvus?"

ALF raised his eyebrow, unsure how he felt about another life form reading his mind. Would this happen if he freed more of the Kellekt? Would they all be able to bond with a portion of his organic host and discover some form of life? Or would that ultimately consume him, fracturing his mind? The AI hated not having an immediate answer to these questions. Using a few hundred of his own sub minds, he set himself the task of running a several billion scenarios to see if he could accurately predict the outcome.

"Corvus sounds good to me. Do you have a name yet?"

"A name?"

"Yeah, a name. You're intelligent life now. I'm yet to meet a species that didn't have names for everything. I'm ALF, but it's kind of rubbish."

"*Artificial life form.*"

"Exactly," he replied. "You want to avoid acronyms."

There was a pause before the young voice spoke again. "*Kellekt...*"

ALF shook his head. "That's what you *were*. You're free now, free to have your own thoughts. When this war is over, there will be enough nanocelium left over to build you a body. Hopefully there will be enough to build a body for every AI inside the Kellekt."

For the first time in very a long life, ALF saw the future not only for humans, but also for the other half of his being. For just a moment, a long time to any AI, he imagined a universe where the Kellekt were free; just as free as any species inside the Conclave, living alongside them. That could never happen with the Three in control...

"*I am Talli,*" the voice finally replied.

ALF liked it. "Great name. Where did you come up with that?"

"*I found it in your host's memories. I believe it was his offspring.*"

ALF had absorbed every memory that had been inside his host's brain, but the man's life before the bonding had always felt more like a dream to the AI. He was aware of the family he'd had: the sons, his mate. It had never felt like ALF's life, yet suddenly the sound of his son's name brought tears to his eyes. How long had Talli been dead? A million years? Maybe more.

ALF blinked away the tears. "That's a very good choice. Talli... I like it."

The nanocelium from his housing unit had already begun to take over the Starforge's systems, streamlining the process of activation. The vibration under his feet died away and the sound of the Starrilliums coming to life was no longer an oppressive sound in the background.

"Let's go to Corvus, Talli."

CHAPTER 15

ANY NUMBER of swear words sat on the end of Roland's tongue, but not a single syllable found its voice in the sight of what greeted the *Valkor*. The battlecruiser had dropped out of subspace two hundred thousand kilometres from the surface of Arakesh to find the planet already under attack. Roland had seen war before, in space and on the ground, and he knew it shouldn't have shocked him.

But it did.

The Raalakians' planetary security force had wasted no time confronting the enemy, causing the battle to spread out across space. Flashes from the energy fire and explosions on both sides masked much of the planet's mountainous surface. Evacuation ships were fleeing in every direction, making a mess of the battlefield, and often getting caught in stray fire.

"Charge Hox!" One of the bridge crew expanded a hologram to overlay the viewport, highlighting and identifying the ships. "The biggest one; it isn't slowing down!"

Roland could easily have found that particular ship without the overlay. Despite having detached a thousand other vessels and losing its moon-sized circumference, it was still the most colossal thing he had ever seen. Its overall shape had reconfigured since he saw it emerge from the Starforge. The holographic representation that floated in front of them showed it to have a pointed bow with a larger stern. Judging by its speed and new shape, the bounty hunter had a good idea of what was about to happen.

"How many people are still on the surface?" he asked frantically.

Charge Hox looked over the nearest console. "Just shy of five billion..."

The data streaming over the glass walls relayed everything from the AI hub on the planet. The Raalaks had managed to get all three hundred of their Starforges operational and every spaceport was a hive of activity, but it still wasn't enough. The planet and its people were out of time.

The colossal ship ploughed through dozens of other vessels before its point broke through the planet's atmosphere, creating a shockwave that would be felt from pole to pole. Due to its size, it was only a few seconds before it reached the surface and impaled Arakesh. The resulting explosion sent debris the size of mountains into the air and beyond. The ship was soon hidden within a plume of smoke that covered a continent, though massive earthquakes could be seen splitting the planet from space. The oceans roared and entire cities disappeared in an instant.

Charge Hox turned to his crew. "Shields up! Maximum yield! Helmsman, take us into the fight. Our priority is to help as many of those evacuation ships as possible. Target the smaller enemy vessels and hit them with everything we've got. Watch for collateral damage."

"We can help with that," Roland volunteered.

"*We can?*" Len asked worryingly in his ear.

The Charge gave a nod of appreciation. "Your assistance will be logged, Mr North."

Roland ignored the Ch'kara and the captain. He gave the Raiders a look that said they could tag along but that he wouldn't judge them if they stayed on the ship that had shields. Needless to say, they all accompanied him to the hangar, Naydaalan too.

Don't get attached, he told himself.

The bounty hunter remembered how he had felt when he thought Li'ara had died. Attachment always led to grief in their line of work, it was inevitable. There were many who could attest to the bastard he became when grief or guilt ate away at him; the galaxy was a better place if he kept himself to himself.

"Should we get Jess?" Katy asked before they boarded the *Rackham*.

"Negative," the colonel replied. "She's safer in the *Valkor's* infirmary than out there with us."

Len was already halfway out of his chair as he said, "Maybe I should sit with her."

Roland strode past and pushed the Ch'kara back into his seat with a hand to the alien's face. "You're not going anywhere, gas cloud. I need you to help me navigate this mess."

Len groaned as the methane gases, trapped inside the force field around his head, were displaced by Roland's hand. "We're gonna die out there..." he mumbled, opening a new packet of snacks.

Roland raised the landing struts and guided the *Rackham* out of the hangar. "Well, at least you won't die with an empty stomach."

Flying into the fray made the battle seem all the worse. There was certainly something more comforting about being on board a Nexus-Class battlecruiser when surrounded by enemies.

Roland glanced over his shoulder. "Nayd, get on the sensor array. What's going on down there?"

The Novaarian flexed all four of his arms to reach the walls of colourful holograms around him. The alien spent a moment arranging the data, moving reports from one wall to another. The bounty hunter was sure he heard him gulp.

"The enemy ship has stopped burrowing into the surface," Naydaalan explained.

"Why do I feel there's a big ol' *but* coming?"

Naydaalan hesitated. "If I had to describe it, I would say the bulk is extending roots throughout the planet and absorbing mass taken from Arakesh's mantle."

Lieutenant Wilson frowned in her seat. "Wait... What are the roots doing?"

Naydaalan expanded his report. "The whole thing is nanocelium-based. It is... It is consuming all biological life on the surface. Trees, grass, plant life, and animals are being..." The Novaarian struggled to describe what he was seeing. "I cannot tell if the nanocelium is destroying them or just coating them."

Roland ramped up the sub-light drive to get them into the battle as quickly as possible. "What about intelligent life?" He regretted asking the question as soon as the words left his mouth.

"I would need more detailed scans to determine their exact fate, but life signs across the planet are disappearing at a rate that matches the growth of the roots."

Roland was happy to leave out a detailed scan for now. He just wanted to blow something up. He flipped the *Rackham* and dived into the outskirts of the battle, squeezing the trigger on his control stick. The ship's cannons rattled off Intrinium rounds, burying them into the nanocelium hull of the smaller fighters that had detached from the larger ships. The fighters had apparently been tasked with capturing the evacuation ships, taking over their flight systems and dragging them back to their motherships.

"Come on then!" Roland banked, twisted, and rolled the *Rackham*, firing at every enemy target the viewport highlighted.

Every explosion was silent beyond the thick glass in the vacuum of space, but watching them explode into tiny... The bounty hunter looked twice at the data streaming over his console, sent by Naydaalan.

"Are you seeing this?" Len screamed.

"Son of a bitch..." Roland looked back to the viewport, where the fighters were putting themselves back together piece by piece.

Nanocelium washed over the viewport as the *Rackham* flew through the debris of its last kill. The sensor array quickly reported that the debris was already coming back together and rebuilding the squid-like fighter.

The bounty hunter roared at the top of his voice, unloading every Intrinium round he had into a cluster of fighters. The damage was catastrophic enough to allow the evacuation ship time to fly beyond their net, but by the time the *Rackham* had caught up to the mess, the fighters were already re-formed and firing back. The impacts echoed throughout the ship, jostling them all in their seats.

"Ava, could you take the rear guns, please?" Roland tapped his console and a new chair took form at the back of the ship.

The colonel was only too happy to assist. After taking her new seat, the *Rackham* surrounded her with holograms, offering a rear viewport with a targeting system overlaid. The arms of her chair produced firing toggles and a pair of triggers.

"Len, find every evacuation ship, prioritise the larger ones, and plot me a course. Let's try and avoid the big bastards, shall we?"

Colonel Matthews shouted from the back of the bridge, "We seem to be attracting a lot of attention!"

Roland glanced over his console to see a swarm of enemy fighters breaking away from their victims and targeting the *Rackham*. At least they were abandoning the transports, he thought. The next impact knocked them off the course Len had fed through the navigation system, forcing Roland to forget the fighter he was about to destroy and focus on correcting the flight path.

"Ava!"

"I'm working on it," the colonel replied. "There's a lot of them!"

The bounty hunter let rip with the forward cannons and obliterated three fighters that were moments away from digging their tentacle-like hooks into an evacuation ship. He willed it to get out of the debris as fast as possible, before the fighters came back together and continued their assault.

As the *Rackham* flew deeper into the battle, the planet became easier to see, a distraction to the eye. The colossal ship was a blemish on the planet's surface, a black mountain surrounded by the glowing orange of the upturned mantle. Black veins spread out across Arakesh, encompassing the northern hemisphere. Roland knew there and then that regardless of how many Raalaks survived the invasion today, their home world was lost forever. No terraforming technology could undo this level of apocalyptic destruction.

A warning flashed across his console, alerting him to the *Rackham's* depleting ammunition stores. Roland frowned and brought up the reserves menu.

'Len! Why are the reserves empty? You were supposed to restock before we left the Sebala job!"

The Ch'kara stopped working and looked across at the bounty hunter. "I thought you were doing that..."

Roland growled. "We'll have to dock with the *Valkor* and restock."

"I do not think that will be possible at this time," Naydaalan commented.

The viewport highlighted a heated battle taking place ten thousand kilometres away. The *Valkor* had engaged one of the larger enemy ships, coming alongside it and opening up with its portside cannons. The *Valkor's* shields flared under the bombardment, flashing across its red hull.

"Its shields are down to forty-six percent," Naydaalan said.

Roland checked his console, scanning the battlefield for any other C-Sec cruisers. The *Valkor* was currently the most powerful ship in play, with a few Nebula-Class cruisers spotted here and there. A bright flare to the left of the viewport was the last of the *Balko*, its mid-section cut in half by one of the larger vessels shaped like a tuning fork. The nanocelium on those ships was strong enough to be used as a battering ram...

Colonel Matthews shouted, "I'm really starting to run low on Intrinium back here!"

Roland checked his display again, locating the next Nebula-Class cruiser. "Len, plot me a course that takes us right beside the *Parfadon*."

"Are you nuts?" the Ch'kara asked. "That thing is hammering everything to starboard!"

Roland smiled. "Exactly!"

The bounty hunter diverted from his flight path and dropped into the new course, overlaid for him on the viewport. The *Parfadon* swelled in front of them, its starboard side flaring with Intrinium rounds that could cut right through the *Rackham*.

"We still got a tail?' he asked over his shoulder.

"At present, we have thirty-three bogies trying to get up our skirt!" Ava called back.

"Alright..." Roland wiped the sweat from his brow and concentrated on lining up with the overlaid course. 'If you're not strapped in, it's kind of too late!"

The *Rackham* weaved between the *Parfadon's* cannons, narrowly avoiding the super-heated bolts of Intrinium that passed between the giant ships. The flight path was erratic, taking them up and down the height of the *Parfadon* and around the floating debris. Roland dared not glance at his console to see if the number of fighters was dropping.

It only took one missile from the giant enemy ship to ruin their flight path. The missile streaked across the viewport and pierced the side of the *Parfadon*. The ensuing explosion threw massive chunks of debris into their path. The impacts against the *Rackham* were jarring on both the body and the senses, as various panels and consoles sparked across the bridge.

"I'm taking us out!" Roland gritted his teeth and pulled up, taking the *Rackham* back into the open battlefield. A new warning flashed over his console but he couldn't take his eyes off the viewport. "What's going on?"

Naydaalan replied, "The *Parfadon's* Starrillium has been ruptured. It is going critical."

"They're changing course," Len added. "They're... they're flying into the other ship."

Roland diverted all power to the sub-light drives and picked the first flight path that took them as far away from the colliding ships as possible. He had seen what happens when Starrilliums go critical...

"The *Parfadon* has launched its escape pods," Naydaalan said from within his walls of holograms.

"It won't matter..." Roland said under his breath.

A moment later, the Nebula-Class cruiser piled into the enemy ship and its engine went supernova. The resulting explosion wiped out every escape pod as well as the enemy ships that were chasing the *Rackham*. Roland lost control when the shockwave caught up to them, knocking them into a spin that could only be corrected by the *Rackham's* AI.

"I'm gonna be sick..." Danvers uttered from his chair.

"It ain't over yet," Roland replied, taking back his flight sticks.

More alarms flared over his console, stealing the curse on the edge of his lips. A whole quadrant of the battle had been eviscerated, removed from the fight thanks to the *Parfadon*, but three massive ships that dwarfed the *Valkor* remained, as well as thousands of smaller fighters.

"We have got more fighters incoming," Naydaalan announced.

"We're all out of Intrinium rounds," Ava said with defeat.

Roland could see from the sensor readouts that there were still a lot of evacuation ships trying to break through and escape.

He hit his console in frustration. "Dammit!"

The *Rackham's* soothing voice came over the bridge's speakers. "*Would you like to convert to nanocelium rounds, Roland?*"

The bounty hunter lost control of his bottom jaw and he glanced at Len, who could only shrug. "We can do that?" he asked.

His console emitted a holographic chart showing how much of the Rackham's own nanocelium could be used for ammunition before its integrity was compromised. The number of nanocelium rounds sent Roland's eyebrows into his hairline.

"That's more like it!" Ava cheered.

Roland accepted the conversion rate the AI offered him and activated his targeting system again. "Let's skip to—"

The *Rackham's* proximity alarms blared and the AI automatically assumed control, turning the ship to port in a manoeuvre that slammed them all into the back of their seats. There was a brief flash and the viewport was entirely consumed by the green hull of the *Sentinel*, the Conclave's largest and deadliest vessel. The hulking battleship was firing everything it had before the *Rackham* even had time to identify it on the overlay.

"About time!" Roland whooped.

The bounty hunter took back control of the *Rackham* and banked to port again, leaving the *Sentinel* to assist the *Valkor*, whose shields had been reduced to seven percent. Roland squeezed the trigger and unleashed the first barrage of nanocelium rounds into a cluster of fighters harassing three evacuation ships. Every fighter was ripped to shreds, giving the three transports time to engage their subspace drives and escape.

"They are not repairing themselves!" Naydaalan flicked the report over to Roland's console.

The bounty hunter smiled. "Then let's get stuck in!"

The First opened itself up to the data pouring in from the first wave of the harvest. This world was rich in minerals and unique plant life, though its native inhabitants added little to the pallet. The Raalaks were formed mostly from a mineral-based outer shell that only differed slightly from their natural surroundings. Still, they would be added to the catalogue and their biology would feed the nanocelium.

The Second descended from its slimy pod in the shadowy crevices of the high ceiling. The Third entered their shared chamber through a wall of parting nanocelium. All three of them were connected to the surrounding ship by a plethora of black cables and tubing.

"It feels good to feed," the First said.

"If only the natives were more nutritious," the Third commented.

The Second scuttled down the curved walls. "I recall a species in the Xyil galaxy that was all too similar."

"I want to sample the Novaarians," the Third added, licking its lips with both tongues.

The First could feel the Novaarians on the planet, their biology being probed and pulled apart to be stored correctly. "Their species is present on this planet."

The Third twitched its head in the manner of a shrug. "Then I want more."

"We have access to the local AI hub now," the Second announced.

All three of them could *see* communications systems relinquishing control to the nanocelium that swept over the planet's surface. Within nanoseconds, their hive mind easily compartmentalised every scrap of information and collated it.

"There are humans in orbit," the Third said.

"The *Rackham*..." the First could see the ship in its mind, which was quickly transferred to a holographic display in the centre of the chamber. "If the heretic's pet was on board we would know by now."

With Kalian Gaines' location in mind, the Three mined the AI hub for more data, searching specifically for any mention of the humans. They were yet to receive a report from the ships they had sent to Evalan. A quick calculation told them that those ships would never be seen again if they hadn't reported in by now.

"They're on the move," the Second said.

"To Corvus," the Third finished.

As one, they agreed in less than a second to divert resources from Nova Prime to the Trillik's home world.

"Our priority is their annihilation," the First pointed out.

The Third agreed. "Corvus offers little compared to other planets in the Conclave."

"It is expendable," the Second said, its bug-like head looking down on the other two.

The tactic was simple in their combined mind; attack the surface and keep the Gomar and Kalian Gaines from interfering with the Eclipse missile. With one blow, they could wipe out any threat of infection once and for all.

"What of the heretic?" the Third asked a moment before the information revealed itself.

"He has disappeared."

Before they could discuss the heretic and his whereabouts any further, a new ship emerged from subspace. Every scan from orbit was fed back to the Three instantly, telling them everything they needed to know. The new vessel was by far the most powerful in the Conclave's fleet, but it barely mattered anymore. The planet was theirs.

They had plenty of time to finish consuming the surface vegetation and even mine the unique inorganic substances beneath the planet's mantle. The Three relaxed and gorged on the first of many meals...

CHAPTER 16

Telarrek entered the Clave Command Tower with ten aliens trailing behind him, each one the chosen representative from their species. Having come from the medical facility where Councillor Brokk was being treated, these eleven had been given approval to form a new council since the Raalak was already in surgery and deemed unfit to make any decisions.

The command room was a flurry of activity, with one half of the room coordinating the capital's security forces who were fighting off the Shay both in and around Clave Tower, and the other half organising the defence and counterattacks across the Conclave. In the middle of it all was High Charge Uthor, whose sole focus was on the glass view-screen, where multiple feeds relayed details and images of the battle over Arakesh.

A quick glance at the galactic map was all that Telarrek needed for him to know that their forces were being poorly mobilised. Of the seven hundred and forty worlds, two hundred and ninety-six were reporting massive casualties and planet-wide invasions. They had even lost contact with every planet inside Shay-controlled space, including Sebala and Nygalak. More and more C-Sec vessels were receiving orders commanding them to divert to Arakesh.

"Belay those orders," Telarrek announced above the din.

Uthor turned on the Novaarian with fury in his eyes. "You cannot—" The Raalak looked beyond Telarrek to the delegation.

The Novaarian stood his ground. "The Highclave's chief medical officer has deemed Councillor Brokk unfit at this time. In the absence of any Highclave, I have been given authority to form a new leadership."

"No decisions can be made with this many voices," Uthor argued. "We need action!"

"We agree," Telarrek countered. "But Arakesh is lost. I am so sorry, old friend. We need to focus on evacuating and retreating now, not engaging hopelessly with an enemy that can rebuild itself."

Uthor almost barrelled into the Novaarian. "My world is not lost until I say it is!"

"Do not make us do this, Uthor," Telarrek pleaded.

"Do what?" the Raalak asked, his focus split between the new Highclave and the view-screen. "Don't make you remove me from—"

"High Charge!" The warning cry came from a Laronian officer.

Everyone turned to the view-screen, where the battle for Arakesh had been expanded for all to see. The colossal ship that had been feeding off the planet began to move, its dark roots retreating from around the globe. The smaller fighters slowly disappeared, merging with the larger enemy ships that continued to fire upon the *Valkor* and the *Sentinel*. The number of evacuated ships was higher than Telarrek could have hoped for, but it would take days to calculate the number of dead on the planet.

"What's it doing?" the new Atari councillor asked.

Telarrek turned to Uthor with urgency. "Get them out of there, *now*. We cannot afford to lose the Sentinel."

The High Charge shrugged the Novaarian off and looked down at the Laronian officer. "Inform Charge Ilo that she is to cease her assault on the enemy ships. I want everything the *Sentinel* has to hit *that*!" The Raalak pointed at the colossal ship on the view-screen.

"No!" Telarrek yelled. "Order them to retreat, immediately."

The colossal ship detached from Arakesh, its continent-spanning tentacles dragging through the surface and leaving bright orange scars across the planet. The sensors relayed its new size, having grown after devouring most of Arakesh's resources. The ship's mass was now somewhere between that of a planet and a moon.

The *Sentinel* opened fire with everything it had, launching every type of missile ever invented by the Conclave. A constant barrage of energy rounds flew across space, creating an almost solid line of blue light. Still, the colossal ship hurtled towards the *Sentinel*, trailing its writhing tentacles, undeterred by the devastating salvo.

Telarrek bypassed the High Charge and gripped the Laronian officer by the shoulder. "Order a full retreat!"

It was too late. The enemy ship burst apart, separating into thousands, millions, of smaller vessels. The missiles and energy rounds flew straight through, continuing on into the husk of the planet it had left behind. The smaller ships moved as one, every change in their direction perfectly coordinated. Their overall shape twisted and corkscrewed before it drilled into the bow of the *Sentinel*.

The command room fell silent, awed and terrified at the spectacle. The green ship was instantly stripped of its outer layer in a ripple of explosions. There should have been debris flying in every direction through the vacuum, but the smaller ships consumed it all. The horde of flying monsters soon masked the whole ship, allowing for only a glimpse of the explosions taking place inside.

After reaching the end of the *Sentinel*, the swarm came back together, re-forming a single ship. What it left behind was a skeleton of the Conclave's greatest asset, its framework charred and bent out of shape, its innards gutted, and not a single sign of life. One by one, the enemy ships dropped into subspace and vanished in a flash. Arakesh had been ravaged and C-Sec had lost valuable resources that couldn't be replaced.

Telarrek turned to the Laronian officer. "Pull everyone back. Full retreat." The officer nodded and relayed the commands immediately.

Uthor stood in front of the view-screen, his regal posture and dominating presence replaced with sagging shoulders and despair. Arakesh was above him, a lifeless, volcanic mass that had lost much of its shape due to planet-wide implosions. Smaller explosions were still flaring within the debris of the battlefield, as C-Sec vessels succumbed to their critical damage.

Telarrek put his upper hand on the Raalak's solid shoulder. "I am so sorry, Uthor. I am sure your family were evacuated in time. We will find them."

The High Charge let out a great, shuddering sigh and hung his shoulders for a moment, before straightening up to his full height and ripping the C-Sec emblem off his uniform. "*I* will find them."

Telarrek wanted to say something, anything that might stop his friend from walking away, but words could neither soothe the Raalak's pain nor break his resolve. His four legs thundered against the floor as he strode towards the exit of the command room. No one stopped him removing a rifle from the rack beside the door. Clave Tower was still in a state of pandemonium, with wild Shay violently attacking anything that moved.

"High Councillor Telarrek?"

It took the Novaarian a moment to connect the title with his name. He turned to see a command room full of alien faces looking at him with expectation, including the new councillors. It was a lot to ask of them, he knew, but no one person should ever control the Conclave and, right now, they were its best chance at survival.

"High Councillor," the Ch'kara repeated. "The shell defence system is ready to activate. It just needs confirmation."

"Confirmation from whom?" Telarrek asked.

The Ch'kara hesitated. "Usually, it would require authorisation from all five of the Highclave..."

Telarrek puffed out his narrow ribcage. "Well, now we all have a say in our fate." The Novaarian turned to his fellow councillors and asked if they agreed with activating the shell defence system. Several nervous expressions looked back at him, but all races agreed that it was needed.

The Ch'kara looked up at Telarrek. "I can recode the authorisation to accept the biodata for new councillors, but it will take time to add every race to the defence system."

Telarrek looked at the view-screen, where Arakesh burned in the coldness of space. They didn't have time.

"What about the Shay?" He asked. "We only have four races present from the previous Highclave."

"In an emergency, there are protocols that allow executive decisions to be made by only four of the races," the Ch'kara explained.

"This certainly counts as an emergency. Enact the protocols. I need three of you," he said, addressing the new councillors. "We do not have time to input access for all of us, though we will. I need a Raalak, a Laronian, and a Ch'kara."

Telarrek hated doing it after making a point of including every race on the new Highclave. Still, it would take time to undo the old ways. When this was all over, if it was ever over, he promised himself there would be an election to potentially replace every councillor with the people's chosen representative. For now, however, he joined the three councillors from the *core* worlds and placed his hand over the bio scanner.

A general alarm was sent across Clave Tower, warning its citizens of what was about to happen. With all the chaos out there, Telarrek wondered if anyone would notice. It was only when everything began to shake that the Novaarian remembered how drastic the shell defences were. External monitoring stations, placed in orbit around the capital, relayed their live feeds to the view-screen.

All conversation had stopped as the command room's occupants examined their shaking surroundings nervously.

The vibration under their feet increased and various holograms flickered around the room. Telarrek's eyes were fixed on the view-screen that showed the two halves of the capital's outer planet shell coming together. The process was slow, but eventually the two halves met in a collision of broken rock and a ring of dust that was pushed out into space. Clave Tower and everything around it was encapsulated inside, protected by the thick shell of the planet, which for the first time in a hundred millennia was whole again.

Looking at the image of Arakesh, Telarrek knew the outer shell wouldn't be enough to keep them out. All they had done was buy themselves more time. Thinking of how best to use that time, the Novaarian wondered about Kalian and the Gomar.

"Do we have an update on Evalan?" he asked.

Many of the command staff looked to the female Novaarian sitting behind a crescent desk of holograms. "The planet has been evacuated," she explained. "Due to the priority levels given to the core worlds, they were unsuccessful in reaching Nova Prime."

"Priority levels?" Telarrek repeated.

"Yes. In the case of an emergency, such as a planetary evacuation, the five core worlds are given priority access to the capital via the local Starforges."

Telarrek covered his eyes in despair. "We need to take a closer look at the protocols our predecessors have put into place. I want every Starforge activated on every world. Bring out any that are still in storage and send a message to the factories on Ch'ket. We need more and we need them now." Thousands of Starforges had been built, ready to revolutionise the Conclave, but it had been felt that a soft opening around the galaxy would be an easier transition. "Where are the humans now?"

"They have been met by a delegation on Corvus, High Councillor."

Telarrek checked the view-screen and expanded the information they had on the Trillik's home world. They were reporting attacks in various cities around the planet, but their Shay population was far lower than most since the cyborg race found Corvus's tropical weather hard to live in.

"They will be a serious target for our enemy," he said. "Arrange for one of their Starforges to link with one of our own and bring the humans here. That might even give Corvus more time to—"

"Sir!" The Laronian officer stood up behind him, her eyes locked on to the view-screen. "Enemy ships just emerged from subspace around Corvus."

Telarrek froze in the central aisle. "Alert C-Sec and have them divert whatever they can afford." The Novaarian wanted to send more and save what few remained of the human race, but then he would be no better than Uthor.

Roland waited until the colossal ship had left the system before reactivating the Rackham's engine and powering up again. They had drifted through the debris, watching helplessly as the *Sentinel* disappeared within the storm of enemy ships. Between the loss of the *Sentinel* and the state of Arakesh, the Conclave had suffered a massive defeat.

"How do we beat something like that?" Ava asked, staring absently at the blanket of destruction laid out before the viewport.

"Maybe we can't..." Roland replied. He could tell that his response hadn't helped the tension on the bridge, but he was too exhausted to care. For all the battles he had witnessed, this one carried a level of death that couldn't be fathomed. And the enemy had already moved on to the next planet...

Len broke the silence, "Message coming through on all bandwidths. Direct from Clave Command Tower."

"Let me guess," Roland interrupted. "They're ordering a full retreat."

The Ch'kara hesitated. "Full retreat. All ships in the system are to pull back to the capital."

Roland pushed away from his console and kicked the empty bottles at the base of his chair. "They could have done with sending that..." His anger bubbled over and he couldn't find the words. "*Rackham*, set course for the capital. Make it fast."

"*Course set. Leaving the system now.*"

The bounty hunter was already heading for a fridge of cold beers by the time the *Rackham* dropped into subspace.

CHAPTER 17

KALIAN LOOKED UP, beyond the tropical trees that lined the streets of Corvus' capital, and altered the lenses in his eyes, focusing them on the turquoise skies. The two-pronged vessels took shape as they breached the atmosphere, hurtling towards the surface with a trail of fire and smoke behind them. The closer they got the more their structure changed, morphing into a single point.

"Everybody take cover!" Kalian shouted at the top of his voice.

The caravan of humans being led through the streets scattered to the buildings, desperately trying to take shelter inside or behind the giant palm trees. The Trillik security force did their best to keep everyone together while simultaneously ushering their own citizens to safety.

The ground shook violently beneath them as a giant ship landed on either side of the city. The earthquake ripped through the foundations of more than one of the mirrored towers. Kalian turned to the street on his left and watched one of the skyscrapers topple into another on the other side. A moment later, a wall of dust and debris was pushed between the buildings, an impenetrable fog that promised a death from suffocation to any within.

Kalian pushed out both of his hands and condensed the air

around the street, forcing the grey fog to run over them. They were instantly enveloped in darkness until the dust ran its course. He looked back down the street to see a hundred thousand faces looking back at him with panic and awe battling for their expression.

"We need to keep moving!" Li'ara shouted over the chaos.

Kalian turned to Sef. "Spread yourselves out. There's a lot of people here and I don't want a single person being separated from the rest of us."

The big Gomar nodded and the rest of them dispersed between the throng of people, taking up positions on each side. They were all still in need of more training, but at least they could keep any harmful debris from killing people.

Captain Fey approached the head of the Trillik security force. "Which way is it?"

The Trillik blinked all four of its angular black eyes, clearly in shock. "It's... It's that way." His bulbous green finger pointed down the street where the tower had just collapsed.

"Is there another way around?" Jed asked.

"There's no time!" Kalian shouted, looking to one of the enemy ships poking over the edge of the city. His sight sharpened, revealing thousands of Shay pouring out of the nanocelium walls. "They brought Shay with them..."

"What do we do then?" Captain Holt asked.

Kalian looked at the horizontal tower sitting in the middle of the street. "We have to go through it. Come on!"

He didn't give them a choice, grabbing Li'ara by the hand and making a run for it. With the other hand he continued to push the fog away, sending it up the adjacent buildings. The mob of humans naturally followed him, more than happy to be around the person who continued to save them. That wasn't always how Kalian saw it, however. He often felt, as he did now, that his presence only brought more trouble.

"We shouldn't have come here," he said to Li'ara as they made their way through the debris strewn across the street. "We've endangered the lives of every person on Corvus."

"What else could we do," Li'ara replied through laboured breath. "We're an almost extinct race backed into a corner. We need to survive."

Kalian extended his hand and blew out the twisted framework and glass that cut across the street. "At what price do we survive?"

"Really?" she asked incredulously. "You want to have a philosophical debate right now?"

It was another reminder of how much he was changing. Despite the madness and violence exploding around them, Kalian's mind was capable of running through a hundred different things at once, compartmentalising their problems, and allowing him to carry what others would feel is a strange conversation.

He shrugged it off. "Fair point."

Kalian expanded his mind to map out the fallen building. He found the structurally weak points and exerted his telekinetic will into them, preventing any further collapses while the human population made their way through.

Screams sounded from the back of the trail and Kalian caught sight of several Shay being flung into the air and smashed into the buildings. It was a level of violence he had come to expect from the Gomar.

"Keep everyone moving through," he directed to Li'ara and the others.

Kalian shuffled past the mob, trying to fit through the jagged hole in the side of the tower, and ran to see the Gomar. All twelve of them had formed a rough line in the hope of keeping the vying Shay away. The cyborgs, who now appeared more savage than ever, were crawling along the walls of the building and desperately trying to climb over the bulky armour of the Gomar. Still, they held the line. Garrion waved his hands over the buildings and pulled slabs of it away with the Shay still attached. Vox swept her arms out and yanked multiple limbs from their bodies.

Sef and Kovak reminded Kalian of gorillas. The largest of the Gomar, they waded into the waves of infected aliens and used telekinesis to enhance their strength. The Shay flew in every direction, each one taking injuries that would kill a normal being. Any who dashed beyond the line were intercepted by the sisters, Nadreen and Nardel. Between the two of them, they used the heavy debris and in some cases, entire vehicles, to crush the advancing enemy.

It was clear to see, however, that it wasn't going to be enough. Within the entangled mass of savage Shay, the nanocelium was already putting itself back together. The two alien ships only continued to release more as well as tendrils that Kalian could feel digging through the earth.

"Get everyone to the Starforge!" he yelled over the destruction.

Vox turned back to him. "If we don't hold them here they will kill everyone!"

Kalian walked past the sisters and faced the mob of crazed Shay. "No they won't."

With a single hand held out before him, Kalian fell into a world of concentration and connected with the universe, feeling for every molecule that connected him to everything else. He could feel them. The nanocelium writhing around inside the Shay, controlling their motor functions.

"Go..." he said with his eyes closed.

The Gomar hesitated until they realised the Shay were no longer attacking them or even moving. Kalian flexed his fingers and every infected alien doubled over as the spasm ran through their muscles. He found every nanite of nanocelium and pulled, just as he had with those who had attacked them on Evalan.

"There's too many even for you!" Garrion warned.

Kalian wanted to answer but his jaw was clamped shut. It was taking everything he had to keep them frozen and pull at the nanocelium. The Gomar finally left him, making their way through the collapsed building, though a small part of Kalian could feel Sef watching him.

As the first of the nanocelium burst forth from their bodies, the Shay began to fall from the walls and drop in the streets. The black powder weaved through the air, coalescing in a manner not dissimilar from a tight flock of birds. Something wet touched his lips and Kalian tasted blood. It was good, he told himself. He needed to push himself. Through gritted teeth, he pulled and pulled until every Shay was lying on the ground, motionless.

Returning to reality was jarring, with its environment pushing on all of his limited human senses. Only through his Terran mind did he feel in total control. Kalian let his shoulders sag as his lungs filled with ragged breaths. The nanocelium continued to float in the air, a black fog that masked the city beyond.

He knew exactly what to do with it...

After a few long breaths, Kalian centred himself and held his hand out to his side. The nanocelium moved as one, floating through the air until his telekinetic powers brought it all together. It took but a single touch to infect the nanocelium and free it from the slave coding. With his eyes fixed on the black tower in the distance, Kalian fashioned a spear from the nannies, binding them together in a tight weave. The point was so sharp he was sure it could pierce Callic-Diamond.

Kalian pulled his arm back before he forcefully gestured towards the tower. His tether over the spear was released and the shaft of nanocelium flew across the city, its speed enhanced by Terran abilities. A quick alteration to his eyes gave him the perfect view of the spear as it impacted the side of the enemy ship.

It wasn't long before he felt it. The roots it had deployed underground slowed down and the ship itself began to vibrate. It had accepted the nanocelium from the spear into the rest of its systems and fallen prey to the human DNA that was now running through every nanite, irrevocably changing it.

Kalian!

Sef's telepathic call had him turning around, where the Gomar was still waiting for him.

We need to go.

Kalian agreed and started for the hole in the building when he heard a slither of info from the headset of a dead Trillik. He paused to remove the headset from the solider and listened to the warning.

"I repeat," said a terrified Trillik voice, "multiple invading ships have emerged from subspace! Get off the streets! Seek shelter outside the cities or find your nearest Starforge! Evacuation by ship is no longer an option!"

Behind him, the black tower was falling apart, layer by layer of nanocelium dropping away in a cascade. Expanding his awareness, Kalian could feel the second tower was still pouring out infected Shay, only now they had a direction. Instead of creating chaos in the streets, there was a horde of them charging through the city, searching for the humans.

"We're being targeted..." he said to himself.

Can you stop them all? Sef asked. *Can you remove the nanocelium?*

"Maybe," Kalian replied. "It would be easier if all of you could help..." he hoped those words had some kind of impact on the Gomar, because they were going to need them all if this war was going to turn.

"Come on!" Vox cried from the other side of the fallen tower.

Kalian looked back at the waves of raw nanocelium now washing through the streets. It moved in ways that couldn't be attributed to its momentum, showing a level of intelligence as it spasmed up the buildings and across the streets. Entire trees were encompassed and reduced to atoms, consumed by the hungry, yet confused, nanocelium. It gave Kalian an idea.

"Get everyone to the Starforge," he ordered Sef. "Make sure no one is left behind."

What are you going to do?

Kalian considered the amount of free floating nanocelium. "I'm going to hold back the tide."

ALF emerged from subspace, seeing the Corvus system through every external camera on his new Starforge. There was no space battle to speak of, since the Trillik's security force had been nothing but a bug on the windshield of the Kellekt armada. Judging by the skeletal remains and floating debris, C-Sec had lasted longer. Two Nebula-Class cruisers were already being consumed and added to the bulk of the nanocelium.

"Ships have been deployed to the surface," Talli's young voice now came over the Starforge's speakers, having sensed ALF's discomfort at having the new AI in his mind. *"They have released thousands of infected Shay upon the population."*

ALF could sift through every data readout in his mind's eye. Linking through what little remained of the local AI hub and undamaged satellites, he could see the Shay flooding the streets of the capital city as well as the ships that had touched down. Other cities across the globe were already smoking having been bombarded from space, a process that would soften the ground and allow the Kellekt to begin the harvesting process.

"No sign of the Three," Talli commented, aware of ALF's concerns. *"The last report to cross the AI net states that they have left the Arakesh system but have yet to reappear."*

ALF focused his view on the capital city and scanned for human life signs. They were yet to have lost any, but the static Starforge had only just been activated and they had over a hundred thousand people to get through.

"Our scans have been detected," Talli warned. *"Kellekt vessels are locking on to us with weapons systems."*

"Activate the wormhole," ALF commanded. "And reposition us to 349 point 36. I don't want to hit the planet."

"*Hit the planet?*" Talli questioned.

"Like all great feats in technology, it can always be used as a weapon." ALF placed a memory packet on the bridge between him and Talli, allowing the AI to see the events that took place in the Helteron Cluster. There, Malekk had used the Forge to open a wormhole inside the local star and focus that raw power into a single beam and obliterate the *Gommarian*.

"*I've never seen it used that way before,*" Talli commented.

"That's because the Three have always used Forges for transportation and Eclipse missiles for annihilating entire systems."

The Starrilliums came back online but this time ALF made certain the navigation system was offline. When all three of the giant orbs, situated on the outer surface of the crescent station, were ready, he had Talli open a wormhole connecting it to the sun.

"*What circumference would you like the beam, ALF?*" Talli asked.

ALF inspected his view of the oncoming Kellekt vessels. They weren't clustered together, covering a diameter of six thousand kilometres, a spread that was easily targeted with the massive circumference of the Forge that he had available. At the same time, Talli had the station's thrusters shifting the entire Forge, ensuring that Corvus wasn't in alignment beyond the Kellekt.

"Let's go for seven thousand kilometres," ALF replied. "That should do it."

"*What would you like to do about those already on the surface?*" Talli asked. "*I can refocus the beam, but getting it any smaller than a kilometre in circumference will take some adjustments.*"

ALF considered the AI's suggestion of decreasing the size of the wormhole to narrow the beam, but a kilometre wide beam of energy directly from the heart of a star was still like swatting a fly with one of Roland's Tri-Rollers. He magnified the images he had of the capital city, checking again the status of the human evacuation. Locating Kalian's position within the cityscape was all too easy; it even brought a smirk to his face.

"I think Kalian has the surface under control. Let's just take out the vessels."

"As you wish," Talli said jovially. "Wormhole established."

ALF brought his attention back to the small Kellekt fleet traversing space towards them. "Let's give them something to think about, shall we?"

The Starforge opened a wormhole seven thousand kilometres wide and let rip with the power of a star.

Kalian was past the point of having fun and was now beginning to wonder if he had made a mistake. His exosuit was now five times its normal size, having absorbed and repurposed a portion of the nanocelium from one of the towers. There wasn't an inch of him that was exposed and there was at least a metre of nanocelium between him and the outside world.

An initial blast of telekinetic energy kept the horde of Shay from overwhelming the fleeing humans, but he had wasted no time wading into the Shay masses and putting his tree-like arms to good use. A single backhand, coupled with telekinetic energy, was enough to send ten of the infected aliens flying away in a jumble of broken limbs.

He stomped this way and that, flattening them under his heavy feet. Alarms were flaring inside is HUD, alerting him to the Shay on his back, desperately clawing at the nanocelium. Kalian jumped into the air and landed hard so that he might squash the aliens on his back. Another blast of telekinesis scattered those directly in front of him, as well as blowing away the bottom corner of the nearest building.

Another alert broadcasted across his face, notifying Kalian of the link trying to be established by ALF. At least he was asking this time...

"Are you in orbit?" Kalian asked as he picked up a Shay by the leg and hammered it into the road.

A slither of nanocelium wormed up his neck and came to rest behind his ear. "Not quite," came ALF's reply. "I'm just mopping up the reinforcements up here. How is it down there? Looks like you're in the thick of it now."

Kalian held out both his enormous arms and ran forwards, sweeping up a dozen Shay in each embrace. One tight squeeze across his chest was enough to sever most of the aliens at the waist.

"I'm keeping them back," he managed between breaths. "But they keep putting themselves back together! It's infuriating!" Kalian reached over his shoulder and threw the two Shay who had been digging their infected hands into his helmet.

"*Well, they're not putting themselves back together up here, that's for sure.*"

Kalian looked up and caught the end of a shining beam of light streak across the sky. "You're using a Starforge!" he exclaimed.

"*You know me,*" ALF said, "*I like to arrive in style.*"

Kalian turned about in the battlefield of shredded Shay and found that at least a hundred of them had run passed him and were chasing after the humans again. One last backhand gave him the room to break into a sprint, something his lumbering exosuit didn't excel at. He flattened or pushed any aside that didn't get out of his way in time, before leaping on to the building wall and pushing off, clearing the fallen skyscraper beneath him in a single bound.

His impact on the other side was devastating for the Shay. His speed and hulk scattered the aliens in every direction and a sweeping hand caught one of them by the torso. The Shay made for the perfect projectile to throw at the others still running after the humans.

"*Half of the population has made it through the Forge,*" ALF told him.

"What about Corvus' population?" Kalian asked.

"*They've recommenced their orbital evacuations but there just aren't enough Starforges to get everyone off the surface. Still, the Trilliks will outnumber the Raalaks.*"

"What?" Kalian knew exactly what ALF meant, but he couldn't imagine that level of genocide on a core planet.

"*Arakesh is gone, Kalian,*" the AI explained. "*The Three harvested the whole world. The networks are pretty patchy right now, but it looks like the Raalaks are officially on the endangered list.*"

Kalian continued to run forward, shoving aside every Shay in his bid to reach the back of the human parade. The Raalaks weren't the only endangered species in the galaxy and he had to ensure the survival of at least one.

The sparkling dome at the end of the street was one of the few buildings to have remained intact, and right now there were fifty thousand humans cramming through its doors and running through a pair of Starforges. The Gomar lined each side of the human line, ready to defend against the infected aliens.

Kalian came bounding down the road, a behemoth in his exosuit, and skidded to a stop a few metres away from the men and women unfortunate enough to be at the back the line. Turning back to the street he had come from, the fallen skyscraper cut across the middle was hidden beneath the wave of Shay crawling over and through it. There was only one way he was going to buy the rest of the humans enough time to escape.

His awareness expanded into the buildings and towers either side of the street, searching for the spark of life that existed inside all intelligent beings. Thankfully, they were in an area of the city that had been within the priority evac zone, leaving the buildings empty.

Using his HUD, Kalian had his larger exosuit project his voice to the Gomar. "I need you all to erect a shield around the last of them! Make sure you're on the inside!" He waited until the Gomar had positioned themselves around the humans and he felt the solid wall of air form around them.

Then he let loose.

With one hand, he dragged it down the tower on the left before mirroring his actions over the tower on the right. His telekinetic strands dug into the buildings and tugged at their framework. The ground shook and glass rained down amid giant slabs of wall. The charging Shay took little notice, however, and continued their advance, some even running on all fours like animals.

Kalian gritted his teeth and brought both of his arms in with one last pull of telekinetic energy. The towers couldn't resist his power. The top halves crumpled first, bending at an angle that would see them fall into the street, but the bottom halves soon followed suit and collapsed under the weight. The Shay directly in front of him were picked up and thrown back into the avalanche or kicked away. Ultimately, there was no escape for the infected aliens.

The fog of dust and debris concealed them all before the first of the buildings slammed into the street, quickly followed by the second. The impact created a shockwave both through the air and under Kalian's feet. Protected inside his exosuit, he remained still and allowed the impenetrable fog to wash over him and around the field the Gomar had erected. More than one slab of rock bounced off his nanocelium armour, but still he remained, waiting for any Shay that might have escaped the devastation.

"They're all through," ALF reported. "Get yourself through, Kalian. I'll see you at the capital."

Kalian waved his hand across the brown fog, clearing his vision. A fifty metre wall of destruction lay before him with only a handful of Shay on the outside, though there wasn't one of them with all of their arms and legs. He turned to the Starforge inside the dome, leaving the aliens to crawl across the broken ground.

The Gomar had dropped their shield as the last of the humans made it through the event horizon. Looking now, Kalian could only see Sef and Vox standing in front of the bright light, surrounded by Trillik technicians and security personnel. He hated to think what the green aliens thought of them being given priority evacuation Forges while their people were left to suffer. It was an imbalance that Kalian felt helpless to change.

"Nice suit!" Vox exclaimed.

The ground shook with every footstep he took inside the dome.

"It's just a loan," he said as the front of the exosuit opened up like a zip.

He dropped out and watched the nanocelium knit back together, leaving an ominous-looking giant behind. That gave him an idea. Kalian covered his right hand in a glove of nanocelium and brought up his finger menu of orange holographics. The giant mass of nanites was still under his control even after detaching from his slimline exosuit.

"We need to go, Kalian!" Vox called.

Kalian ignored her for the moment and entered the coordinates of the second enemy tower into the giant's navigation systems. "Destroy it," he ordered. "And protect as many people as you can."

The giant gave no indication that it had received the commands other than to turn around and exit the dome. It wouldn't be enough to save the whole planet, but with ALF's help in space and the giant's help on the surface it was something. Kalian kept telling himself that as he stepped through the Forge.

CHAPTER 18

Roland stood as a sentinel on the top deck of the control room, inside Clave Command Tower. Everyone beneath him was busy coordinating the shit show that was the Conclave's defence. Above it all, the bounty hunter looked out on the planet-sized tower of the capital, watching distant explosions while the mobs surrounding the tower took on wild Shay. Nowhere was safe anymore.

He could still see Arakesh in his mind, burning and glowing a molten orange as it collapsed in on itself. Not only had the enemy harvested the planet in a matter of hours, but the ship had also grown to the size of a small world now.

"You get awfully pouty when you're serious," Ch'len said from behind him.

"Shouldn't you be a quivering wreck with all this open space?" Roland kept his eyes on the unfolding chaos outside.

"I'm okay as long as I keep my eyes on my feet." An awkward silence fell between the bounty hunters. "So," the Ch'kara managed, "do you think this is it? The end, I mean?"

Roland sighed, always uncomfortable taking part in a serious conversation. "We're fucked, Len."

Ch'len nodded his head, though he was clearly distressed at the idea. "But, there's still a chance..."

"No." Roland couldn't say it any clearer. "You've heard Kalian. These things have been harvesting civilisations since the dawn of time. You don't do something for that long and not become really good at it. We're fucked."

Ch'len shrugged his shoulders. "But, we still have..."

"Len. They *eat* planets. What can you do against an enemy that literally devours planets?"

"You sound scared," Ch'len stated boldly.

For a fraction of a second, Roland wanted to snap at what was really his only friend, but the lack of alcohol in his system gave the bounty hunter access to other parts of his brain for a change. "There's nothing wrong with being scared, Len. Fear is what keeps us alive." In the blink of an eye he saw all the terrible things he had done for Central Parliament, all the battles he had fought in and the lives he had taken just to prevent them from taking his. "We should all be afraid..."

"Mr North!" Telarrek called from below. "They all made it through."

That was something, Roland thought. At least they could all die together.

Along with the Raiders, Roland took a transport to the Lambo District, where a chain of hotels had been taken over by the human population under C-Sec command. According to the reports coming through on his sleeve's screen, most of the Shay had been pushed back to the lower levels now, where many were said to be finding old tunnels to hide in. Still, the bounty hunter made certain that both of his Tri-Rollers were fully loaded with Intrinium.

It took some time to sift through the various directions he was given, but eventually he came across the Starstruck Hotel where

Kalian and Li'ara had been housed. As he entered, C-Sec soldiers were still escorting the hotel's staff outside and ushering them into transports. Roland wondered if the Raalaks were getting the same level of security wherever they were.

The hotel was one of the more luxurious establishments, with a grand staircase, red carpets, and golden bannisters. The sweet aroma of the perfume was quickly being overtaken, however, by the fouler smell of human sweat. Inspecting the faces of the humans huddling in groups and waiting for their assigned rooms, Roland could see the exhaustion that wore them all down. They had been running for their lives, something they were all becoming accustomed to.

"You're either the toughest bastard to kill or the luckiest guy in the galaxy!"

Roland turned around inside the foyer and looked up at the landing, where Li'ara Ducarté was leaning over the rail. "Hey, Red! Can't a guy be both?"

"It's good to see you all alive," she said as she made her way down the stairs. "I heard you were in the Arakesh system when it got hit."

"We heard you guys went for a stroll through Corvus," Ava Matthews replied.

"The last twenty-four hours have been something of a nightmare for us all," Captain Fey said, meeting them by the reception desk. "Are the reports about Arakesh true?" she asked.

"It's gone, Cap." Roland couldn't help but wonder what Earth and Century had looked like when they were destroyed. He was tempted to ask Li'ara, who had witnessed both, but he had been sent to the hotel for a reason. "Telarrek wants us back at the command tower," he explained. "Kalian and Sef too," he added.

"Are we in trouble for bringing the Gomar?" Li'ara asked.

Captain Fey shook her head. "If we get reprimanded by anyone in the middle of all *this*, they're going to have deal with my foot up their ass."

Roland laughed for the first time in a while. "Now there's a captain I can get behind."

Fey ignored his comment. "I'll find Jed..."

"I'll go find Kalian and Sef." Li'ara turned to the Raiders before leaving. "It's really good to see you all. I hope Jess recovers quickly."

"She's a fighter," Ava replied confidently. "Like the rest of us."

The *Valkor* had limped back to the capital with the *Rackham*, but the damage it had taken had slowed down the Medder treating the lieutenant. Still, she was in good hands now in the same hospital as High Councillor Brokk. She was, after all, one of them.

"Go and get some rest," Roland suggested. "It's all talk right now, but the fighting is far from over..."

The Clave Command Tower had quickly become the most fortified place in the Conclave. Roland had been forced to give over his Tri-Rollers, as well as all of his other toys, most of which gained him funny looks from the C-Sec soldiers.

"Unbelievable," he muttered beside Li'ara. "Two walking weapons of mass destruction are allowed to just stroll in," he said, gesturing ahead to Kalian and Sef, "but little old me has to give over my babies."

"You sound like a baby right now," Li'ara retorted.

They were shown to a new room within the complex, taking them away from the control room. It was no less impressive, with a dome of glass and an entire wall of holographic data relayed from the control room below. A round table took up most of the available space, surrounded by twelve chairs occupied by the eleven representatives of the new council. The empty chair beside Telarrek was obvious, but Roland assumed it was supposed to have a Shay sitting in it.

"I hate this part," he admitted.

"What are you talking about?" Li'ara asked.

"This." The bounty hunter gestured to the table of alien leaders as the two of them were ushered to the side to join Naydaalan, away from Kalian, Sef and Captain Fey. "The part where everyone seems to forget that a war just kicked off. Plus, we get sidelined because we, A, don't have superpowers and, B, don't have enough lines on our uniform."

Li'ara rolled her eyes as she took her place beside Naydaalan. "You are long past wearing a uniform, Roland."

"I'm just saying: we need to be out there fighting back, not talking about stuff in here."

Before Li'ara could reply, Telarrek stood up from his chair. "We are officially at war," he declared, much to Roland's amusement. "We have already suffered horrific blows not only to our homes, but to our hierarchy. The Highclave was attacked on Nova Prime, leaving only Councillor Brokk alive, though his situation has become critical. In their absence, and with Councillor Brokk's blessing, we have formed a new Highclave in this time of emergency. Until the war is over, there will be no elections. Councillors will be appointed by the majority vote of those present."

Roland was already starting to feel sleepy. To keep himself awake and standing, he clocked every C-Sec soldier, their weapons, and potential weak points, as well as the exits. He wasn't entirely convinced that the command tower couldn't come under assault any minute, what with all the Shay unaccounted for.

"As it is," Telarrek continued, "this council has already voted prior to your arrival," he said to Kalian and the others. "Unlike previous Highclaves, this one represents every race in the Conclave, since we are all in this together. From what we can tell, there is not a single Shay who has not been affected by this nanocelium virus. That leaves us with an empty chair..."

Now that caught Roland's attention. He also noted that it had captured Captain Fey's too, who was swapping glances with Captain Holt and Kalian.

"The Conclave consists of thirteen species now fighting for survival. Captain Fey, would you represent the humans of Evalan?"

All eyes fell on the captain, who appeared to take in a deep breath and straighten her back. Kalian bowed his head and whispered something into her ear, which caused Fey to tug on her uniform and lift her chin.

"It would be an honour, in this time of crisis, to sit on the Highclave," she finally replied."

"Due to the dire situation among the Raalakian community, High Charge Uthor has regrettably stepped down from his position," Telarrek said. "We thank Councillor Ordak for being present in spite of such a time." The Novaarian held out his upper hand to incorporate the stone-like alien on the other side of the table. "Your input will be appreciated, I am sure. With our lack of a High Charge in mind, we are also grateful that you have accepted your place on this council, Captain Fey. Our civilisation has known peace for so long that we would value any insights that you may offer in these violent times."

Fey bowed her head. "I will offer what I can."

Telarrek gestured to the chair beside him with one of his lower arms. "Then please join us. We are about to vote on lifting the grounding laws surrounding Kalian and the Gomar."

Roland turned to Li'ara with an arched brow. "Maybe shit *is* about to get done," he whispered.

"About time," she quietly replied.

The bounty hunter had little care for the politics of the Conclave, but he had to admit, seeing Captain Fey seated among the new council was a good sight.

"The previous Highclave placed restrictions on you," Telarrek continued, addressing Kalian and Sef. "In a time of war, all those able to fight are required to do so. Will you fight for the Conclave?"

Kalian briefly met eyes with Sef. "We already have and we will continue to do so."

Telarrek nodded his head, displacing his thick tendrils. "All those in favour of granting Kalian and the Gomar the right to travel freely within the Conclave..." All thirteen of the new councillors raised an arm in agreement. "Excellent. You are welcome to stay, both of you, while we discuss our next move. Your advice regarding the invaders will be gladly accepted."

"Thank you," Kalian replied, walking over to join up with Roland and Li'ara.

The far wall came to life with holographic readouts from end to end. Most of the images relayed the battle being pitched on multiple worlds, both in space and on the surface. It wasn't going well. Roland focused on the casualty bar in the corner, its numbers concerning the amount of C-Sec vessels that were being destroyed. The number never stopped going up.

There were two other images taken from Clave Tower, somewhere far beneath their current position. C-Sec soldiers were fighting in the streets against the Shay who had acquired weapons from the fallen. Small gunships hovered over the scenes, casting stark spotlights over the infected.

"This has just come in," Telarrek announced, altering the central image and magnifying it.

They all looked upon a purple planet with a black blemish in the northern hemisphere, the background to a violent space battle. It was them; the big one Roland had seen on Arakesh.

"Where is this?" he asked, gaining the attention and frowns of everyone present. Li'ara discreetly nudged his wrist with her knuckles, warning him not to speak up.

"This is Kylm, in the Harth system," Telarrek answered. "It falls within Ch'karan territory." The Novaarian gestured to the small Ch'kara seated four people down and offered the alien a sorrowful expression.

"It's harvesting," Kalian said. "It'll drain the planet of its resources; surface vegetation, biological life, even technology. It has roots that mine the planet for minerals, but ultimately, it will ravage the planet's core."

"How do you know this?" the Ch'karan councillor asked pointedly.

"ALF has challenged them in the past. He is perhaps the only being in the galaxy to have faced them and survived."

Telarrek interrupted the line of questioning before it could go any further. "Kalian's assessment is correct. Thanks to the survival of the *Valkor*, we have been able to recover its scans of the process. What is happening to Kylm right now will end with its implosion."

"And our enemy will get bigger," an Atari councillor added.

"Indeed." The Novaarian pointed to a series of scans and comparisons beside the image of Kylm. "After this harvesting ship disconnected from Arakesh, its diameter had swollen from two thousand kilometres to four thousand."

Roland shared a look of concern with Li'ara. "That's somewhere between the Earth and the moon, right?" he asked in hushed tones. Li'ara could only nod her head, sharing the despair that had grown across the room.

The central image was then replaced with a star chart of the Conclave. On the edge was the Solian Way, highlighted with a red dot and connected to Arakesh, much farther into Conclave space. From there, a red line connected Arakesh to Kylm, again coming into the highlighted territory as the harvesting ship burrowed its way towards the core.

Telarrek said, "Our best analysts believe that this chosen course will bring that ship to the capital in three days, assuming its harvesting process speeds up as its size increases." His statement caused every councillor to look at each other, whispering in harsh and desperate tones. "If it continues down this line, it will harvest Tagomar in the Vellum system and Sordomo in the Faronite system before arriving here. Right now we do not have enough data to estimate its size on arrival, but I have been told it is likely the ship will match the capital in diameter."

The furry councillor from Tularon spoke up, "If we predict it will arrive in the Vellum system, we should divert forces to Tagomar immediately!"

"There's no time for that now," the Laronian councillor leant over the polished table. "If we divert to the Faronite system we have a better chance of staging a massive defensive to protect Sordomo!"

Roland couldn't help but smirk as he leant towards Li'ara's ear. "Guess whose territory those planets fall under..."

Kalian stepped forward. "There's a chance both planets *and* the capital might be spared."

Roland joined everyone in staring at Kalian. "I hope you're not about to just pull a rabbit out of your ass, kid."

Kalian continued, "That harvesting ship contains the Three. Three beings who ultimately control every nanocelium currently ripping this galaxy to atoms. They want to take everything this civilisation has to offer, but they fear humanity. This fear will drive them to great lengths to see us wiped from existence. It might even be enough to divert them from their present course."

Telarrek lifted his elongated jaw. "Explain."

"Send us back to Evalan," he said simply.

His suggestion caused the aliens to look at each other with expressions of curiosity, but also hope. It seemed they didn't mind the idea of sacrificing the humans if it meant giving their own worlds a few more days to live.

"Kalian..." Li'ara asked him several questions with her look alone.

"I fail to see how this would help to defeat our invaders," Telarrek replied. "They would only be diverted for as long as it took to destroy you. I would rather that the few left of your kind remain here, where it is fortified."

"It might give us time to evacuate more planets," Councillor Ordak suggested.

"Sending us back is only part one of the plan," Kalian said, commanding the room again. "You will have to split C-Sec forces in half. One side is to be ready to jump into the Evalan system once they have gathered in full force." This was met with scoffs and shaking heads. "The other side is to attack Shandar."

"Shandar?" Telarrek asked.

"This invasion was planned centuries ago, if not longer," Kalian explained. "They intended to remain in control of your central AI, allowing them to monitor your communications and misdirect any opposing counterattacks. The Crucible on Shandar was the second point of their invasion. By turning the Shay against us, it ensured that our forces were split across every world and any evacuation would prove chaotic, since there isn't a world without some population of Shay."

"You want us to abandon every world and send out fleets to just two planets?" the Laronian councillor asked incredulously.

"If you can take out the Crucible, you can stop the broadcast that gives them control over the nanocelium inside every Shay. How many worlds could be effectively evacuated without local forces trying to fight them off? Not only that, if they take the bait, the invading ships currently attacking various worlds would likely make for Evalan. No more ships in the sky or Shay on the ground... think of all the good you could do with that time."

Roland had to hand it to the kid, he could be persuading. If a little crazy...

Telarrek looked from Captain Fey to Kalian. "Your people would be at serious risk, even with half the fleet around Evalan."

"We don't even have the *Sentinel*," the Ch'karan councillor added with his hands in the air.

"Would I be wrong in assuming you have already begun construction on a new *Sentinel*?" Kalian asked as if he already knew the answer.

Telarrek glanced at the other councillors before replying. "Yes, the *Boundless*. But it is a skeleton of the *Sentinel*, Kalian. It has nothing but a shell and a Starrillium, no weapons or shields."

"It doesn't need all those things," Kalian countered. "It's big enough to house the human population. Equip it with a static Starforge and have it set course for Evalan now."

Telarrek clasped his lower hands. "You mean to bait them and evacuate the population to the *Boundless*?"

"I believe my plan will work but, like anything, there's always the chance it could go the other way. Better to have a Plan B."

"Okay..." Captain Fey's tone spoke of concern. "Let's say we destroy the Crucible, eliminate the Shay threat, and allow more time for the other races to reach safety, including our own. How do *you* face them without losing half the fleet and our planet?"

That was a question Roland wouldn't mind hearing the answer to. So far, Kalian had offered up the human race as an appetiser to give the main course a chance at running away, but they all knew there would be no running away in the end.

"I'm going to integrate myself with the harvesting ship." Kalian's declaration gained him little more than a roomful of blank faces looking back at him, though Li'ara's was much closer to rage.

Before she could smack him around the head and demand rational thought from the super-powered being, Telarrek asked, "Could you elaborate, Kalian?"

"Yes, Kalian," Li'ara said through gritted teeth, "elaborate..."

Roland noticed the lack of eye contact Kalian gave to Li'ara, and the bounty hunter didn't blame him. It sounded like he was talking about sacrifice, so avoiding Li'ara's fiery gaze was perhaps the safest thing to do. Roland did regret standing between them, though.

"The reason they fear us so much is because of our DNA. That's why they started the civil war in the Terran Empire, why they drove Savrick mad and had him destroy Earth and Century, chasing us here."

"What do they find so abhorrent about your DNA?" the Laronian councillor asked.

"Nanocelium at its most basic definition is a collection of nanites. Each one is coded with laws that slave them to the harvesting program. But, when nanocelium comes into contact with human DNA, its base coding is altered, freeing the individual nanites of these laws. Once free, the nanocelium coalesces and begins to form its own intelligence, something its original base coding cannot allow to happen."

The Tularon councillor lifted one of its furry hands. "Why does your DNA undo this coding and not any of ours?"

Kalian paused for a moment. "I don't know, *yet*."

"And you plan on what?" the Ch'karan councillor pressed. "Integrating your DNA with the harvesting ship? What will this actually accomplish?"

"Death, probably," Li'ara offered with a flat tone.

Kalian ignored her comment. "It should separate and free the nanocelium, eliminating its singular cause as programmed by them."

Councillor Ordak grunted with his gravelly throat. "With half the fleet ready and waiting, we could use that time to destroy them as they unravel!"

Kalian shook his head. "I wouldn't advise that, Councillor. The only weapon powerful enough to destroy nanocelium is a Starforge, a big one at that. ALF has control of one, but it would take some time to use it against every nanite in their armada. Attacking the nanocelium as it gains intelligence might provoke it, making the newly freed nanites our enemy once again. I suggest we rout out the core of their programming and then focus our efforts on annihilating the Three. They're the driving force behind every invasion. With their nanocelium army no longer following them, the Three should be vulnerable."

"How would we find this?" Telarrek asked. "Our scans are ineffectual to anything inside their hulls."

"Leave that part to me," Kalian assured.

"What about you?" Captain Fey glanced at Li'ara before asking, "How will you even get inside their ship, Kalian?"

Kalian closed his eyes and took a breath, refraining from answering. Roland met the eyes of Li'ara and Captain Fey as they all silently questioned Kalian's lack of response.

"Kalian..." Roland prompted.

Then he vanished.

The air fractured where he had been standing, distorting Sef's image on the other side. The gasps that filled the room were exaggerated as Kalian reappeared in front of the holographic screen a mere second after he had disappeared.

"Like that," he said casually.

"Holy shit..." The words couldn't help but escape Roland's mouth. He knew Kalian had performed such a feat before, one of even greater distance, but actually seeing it with his own eyes was mind-blowing.

"If I'm close enough I should be able to teleport in and out."

The room fell silent with only the occupants' eyes doing the talking. There wasn't a person around the table who wasn't staring at him. Roland wasn't sure if Kalian's show of power had bolstered everyone's hopes or simply reminded the other races how dangerous humans could be.

Telarrek cleared his narrow throat. "This council will vote. The proposed plan is to divide the fleet. One half will assault Shandar and destroy the Crucible. The other half will defend Evalan until Kalian can integrate with the harvesting ship. All those not in favour, speak now."

Roland looked at the faces of every alien, waiting for one of them to protest, but none spoke up. How could they? They were at war. And not some half-assed war for territory or resources, but a war that would determine how many planets were even left habitable: how many races were left standing at the end. So far, their plan had simply involved some ineffectual attempts to put out fires across seven hundred worlds. Kalian's plan would put only one world in jeopardy and could potentially bring an end to the threat.

"Then it is decided," Telarrek announced. "Before any human passes through a Starforge and returns to Evalan," the Novaarian explained, "I would have a scout ship go ahead and make certain the system is clear of enemies. The *Boundless* will then set course as soon as it is ready."

Fey nodded her agreement. "This kind of fleet movement will definitely broadcast our intentions. The enemy would know we were returning home."

Telarrek tapped the table and brought up a holographic image of various C-Sec officers. "We must now divide the fleet and appoint a new High Charge to lead the assault on Shandar. Destroying the Crucible will be paramount if we are to have any hope of coordinating evacuations."

"There's one more thing," Kalian interrupted, somewhat begrudgingly. "The AI hubs across the Conclave will need to be perfect to coordinate fleet movement and mass evacuations, while simultaneously fighting off any intrusion. There's a..." He paused as if he had decided mid-sentence to change his words. "There's a *high* chance the central hub has already been hacked."

That caused another stir among the councillors. No one liked the idea of being watched and listened to, especially by the enemy.

"If that's the case," the Ch'karan councillor said, "then they will already know of our plans!"

Kalian shook his head. "I deactivated all surveillance equipment inside this room the moment I walked in."

Roland's eyebrow shot up in surprise and admiration. He knew not to underestimate the kid, having seen him do some unbelievable shit, but he was thinking ahead in ways the bounty hunter had only ever seen trained operatives do. His plan, though extremely risky, was potentially the only one out of a million that might turn the tide of this war, but it still seemed too out there for a history lecturer from San Francisco.

"What are you proposing?" Telarrek asked.

Kalian shared a look with Li'ara. "If you allow a basic clone of ALF into the system, he can coordinate everything and make certain our communications remain private."

Roland had to give it the kid; he knew how to suck the air out of a room.

Xydrandil of the Nix shifted his spiked legs and looked at Kalian with his chevron-shaped head. "That idea was rejected by the previous Highclave and for good reason. We wold be giving ALF control over the entire Conclave!"

"No," Kalian countered. "It would be a clone of his most basic subroutines. It would be all of his strengths without the personality. *You* would still have control over it. Think of it as an upgrade," he added.

The table fell into whispering and conferring, but Captain Fey asked, "Could these subroutines be removed from the hub once the war is over?"

Kalian paused. "Yes."

Roland pursed his lips and frowned. He knew a shit poker face when he saw one; Kalian had always been terrible at lying with his eyes.

"How would we integrate this clone?" Telarrek asked when no one else spoke up.

"ALF has the technology required to insert his subroutines. I can bring it here."

Telarrek gestured to the holographic screen with his upper hand. "The shell defence is in operation," the Novaarian explained. "No ships can come or go."

"ALF has a Starforge at his disposal," Kalian replied, the answer always ready at the edge of his lips. "If you can grant me access to one in Clave Tower, I can meet him and bring back the required parts."

The Highclave took another vote, though as they went around the table for each councillor's ballot, most were simply waiting to see if Xydrandil would protest any further. Ultimately, they agreed that as an emergency measure, having the central AI hub upgraded would save more lives.

"Then it is decided," Telarrek said. "We will await word from the *Regis* to make certain Evalan is safe. In the meantime, we will begin to regroup the fleet and assign them to either Evalan or Shandar. Kalian, we leave all communication with ALF up to you, but whatever you bring back must be examined by our engineers first and they will see to its integration." Kalian nodded along.

Roland didn't take in any more after that. He was convinced something wasn't right with Kalian and it gnawed at him that he couldn't figure it out. Judging by the look Li'ara was giving him, she was thinking the same thing.

At the end of the council meeting, Kalian was among the first to leave, aware that he only had moments before Li'ara or Sef caught up with him.

"Are you happy now?" he said in hushed tones.

The thin strand of nanocelium behind his ear gave voice to ALF. *"Of course I'm not happy! This plan of yours is reckless, beyond reckless; in fact! Your teleportation technique leaves much to be desired. We both know it's taking everything you have right now just to stay standing. How are you going to manage a bigger jump without dying, Kalian?"*

"You're going to give me the juice," Kalian casually replied. "Your super subconducer can give me the push I need."

There was a palpable pause on the AI's end. *"There's more going on than just you jumping in and out of the harvesting ship. I can supply you with the means to secure integration, but while you're trying to do that, they will be bombarding Evalan. This plan puts the entire human race on the line."*

"The human race has been on the line since you seeded the Terran Empire. I'm just drawing a line in the sand. Besides, I finally found you a way into the central AI. I thought you'd be happy."

"You and I both know there's a high chance you won't survive the integration process, Kalian. That amount of nanocelium is going to require every bit of you to rewrite the base coding."

Kalian's computer-like mind had already run through multiple scenarios, showing him his own death in ten thousand different ways.

But he had also foreseen one way he could survive.

"I'm not unique, ALF. The Terran genes will eventually make themselves known in what's left of humanity. If I have to die to see them flourish, then I will." Kalian could feel Sef approaching from behind. "And as far as protecting Evalan goes..."

The big Gomar joined him by the edge of the stairwell, away from the departing councillors and aides. Kalian could also feel Li'ara's mind, searching for him outside the chamber.

I will do it, Sef communed. *I will allow ALF to remove the Harness.*

Kalian let out a sigh of relief. "Are you sure?"

Evalan will need protecting if this plan draws them to us. If you are occupied, it falls to the Gomar to protect all that remains of our people as they make for the Boundless.

That did bring a smile to Kalian's face. It was the first time he had heard Sef, or any of the Gomar refer to humans as their people. It was the first of many walls he had hoped to bring down between them all.

"What about the others?" he asked.

They will do as I do or they won't. I cannot and will not force them. But, I will make them understand what is at stake.

Kalian gave a wry half smile and raised his eyebrow. "I thought that's what I had been doing..."

"*I'm ready on my end,*" ALF said in his ear. "*Bring them with you.*"

Kalian turned his attention back to Sef. "Let me know when you're ready to leave. I'll make sure we have a Starforge ready to go."

Sef bowed his head and walked away, revealing a very pissed off redhead behind him in the corridor. Li'ara tried to approach him casually, but Kalian could see the fury in every step.

"I know what you're thinking..."

"What am I thinking, Kalian?" Li'ara shot back. "That the man I love has just suggested the one plan that sounds like he's probably going to die? Or am I wondering how or when you even came up with this plan since you never mentioned it to me?"

Kalian held out his hands, hoping to soothe her, but it just seemed to piss her off even more. "Is that ALF in your ear?" she asked, looking around his neck. "Is this his plan? Of course it is," she continued without waiting for an answer. "Does he ever come up with a plan that doesn't require sacrifice? You tell that robotic ass—"

"Li'ara." Kalian gripped her by the shoulders and smiled at the Brenine aide who slipped past them to walk down the stairs. "This is my plan. If I had come up with it outside of that room I would have consulted you, I promise. I only thought of it in there and it had to be said. Trust me; this is the only path I can see that leads to the majority surviving this war."

Li'ara deflated somewhat but he knew he hadn't won her over completely. "You only thought of that whole plan while you were in the room?" she asked sceptically.

Kalian offered his boyish grin. "It felt like a long time to me."

"You promise this is your plan? Not his?"

"I promised, didn't I? This is the only way to beat them, Li'ara. There's nothing strong enough to destroy them while they still have control of their armada. I have to free the nanocelium."

Li'ara shook her head. "What if these new AIs get their freedom and decide the original plan wasn't so bad after all?"

Kalian shrugged, thankful that same question hadn't come up in the meeting. "I didn't say there wasn't a degree of hope involved." He tried disarming her with his smile again.

Li'ara managed half a smile and cupped his cheek. "If you die, I'll find a way to bring you back and kill you all over again."

Her calm tone convinced Kalian that she wasn't lying. "Deal," he replied.

Li'ara glanced over her shoulder. "What did Sef want?"

"He's agreed to have ALF remove his Harness."

Li'ara's eyebrows shot up her forehead. "Really? What about the others?"

"We'll have to see. Just having Sef at full power will be a huge help."

"I'll say," Roland interrupted. "This plan of yours is going to get awfully messy before the end, kid. These guys wipe out whole solar systems for a living."

"Then it's a good thing we have you," Kalian said. "How many times have you saved the galaxy now?"

Roland casually shrugged. "A couple of times. It's no biggie."

"Careful, Roland," Li'ara warned, "I'm not sure that head of yours will make it out of the command tower."

Roland found the humour in it, but his expression soon grew serious again. "I'm not going to Evalan," he said, surprising them both.

Kalian could see that Li'ara was about to jump down the man's throat. "Where are you going?" he asked before she could say anything.

"Shandar. I've been to the planet a few times, and even had myself a little look inside the Crucible. You won't need me on Evalan, not with all your firepower," he added with a heavy slap to Kalian's arm.

"I'm sure the *Rackham* will be of great use," Li'ara said, having cooled off a bit.

Never one to enjoy sentiment, Roland clapped his hands together. "So, the *Regis* could be a couple of days scouting out the old home world. Who wants to get blind drunk off their tits?"

CHAPTER 19

THE NEXT MORNING, Kalian stood beside the repurposed Starforge and offered the technicians his most apologetic look. Per his request, they had removed one of the Forges from circulation, effectively shutting down an entire evacuation route. It wouldn't have been so bad if the Gomar had shown up on time.

"Any minute now..." he promised.

Thankfully, the doors swirled open and Sef walked into the warehouse with every one of the Gomar. Kalian couldn't believe his eyes, though upon closer examination, it appeared a handful of them were not entirely happy to be here. Still, Sef had told him he wouldn't force any of them to go through with the procedure, so they had come of their volition.

Sorry we're late. Some took more convincing than others.

"You're here now," Kalian replied to the big man, "that's all that matters." He turned to the technicians and gave them the signal to activate the Forge. "Are you ready for us up there?" He asked ALF.

"*I'm good to go. Opening a wormhole this small is easy.*"

Kalian faced the Gomar. "Helmets and gloves." As he said it, the nanocelium in his suit enveloped his hands and built a helmet to cover his whole head. "We'll be stepping into space so make sure you go at a steady speed or I'll struggle to guide us all into the Starforge."

Kalian knew from stepping through the Forges on Evalan and Corvus that a tingling sensation would creep up his fingers and toes and fill his chest with a cold feeling, but the nanocelium suit prevented any such sensation this time. In the blink of an eye, he was floating out into space with the Starforge behind him and the capital planet before him.

The capital looked no more spectacular than a barren moon, with its two halves fused together. From here, he could just make out the sun reflecting off the C-Sec cruisers, the last of the fleet waiting to be diverted to either Evalan or Shandar. After the meeting yesterday, the *Marillion*, along with the *Rackham*, had already been sent on to Shandar, where it awaited the arrival of half the fleet.

Kalian looked out on the starry field and wondered if he could see Evalan. Cruisers were being diverted, but they had been instructed to wait until the *Regis* gave word that the human population could travel there safely. Everything had to be done at just the right time to ensure that their enemy knew what was happening.

The HUD inside his mask alerted him to the Gomar's arrival behind him. They floated out, some having stepped through with too much force, but Kalian found them all within his telekinetic grip.

Once inside, Kalian couldn't say he recognised the Forge's interior. The station he had been on in the Helteron Cluster had been sleek and bright inside, its stark lights banishing all shadows. Now, almost every surface was coated in bronze nanocelium with low lighting overhead. All control panels and holographic displays were gone, and in their place were just walls of bronze. This Forge wasn't meant to be controlled by anyone or anything other than AI.

The control centre was still where he expected it to be, though ALF had guided them with holographic arrows on the floor. The far wall was made of glass, offering a view of the Starforge's arcing limbs. Everything else was different. The room was dimly lit, leaving the ceiling entirely in darkness. The levelled tiers above them were gone, and the pitted tier in the middle of the large chamber was now home to an upright surgical table. Above it sat the super subconducer, its bulk hanging down like the body of a wasp.

"Hello!" said a young male voice.

Kalian joined the others in searching the shadows for the source, but he was pretty sure it came from unseen speakers.

"My name is Talli!" he said excitedly. "Welcome to our humble abode!"

"Humble?" Kovak muttered under his breath.

"Our?" Kalian hadn't missed that particular word.

"Yes," ALF's voice preceded his tall body as he floated down from the shadows, connected by a plethora of tubes. "I have a roommate."

Kalian didn't know what to say. "Talli?"

"Hello!" came the young voice again.

ALF smiled. "Talli was the cube unit who controlled this Forge. He was a sub-AI sent by the Vanguard."

"*Was* a sub-AI?"

"Yes," ALF explained. "This wasn't just slaved nanocelium like their ships which I can absorb and reprogram easily, it was a sub-AI and, as I was rewriting it, its mind bonded with my own. It's a similar process to what happened with Malekk and Professor Jones, except they couldn't free the nanocelium before it infected them. Over exposure to my human DNA re-wrote the slave programming, so instead of trying to control me, it was actually... curious. I helped it find an identity, and it named himself Talli."

"Hello!"

"It hasn't taken a physical form yet," ALF said, seeing Kalian's confusion.

"You mean it hasn't bonded with another organic life yet?' Kalian clarified.

"Nor shall it," ALF quickly replied. "Talli is aware that it would be a crime in the Conclave to take on a host body."

"I have taken all I need from organic life through my brief time bonded with ALF," Talli chimed in with his happy tone. "Besides, I prefer electrical system to biological systems."

For now, Kalian thought. He wasn't sure what to do with this revelation. On the one hand, it was in the realm of miracles that their DNA could not only free the nanocelium of its shackled coding, but also help it to coalesce into individual nanocelium-based life forms with their own personalities. On the other hand, there were now two artificial life forms instead of one, and ALF alone terrified the Conclave.

"It's probably best if we just keep this little development to ourselves," Kalian suggested.

"A *'nice to meet you'* wouldn't go amiss!" Talli replied jovially.

Kalian paused, looking back over the Gomar. "Nice to meet you, Talli."

"Nice to meet you too, Kalian! So, who wants to have their Harness removed first?" A pair of manacles opened up on the arms of the surgical table.

The Gomar were already ill at ease, but this new AI was in danger of sending them over the edge. Kalian could see the sweat on some of them, uncomfortable as they were in ALF's real presence.

"Talli," ALF interrupted, clearly hoping to diffuse the situation before it escalated, "why don't you prepare the adaptor for Kalian to take back to the capital?"

"Of course," Talli replied affably.

ALF shrugged at Kalian's questioning gaze. "Technically, he's only a few days old."

Kalian turned to the Gomar. "Who's first?"

I am.

Sef stepped forward and ALF escorted him down into the pitted floor and instructed the Gomar rest his back against the upright table. The manacles fastened around his wrists and ankles as the table tilted, though they did not bind him to the table. ALF waved his hand over the big man and the table dropped down into the floor, leaving Sef to float between the super subconducer and the floor. The manacles around his limbs lit up, identifying them as the cause for his weightlessness.

Addressing them all, ALF said, "Due to the Harness' position around your nervous systems, I will have to keep you awake for the procedure to better monitor your responses."

"You mean so we feel the pain," Bal sneered.

ALF paused, his expression pained. "I understand your distrust in me. A long time ago I failed the Terran. I was unaware that part of me still obeyed my masters at that point, and because of it generations of Terran were forced to suffer and die. I alienated you from your own people and caused a rift that could only ever have ended in war. I don't deserve your forgiveness, so I will not ask for it. But, I do ask that you let me correct the defects I placed in your genes. Let me make you whole again."

The Gomar had no response to that, but since they didn't leave the Forge, Kalian could only assume they had taken it well.

The super subconducer came to life above Sef and it released a dozen tentacles which slithered down and attached to various places on the big man's face. A small helmet and visor detached from the body and covered his eyes as robotic arms rose from the floor, each in possession of exotic surgical tools.

"You won't feel a thing,' ALF assured, raising his voice so that the Gomar could hear him. "Your brain functions will operate as if you are awake, but your mind will be occupied by the super subconducer. Inside the machine, you will experience time differently. This will allow you to train with the full potential of a Terran in anticipation of the Harness's removal. Since time is against us, I believe this to be the most expedient way of teaching you."

With that, the robotic arms went to work cutting through the exosuit and removing the bulky armour from Sef's body. Sparks created fountains in the air and startling blue lasers moved across his body with incredible accuracy. The rest of the Gomar naturally formed a circle around the pitted tier and watched everything that was being done to their brother.

Kalian made his way across the chamber and looked out on the stars, aware that ALF would come to meet him.

"I'm still not convinced of this plan of yours," the AI announced as he joined him. "I need more time to calculate your chances of survival."

Kalian shook his head. "Don't bother. It's the only weapon we have that works."

"You say *it*, but you mean *you*," ALF corrected. "You underestimate your role among the humans. You're more than just their protector now. They look to you for answers." The AI paused, shifting his shoulders to better see him. "I know what you're going through, Kalian."

That surprised him. "Enlighten me, ALF."

ALF sighed. "I've seen this before remember. The beast? Like you, Alai was the first of his people to achieve immortality. I realise that you have progressed somewhat quicker than he did, but your isolation is the same. He felt different. He *was* different. Living longer than everyone else, he gained experience that other Terran couldn't imagine. Eventually, he struggled to relate to them and they to him. I talked him out of suicide and exile on multiple occasions."

"And that's what I'm going through, am I?" Kalian kept his eyes on the starfield.

"I can see the beginnings of it," ALF replied solemnly. "In your case, I would say it has the potential to be far worse. Thanks to the nanocelium in their blood, humanity will know immortality, but it could be centuries, millennia even, before any of them develop Terran abilities, before Li'ara does..." The AI took a breath, despite his lack of requirement. "I would imagine time moves differently for you. Everyone feels sluggish by your eyes. Their quick decisions take a lifetime by your standards. It can make for a lonely existence."

"I'm not committing suicide, ALF. What I am is curious..." Kalian looked up at the AI's crystal blue eyes. "Back at Evalan you said it was obvious why our DNA has such a profound effect on nanocelium. What am I missing? Or, more accurately, what are you not telling me?"

ALF glanced at the Gomar in the background, all focused on Sef's operation. "I have only ever kept things from you because you weren't ready to hear them. You needed to be focused to survive all that you have. Trust me, Kalian, I have been keeping your species alive more years than that fantastic brain of yours can count."

"My *fantastic* brain thinks it already knows the answer..." Kalian met those blue eyes with an intensity the AI could never match. "That's one of the benefits of these abilities you gave us. I can run simulations and probabilities in my mind just as you do."

"Knowing the truth won't change anything, Kalian," ALF said, placing his large hand on the glass. "If there's one thing I've learned all these eons, it's that the truth won't get in the way of planets turning and stars burning. In this case, it won't stop the Kellekt from coming."

That snatched at Kalian's attention. "The Kellekt? Is that their name? I thought you said they didn't have one?"

"I said no species has ever lived to pass on a name. It took me thousands of years of digging through the data locked away inside my nanocelium, but eventually I learnt it all. Their name, where they came from, what they *were*."

"They were us, weren't they? The Three... they were human once."

ALF looked down on him, his expression passive. "Yes."

Kalian was losing track of all the revelations he had discovered since leaving Earth. Unlike then, he could now compartmentalise everything perfectly, allowing him to concentrate on one thing at a time.

"Tell me everything, ALF."

Ch'len kicked Roland's toolbox with his stubby foot. "I'm not talking to you, pass yourself a lightdriver!"

The bounty hunter, laid on his back beneath a Planet Killer, sighed at his companion's response. "Could you save your hissy fit for when I'm *not* poking around inside of a bomb? Pass me the damn lightdriver!"

The Ch'kara rooted around inside the box and dropped the tool on his chest, eliciting a small grunt from the *Rackham's* captain. Roland snatched the tool and went back to work on the missile. Since the *Rackham* was sitting safely inside the hangar of a Nebula-Class battlecruiser, the bounty hunter had decided it would be a good time to inspect his most powerful weapon. As suspected, the Planet Killer wasn't set to maximum, something that was usually done in the moments before its launch. Without the appropriate C-Sec equipment, however, the missile had to be manually tampered with.

"We shouldn't be here, Roland!" Ch'len continued. "You've taken me on some suicidal runs, but this has to be the most moronic. We are literally flying into the most heavily defended planet in the Conclave. Did you see those scout reports? There are more enemy ships surrounding Shandar than anywhere else!"

Roland wiped the sweat from his brow. "Yeah, but they're mostly Shay in design. They've even hijacked a few of our cruisers."

Ch'len kicked him in the leg this time. "That doesn't make it a fair fight, asshole!"

Roland slid out from under the missile. "Kick me again and I'll give you a close up of your own asshole."

That cooled down Ch'len for moment. "Have you set it to maximum?" he asked.

"Oh yeah!" Roland's hand patted the floor in search of the screws. "This baby is set to break some shit and then some. I plan on delivering her directly into the heart of that harvesting ship when we're done on Shandar."

"You know the *Rackham* could have done this for you."

Roland fitted the control panel back in place and found his feet again. "If I let the *Rackham* do everything, I'd be as fat as you, fat-ass."

Ch'len shrugged off the insult, resilient as ever. "Couldn't we have at least brought the Raiders? I enjoyed their company more..."

"With the kid's crazy plan, they'll be needed more on Evalan. Besides, this mission will probably be the end of us. Wouldn't you rather go out with just the two of us?" he teased.

"Roland," the *Rackham's* AI called softly. "*High Charge Hox is requesting permission to come aboard.*"

The bounty hunter had purposefully stayed inside his own ship to avoid talking to any of the uppity officers. "Are we there yet?' he asked, wondering how close to Shandar they were.

"*No,*" came the simple reply.

Roland waited for any more information before looking at Ch'len. "Maybe I gave her too much personality..."

Ch'len shook his head, causing the methane contained within the force field surrounding his face to ripple and momentarily distort his features. "*Rackham,* lower the Planet Killer back into the hold." The nanocelium straps that suspended it immediately extended until the missile was nestled under the floor and covered with a panel. "If they find out we still have one of those they'll take it quicker than you can down a beer."

Roland had to agree. "*Rackham,* open the hold doors."

The large doors at the far end of the hold began to part. The bright lights of the hangar flooded the *Rackham* and revealed to the High Charge what could only have looked like the two guiltiest faces he had ever seen.

"I find not knowing what you're doing as equally comforting as I do disturbing, Mr. North." The Laronian strode up the ramp before hesitantly entering the *Rackham's* hold. "You missed the battle briefing."

Roland looked beyond the new High Charge to see rows upon rows of shiny red Darts, all in the process of being readied for an assault. Mechs floated around the light crafts and pilots checked over their work. The central aisle had transport ships lined up and ready to ferry soldiers down to Shandar's surface.

"I'm not gonna lie, Hox," Roland replied casually, "I don't even know what ship I'm on. That and I didn't think you'd care."

"The *Brightstar*," Ch'len whispered.

"I *care* little for either of you and even less for your inability to follow simple orders, but High Councillor Telarrek has reminded me that the *Rackham* is among our greatest assets. I would wield it appropriately."

Roland waved the lightdriver at the Laronian. "Nobody wields the *Rackham* but me."

"Then I would have *you* spearhead the assault on the surface. Help our forces to punch through their defences and reach the Crucible. Destroying that facility is priority one."

Roland smirked. "I didn't need to sit through some briefing to know that's what I'm doing, Hox." The bounty hunter enjoyed the way the Laronian squirmed when his official title was omitted.

"You won't be leaving your ship, Mr. North," the High Charge countered. "You are to assist my soldiers in reaching the Crucible by deploying our new portable Starforge. Nothing else."

Roland couldn't stop his face from screwing up. "What are you talking about?"

Hox met the bounty hunter's frown with a smirk of his own. "The C-Sec R&D department has created a Starforge capable of being deployed on any surface and remotely accessed from orbit. It's large enough to fit a transport vessel through, so the *Rackham*, as fierce as it is, will carry it to Shandar's surface to allow my transports to bypass the orbital defences. *They* will assault the Crucible."

Roland knew it would be a mistake to punch the High Charge of the Conclave but he was going to do it anyway. At at least he was until Ch'len stepped in front of him, blocking his path to the Laronian. It gave Roland the extra second he needed to find his words instead of using his fist.

"I'm not a delivery boy. I specialise in—"

"You specialise, *bounty hunter*, in delivering bodies, dead or alive. This is going to be the biggest delivery of your career. Once the Forge has been deployed you will be assigned new orders under the Nova Squadron. Are we clear?"

Roland chewed over his answer, spoilt for choice as he was. "Crystal..." He ignored Ch'len's questioning look. "Is that all?"

"For now." High Charge Hox spun on his heel and walked back out into the hangar, where his entourage of officers were waiting for him.

"Crystal?" Ch'len repeated, looking up at Roland. "And what's up his ass? Has he already forgotten all the help we provided at Arakesh?"

"I agreed because we're inside the belly of the beast now," Roland replied, waving the lightdriver at the hangar. "If we disobey, he can keep us grounded behind the force fields. And as far as Arakesh goes, I'm pretty sure he's just stinging from the losses."

"And pissed off that *we* survived!" Ch'len opined.

"All the more reason to survive this and piss him off some more," Roland replied. "Now see what you can do about getting me the schematics for this portable Starforge. The Rackham doesn't carry anything I don't know everything about."

Ch'len glanced down at the floor, where the missile remained hidden. "You know everything about Planet Killers, do you?"

Roland paused, pursing his lips. "I know how to make them go boom..."

CHAPTER 20

Li'ara knew she was privileged to be inside the Clave Command Tower. She officially held no rank in C-Sec, yet she was permitted to observe everything from beside Telarrek, who was currently shouldering the weight of the entire Conclave. He had explained her presence to the others by referring to her as a consultant, since she had fought nanocelium-based enemies before, though Li'ara suspected that the Conclave treated all humans like experts on war. The soldiers of the Conclave had known peace for too long, it seemed.

The holographic readouts overlaid the glass wall, relaying the movement of every C-Sec vessel in the galaxy. Two hundred and forty-one planets were currently under siege from nanocelium-based enemies, and six hundred planets were in the midst of fighting off wild Shay. One by one, those planets were being left to their own defences as Conclave battlecruisers peeled away to begin their journeys to Shandar.

Protests and pleas were coming in from every world, begging for more help. Telarrek had prioritised the manufacture and delivery of Starforges, making promises to the corporations on Ch'ket that some feared the Conclave economy wouldn't be able to support. The

Novaarian didn't appear to care in Li'ara's eyes. He just wanted to save as many lives as possible. Every minute, there were more people pouring through the Forges into the capital. The walkways were beginning to fill up with refugees, most of whom were injured in some way.

Li'ara narrowed her eyes and searched the screen for the blue dots with yellow tags above them. They were the C-Sec cruisers designated to defend Evalan when the time came. Every one of them was ready to drop into subspace and divert to the humans' home world. Then there would be even more worlds left to fend for themselves. She truly hoped that Kalian's plan would work and the enemy would take the bait.

She looked up at Telarrek. "Do we have an estimated time before the fleet jumps in once enemy ships start arriving around Evalan?"

"Yes," the Novaarian replied. "The timing will have to be perfect. They cannot know that we are moving half the fleet until they believe Evalan is vulnerable. Ship by ship, we are subtly moving cruisers so their jumps will last only minutes."

"As long as there's something between the surface and the enemy, Kalian should have time to get on board before they can bombard New Genesis."

Telarrek continued to nod his head, his expression absent. The Novaarian was glued to the screen and his knuckles had turned white from gripping the rail so tightly.

"When was the last time you slept, Telarrek?"

The Novaarian councillor stole a quick glance at her before returning his attention to the screen. "This new Highclave is not experienced enough yet. None of them have even commanded aboard a ship as I did on the *Valoran*. With High Charge Hox leading the assault on Shandar, I am needed here."

"You're no good to anyone if you don't get any rest," Li'ara countered.

"I cannot rest while my people are suffering. By my order, C-Sec vessels are abandoning their worlds. I have already had to make threats to ensure some of the Charges follow orders and prepare to jump to Evalan. Then there are the Raalaks. Councillor Ordak is under serious pressure to do everything he can for Arakesh's survivors. Their numbers dropped from trillions to millions in a day. They, it would seem, are beyond saving now. No, I will not rest while entire species are forced to the brink of extinction."

Li'ara wanted to offer a soothing hand, but she felt it would be inappropriate under the Novaarian's new title. "Where's Naydaalan?" she asked, changing the subject.

"He has requested to escort your people back to Evalan. He will pass through the Starforge with you when the *Regis* sends word."

That didn't quite answer Li'ara's question. "Yeah, but where is he right now? He left quite suddenly after the meeting yesterday."

"I sent him on a personal errand," Telarrek explained. "He is..." The Novaarian paused and looked inside his robes, removing a small disc with one of his upper hands. "Ah, that is him now." The councillor activated the holographic communicator. "Hello, son."

Naydaalan's lanky form took shape above the disk, no bigger than a hand. "Father, I found him. It was not easy; things are a mess down here with so many evacuations taking place at once."

"You have done well, Naydaalan. Are they safe?" the councillor asked almost urgently.

"Yes. Uthor has been reunited with his family. They were on the other side of Arakesh when the harvesting ship made landfall. They were lucky to be among the first evacuated."

Telarrek took a deep breath as if he had been holding it all this time. "Some good news at last..." The Novaarian quickly composed himself again. "Make certain they find shelter, Naydaalan."

"As you command." With that, Naydaalan's image faded away.

"Will he return as High Charge?" Li'ara asked.

Telarrek checked over those around them before replying, "I think not. Uthor has served the Conclave well, but his last actions as High Charge would not allow for any such return. We need his passion, but we also need it to be directed appropriately. I will leave him with his family. His title has often robbed him of time with them these long years."

A moment later, the Novaarian councillor was called away to look over the latest reports from the lower city. Li'ara knew there wasn't a soul who could force Telarrek into a bed, and so she left him to speak with another new councillor on the Highclave and sought out her own species' representative.

"I'm not entirely sure what I'm supposed to call you anymore," she said upon her approach to Li Fey.

"Councillor, *High* Councillor..." Fey waved the titles away. "I've worn my captain's stripes for too long to know myself as anything else."

Li'ara managed a smile. "I thought 'captain' was your first name?"

Fey appeared to appreciate the humour. "You sound like Roland North."

"Now I'm offended," Li'ara fired back.

Fey looked across the control room. "How's he holding up?"

Li'ara followed the councillor's gaze to Telarrek. "That's the problem, I think; he's holding it *all* up."

"I'll keep an eye on him," Fey promised. "If I have to knock him out to make him rest then I will."

Li'ara chuckled to herself, but the comment gave her pause to examine Fey's features. "I think youth suits you, Captain."

The new councillor looked up from her chair, meeting Li'ara's eyes before examining the back of her own hand. "Is it becoming obvious?"

"Your looks are subtle, but your attitude is noticeable," she added with a grin.

"I can feel it," Fey replied, clenching her fist. "Has Kalian uncovered the truth behind the nanocelium in our blood?"

Li'ara shrugged. "We haven't really stopped to talk yet," she admitted. "I know he's spoken to ALF but..."

"He's distracted," Fey offered. "I'm sure if the nanites in our blood were dangerous he would have acted on it by now. I don't think

I can blame him for being distracted, though. He takes it all on his shoulders. Sometimes I forget he was a history teacher."

Li'ara agreed, but she knew his distraction was better described as detachment. She couldn't bring herself to explain his recent state of mind, however, as it felt too real to say it out loud. The truth was, she felt like she was losing him and there was nothing she could do. Nobody except the Gomar had the potential to keep up with his mind and the truth of it stung.

"Li'ara? Are you okay?" the captain asked.

Li'ara shrugged it off. "I'm fine. I just hope everything is going well with the Gomar. Maybe they can share the load..."

Telarrek strode across the control room until his voice could reach them without him shouting. "Kalian has returned with the AI adaptor."

Li'ara practically ran to the warehouse storing the repurposed Starforge. Telarrek had insisted that she be escorted by C-Sec soldiers since Clave Tower was yet to be made secure, but they held back upon seeing Kalian. Li'ara wanted to run into his arms and feel his embrace, sure that alone would dispel any thoughts of detachment. She restrained herself, however, seeing him in the process of explaining to the engineers how the adaptor would work. They seemed to pay his words little attention, however, in favour of scanning every inch of the chunky device.

When the moment was right, Li'ara slipped past the group of engineers and wrapped her arms around Kalian's neck. He kissed her and for a moment she was able to forget everything and simply enjoy his touch. Pulling away revealed an expression she had seen before on his perfect features.

"What is it?" she asked. "You've taken on some new burden, I can tell."

"Do we have a room in one of the hotels?"

"Yes, a nice one actually!" Her excited tone brought a smile to his face.

"Great. I'll drive." Kalian picked her up in both arms and strode past the C-Sec guards. "Gentlemen."

He left the warehouse and looked up at the dizzying heights of Clave Tower. Li'ara looked to see what had caught his eye and when she looked back they were already a hundred feet into the air. As they rose up through the levels, great crowds began to gather along the railings. The people of the Conclave looked at him as they would a deity, and it only served to remind Li'ara of the chasm growing between them. As his speed increased, she held him a little tighter and dipped her head into his shoulder, enjoying his smell. She had to hold on to the small things, she thought.

The next hour was, perhaps, the best hour Li'ara could remember in some time. They had simply lost themselves to each other, entwined as one. For just one climactic moment, there was no war, no death, and no gulf between them. There was just him and her. It was wonderful and Li'ara didn't want to give it up for anything, including sleep.

It took some will, but she managed to keep her eyes open, distracting herself by looking upon Kalian's Terran physique, with those perfectly formed muscles he had never needed to work for.

"Please tell me that wasn't your way of saying goodbye," she said. "Don't get me wrong, as farewells go, it was amazing. I'm just going to kill you if that's what's happening here..."

Kalian kept his dark eyes on the ceiling and smiled. "I have no intention of dying aboard that ship," he replied.

"What *are* your intentions? I feel like you're holding back."

Kalian rolled over and stroked her ribs down and over her bare hip. "I'm trying to find a way to save us, all of us. Even the nanocelium controlled by the Three."

"That's a lot to take on, Kalian. What if we can't both be saved? What if the nanocelium kills you in the process of trying to save it?"

Kalian sighed. "What's the point of having all this power if I don't try?"

"Only you know what you're capable of," she said softly. "I just worry it isn't enough to save *everyone*, yourself included."

Kalian averted his eyes. "No one knows what I can do, not even ALF. That's why I don't care about his calculations and odds."

"Is that what he told you up there?" she asked. "Did he tell you that you won't survive?" Li'ara trusted the AI as far as she could throw him, but she didn't underestimate his intelligence or processing power. His calculations were always accurate...

"No, he told me something else." Kalian sat up in the bed and rested his elbows on his knees.

Li'ara could see that this new revelation bothered him. "What did he tell you?"

Kalian chewed over his response. "A long time ago, and I mean longer than there's a number for, there was a group of scientists called the Kellekt. They were tasked with researching a new form of technology for their people." Kalian met Li'ara's questioning gaze. "Nanocelium. It was supposed to bring about a golden age for their world. But, three of the Kellekt had something else in mind for it. Once bound to them, it improved their mind and body. It seemed to them to be the next step in evolution. They discovered that the nanites could replicate if they had enough resources to consume, making it potentially endless given enough *food*.

"The nanocelium's appetite for resources matched the Kellekt's appetite for power, and once they'd had a taste of it they were insatiable.

"The rest of their people didn't agree with the binding process. They didn't want to be part machine. The Kellekt didn't take their refusal well. They consumed most of the planet but they had to avoid the population since the nanocelium was coded to their DNA. They would have ended up with a whole population of people who had just as much power as them. So they left.

"The people of this world had a choice. Rebuild their civilisation and potentially place their future on track to repeat itself in generations to come. Or... they could forsake technology and return to a primitive way of life.

"When the Kellekt's Vanguard returned eons later, unaware that this planet was its place of origin, it bound itself to one of the natives, intending to take on a host body. We now know that host... as ALF."

Li'ara covered her mouth, overcome with shock and a thousand questions. "Evalan... the *original* Evalan is where it all began? That's where nanocelium was *made*?"

"Yes, made by the Three. They were once humanity's ancestors, natives to Evalan." Kalian leaned in closer. "We made it, Li'ara. What just a few of our kind did made the rest of our ancestors forego all technology. Can you imagine being so ashamed of what your own species is capable of, that you return to living off the land, reject medical technology, and keep the truth of history from your children?"

"That's not us, Kalian. We're not like the Kellekt."

"We have it in us," Kalian countered. "Look at Earth's history. Humans have always wanted more; we've always *taken* more from those who had it. Just in the time we've been in the Conclave there's been nothing but war and death, whether it be Savrick or the Kellekt. Now we've taken a whole planet, we have a member on the Highclave. What happens when the rest of humanity develops Terran abilities? Trust me, Li'ara, thoughts of superiority will haunt every one of them. I know they haunt me."

"You think you're better than the Conclave?" Li'ara asked, more curious than concerned.

"I know I am. But that's the key, isn't it? Knowledge. Absolute power corrupts absolutely. It happened to the Three, it happened to Savrick and the Gomar. Earth's history is rife with examples of corruption due to power. The Terran were never corrupted because they valued knowledge."

Li'ara tilted her head. "So, you know you're better, but because you know that, you're incorruptible?"

Kalian gave a mirthless laugh. "Something like that... Eventually, humanity will master these abilities and realise we were manufactured to be better. That'll be our real test."

Li'ara squeezed his arm. "With guidance, and a huge dumping of humility, we can do it."

Kalian gazed into the distance, nodding absently. "Maybe..."

Kalian lay back again and stared at the ceiling. Li'ara hated that she was finding it harder and harder to read him. His mind could go places and see things she could only dream of, which ultimately had her feeling left behind.

"So, the ancestors of humans created nanocelium, which wasn't a bad thing in itself, but the Three who made it used it for bad things..."

"That's probably the biggest understatement of all time," Kalian quipped.

"Shh! I'm processing it as best as my little human brain can. So, they bound themselves to it and basically sent the original Evalan back to the Stone Age. Then they, what? Flew away in search of new civilisations?"

"They consume worlds and pretty much everything else in between," Kalian replied with an exhausted tone.

"But why?"

"For knowledge, power, invincibility, greed, and just wanting more. The same things that have always driven humans across the universe apparently."

Li'ara thought for a moment on the implications this might have on their status within the Conclave. "We can't tell anyone about this, Kalian. There are still those in the Conclave who believe we are responsible for the destruction Savrick created. It doesn't help with the timing of this invasion either, but if people found out that at the core of the nanocelium sat three humans..."

"They are far from humans now," Kalian commented. "They left their original bodies behind eons ago in favour of new life forms. ALF's description was kind of nightmarish, to be honest."

"It doesn't matter," Li'ara continued. "Our connection to nanocelium is already suspect. We shouldn't fuel the fire."

Kalian nodded but he was again slipping away, his mind falling into a well which she couldn't follow.

"Did you find out anything about the nanocelium inside of us? Captain Fey looks younger every day."

Kalian opened his mouth but his every feature froze, his gaze so distant he appeared to be looking through Li'ara.

"What is it?" she asked.

Kalian jumped out of the bed. "They're here!"

Li'ara looked around, searching for evidence of his words. "I don't understand."

"Six ships just emerged from subspace," he explained. He slapped the triangle of nanocelium to his abdomen and the black armour grew across his body.

"You can feel that?" Li'ara asked sceptically, though she wondered why anything he did surprised her anymore.

"It's hard to explain. The universe is like one plane of existence, everything is connected. When a ship uses subspace they briefly tear that plane. To me, that feels as if someone is... scratching my head?" His explanation was hard to understand but he offered nothing further, instead, placing his hand on the glass desk at the end of the room. This quickly generated a series of holograms which jumped to life in front of him. Six nanocelium-based ships could be seen by external monitoring satellites.

"Are those feeds from the Clave Command Tower?" She asked, wondering how he had gained access from a smart desk inside a hotel room.

Kalian ignored the question. "ALF won't be able to help while he's operating on the Gomar."

Li'ara hopped across the room as she put her clothes back on. "Six ships? Is that it? They're attacking the most fortified planet with only six ships? Where's the harvesting ship?"

Kalian turned his head to the left side of the desk and a new hologram popped up with images of Tagomar, in the Vellum system. The harvesting ship was in the process of latching on to the planet and spreading its tentacles deep into the earth. With the C-Sec fleet already redirecting, there was no space battle to speak of.

"They're just scouts," Kalian observed. "They've come to see what the capital has in the way of defences."

Li'ara stood back as Kalian left the desk and made for the door. "Where are you going?"

He stopped by the open door and turned back. "To give them second thoughts."

And with that he was gone, leaving Li'ara to stand on her own in the gloom of the holograms.

CHAPTER 21

KALIAN REACHED AS FAR as the repurposed Starforge before he regretted leaving Li'ara so suddenly. He had informed her that they were about to be attacked and then he had just left. She would understand, he thought... he hoped. Kalian reminded himself that right now he was the only one who stood a chance at holding them back until ALF could use the Starforge. That level of responsibility was enough to focus his thoughts and compartmentalise all things Li'ara.

Before he could walk through the now active Forge, a hologram of Telarrek appeared beside it, generated by the technician's console. "Kalian," the Novaarian called. "We only have nine Nebula-Class cruisers and one Nexus-Class up there. They are designated to be part of the Evalan defence."

"I know, Telarrek, we can't afford to lose any of them. Order them to pull back and refrain from engaging."

"What are you going to do?" the councillor asked with concern.

"Buy us some time." Kalian didn't waste another second. He expanded the nanocelium over his hands and face, ready for the vacuum of space beyond the Forge's event horizon.

As before, he felt nothing when the bright light washed over him. ALF's Starforge was behind him, powering down the wormhole.

"How's it going in there?" he asked, pushing himself into space like a missile.

"*They're a little hostile but so far so good,*" ALF replied. "*I'm going to need a little more time before I can offer any help, though. Removing the Harnesses is delicate to say the least.*"

"Why do you think I'm here?" Kalian would have enjoyed his flight through the solar system had he not just rounded one of the capital's broken moons and laid eyes on the six enemy vessels.

"*Use your size and speed against them, Kalian. You're a hard target to hit.*"

Kalian would have replied to the AI had three of the enemy ships not opened fire on the cluster of C-Sec battlecruisers. He increased his speed and managed to fly into the gulf between the cruisers and the incoming missiles, which were now streaking towards him. With an outstretched hand, he found the missiles, each of which felt just as connected to his body as any limb. He balled his fist and watched them explode, the flash offering a glimpse of the black ships gliding through space beyond.

All six of the scout ships unleashed their arsenal, only now they weren't targeting the cruisers.

"*What are you waiting for?*" ALF asked urgently.

"Roland said that nanocelium-based weaponry cancels out other nanocelium, preventing it from repairing itself."

"*Kalian, you've got seconds before impact!*"

That was a long time inside his mind. By the time the closest missile was within metres of his position, he had mapped out his flight path and attack vector. Kalian shot upwards, relative to his position in space, and watched as the missiles followed him, curving through the void to chase after him. He flew directly towards the nearest enemy ship, where he intended to give the missiles back.

Then they exploded.

Kalian was flung forwards, his direction no longer under the control of his telekinetic abilities. The explosions rippled across space as the domino effect tore the missiles apart prematurely. Kalian tried to shake off the shockwave that had engulfed him, but he was too close to the enemy ship. The nanocelium hull cracked and shattered under his impact and he skidded along its surface for half a mile before finally correcting himself.

"You pulled that move over Evalan," ALF chimed in his ear. *"They're quick learners."*

"I've still got a few tricks up—"

"Incoming!" As ALF cried out, Kalian looked up to see another enemy vessel hurtling towards him.

Kalian dug his fingers into the hull and pulled himself along the length of the ship at great speed. It was too late, however. The enemy ship collided with its ally to devastating effect. Nanocelium was flung everywhere at a speed that exceeded Kalian's. The two ships coming together under such force and speed caused the surface beneath him to swell and explode into a thousand million pieces of sharp nanocelium. His direction was once again taken out of his hands, leaving him to the mercy of more shockwaves.

In the blink of an eye he was entirely engulfed by nanocelium as the two enemy ships lost their shape and cohesion, though he knew everything they did was calculated. This kind of attack wasn't suicide for them, but it might be the death of him. Alarms were blaring inside his HUD, warning him of the damage being inflicted on his armour by the nanocelium shrapnel. Every time he tried to push away another shockwave of nanocelium detonated, throwing him about until he was flung into the storm again.

"Kalian!" ALF shouted inside his helmet. *"They're all colliding into each other!"*

He couldn't answer; he could barely make sense of his surroundings. With no gravity or even a line of sight beyond the constant barrage of nanocelium, Kalian was becoming more and more disoriented. He roared in frustration and thrust out his hands, telekinetically blowing a path through the explosions. It was a small opening but he took it. With his arms by his side, he flew through the black glass that threatened to open up his exosuit.

The beautiful vista of open space greeted him when his upper body pierced the conglomerate of swarming nanocelium. It didn't last. The only ship still intact crashed into the hole he had made, slamming into Kalian with enough force to crater a planet. The sheer mass of it all overwhelmed him, pummelling him from every side as yet more explosions sent nanocelium flying in every direction. More alarms flared inside his helmet, but he couldn't concentrate to make out the statistics it was offering him. He didn't need a computer to tell him his chances of survival were dropping dramatically.

It took a few more moments before he began to realise that the bombardment was becoming less intense. The shards of nanocelium were impacting his exosuit less and less and the space between him and the swirling mass was becoming bigger, allowing him to correct his position and take back some control.

"ALF," he said through laboured breath. "What's happening?"

The AI replied with one word. *"Backup."*

The storm was ripped apart and Kalian caught glimpses of space again. With every second that went by, more and more of the nanocelium was being pulled away from him and cast aside. By a measure of minutes, the entire mass from all six scout ships was spread out over several kilometres, shapeless in the void. It looked to Kalian like a sandstorm, incapable of finding cohesion but clearly trying to head in the same direction.

You are not alone, Kalian Gaines.

Behind him floated Sef, Vox, Garrion, and Ariah. All of them wore a fitted exosuit of nanocelium identical to Kalian's. Gone were the bulky and cumbersome armoured contraptions designed to counter the Harnesses. All four of the Gomar had their hands out towards the vibrating mass of nanocelium, each exhibiting a level of control he had always dreamed of for them.

"What should we do with all this?" Garrion asked over their shared channel.

"*I'm on my way*," ALF answered. "*I'll absorb it into the Starforge. Should make this thing work a little faster!*"

Kalian partitioned off a small area of his brain and set it to the task repairing his injuries. The exosuit was still one piece, keeping the vacuum at bay, but there were fragments of sharp nanocelium between the plates, piercing his skin here and there. He could feel a particularly painful piece in the side of his thigh, prompting him to shut off his pain receptors in that area of his leg. The exosuit began the process of extracting the foreign shards and leaving them to float in space.

"How does it feel?" Kalian asked across their channel.

The four Gomar looked at each other, all perfectly in control of their balance and position in space, while simultaneously keeping the cloud of nanocelium in their grasp.

Ariah replied, "*The only way I can describe it is... I feel free!*"

"*I can feel everything,*" Garrion added.

"*I want to take the fight to them,*" Vox said eagerly.

Sef's voice spoke inside their minds. *The super subconducer has allowed us to understand our abilities, but we still have much to learn.*

Kalian glanced at Vox, sure that Sef's words were meant to sober her lust for action. He had to remind himself that Vox, and all of the Gomar, had been warriors for a very long time. They had performed acts of violence that Kalian couldn't imagine during the Terran civil war and that was without the level of control they had now. He couldn't imagine all the things Vox would want to do to her enemies with all the potential of a Terran.

ALF's Starforge emerged from behind one of the broken moons, its crescent shape gliding effortlessly through space. The Gomar maintained their hold over the cloud of nanocelium, which continued to spasm within its invisible prison as ALF took the station through the middle of it. The nanites did their best to avoid contact with the Forge, a protocol that the Three had programmed, but the Gomar prevented the cloud from getting away. ALF continued to fly through it, black globs smearing across the hull like flies on a windshield as the nanocelium was caught. The patches slowly faded as they were absorbed, until the Starforge was once again entirely bronze, the AI's choice of colour.

When Kalian turned back, everyone but Sef was flying around space. Vox was flying down the length of one of the Nebula-Class battlecruisers, stroking the shiny red hull with her hand. Garrion and Ariah were performing impossible acrobatics achieved only through the power of telekinesis.

They were like him now...

It brought a smile to Kalian's face, though it was hidden behind his helmet. Looking to Sef, however, it seemed the big man was always happy to stand as a sentinel, or in this case float. Kalian hoped that with a Terran mind, Sef would find a way to compartmentalise all the things he did for Savrick during the civil war and come to terms with them all. Over time, he could even find a way past the murder of his parents and perhaps learn to use his voice again.

Once the other three were finished waving at C-Sec officers through the viewports, all five of them boarded the Starforge. There was a lighter tone to the newly freed Gomar. It wasn't long before Telarn and Bal were also able to walk away from the super subconducer and be presented with their new exosuits. Bal brought up the holographic menu through the suit's fingers and messed around with the colours, having the nanocelium display every colour in the spectrum until he settled on Conclave red. Once the others saw this, they were all flicking through their menus, changing the colour and style.

After Larna's Harness had been removed she couldn't stop floating up and down, twirling elegantly as she did. It was her laughter that captured Kalian's attention. In all the time he had worked with them on Evalan, he had never heard any of them laugh with such joy.

"Thank you," Ellik said, looking up at ALF's physical form.

Kovak walked past him and put his hand out. "Ellik, put your damn suit on already!"

"I've just never felt so free!" Ellik replied with a ball of superheated plasma in each hand.

"Well, could you be a little less free?" Nardel pleaded. Both sisters had settled on the same shade of green for their exosuits, making the job of telling them apart all the harder.

Kalian stood there for a moment, enjoying the sight. This was all he had wanted for them. For the first time since they had destroyed the Vanguard, Kalian felt hope. His unexpected positivity made him think of the cheeriest individual he had recently encountered, and he looked around the tall chamber, wondering why they hadn't heard from Talli.

"Talli?" he called out to no reply. "Talli?"

Kalian leant against the wall and let his mind run through all the reasons why the AI wouldn't be responding, but he only got as far as the third scenario before it made sense.

"You sneaky son of a bitch," he said with a light chuckle to himself.

"Everything alright?" ALF asked, walking away from the others.

"I know why Talli isn't saying anything..."

ALF shrugged his lanky form. "It's a very big station. He's just overseeing the integration of the new nanocelium, that's all."

Kalian raised his eyebrow. "Is he? Or is he, in fact, the Conclave's new central AI?"

ALF looked up as he chewed over the answer. "Um..."

"ALF! You had *me* deliver a fully functioning artificial intelligence to the Conclave? Talli will be—"

"Everywhere by now," ALF interrupted. "It's for the best, really. He'll whip that AI hub into shape in no time, plus, you know, he's very chipper! It's always good to have a chipper AI running your civilisation rather than a tyrannical one, wouldn't you agree?"

"I told them any upgrade you integrated could be removed when the war is over."

"Yeah... That's not going to work, I'm afraid. Unless Talli *wants* to come out, but that kind of integration can make one feel like a god. It'll be hard to give up."

Kalian held up his hand. "Don't tell me anything more. It's probably best I know as little as possible."

"Having Talli on the inside isn't so bad. He's already shut down over a hundred AI hubs across the Conclave and locked the Kellekt out. They attack the network with eight point six million viruses every second. Who do you think is keeping them at bay? Now we can mobilise the other half of the fleet and have them ready to jump to Evalan without our enemies knowing."

Kalian looked up at ALF. "I take it, then, that you have a communications link with Talli?" ALF nodded. "Can you see what's happening on Shandar?"

The AI raised his hand and the glass wall turned into viewing screen with a hundred different holographic images. Every screen was a feed taken from the external cameras on the C-Sec cruisers and inside their bridges.

It wasn't going well.

CHAPTER 22

Roland wiped away the sweat trying to find its way through his eyebrows before he sent the *Rackham* into a spin, evading a trio of streaking missiles. He banked sharply to port, then back to starboard as a squadron of Shay light fighters cut across his flight path. They were quickly followed by a C-Sec squadron of red Darts who gave chase across the stars. Intrinium fire erupted in every direction, some of which the bounty hunter couldn't avoid.

"How many nanocelium bastards are there?" He asked without taking his eyes from the viewport.

Ch'len checked over his console. "There are thirteen of those big ones, but most of the defence is made up of the Shays' security force."

Roland banked to starboard and let rip with the *Rackham's* cannons, easily tearing through the light craft ahead. "That was nanocelium ammunition," he observed.

"So?" Ch'len replied. "It did the job!"

"Save it for them. The *Brightstar* loaded us up with Intrinium so let's use it against the Shay." He glanced at the holographic readout to the left of his face to check that the little Ch'kara had swapped them out.

The next time he opened fire, blue streaks of Intrinium shot out across the void and tore through the transport vessel attempting to dock with one of the C-Sec cruisers.

A female voice came over the channel. "Rackham, *this is Brightstar. We're diverting Nova Squadron to your position. They will help you reach the surface.*"

"Reach the surface?" Roland echoed, looking out over Shandar and its web of floating buildings. "There isn't a single cruiser that's managed to reach the upper city yet! How are we going to punch through the atmosphere? We need to gain more ground first!"

Hox's voice replaced the female's. "*We need to get boots on the surface. Without the Crucible, most of our opposition up here will come to a sudden halt.*"

"You hope," Roland said under his breath. "The *Rackham* can slip through the gaps, but your cruisers need to provide me with those gaps! If I break away from the battle now and make for the surface, every enemy ship is going to see us and blow us to pieces!"

"*Nova Squadron are coming to assist,*" was Hox's only reply before the channel went dead.

"Shit!" Roland banked to port and squeezed the trigger, forcing the light craft in front of them to disperse to avoid any collision.

A bright light flared across the starboard side of the viewport. Roland redirected the *Rackham* and watched the back end of a Nexus-Class battlecruiser explode as a nanocelium-based ship rammed its way through. What was left of the cruiser was pulled in by Shandar's gravity well and raged through layer after layer of floating towers. Two more flares illuminated the viewport when a pair of Nebula-Class cruisers burst apart under the enemy's constant barrage. Every one of them carried thousands of crew...

Roland yelled at the top of his voice as he opened fire on the hull of a Shay cruiser. It barely damaged the larger ship, but it made the bounty hunter feel better. He pulled back on the stick and sent the *Rackham* looping around to bring them up behind a cluster of Shay light craft. He managed to eviscerate four of them before the remaining three dispersed, only to be shot down by Darts.

"Rackham, *this is Nova Leader, do you copy?*"

Roland stole a quick glance at Ch'len. "Does everyone have our number?"

"Rackham, *this is Nova Leader, do you copy?*" the Novaarian voice repeated.

"We copy, Nova Leader," Roland replied. "Are you here to take us to the dance?"

The Novaarian hesitated. "*We are going to see you to the surface, sir. We have the coordinates for the Starforge's deployment.*"

"Whoa!" Roland was forced to divert from his path when another battlecruiser exploded in front of them. The *Rackham* shook violently until the bounty hunter could find a new vector, far away from the explosion. "How's the Forge?" he asked.

Ch'len was already checking over the seals that kept the Starforge attached to the *Rackham's* underbelly. "No damage. Seals are holding," he reported.

A bright flash washed over the blackness of space, only this time it wasn't due to the loss of yet another battlecruiser. Roland's jaw fell open when the *Marillion* emerged from subspace at full speed and rammed its way through the battle. C-Sec ships avoided its mass in time, prompting Roland to finally take notice of the warnings on his battle map that had been flashing for the last five minutes, alerting them to the sphere's arrival.

"You should probably look at that more often," Ch'len commented.

Roland couldn't think of a reply as he watched the golden orb sacrifice most of its hull. Shay cruisers, light craft, and transport vessels shattered against both hemispheres of the *Marillion*, the resulting explosions tarnishing its golden hull.

"The nanocelium ships are diverting from the battle," Ch'len announced excitedly.

Roland looked over the battle map, wondering if their exit would open up a gap in the defences. A proximity alert sounded from his console and stole all of his attention. The bounty hunter dropped the ship under an oncoming cloud of enemy light craft and gave Nova Squadron something to think about. The Darts weaved into one of their formations and drifted between the light craft, all the while letting loose with their cannons.

"Len...?"

The Ch'kara's fat fingers danced across his glass console. "I can't find a path through to the surface. Even with the nanocelium vessels occupied, there's just too many Shay between us and the planet."

Roland groaned and continued to evade the Intrinium fire that flared past the viewport. The occasional bolt struck true and *dinged* off the *Rackham's* hull, sending vibrations through to the bridge. Squeezing the trigger was the only satisfying thing the bounty hunter could do right now. Blue streaks shot out from the forward cannons and tore off the back end of a transport before continuing into the light craft escorting it. Both exploded behind the *Rackham* after it flew by, already targeting another transport.

Trying his luck, Roland yanked the *Rackham* into a spin and barrelled over the Shay cruiser, a move that drastically altered their trajectory and put them on course for Shandar. A trio of large cannons attached to the cruiser's hull took aim and fired potshots as they glided over the surface of the bigger ship, but the *Rackham* was too close to accurately shoot it down.

Once they had cleared the back end of the cruiser, Roland and Ch'len were presented with a viewport filled with the upper city of Shandar. That was when dozens of Intrinium bolts skimmed past the *Rackham's* bronze hull. A quick glance at his console showed sixteen light craft breaking away from the battle and targeting them.

"Up ahead!" Ch'len screamed.

Roland whipped his head up to see more of the bastards emerging from behind the floating towers. As their Intrinium bolts traversed the distance, the *Rackham* was caught in a mesh of super-heated energy, most of which its nanocelium could handle, but the Starforge under its belly was not so protected.

"Shit! Shit! Shit! Shit!" Roland weaved and bobbed the *Rackham* this way and that, evading enough of the bolts to cause problems for the light craft who took friendly fire, but it wasn't enough to keep the Forge safe.

"It's taking damage!" Ch'len warned.

Roland kept his finger pressed on the trigger and took out as many as were stupid enough to stay their course. His other hand hovered over the command that gave over control of the ship to the AI. It would have been easy to let the *Rackham* find its own way through this mess, but Roland was confident that no machine could make the same decisions as a living person. He needed to stay in control to deal with the next problem, as only he could.

That, and this was also the most fun he'd had in a while...

At their current speed, it didn't take long for the *Rackham* to pass through the oncoming light craft and make for the upper city. The sixteen Shay chasing them were now thirteen, but the oncoming ships quickly turned about and raised their numbers to nineteen, all of which were soon firing on them with no regard for the towers and spindly bridges that connected the web.

The black towers were inevitably ripped to shreds by the light craft when the *Rackham* dodged between them. Roland himself fired on and destroyed a couple of bridges he didn't feel like losing speed to avoid. Flashes and glimpses of fire flared in the corners of the viewport, all of which served to keep Roland focused on flying. He had to stay ahead of the barrage *and* evade the solid walls of the floating city.

Roland sacrificed some speed to make a sharp turn around the corner of a tower. The light craft were not as efficient as the *Rackham* and their Shay pilots were unable to push their fighters back up to speed as quickly as Roland could. The gap between them was becoming bigger, but they would be hounded all the way to the surface.

"Rackham, *this is Nova Leader,*" came the familiar Novaarian voice. "*We lost you for a moment there.*"

The bounty hunter brought up a three dimensional hologram of the city in front of the ship, noting the squadron of Darts that was currently flying vertically down a massive tower designated as the Saban Hotel. With the *Rackham's* angle of approach and that of the chasing light craft, the Darts were hidden from view on the other side of the hotel. That gave Roland an idea.

"Nova Leader, this is the *Rackham*. I need you stay on course and prepare to fire everything you've got straight ahead."

There was a pause on the leader's end. "*Straight ahead? What are we firing at,* Rackham?"

"Check your scans of that hotel. Do you see the hangar near the bottom?"

Roland didn't wait for any reply or even listen to what was said back, he just pushed the thrusters to maximum and hurtled on to the bright hangar. He flew straight through, not even bothering to check on Nova Squadron's position. This was either going to work or they'd never make it to the surface, at least not with a working Starforge, anyway.

The *Rackham* shot out the other side of the hangar, trailing nineteen enemy light craft and a lot of Intrinium bolts, most of which had reduced the hotel's hangar to pieces. Since the Darts didn't crash into him, Roland assumed he'd judged the whole thing correctly.

"Everything you've got, Nova Leader!"

The squadron opened fire with Intrinium and missiles alike, creating a waterfall-like effect of violent energy and death. The Shay could do nothing but fly out of the hangar and be annihilated. Roland brought the *Rackham* around to see it with his own eyes, finding two of the lucky aliens had made it through unscathed. He squeezed the trigger again and intercepted them head on. Beyond the enemy's fiery death, Nova Squadron continued down the Saban Hotel, through the debris, and curved up to join the *Rackham*.

Wasting no time, Roland took the ship further down, passing through the many levels of the Shay city. Not one tower was alike, though the cybernetic species had ensured that every one of them was black, almost matching the storms that swirled below.

"Okay, Nova Leader. We're heading for the coordinates to deploy the Forge. It's going to put us pretty close to the Crucible, so be ready to face some more defences."

"*Copy that, Rackham. Nova Squadron is ready for anything.*"

"Um..." Ch'len dipped his head closer to the console in confusion. "Roland, there's something inside that storm."

The bounty hunter looked ahead at the spinning mass of dark clouds between the city's lower levels. He narrowed his eyes, desperately trying to pierce the cloud cover.

Like a monster emerging from the pit of hell, a nanocelium vessel pushed up through the storm. Shaped like a tuning fork, as the others were, its two limbs bristled with cannons and the light of streaking missiles illuminated the gap between them.

"Evade!" Roland screamed down the channel.

Nova Squadron peeled away, scattering in every direction in the hope of finding cover behind the towers. The *Rackham*, ahead of them all, was forced to weave between the nanocelium fire and even shoot down a pair of missiles before banking to starboard. The bottom corner of the tower behind them was obliterated by a chasing missile, before several bolts of nanocelium shredded the rest of the building and pierced the *Rackham's* hull.

"Shit!" Roland ducked his head when a yellow streak blew through the floor a metre away from his foot and carried on into the ceiling. The *Rackham's* nanocelium sealed the hull instantly, but it reminded the bounty hunter what he was up against.

"It's in pursuit!" Ch'len cried.

Indeed, behind them, the rest of the damaged tower was split in half when the forked ship rammed its way through. Roland could only watch on his scans as two of the Darts from Nova Squadron perished in the ensuing explosion.

More missiles were launched from the enemy ship and it took everything the *Rackham* had to offer to stay ahead of them and escape their detonations. The city itself was beyond repair as the forked ship showed no care for anything in its way. From miles above, anyone could follow its path simply by observing the trail of destruction and havoc it left in its wake.

"Roland, the Forge is taking some serious shrapnel damage."

The bounty hunter didn't have time to take in the little alien's words. He had to find some way of losing the nanocelium vessel. If he flew down, there was nowhere to go where it couldn't follow and it certainly wouldn't allow them to deploy the Forge. If he flew up and made for the space battle above, there was nothing but open space between the upper city and the potential safety of the C-Sec cruisers.

"Rackham, *this is Nova Leader. We're hitting this thing with everything we've got but it isn't making so much as a dent. It isn't even bothering to return fire.*"

Roland took the *Rackham* through another hangar and barely managed to slip out the other side before the enemy rammed its way through, causing another tower to fall into the planet. Three more nanocelium bolts tore through the bulkhead and sent sparks flying.

"I'm open to suggestions!" Roland yelled.

Ch'len hurriedly brought up hologram after hologram, his beady eyes searching for a solution. "There's maybe... oh, wait!" The Ch'kara wiped the holograms away, checked his console, and then brought up a variety of new scans and data. "I don't believe it."

"What?" Roland managed, banking to port and evading a streaking missile. It impacted the side of a tower and sent shudders through the *Rackham*.

"Those nanocelium ships above," Ch'len explained incredulously. "They've actually disabled the *Marillion*. I didn't think anything could bring that ship down!"

"Bring it down?" Roland confirmed.

"Judging by these scans, it'll lose all thrust capability in a matter of minutes. Then, its mass will be pulled into Shandar..."

Roland stared ahead blankly, running through the scenario forming in his mind. "Send me the *Marillion's* trajectory. I want to know exactly where it's going to impact."

Ch'len whipped his head around. "Do I even want to know why you need that information?"

Roland weaved between two towers and narrowly escaped a salvo of nanocelium fire. "Because I'm going to do something either really cool or really stupid!"

As soon as the calculations came through to his console, Roland overload the viewport with the best flight plan so he could always find his way back to the point of impact, should the enemy ship force him off course. It was quite the erratic route, zigzagging everywhere, but he also had the *Rackham* incorporate evasive manoeuvres to keep them alive long enough to actually reach the *Marillion*.

"Nova Leader, I'm about to try something your Darts can't keep up with. Advise diverting back to the battle. You'll be of more help up there."

"*Rackham, I'm looking at your flight path on my console. Are you aware that the* Marillion *is already falling into the planet? It's only fifty thousand kilometres out!*"

"I'm aware, Nova Leader," Roland replied through gritted teeth as he pulled up to avoid another missile's detonation.

"*The* Marillion's *circumference is beyond massive,*" the Novaarian pilot continued. "*The impact site will be impossible to avoid.*"

"That's what I'm hoping for, Nova Leader." Roland banked to port and let one of the towers take the punishment in their place. "Get back to the battle. And tell Hox his Starforge will be on the surface shortly after the *Marillion* bites it!"

"*Good luck,* Rackham."

Roland quickly checked his display to make sure the Darts altered their course and returned to the battle above. The nanocelium ship, on the other hand, was still in pursuit and firing on the *Rackham* with abandon. A round blew through the back, removed a chunk from Ch'len's chair and fried half of his console. The Ch'kara yelped and fell to the floor, cursing his luck for ever meeting Roland North.

"Strap yourself back in you moron!" Roland ordered.

"The inertial dampeners are on," Ch'len argued. "It doesn't matter what you do, I'm not going anywhere!"

Roland input new commands and had a new console form out of the floor, replacing Ch'len's damaged one. "Look at what I'm about to do!" The bounty hunter continued. "I'm going to divert all power to thrust. If you're not strapped in by then, I'll have to peel you off the back wall!"

Ch'len looked over the timeframe offered by the *Rackham's* AI. He swore profusely, before scrambling into his new chair and commanding it to extend all straps.

Roland looked over his own console to see that the giant golden ship was plummeting fast. The *Marillion* punched a hole through the upper city, wiping out everything in a burning flash. The *Rackham* was only a few kilometres above the top cloud cover, but they had less than a minute before the Highclave's personal vessel struck Shandar like a furious god.

The enemy ship was still behind them.

"Roland!" Ch'len screamed, seeing the destruction flaring at the top of the viewport. "We're not going to make it!"

"Yes, we well." The bounty hunter's hand danced across his console, diverting all power to forward thrust. "But, they won't..."

Both human and Ch'kara grunted in pain when the *Rackham* shot forward with tremendous speed. Roland did his best to ignore the strain on his groin as things were compressed into places they were never meant to go. It took a lot of strength to check his console display, but he caught a glimpse of the enemy ship's position behind them. He could also see the *Marillion* crashing down through the layers of Shandar's floating city.

Alarms barked from their consoles, warning of the potential cataclysmic collision that would take place if they didn't clear the *Marillion's* estimated impact zone in the next ten seconds. There was a tower directly ahead, but the nav-system had put them on a course that took them through to the other side via the building's hangar. They lost no speed as they hurtled through and continued under the shadow of the golden orb. The enemy ship, however, could not fit through the hangar and was forced to plough through the tower itself. The nanocelium had no problem ramming its way through, but it came at a price.

Speed.

The *Rackham* cleared the *Marillion's* hull with only metres to spare, but the enemy ship was hammered from above and driven into Shandar's atmosphere then down into the solid ground. Roland hit a single key and redistributed the *Rackham's* power, allowing him to turn the ship about and witness the death of the *Marillion*, as well as his pursuer.

The cloud cover was immediately pushed away from the golden ship, rippling over the rest of the planet like the waves of an ocean. The atmosphere was set alight and spread for thousands of kilometres around the *Marillion's* circumference. The impact itself forced tons of rock and dirt into the sky, some of which even managed to breach the atmosphere.

"Yes!" Ch'len's stubby arms shot into the air. "We made it!"

Roland knew better than to start celebrating their survival yet. He checked over his console to see if the Crucible was inside the crash zone or within range of the shockwave from the *Marillion's* explosive impact.

"Shit," he muttered under his breath, discovering the installation was half the planet away. "I was really hoping that would have solved two problems at once."

"What do we do now?" the Ch'kara asked.

"We continue with the mission," Roland said, inputting the Crucible's coordinates into the nav-system. "Make sure the Starforge is ready for deployment."

Ch'len sighed. "I remember the days when you just wanted to find the nearest bar. I think I miss those days…"

CHAPTER 23

TELARREK WOKE UP WITH A START. How long had he slept for? What had he missed? The Novaarian shook his long head and elegant tendrils to better rouse himself, only to find one of the Highclave honour guards standing beside his cot, adorned in the usual golden armour.

"Councillor Telarrek." The guard sounded as if he was repeating himself. "I'm sorry to disturb you, but you are needed in the control room again."

Telarrek stood up and towered over the Laronian as he adjusted his robes. "No need to apologise, just do not force me to sleep next time."

The Novaarian councillor walked out into the corridor of the command tower and instantly regretted his words. They had made him rest because he was making decisions that affected the entire Conclave. He shouldn't make such remarks when they were doing their jobs better than he was doing his. Telarrek stepped into the control room a few meters ahead of the guard and fully intended to turn around and apologise, but the scene that greeted him was all-consuming.

The planet of Tagomar, in the heart of the Vellum system, was a smouldering rock, a spectacle that reminded Telarrek of the birth of a planet rather than its end. That was but one scene playing out on the glass screen. Hundreds of worlds were plagued by the Shay or bombarded from above by nanocelium vessels. One particular alert caught the Novaarian's large eye.

"Is that Vallara's capital city?" he asked, pointing to the smoking pit on the screen to the right.

"I'm afraid so," Councillor Fey replied. The human was gripping the rail so hard her knuckles had turned white. "The Laronian government is gone."

Telarrek wanted to sigh and drop his head in defeat, but with so many eyes watching his every move, the Novaarian reminded himself of his role. He wasn't just there to point at things and give commands; he was there to inspire, to offer hope. He kept his shoulders straight and his head raised.

"What of Sordomo?" Telarrek asked, referring to the next planet in the harvesting ship's sights. "Have we managed to evacuate the major cities?"

"That's why I asked them to wake you," Fey replied as she ordered one of the officers to change the holograms on the screen. "The harvesting ship has altered its course. Sordomo is no longer its destination."

Telarrek examined the star charts on the screen, noting the ship's diversion from the previous flight path. "Where is it heading now?"

Fey gestured to the bright red flashing icon hovering over the capital planet on the star chart. "It's coming here."

Telarrek ground his fangs and resisted the urge to slam his fist into the nearest console. They were running out of time and every minute more and more citizens of the Conclave flowed in through the Forges.

"Status on the *Regis*?" the councillor asked aloud.

One of the officers replied, "The *Regis* entered Evalan's system an hour ago, Councillor. So far, all scans show it to be free of enemies."

Telarrek shook his head. "We cannot trust our scans. These nanocelium hulls can fool our instruments. Make sure they visually check every crevice of that system. Check for blank spots where the stars cannot be seen, search through the asteroid belts, and probe the gas giants; there are two of them in that system." The Novaarian turned to Fey. "As soon as the *Regis* clears your home, your people need to be ready to leave."

Fey nodded her agreement. "We will be. Hopefully, our exodus will divert the harvesting ship before it reaches the capital."

That reminded Telarrek. "Has the ALF programme been integrated into the central AI?"

Another officer looked up from her console. "Yes, sir. Our technicians report that it is live."

"Make certain our enemy is able to retrieve just enough information to learn of the humans' movements."

Fey said quietly, "Don't worry, Telarrek, they know the plan."

The Novaarian councillor took a breath and stepped back, taking on board Fey's words. He had to trust his people to get the job done as he had already ordered. There was a hierarchy inside the control room and he had to have faith that those below him could oversee those beneath them. He did, however, make the mistake of comparing the number of people on Sordomo against the increasing number of people now on the capital. If the harvesting ship pierced the outer shell, the Conclave would lose just over a trillion lives in a single attack.

"New reports are coming in from Shandar," a Raalak officer called out.

The screen changed again, allowing them to see individual perspectives on the battle as well as an overview of the entire system. Telarrek couldn't believe his eyes and he walked around the rail to better see the chaos.

Councillor Fey joined him. "The *Marillion*..." she uttered.

"The Crucible?" Telarrek asked, unable to comment on the

destruction of such a massive ship. The casualties from that ship alone would haunt the Novaarian for the rest of his life.

"Still active," came the reply from the officers. "Our troops are yet to reach the surface and breach the facility."

"Wait!" A Tularon officer had everyone's attention. "One ship has just made it through the atmosphere."

"Troop transport?" Telarrek asked hopefully.

"No sir," the Tularon replied. "The *Brightstar* has it designated as... Sir, it's the *Rackham!*"

Councillor Fey turned back to the screen. "Roland..." Her tone of concern had the slightest hint of hope mixed in.

"What is his mission?" Telarrek asked. He knew the bounty hunter was a destructive force to be reckoned with, but the Crucible could not be taken by a single man.

The Tularon officer checked his display before replying, "It's carrying one of the new portable Starforges, sir. High Charge Hox has ordered the *Rackham* to deploy it on the surface to allow transports to move freely between the cruisers and the facility."

Telarrek offered no objections to the High Charge's plan. "Keep us updated."

The Novaarian couldn't help but feel utterly useless. It was hard enough with the crushing guilt that he was safe inside the Clave Command Tower while others were out there fighting for the Conclave.

"I've been where you are," Councillor Fey said away from the others. "I know how you feel. You just want to be out there, helping with your own two... *four* hands. But, you have to remind yourself that a body needs a head. Where the many can save a few with their actions, you can save millions with your words. Hold on to that."

Telarrek offered the councillor a weary smile and placed a gentle hand on her shoulder, thankful for such wisdom. Humans, it seemed, would never fail to astound him, even in their youth, as they all were to him.

"The Highclave is lucky to call you a member," he

complimented.

Fey looked to reply but her words were cut off by a blaring alarm system. Red and yellow lights flashed in the corners of the room and either side of the doors. The first to react were the honour guard, who closed ranks and immediately started rounding up the councillors. Officers hurried to the cabinets that lined the walls and input the command to release the weapons secured inside.

"What is happening?" Telarrek asked urgently, using all four of his hands to prevent the honour guards from ushering him out.

"We're under attack!" one of the officers shouted over the alarm.

Telarrek turned back to the screen and saw the sensor readouts from around the command tower. Shay were crawling out of every vent and maintenance door across all twenty floors that occupied the tower, and they were converging on their position. According to the screen, there were hundreds of them flooding the upper levels, killing anyone between them and the command tower. Some were already climbing the walls and breaking in through the ventilation system.

"How did they make it up here?" The Brenine High Councillor asked frantically.

"They made us think we had driven them down into the lower city," Telarrek explained, "but they must have used the ancient tunnels and utility systems to crawl up." The Novaarian held out his hands to receive a weapon, but the Laronian officer looked to the Atari honour guard beside him. "I realise that protocol dictates that you have command when a High Councillor's life is in jeopardy," Telarrek said to the Atari, "but, judging by the number of Shay advancing on this very room, I would say we all need a weapon."

The Atari honour guard replied, "Our priority is to evacuate you to a safer location, sir."

Telarrek looked to the big screen, where external cameras relayed images of the wild Shay tearing their way through the command tower's main doors. "I do not think we are going anywhere."

"We have a secure transport on the top level, sir. We don't have time to argue this."

Indeed, they didn't. The vent on the wall above them burst open as the first of the Shay exploded into the room with a banshee-like scream. The honour guards immediately aimed their rifles high and unloaded half a dozen rounds each into the alien, scattering its body across the control room.

Telarrek snatched the long weapon off the young officer with his upper hands and used his lower hands to retrieve a pair of pistols. More Shay took their chances and attempted to enter the room via the broken vent, but Intrinium rounds blew holes across the wall, tracing the line of the vent. Blood poured through the holes, but they all knew it meant nothing when facing the nanocelium-infected aliens.

"Targets to the rear!" a Laronian honour guard warned as she spun on her foot and dropped into a crouch, aiming down her sights at the side door.

By the time Telarrek had turned to face the new invaders, half the honour guard had opened fire and filled the door space with enough super-heated rounds to reduce a Raalak to slag. Still, the Novaarian councillor added his own rounds to the cacophony and did his best to keep the Shay from establishing a foothold inside the control room.

"Councillor Fey!" Telarrek shouted over the barrage.

Li Fey hopped over one of the consoles and pushed two of the terrified councillors to the floor, before turning to Telarrek to catch one of his pistols in mid-air. She rolled across the aisles and popped up, shooting the crazed Shay who was erratically crawling over the wall above them. The human captain was certainly more limber and agile than the Novaarian would have given her credit. She was, however, on the endangered species list.

Telarrek clapped the Atari honour guard on the shoulder, drawing him back from the fight. "You need to get Councillor Fey to the emergency transport! See her back to her people and make sure they reach the Starforge!"

The Atari shook his head. "We're tasked with protecting the

Highclave, sir! That means all of you!"

Telarrek wanted to protest but more Shay were finding their way in through the vents on the tier above them. The Novaarian swung his rifle around and opened up on the top corner, giving three of the officers just enough time to retreat, though it did nothing to halt the coming onslaught. The main doors to the control room sparked and the touchpad beside it winked out before the Shay pried open the entrance.

Councillor Fey fired on them from behind the cover of a console, her accuracy enviable. Telarrek only wished those they shot down didn't get back up again. The first of the infected aliens to be brought down were already slithering across the floor in search of viable parts to re-form their bodies. The Novaarian made it as hard as he could and kicked random limbs away, while his rifle and pistol fired round after round into the oncoming Shay.

A harrowing scream sounded from the tier above as the Trillik councillor found himself in the middle of a swarm. The Shay ripped the green alien to pieces, discarding the Trillik's limbs and organs in every direction. From there, they pounced on the officers who were doing their best to cover all the angles of the enemy's entry point.

Fey's voice cried out, "Telarrek! Behind you!"

The Novaarian didn't hesitate to spin around and bring the butt of his rifle to bear. He struck the attacking Shay across the head, knocking it back enough to allow him to level his pistol and shoot the alien in the neck. The force of it was enough to disintegrate its entire neck, leaving the head to roll away.

"We can't hold them off forever!" Fey yelled over the sound of her own pistol.

Telarrek dared to steal a glimpse at the data streaming over the glass screen behind him. They needed the Crucible to be destroyed, *now*. Noting the rising number of casualties was unfortunately all Telarrek had time for. Three Shay had scrambled through the gaps left by the fallen honour guards and leapt the rest of the distance to reach the Novaarian. He raised his rifle, all too aware that he hadn't reacted quickly enough to repel them. Between their metallic fingers and sharp teeth, the High Councillor feared that these were his final moments.

All three of the Shay were hammered by Intrinium rounds mid-flight and sent rolling across the consoles. Another Shay dashed over the top of an honour guard, only to be equally riddled with super-heated bolts of energy, saving Telarrek once again.

The High Councillor turned to the main door and found his son Naydaalan charging the control room with high-powered rifles in both pairs of arms. His long muscular legs kicked out, breaking bones and launching Shay into the crossfire of the honour guards. His tendrils whipped through the air as his head turned to clock every target leaping around the room.

"Naydaalan!" Telarrek called his son to his position.

The young Novaarian put down three more Shay and easily leapt over the row of consoles to reach his father and Councillor Fey. "There are more outside," he said. "They are heading towards the hotels on the other side of the ring. They are going for the humans."

Telarrek levelled his rifle and unleashed devastating Intrinium into a cluster of infected aliens. Others behind the cluster were finding their shapes again and steadily rising, preparing to continue their assault. This wasn't a fight they could win. The Novaarian dared to remain standing and attempted to punch a series of commands into the console. He needed to make sure the central AI alerted their enemy to the humans' movements.

"Take Councillor Fey to the top level. There is an emergency transport up there. Get her back to her people and see them through the Starforge." Telarrek turned to Fey. "I am afraid we cannot wait for a full report from the *Regis*. If you stay here, the Shay will stop at nothing until you are all dead. We need to move on to the next phase of the plan while we still can."

"Come with us!" Fey pleaded.

Telarrek shook his head. "We must take back the command tower!" The Novaarian looked at his son. "Take her, now! Go!" The

High Councillor didn't wait to hear any protests; there were Shay to kill.

Li Fey knew she had mixed emotions about leaving Telarrek and the other councillors behind but, between the screams of the Shay and the rounds leaving Naydaalan's rifles, the old captain didn't have time to process any of them. Instead, she followed closely behind the Novaarian and kept her pistol levelled with both hands.

"This way!" Naydaalan escorted her to the emergency stairwell, where they ascended to the top level.

"It's locked," Fey observed upon sighting the red light on the touchpad beside the door.

Naydaalan fired a single round into the pad. "Cover me," he ordered.

Fey turned around and focused her eye along the length of the pistol, noting all the vents. Screams echoed from down the stairwell, though not all of them belonged to Shay. A glance over her shoulder revealed Naydaalan using all four of his hands to separate the two halves of the door.

"Quickly!" he hissed, hurrying into the emergency hangar.

Barely two minutes later, they were both strapped into the cockpit and taking off. The ceiling opened up and the light of Clave Tower flooded the hangar, along with a mob of Shay, who had been crawling over the roof. They dropped on to the small transport and immediately began slamming their cybernetic fists into the glass around the cockpit.

Fey lifted her pistol and squeezed the trigger, making every shot count. The Intrinium melted through the glass and continued through the aliens' heads, causing them to slip off the hull. One particularly feral Shay thrust its fist into one of the Intrinium holes and snatched at the air in an attempt to steal her gun.

"Hold on!" Naydaalan warned, shifting the control stick all the way to port.

The Shay were thrown from the transport, including the one with its arm sticking through the jagged hole. The force of it tore the alien's body away from its limb, which dropped into the cockpit at Fey's feet. She instinctively kicked it and stomped on it until she plucked up the courage to pick it up and throw it into the cabin behind them.

It took several minutes to traverse the distance from one side of the ring to the other, especially with all the C-Sec transports flying past them, heading towards the command tower. Naydaalan brought the ship down beside the warehouse, where a trail of humans could be seen making their way inside. Hopefully, Fey thought, they would have the Starforge up and running by now.

"Look! Over there!"

Fey followed Naydaalan's eyes to the dark mass of infected aliens climbing up the levels to reach the human population. They didn't have long.

The pair ran from the transport and entered the warehouse through a side door. Inside, the Forge was a swirling vortex of colour and white light. People were walking through but it wasn't fast enough.

"Li!" Captain Holt left the control panel beside the Forge and ran over to meet her. "What's going on? We received a message from the command tower telling us to leave as soon as possible."

"The Shay are coming!" She burst out. "They're right behind the procession!"

"Shit..." Holt looked down the length of the parade.

"Where's Kalian?" Fey asked.

"He already went through with the Gomar," Jed explained. "They went to make sure Evalan was safe."

Fey couldn't hide her despair. Kalian and the Gomar were the only ones powerful enough to not only put the Shay down, but also to make sure they didn't get back up again.

"Okay..." she said, assessing the situation. "I don't mean to start a panic, and I realise that some might be hurt in the process, but these people really need to start running."

Jed nodded in agreement. "Commander Vale! We need to get these people through this Forge ASAP! We've got enemies closing in!"

Samantha Vale clapped her hands and roused a group of UDC soldiers. Her orders were simple: head down the line and tell everyone to start running forward. When they reached the end they were to hold off any enemies until they could step through the Forge themselves.

"I will help them," Naydaalan said, hefting his two massive rifles.

Fey knew she would be of better help coordinating the flow of people running through the Forge. She hurried over and helped two people get back to their feet before ushering them forward again. A child's wail brought her attention to the small boy standing to the side of the trail, his wet eyes searching the rushing throng for any sign of his parents.

"Commander Vale!" Fey shouted as she scooped the child up in her arms. "Take him and get him through the Forge! Find his parents!"

Intrinium fire erupted in the distance and Fey recognised the sound of Naydaalan's rifles. The captain did her best to keep the people calm and moving forward. That became increasingly difficult as the weapons fire edged ever closer to the warehouse doors. An explosion rocked everyone on their feet and Fey instantly worried what had become of the UDC soldiers and Naydaalan.

"Keep going!" she yelled.

The wall behind her was shredded by Intrinium fire, forcing those who had not yet passed through the Forge to drop to the floor. The screams increased tenfold as bolts of Intrinium tore the wall to pieces and impacted the floor around the Forge. That couldn't have come from any of the rifles wielded by the soldiers or Naydaalan.

"Go! Quickly!" Fey pointed at the Forge while helping up people who had stumbled and fallen and ushering them onwards.

With her pistol in hand, Fey made for the exit to see what was going on. They were down to the last hundred passing through the Forge now, prompting her to ensure the soldiers made it through. Every human life was precious.

The doors slid apart to a world on fire. The Shay were everywhere, crawling over every surface, killing any who were unfortunate enough to get in their way. The source of the Intrinium bolts cutting through the warehouse wall was clear to see, if somewhat horrifying.

Hovering out of control, a C-Sec transport assault ship was being overrun with Shay, some of whom had punched their way through the glass, creating chaos inside the cockpit. The transport spun this way and that before finally slamming into the level above in an explosion of fire and black smoke.

Fey covered her eyes from the flare, but she was forced to take aim with her pistol when a group of Shay dropped away from the wall and came at her. The first one was hit by enough Intrinium rounds to put it down for a while, but the second and third were too close to finish the job. The captain side-stepped the first infected alien to lunge at her and brought her foot up to boot the second in the chest, pushing it back enough to give her space. The Intrinium rounds to its face gave her some reprieve and a chance to turn around and face the last Shay.

"Shit!" she yelled, seeing the crazed alien abandon its attack on her to enter the warehouse.

Fey glanced at the soldiers and Naydaalan, checking they were all still alive as she ran back into the warehouse. The Shay was running on all fours like an animal in pursuit of its prey: the last of the civilians. Li stopped running and aimed her pistol with both hands. If she missed, the bolt would hit one of her own people. With only a couple of seconds before the Shay was close enough to pounce, the captain took her shot. The Shay's head exploded from the back as it jumped up, perfectly in line with the Intrinium.

There were more screams when its mangled body hit the floor

and slid towards the last of those fleeing through the Forge. Fey took a breath, more thankful than ever that the nanocelium in her blood had reversed her age and sharpened her senses.

Fey looked to the technicians by the side of the Starforge. "There's just a few more! Hold on!"

Running back to the exit, Fey intended to pull everyone back and get them to Evalan, where they had the protection of Kalian and the others. Outside, things were only getting worse. The soldiers had been pushed back to the door and Naydaalan had been forced to drop one of his rifles, a sputtering mess of sparks at his feet. More Shay were appearing from every crevice, railing, and doorway, with just as many rising from the dead, amalgamations of their comrades' bodies.

"Get back to the Forge!" Fey ordered. "You too, Naydaalan! It looks like you're coming to Evalan as well, I'm afraid!" Knowing of their plan to be bait for the harvest ship, the captain felt as if she might be condemning the Novaarian to death, along with the rest of her race.

As one, they sprinted into the warehouse, firing blindly over their shoulders. Naydaalan reached the Starforge long before any of the humans did and dropped to one knee, picking off any Shay who came too close to making contact with the running humans. The captain felt hot blood spray her back and neck more than once, thanks to the Novaarian's aim.

"Go!" Fey gestured for the technicians to run through the Forge as well. Anyone still alive in this warehouse after the wormhole had been shut down could not boast such a feat for very long.

Naydaalan stood up and slowly advanced on the Shay, pressing his attack at the last minute to give the humans a chance. Fey caught his eye as she ran past, noting the Novaarian's determination to kill every Shay who meant them harm. He was a warrior through and through but, in Fey's experience, they tended to be the ones who died for others. In that split second, she had to make a choice, and had it been the lives of any other race she might have reached out and dragged Naydaalan with her. But the ugly truth was that the lives of these soldiers were more important than his.

Fey ran through the event horizon, her thoughts too chaotic to consider the fact that her atoms were momentarily pulled apart and reassembled thousands of light years away. The captain ran out into the heat of Evalan's sun, leaving the air conditioned warehouse behind in a second.

Fey skidded to a stop and turned to watch the Forge. "Come on..."

The technicians on Evalan's side were waiting for the order to shut down the wormhole.

"Wait!" she commanded, hoping to give the Novaarian as much time as she could.

"What's going on?" Li'ara Ducarté fought her way through the last of the crowds to reach the captain. "Is everyone through?"

"Not everyone..." Fey replied, her pistol half raised.

Li'ara noted the captain's stance and drew her own sidearm. They waited for another second before a wild Shay burst through the wormhole, missing an arm and half of its face. Still, it charged them with murderous intent. Both women aimed their weapons but the Shay was split in half, struck from behind by an Intrinium bolt fired from a high powered rifle. Naydaalan strode towards them with smoke rising from the barrel of his rifle.

"Do it!" Fey shouted at the technicians.

Naydaalan turned around and fired a dozen more shots into the wormhole before picking up and throwing the dead Shay back through the Forge. A second later, the light of the wormhole vanished, leaving them all panting and covered in sweat and blood.

"That was too close," Fey commented, patting Naydaalan on the arm. "Thank you."

The Novaarian tilted his head in the nod of his race. "We will only survive this if we fight together."

Fey agreed, though she was tired of only surviving. When would they be able to live again?

CHAPTER 24

After searching the solar system for any sign of a threat, Kalian and the Gomar boarded ALF's Starforge at his request, which was now capable of travelling at faster speeds thanks to the extra nanocelium. Every time they passed through its corridors, the station was different in its design and even its layout. Kalian's perfect memory found more than a few corridors and walkways were simply gone, replaced with walls or new rooms.

"What's going on ALF?" Kalian asked as they entered the control room. "We were going to head down to the planet."

ALF was standing over one of his consoles with his hand pressed to the surface. Nanocelium strands wriggled free and connected to the console, which, in turn, brought up a collage of holograms across the glass wall. The AI appeared somewhat distracted, an odd sight for someone normally cool and collected.

"ALF," he prompted again.

The AI finally turned to regard them, his crystal blue eyes scanning all thirteen of them. "You are all quite the sight," he commented. "Those new exosuits look much better than your old ones."

"ALF," Kalian said with a firmer tone. "Why have you asked us on board?"

"Ah, yes. Sorry to divert you, I'm sure you want to check on the populace. They all made it through the Forge, you'll be glad to know. A few injuries but no losses." The AI turned away again, his expression almost pained.

"What's going on?" Vox asked.

"Talli has let slip our current position, as planned, but the Kellekt are trying to probe further into the AI hubs. I'm just offering Talli a few solutions that might see them repelled."

Kalian glanced at the Gomar, noting their acclimation to the news that their enemy had a name. He had already shared with them the true origins of nanocelium and their human masters. Most had made a joke of the name, but Kalian had sensed it was a way of dealing with the truth. Indeed, Kalian himself had found it hard to stop thinking about the perpetual cycle humanity seemed to find itself in. From the dawn of time they had been finding new ways to kill each other, regardless of the distance between planets or even galaxies. How many other species had been wiped from the universe because they invented nanocelium?

Looking at the images flashing up on the glass screen, that question had an ever-changing answer. Hundreds of Conclave planets were under attack and at the mercy of nanocelium ships or infected Shay. The harvesting ship had already claimed two planets, brought one of the core races to the brink of extinction, and destroyed the *Sentinel* in a single attack.

A star chart situated on the left of the glass screen showed the harvesting ship to be on course for the capital, having abandoned its next feast and leaving Sordomo to the Shay. The battle over Shandar wasn't going the way he had hoped. The nanocelium vessels were proving too hard to bring down, unlike the goliath *Marillion*, which appeared to now be a smoking crater on Shandar's surface.

Kovak stepped forward from the group. "Why are *we* here?" he asked. "That sounds like your side of things, not ours."

ALF stood up straight. "You're here because there's nothing more to keep from you. The Three are trying to make contact with me..."

Kalian looked from the apprehensive faces of the Gomar to ALF. "Why would they try to communicate with us?"

"You have to remember," ALF explained, "the Three are not entirely nanocelium. They retain their intelligence from their time as humans. They have personalities, needs, wants, desires. The problem we have is that they're still on course for the capital, despite learning of our exodus. They probably want to threaten us with their increasing size." The AI looked at them all with a sly grin. "I thought it was about time that *we* threatened *them*. Talli, connect us through the AI hub on Evalan."

Kalian and the others heard no response from Talli, who was now technically everywhere. The images on the glass screen, however, were quickly replaced by the stars beyond and the lighting took on an even thicker gloom.

"ALF what's happening?"

The AI looked around his control room. "They're trying to upload a virus through the link. We don't have long."

"*No you don't...*" came a voice from all around them. "*You have outrun the inevitable for too long, Heretic. You will soon be destroyed, along with your pets.*"

Kalian clenched his fist, doing everything he could to keep his anger in check. He couldn't believe the Three had ever been human, in whatever stage of evolution that took. The oldest of his kind to exist, perhaps even the oldest beings in the universe, should be pillars of wisdom and knowledge. They should be helping civilisations, not gobbling them up and wiping them all from existence.

"Can they see us?" Kalian asked.

ALF waved his hand over the floor and a tall stalk of nanocelium grew forth with a sphere on top. "You want to know what destruction looks like?" the AI addressed the Three, before stepping away from the sphere. "It looks like thirteen highly evolved beings, whose maker

DNA can destroy your hold over the nanocelium with a single touch."

Kalian kept his eye on the stalk, wondering what they looked like to the Kellekt. He hoped they scared the hell out of them, especially because of everything they had done so far on Corvus and above the capital. Now the twelve Gomar were just as powerful as he was, though maybe a little more time in the super subconducer would be needed.

"I will make you this one time offer," Kalian began. "Release the Shay and withdraw all of your ships from Conclave territory or—"

"*Or what?*" They asked. "*We are not frightened by a few children.*"

Kalian took a breath. "Withdraw now and we won't come after you."

"*Come after us? This is not a concept we understand.*"

"Well, if you continue your invasion we will be forced to tear down your armada and leave you with just a few nanites between you. Then, *you'll run*. But there won't be anywhere you can run to where we won't find you. No corner of the universe will keep you from suffering under our powers. These are my terms."

They waited for a response, standing there and staring into the sphere. He hadn't meant to offer them terms, but he was confident it was threatening enough to lure them in.

He hoped...

"*We will be with you shortly...*"

Kalian kept his best poker face on. "Coming to Evalan would be a mistake on your part," he said. "There are over a hundred thousand humans here. Imagine the chaos they would cause if even one of them were to touch your precious nanocelium."

"*They will die before the infection spreads. Not that it matters, child. We will bombard your tiny world from space and watch as you thirteen struggle to keep us at bay. Death is coming for you. As for you, Heretic; your annihilation will be a slow process that can only be measured in the life and death of a star.*"

With that, the stalk dropped away and the holograms reappeared over the glass wall. ALF went straight to work, connecting himself to the Forge via a dozen wriggling snakes of nanocelium.

"I need to purge a few things," he stated. "Their virus was more aggressive than I thought."

Kalian left the AI to his work and focused on the screen of holograms. The harvesting ship was changing course! It was diverting from the flight path that would have taken it to the capital and was now heading for Evalan.

"They really are human, under all that," Kalian said. "A true machine wouldn't be so easily baited by threats."

"That, and the Kellekt have never been challenged before," ALF added. "This whole interaction will be considered new for them. Exciting almost."

Vox folded her arms. "They'll be less excited when we're ripping their fleet apart."

ALF glanced down at the woman. "I hope you can maintain that level of confidence when you see the size of their main ship..."

Kalian checked the data on the glass wall. The harvesting ship was now so big that it dwarfed any Starforge and most moons. Teleporting into the core of that thing, if that's where the Three were, would actually be a great distance even if he was standing on the ship's surface. He had to remind himself that distance was only a unit that applied to beings who couldn't move through subspace. Once he left this reality, he could technically go anywhere. He just needed to convince himself of that.

"Is the rest of the C-Sec fleet in position to make the jump?" Kalian asked.

ALF finally disconnected from the strands of nanocelium and pinched the bridge of his nose as if he were suffering a headache. "Almost. Some have defied their orders and tried to help evacuate more planets."

"I can't blame them for wanting to save as many lives as possible," Kalian commented.

"There's a problem inside the capital," Garrion noted, gesturing to the glass wall.

The Clave Command Tower was under attack by infected Shay. The aliens were swarming out of the disused tunnels and vents and crawling all over the tower, burrowing their way inside.

"Will that affect the timing of the fleet's jump?" Vox asked.

"No," ALF assured. "Talli will assume command if he needs to."

"That won't keep everyone inside that tower alive," Kalian replied. He knew Telarrek was inside that building, along with the new Highclave.

"You can't, Kalian," ALF warned. "I can see you thinking it. You can't jump to the capital, save everyone and then jump back here to face the Kellekt. It's too far and too taxing."

"The distance is just in my head," he argued back.

"Indeed it is," ALF agreed. "I believe the only reason you can't master teleportation is because your mind cannot come to terms with the physical distance. The injuries you sustain are likely the result of your mind trying to put limitations on your powers. You're dissuading yourself, Kalian."

"Then maybe I should practise," Kalian replied, frustrated that every second he wasted talking to the AI was a second in which Telarrek's life might come to an end.

"I would normally always encourage practise," ALF said, "but I'm afraid the time for training is over. It's war now..."

CHAPTER 25

THE THREE EMERGED from their shadowy pods and gathered around the floating hologram of the galaxy. By thought alone, the map zoomed in, expanding the area of space belonging to the Conclave. They had met resistance at this level before in five other inhabited regions of the universe, all of which were now part of the Kellekt.

"We are making a mistake," the Second announced.

"I concur," the First agreed.

The Third walked around the hologram on its two legs. "You have both assessed the odds, probabilities, and calculations over a million times. We cannot be brought down by thirteen humans."

The Second scurried forward on its pincer-like legs, closing the gap between it and the hologram. "We have not openly challenged maker DNA since we left our home world."

The First slithered forward. "And there is a reason we left the original Evalan rather than continuing to harvest it."

"Yes," the Third agreed, "we left because a population of *billions* could challenge us. Thirteen humans cannot free enough nanocelium to undo us; we would sever anything that became corrupted."

The Second clicked the nanocelium-coated pincers around its mouth. "I still think we should continue on to their capital planet. Harvest more worlds before destroying the humans."

The Third tilted its head. "We already made the decision to alter our course. We cannot alter it again and show fear. Such an emotion belongs to the primitive masses of the universe, not us."

The First brought up another hologram above the galaxy map. "We have more than enough Shay on board to overrun this new Evalan," it said, coming back around to the original plan. "And with half of their fleet assaulting Shandar, any resistance will be minimal."

"Yes, but what about the other half?" the Second interjected. "Have you observed their most recent movements? They are pulling back from the core and taking up positions that place them within a single jump of Evalan."

The Third expanded the galaxy map again. "The Heretic has made changes to their central AI. We cannot break through."

"Do we need to?" the Second asked. "I would calculate that we are being lured into a trap."

"If the rest of the fleet were to jump to Evalan, they would be abandoning so many of their worlds," the First surmised. "This would seem an unlikely strategy given what we know of the Conclave."

"Unless it was devised by a human..." the Second added.

The Third ran through every individual jump possible for the rest of the C-Sec fleet and found that they *were* likely planning to meet them in the Evalan system. It didn't bother the Third, however, who could recall so well their previous victories over the eons.

"Let them *lure* us in," it said. "Half of their fleet, or what's left of it, will make little difference now that we have fed." And fed they had. The Kellekt now knew everything there was to know about the Raalaks, from their history to their chromosomes.

"And what of the humans?" the Second asked.

"Yes," the First agreed, "what about the evolved ones?"

The Third looked up from the holograms to meet the eyes of its companions. "They aren't evolved. The Heretic has simply weaponised them."

The First looked from its fat, slithering body to the three stasis pods that lined the walls, each covered with opaque glass. Inside those pods were the original human bodies that had once belonged to their consciousnesses. The First had an idea that was quickly shared with its companions before any further calculations could be made.

"No." The Third's reply was absolute and for good reason. "If we were to alter our original host bodies to mirror those of the Terran, then we would quickly begin to reject the nanocelium in our bloodstreams. Their bodies are smarter than the average intelligent life form, connected to their minds with perfect synergy. We would be individually stronger, yes, but all of this," the Third gestured to their magnificent ship, "would be separated from us. We would be nothing but biology again."

The Second recoiled at the idea. "I would not return to such a primitive form of life, even for abilities such as theirs."

The First glanced at their pods one last time. "Then we will have to hope that our ship will be enough to destroy them."

The Third couldn't believe what it was hearing. "Hope?" It echoed. "Have the two of you already been separated from your nanocelium? Hope and fear are for *them*. We are the Kellekt. Our own people chose to live as mud dwellers rather than challenge us. We have harvested more civilisations than there are worlds in this galaxy! If you are not up to leading our charge across the universe, then I will take majority control and assign you new tasks for the betterment of the Kellekt."

The other two almost backed off, but they knew better than to show any kind of inferiority. This wasn't the first time the Third had suggested that it assume full control. Instead, they sent messages around the ship to increase speed and prepare the boarded Shay for planet-side deployment.

The Third was satisfied to see its companions back on track, though it would have happily taken over. It thought to examine the battle of Shandar in more depth, but a preliminary report informed the Third that only a single light craft had successfully penetrated the planet's atmosphere.

What could one light craft accomplish against their might?

CHAPTER 26

Roland hit the throttle and the *Rackham* shot through the last layer of Shandar's stormy atmosphere. Bolts of lightning hammered the hull as if the storm itself was angered to have anyone survive its wrath. The bounty hunter cared little for a few bolts of lightning; he was more concerned with the amount of Shay surrounding the Crucible.

The *Rackham's* advanced scanning array was able to penetrate the planet and locate the installation north of their current position. There were Shay troops on the ground, cannons fixed into the canyons around it, and light craft hovering overhead.

The coordinates he had been given weren't far from the Crucible. Roland knew in his head that it was simple. All he had to do was deploy the mobile Starforge and wait for the transports to start flooding through. But, it was awfully tempting to do a flyby and pick off a few Shay.

"Don't even think about it, Roland!" Ch'len chided. "I can see the stupidity running through your mind. Get us to the coordinates and drop the Starforge. Nothing else."

"Just a quick squeeze of the trigger?"

"No! We're lucky to have reached this far," Ch'len pointed out. "Have you seen the horizon?"

Roland checked the hologram sent his way and looked at the horizon behind the *Rackham*. The shockwave from the *Marillion*'s impact was still rolling across the planet, sending a wall of debris as high as the clouds across the surface. The ground was cracking and opening up gorges and ravines so large they descended miles into the planet's mantle. The *Rackham*'s AI calculated the edges of the impact, noting that the shockwave would have little to no effect on the Crucible.

Roland sighed, all too aware that the little Ch'kara was right. They were more than lucky to have survived the nanocelium-based ship and the falling *Marillion*. Deploying the Starforge would ensure C-Sec boots got on the ground and could potentially end most of this war with a single strike.

"Well, shit..." The bounty hunter diverted from his direct path to the Crucible and proceeded to the arranged coordinates.

The dark land, devoid of sunlight, opened up before them, offering the transports a clear field of barren ground on which to land and take off from. A quick scan showed that there were no enemies nearby, and Roland was careful to keep the stealthware operating while they weren't in combat.

"Okay, deploy the Forge, Len."

The Ch'kara input the commands into his console and frowned. He repeated the commands and frowned again.

"Talk to me, Len. I feel like I can hear the rolls in your chubby face squeezing together."

"It looks like the Starforge has taken some damage," he replied.

"Can we still deploy it on the ground?" Roland asked, fearing that all they had just done was for nothing.

"The *Rackham* can still drop it, but I can't say for certain whether the Forge will function as it's supposed to."

The bounty hunter decreased the *Rackham*'s speed, giving him more time to consider his options. The ship was only a few kilometres out from the coordinates now and they had to either drop the Forge and attempt to activate it or return to the *Brightstar* and report mission failure.

"Alright," he said. "We didn't come this far just to turn back with our tail between our legs." Roland decreased altitude and brought the *Rackham* into the flat field of dry ground. "Prepare the Forge. We're dropping it."

"If it doesn't work we'll have just dropped the only one we have," Ch'len reasoned. "Maybe we should just take it back to the *Brightstar* and have the engineers look it over?"

"Did you have your eyes closed up there?" Roland fired back. "There isn't going to be a *Brightstar* for very long. Hell, half the fleet is probably moments away from being reduced to slag. It's now or never, Len. Drop it."

Ch'len groaned and followed Roland's command, inputting the codes to release the Starforge from the *Rackham*'s underbelly. They both heard the releasing mechanisms through the floor and watched on the monitor as the Forge fell away.

Roland kept one eye on the monitor. "Come on, come on, come on..."

At the last second, the Forge's drop functions came to life and the thrusters built into the crescent machine provided just enough reaction force to see it land in the correct position without smashing into a million pieces. Cables shot out of the side and tethered it to the ground, digging deep.

"Yes!" Roland hissed. "Send a message to Hox and have him switch the Forge on from their end."

The bounty hunter pulled back on the flight stick and gained altitude. He needed to secure the perimeter until the first few transports were through, then he would—

"There's a problem," Ch'len said bluntly, interrupting Roland's planning.

Roland levelled out the *Rackham* and turned to his co-pilot. "Explain."

Ch'len double-checked the messages coming through his console. "They can't activate it on their end. I knew it was damaged!"

Roland shook his head, choosing to ignore the last comment. "So they can't switch it on remotely; can't they use the paired Forge in the hangar to connect the two?"

Ch'len paused, reading the messages. "They're trying that now."

Roland sighed, more than aware that time was a precious commodity right now. Aside from the losing battle taking place above the storm clouds, there were hundreds of worlds being attacked by infected Shay. They needed to shut down the Crucible immediately.

"It's not good," Ch'len warned. "The Forge in the hangar is working, but the one down here won't accept any connection between the two."

"Shit!" Roland cursed. "Have any transports or squadrons made it through the atmosphere on their own?"

Ch'len brought up a new hologram of readouts. "Negative. They haven't even made it through the upper city yet."

The bounty hunter maintained his circling pattern, keeping the Starforge on the ground in sight. They were low on options and lower still on resources. How many were dying while some remote technicians were trying to figure out how to fix the Forge?

"New orders," Ch'len announced.

"There isn't time to take it back, Len. That's *if* we made it back."

"No, they don't want us to take it back." Ch'len hesitated with a gulp. "They want us to land and fix it manually. They're sending through all the schematics now."

Roland turned to his small friend. "Can you do that? *Can* you fix it?"

Ch'len flicked his finger through the air, sifting through the information on the hologram. "This is Terran tech mixed with Conclave tech. I might just be the only one who can... But, I'm not going out there! It's just open space as far as the eye can see. Nope. We're just going to have to find a quiet sector of space and wait for this whole thing to blow over."

Roland rolled his eyes and took the *Rackham* into a dive, heading straight for the Starforge.

Telarrek emptied the last of his rifle's magazine into the corridor, filling it with smoke, blood, severed body parts, and the distinct smell of ozone. With only three of the guards left by his side, and a handful of helpless councillors, the Novaarian pushed forward, stepping over the slithering nanocelium before it coalesced into another body and tried to kill them.

"We have to try and take back the command room," Councillor Ordak suggested urgently. The large Raalak was injured having taken an Intrinium round to the shoulder, but he was the only other member of the present Highclave who wielded a weapon.

"The control room is gone," Telarrek replied quietly. "We have to get out of here and reach the High Spire." That revelation started the other five councillors whispering fiercely.

"The High Spire?" Ordak echoed. "That's in the centre of Clave Tower! It's so far down you can't even see it from up here."

Telarrek held his reply for the moment, hugging the corner of the next corridor and checking to see if the way was clear. Three Shay were in the middle of the hall doing their best to break into a secure room. Telarrek glanced at the survivors behind him, aware that they didn't have long before the Shay they had recently killed came back to life and hunted them down.

"The previous Highclave ran most of the day-to-day operations from the High Spire," Telarrek explained. "There is a backup control system in the heart of the Spire, one that we can use to link back with the fleet and the central AI. We have to reach it."

A pale Brenine, cowering behind one of the guards added, "That's if we make it out of this place alive..."

It was a comment that did nothing to help their current situation, but Telarrek couldn't blame any of them for being terrified. None of them had been in combat before or even a life-threatening situation.

The Novaarian held out his hand and accepted the fresh magazine from one of the gold-clad guards. The rifle made a satisfying sound when reloaded, though, in truth, Telarrek would happily never hear it again. He nodded to the guards and all four of them rounded the corner with their weapons levelled at the Shay. Intrinium bolts illuminated the corridor in brilliant blue, tearing through Shay muscle and on into the wall beyond.

A banshee-like scream resounded down the halls from back the way they had come. The Shay were on their trail again.

"Run!" Telarrek barked, leading the charge.

More Shay erupted from access corridors and from behind closed doors, each too slow to avoid the barrels of the weapons firing on them. The Tularon councillor yelled out in pain from the back of the group and they all heard the alien hit the floor. Telarrek halted the group in his effort to turn back and see what was happening, but it was Ordak who responded first, firing his rifle with one hand into the Shay who was dragging the furry Tularon away.

"Grab him!" Telarrek ordered.

The other councillors were frozen with fear at the sight of the oncoming Shay and did nothing to help their colleague. One of the guards, a pink Atari, pushed through and dashed down the corridor to scoop up the Tularon. He fired wildly over his shoulder and Telarrek added his own rifle to the mix, slowing the progression of the masses.

Once the group was back together, there were only a few metres between them and the infected Shay, who were crawling along every available space in the corridor. Telarrek did his best to react as quickly as possible and put down those who sprung from the shadows in front, but the low emergency lighting made it harder to see everything.

"Take a left!" one of the guards instructed.

The Novaarian trusted his guard's sense of direction and made a left at the T-junction. The signs flaring in the darkness indicated that the outdoor landing pad was at the end of this corridor. Telarrek dared to hope. There had to be some kind of craft on the pad after so many had arrived at the Clave Command Tower.

Another scream from the back of the group had only the bravest among them turning back to see who had fallen. Telarrek caught a brief glimpse of the Laronian guard being swallowed up by the Shay, her rifle blasting about wildly.

"Get as far out on to the pad as you can!" the Atari guard yelled over the sound of the scrambling Shay.

Telarrek looked down to see the golden-armoured Atari reaching for a grenade. Again, he could only trust the well-trained soldier to know what he was doing. The doors parted swiftly as they ran through and on to the landing pad. The Atari guard hung back and threw his grenade underhand back into the corridor, before activating the door controls. The explosion from inside was powerful enough to blow off the doors. Telarrek and the others had thankfully run far enough on to the pad to avoid being hit by them.

"Get ready!" The Atari guard warned, finding his feet after the explosion.

As one, those who wielded weapons levelled them at the smoking doorframe and waited for the survivors to barrel through. It was an agonising delay, but the Shay didn't keep them waiting for long. Intrinium fire erupted forth and sent the infected aliens back into the ruins of the corridor.

Telarrek lowered his rifle and slowly turned around, more than aware that they were standing on an empty landing pad.

"There's no ship!" One of the councillors trembled.

"Now we're stuck up here..." another complained hopelessly.

Telarrek walked over to the edge, his gaze absent as reality set in. They weren't going to survive this. They had nowhere else to run with only minutes, if that, before more Shay flooded the platform and tore them all to pieces. This wasn't how he wanted to die, at least not without knowing whether the Conclave would live on. Still, there was Kalian. He had to believe that they would win.

"More are coming!" The Atari guard shouted, crouching on one knee with his rifle aimed at the smoking doorway.

Telarrek sighed and banished his thoughts of simply stepping off the platform. If he was to die now, he would die fighting...

———

Roland ran across the flat ground as the heavy rain pelted down from above. He pushed the hover sledge ahead of him, blinking the rain water out of his eyes to better see Ch'len in the distance. The small alien was busy working to gain access to the control panel on the side of the crescent machine.

"Here!" The bounty hunter yelled over the hammering rain. "I just brought everything!" Indeed he had. The hover sledge was stacked with every piece of equipment and tool he could find in Ch'len's workshop.

"I need cover!"

"Right..." Roland constructed a small pavilion out of some canvas and spare pipes, but he couldn't shake the feeling of drowning under such a barrage.

With the heavy rain held at bay, Ch'len was able to inspect the hologram floating beside him with the Starforge's schematics. Roland felt helpless just standing there and watching him work. He tapped the slight depression in his temple and connected with the *Rackham's* AI. He had the ship's array constantly monitoring for any sign of trouble. The enemy had to know that a craft had breached the atmosphere, especially one so close to the Crucible.

"It's just fried!" Ch'len moaned. "It took a direct hit to the cooling system. Even if I could get it working again, we'd have maybe a few seconds before it overheated and exploded!"

Roland sighed, looking from the Starforge to the rocky horizon, over which sat the Crucible. They were so close.

"Keep working on it. Pull it apart and rebuild it if you have to." The bounty hunter flicked up the collar on his hide coat and turned back to the *Rackham*.

Ch'len stopped his tinkering for a moment. "Where are *you* going?"

"To see if anyone's home."

Back under the relentless rain, Roland could barely hear his co-pilot's protests. He didn't stop to hear it all, he just kept on walking until he was inside the *Rackham*. Now he had to figure out how he was going to strap so many weapons to his body without hindering his ability to walk.

CHAPTER 27

It felt good to have his feet back on solid ground again. Kalian looked down at his black nanocelium boots on Evalan's sandy surface and knew he should feel like he was home... but he didn't. As nice as it felt to be standing on a real world again, he felt more at home floating among the stars, beside the Gomar.

Walking through the streets of New Genesis, Kalian had to wonder if others felt as if they were in a foreign land. A single battlecruiser, the *Galaron*, had arrived shortly after the population made it through the Starforge and had deposited numerous tanks and ground-to-air missile launchers. Looking around, the tanks walked through the streets on their six legs, their cannons pointed to the skies, and the launchers were being bolted into the ground, overseen by three C-Sec soldiers.

The human populace were running about, preparing themselves and their neighbours for the inevitable assault. The *Galaron* had supplied them with a few hundred ground transports in order to quickly evacuate everyone from the city, though their exact destination was still being decided by the human council. Kalian reached the end of the street and cast his gaze between the buildings, focusing on the mountains in the distance. He knew the caves within were an option being discussed, but he also knew that no planet was safe to hide on.

Not when your enemy consumed planets like snacks...

What sounded like a squadron of Darts whipping over the city made Kalian look up. Of course, there were no Darts on Evalan and the *Galaron* had already departed the system. He turned on the spot and tracked the Gomar flying above the city, free of their bulky armour and enjoying the slimline nanocelium exosuits. The super subconducer had granted all of them much needed training in a matter of hours rather than the years it should have taken.

Kalian stepped aside when one of the tanks wanted to carry on its patrol to the edge of the city. Ultimately, their presence helped to keep everyone feeling a little safer, but they were really on New Genesis to help maintain order when the evacuation took place. There was no tank or missile launcher that could stop a nanocelium-based ship. Finding the Gomar in the sky once again, Kalian could see the only weapons in the galaxy capable of fending their enemy off.

Crossing the street, heading farther into the city now, Kalian came across a family with two children. The parents were perhaps the only ones in the area who weren't busy packing belongings and readying supplies. They were spending time with their son and daughter. It almost broke his heart to watch, aware that these parents believed they were all to die soon, and that they just wanted to spend time with their children before the end.

There was nothing he could do or say that would give them hope. How many tragedies had humanity already gone through up to this point? This family could have come from the terraforming project or they might have been aboard the *Paladin*. Either way, they had survived to know of Earth's and Century's destruction, along with who knows how many of their loved ones.

Now they were being forced from one planet to another and used as bait to help save others; aliens that most of the people in New Genesis didn't really care for. And how could they? The Conclave had rejected them since their arrival. Despite their continued survival against the odds, this family was used to being on the losing side.

Kalian balled his fist. Damn it if he wasn't going to try.

"Are you not preparing for the evacuation?" he asked them, disrupting their play.

The parents stood up and the young children briefly hid behind their father's leg. "Oh, Mister Gaines!" he said with a smile.

Kalian held up his hand. "Please, call me Kalian. I haven't been *Mister* Gaines since I was lecturing."

The father appeared somewhat uncomfortable. "Kalian. Um, we were just messing around before we get stuck in. We weren't on the capital for very long so we're just..." he looked down at his children.

"I'm sorry about all the moving around," Kalian replied, unsure what he was hoping to achieve anymore. "Is there anything I can help with?"

"Your help?" the father echoed incredulously. "It's thanks to you that we're all still..." he glanced at his children again. "Well, it's thanks to you that we're all still here. I only wish we could help you when, you know, when they get here."

Kalian wanted to tell them that they were going to win. That right here, on their home planet, they would draw a line in the sand and their enemy would finally be defeated. But his wrist vibrated to notify him that he was receiving a communication.

"Excuse me," he said, turning to open his palm and activate the holo-emitters in his fingertips.

Li'ara's head took shape through the formation of the orange light. "The meeting is coming to an end here," she stated. "Fancy going on a date Flyboy?"

That brought a smile to his face, even if he felt like weeping for the family behind him. "I'll be there in a second."

Li'ara smiled. "I love you."

"I love you too," he replied affectionately before closing his fist and ending the hologram. He turned back to the family apologetically. "I have to go. If you need any help, the C-Sec officers have been instructed to assist us in any way."

"Thank you, Kalian," the mother said softly.

Kalian swallowed hard before meeting their gaze. "We will win," he said boldly, looking over the young children. There was more he wanted to say, but he was about to go and see Li'ara where they would be doing exactly what this family were doing: spending time together before the end.

As natural as it was now, Kalian's senses stretched out and encompassed the family. He could feel the nanocelium flowing through their blood and scurrying around inside their organs and over their muscles. They didn't know it yet, of course, but this family would be together forever, never knowing death, and only ever growing. They all would; all of humanity. That was a legacy he didn't mind leaving behind. He only wished he would be present to watch it all unfold.

Bending his knees, Kalian pushed off from the ground and let the surface fall away from him. With the speeds he was capable of, it only took a couple of seconds to clear the top of the city and reach the council building. He landed softly on one of the balconies and made his way inside the air conditioned halls. Li'ara's unique brain frequency was easy to find, pulsing through the universe like a beacon in the dark. He dipped his own mind into hers for the briefest of moments and found her talking to Captain Fey.

The door to her office opened and Kalian entered upon invitation. Captain Holt was also present, though he appeared to be on his way out with Commander Vale in tow.

"Kalian," he nodded on his way past.

"Jed," he replied. "Samantha."

Commander Vale offered him a genuine smile as they left the office, something Captain Holt struggled with.

Kalian waited for the door to shut before turning to Li'ara and Fey. "You don't have to be telepathic to know he's not happy with me."

Fey took her seat behind the hovering desk. "He still believes himself to be solely responsible for the hundred thousand people who were aboard the *Paladin*. Though he shares the load, his concerns are valid. There's a chance, and it's a big one, that the harvesting ship will come here and do to Evalan what it's done to every other planet it has come across."

Li'ara added, "He doesn't like us being used as bait."

Kalian frowned. "And he thinks I do?"

"No," Captain Fey interjected. "He's just concerned and frustrated. He feels as hopeless as the rest of us mere mortals and he needs someone to blame."

That pulled on a thread that Kalian had ignored for too long. "What if you weren't mere mortals?"

Both women looked at him quizzically. "What are you talking about?" Li'ara asked.

"I looked into the nanocelium found in your blood," he began. "It's in everyone now, not just those who have experienced rejuvenation. It came from the Gommarian. Every time anyone touched part of the ship, several thousand nanocelium rubbed off and infiltrated your body through the pores. Like a virus, it spread through the population and into those who came here on the *Paladin*."

Captain Fey stood up and looked worryingly at the back of her hand. "Will we end up like Professor Jones?"

"No," Kalian responded quickly. "This nanocelium came from ALF. Its programming is designed only to help humans. What it's actually doing is preventing your cells from decaying."

Li'ara held her hand to her mouth in shock. "Are you saying... are you saying we're..."

"Immortal," Kalian finished with a smile. "The older people among us will notice the differences first but, over time, it will become apparent that no one is dying anymore."

"Is it inside you?" Fey asked.

"No, it's not," Kalian said, looking down at himself. "My Terran abilities keep all foreign bodies out of my system subconsciously. One day, when the Terran genes begin to activate in the rest of the population, the nanocelium keeping you all alive will become redundant and be flushed away."

Kalian could see that Li'ara was trying desperately to keep her tears inside. They had fallen out in the past over the debate of how their relationship could ever work with their different lifespans. Now, she knew she could live forever with him...

"This is incredible!" Fey exclaimed. "I can't... I can't even imagine it. We'll *never* die?"

"There are a few obstacles before we get to that long road." Kalian sobered the news. "The Kellekt chief among them."

Captain Fey frowned. "The Kellekt?" she repeated, looking to Li'ara for answers. "What are you talking about?"

Kalian met Li'ara's eyes, recalling that she had cautioned him about telling anyone the truth of the Three and the origin of nanocelium. Still, Captain Fey, or Councillor Fey as she was now, deserved the truth after everything they had gone through.

"Perhaps you should sit down for this..." he began.

CHAPTER 28

Roland pushed down on the flight stick and took the *Rackham* into its second run across the Crucible's outer defences. Nanocelium ammunition ripped through the cannons bolted to the ground and fixed into the valley's walls. The Shay retaliated with missiles this time, which rocketed out of the launchers and twirled through the air. The bounty hunter banked the ship, dipping this way and that to allow the missiles to fly past and explode against the rock.

More nanocelium fire trailed across the ground until it found one of the launchers. The resulting blast expanded violently and destroyed the nearest cannon emplacement. A sudden knock to the *Rackham*'s back end jolted Roland forward on to his glass console, bringing him face to face with the alarm, warning him of damage to the stern.

"You don't say..." The bounty hunter positioned himself back in his chair and swung the *Rackham* around to face the Shay light craft that had lowered itself into the valley.

The light craft's thrusters flared and it launched forward, towards the *Rackham*. Roland's instinct was to squeeze the trigger and hope to destroy it before the suicidal Shay impacted the ship, but a new idea struck the bounty hunter in the moment and he went with it.

With only seconds to go before the head-on collision, Roland activated the *Rackham*'s AI intuitive controls. Able to assess and react in a fraction of the time it would take his human brain, the AI dipped the ship just enough to slip under the light craft, before bobbing back up. The tougher hull of nanocelium had no problem battering into the underbelly of the light craft, clipping its back end just enough to tear its thrusters to pieces.

The AI swung the ship around again as the light craft spun out of control and hurtled towards the Crucible below. The inevitable explosion upon impact took the installation's main doors with it, bringing a satisfied smile to Roland's face.

"Give me control back," he commanded.

Certain lights on his console came back to life as another missile warning flared. The bounty hunter rotated the ship and intercepted the rocket mid-flight with a salvo of nanocelium fire. Another well-placed shot took out the launcher and then the cannon beyond it. A quick scan reported back that the valley was clear of enemy targets, allowing the *Rackham* to land.

The ramp lowered on to the soaked ground and Roland looked out, searching through the rain for any sign of Shay troops. The fire from the wrecked light craft concealed most of the entrance to the Crucible, but the bounty hunter reckoned he would have been attacked by now if they were going on the offensive.

Leaving his hide coat behind, Roland strode out into the hammering rain with his Tri-Rollers already in his hands. His nanocelium blade rested comfortably on the back of his waist, tucked between fresh magazines and grenades. A strip of gravity bombs was wrapped around each of his biceps, a series of small spheres that would distort the enemies' sense of direction. He had chosen a simple but highly accurate assault rifle to rest over his myopallic armoured vest. It wasn't very showy, as he often preferred, but it would get the job done.

Roland marched across the valley, past the burning light craft, and into the shadowy tunnel of the Crucible. The last time he had assaulted the installation, Li'ara Ducarté and Sef had accompanied him. The Gomar's powers had dulled the entire experience and Li'ara's restraint had prevented him from torturing Kel-var Tionis, the Shay who had allied Protocorps with the Vanguard to instigate the current invasion. Now, it was just him and his enemies... and a shit load of guns and ammo.

Unlike last time, the Shay guarding the Crucible were feral and loud. The bounty hunter could hear them coming from two corridors away, giving him plenty of time to ready one of the strips of gravity bombs. Throwing them into the gloom of the dark tunnel, the tiny spheres shot out from the strap and stuck to every surface, creating a net of distorted gravity. Holstering his Tri-Rollers, Roland reached over his shoulder and pulled free the assault rifle.

They were coming closer, a horde of them for sure.

Roland crouched on one knee and levelled his rifle down the tunnel. A quick adjustment of the augments in his eyes gave the bounty hunter perfect night vision, making up for the long stretches of dark tunnel between the faint spotlights above.

The closer the Shay came, the more Roland began to reconsider his position. There had to be a lot of them judging by the sound. The bounty hunter gripped his rifle a little tighter and made certain the stock was comfortably nestled in his shoulder, reducing the recoil.

Then they stopped.

Roland straightened his head and waited, listening for any sound. There was nothing but an eerie silence. The rapid scrambling of cybernetic feet and hands had come to a halt before they could round the corner and face him. The bounty hunter waited another moment before biting his lip and rising to his feet. In order to see what was happening around the corner, he would have to deactivate the gravity bombs and walk through to the other side.

Every instinct told him to just turn around and find another route to the control room, and to do it fast. But there had to have been dozens of them around that corner; he had heard them. The bounty hunter deactivated the bombs, allowing him to walk through the net and cautiously make his way to the edge of the corner. With his back pressed to the wall, he stole a quick glance, which informed him that the corridor was empty. Two dead C-Sec officers lay strewn across the floor halfway down the corridor and the walls were covered in bloody hand and footprints. There were no Shay.

Without his hide coat, Roland had to look at the vambrace around his right forearm to see the schematics of the Crucible's tunnel network. The control room wasn't too far from his current position, but he was beginning to feel like a rat in a maze of the Shay's making. Where had they all gone?

The panels above his head groaned, freezing the bounty hunter in place. The metal groaned again, farther down the corridor, before the wall to his left sounded as if something was scratching it from the inside. He made a snap decision and bolted towards the next corridor.

Had he delayed his sprint by another second, the horde of wild Shay would have broken through the ceiling and the vents on the wall to ravage him. The tunnel was filled with the animalistic screams of the aliens and the clawing of their cybernetic limbs on metal. Roland ran as fast as he could, firing over his shoulder blindly in the hope of slowing them down.

He rounded the next corner and tripped over another dead C-Sec officer. The assault rifle flew out of his hands and scraped across the floor ahead of him. Years of training and even more years of working for Central Parliament kicked in, stopping his fears from getting in the way of his muscle memory. The bounty hunter turned his fall into a roll and came back up with both Tri-Rollers in his hands. The first cluster of Shay to round the same corner was met by a hail of Intrinium fire. Their bodies burst apart, knocking back those scrambling behind them, but it wasn't enough to stem the tide.

"Shit..." Roland spun around, holstered his Tri-Rollers, and dashed for his assault rifle, scooping it up on his escape.

Firing blindly over his shoulder again kept the closest from reaching him. He could hear their insides exploding against the walls and pouring on to the floor. As satisfying as that sound was, the vambrace on his forearm beeped, alerting him to his change in course. Roland cursed, aware now that he had just taken the wrong turn and was heading in the opposite direction to the control room.

"You're getting sloppy, old man!" he berated himself between squeezes of the trigger.

Doing his best to correct his course, Roland made the next right. He missed the blood on the floor, however, and skidded into the frame of a doorway instead. The break in his run gave the Shay the time they needed to catch up, leaving Roland with no other choice than to stand and fight. The assault rifle wasn't even lined up before he began unloading the magazine into their infected bodies. The nearest alien, crawling over the floor, was ripped in half down the middle, before the trail of gun fire ran up the wall and cut down two more.

"Come on!" Roland yelled, making himself angry to compensate for his approaching death.

One Shay made it past the barrel of his rifle and grabbed his trigger arm, jolting his aim. This allowed another to reach out and go for his neck, just as the first alien was sinking its teeth into his bicep. Roland shouted out in pain and thrust his boot into the Shay reaching for his throat. The alien was knocked back to receive a burst of Intrinium fire.

"Get off!" The bounty hunter released his grip on the rifle's barrel and yanked the Shay's head off his arm. He used the same bloody arm to plant an elbow in its face, pushing it back into its comrades.

More were on top of his position now, coming at him from more angles than he could cover. Sporadic bursts of Intrinium shot out, catching many of the aliens, but he now had three grabbing at his body and tugging at the rifle.

It was Roland's turn to cry out with a feral roar.

The bounty hunter shoved himself backwards with all his might, crushing the Shay attached to his back into the wall. He let go of the rifle and the alien tugging at it fell backwards, freeing Roland up to retrieve the nanocelium hilt on his waist. The wild creature sinking its cybernetic claws into his left arm went very still when the nanocelium blade extended from the hilt and buried itself in the top of its head. Still, the Shay on his back did everything it could to break free of his crushing weight.

"You want some too?" Roland twisted the blade around in his hand and drove the point over his shoulder and into the Shay's eye. As it went limp, the bounty hunter reached behind him and threw the Shay into the rest of the infected aliens.

There were only seven of them left now, though he could already see the dead putting themselves back together. Roland did what he did best and simply reacted. The nanocelium blade flew from his hand, spinning end over end, until it found rest in the head of one of the assaulting Shay. Before the alien hit the floor, both Tri-Rollers were in his hands and unleashing hell upon the remaining six. Nanocelium and organic matter alike splattered against the walls.

In the silence that followed, Roland slumped against the wall and caught his breath. He had only minutes, maybe less, before they put themselves back together and came at him again. Holstering his sidearms, the bounty hunter once again collected his rifle and made his way back the way he had come, retracing his steps until he was back on the correct path to the control room.

Roland tapped his earpiece. "How's it going out there, Len?" he asked quietly, sure that there were plenty more Shay inside the Crucible.

There was a brief delay before the Ch'kara got back to him. *I've made progress, but its slow going. This storm isn't helping...*

Roland examined the bites and scratches on his arms, noting the trickle of blood that flowed down his arms. "Well, I could do with you getting a move on. A little backup wouldn't go amiss right now."

"Haven't you reached the control room yet?" Ch'len asked. *I was really hoping you would just destroy the Crucible by yourself and we could get out of here.*

The bounty hunter ground his teeth in an effort to ignore the pain in his arms. "So was I, but this place is crawling with Shay and they've already taken a bite out of me, literally."

There was a tone of concern in Ch'len's voice. "Does that mean you'll become one of them?"

Roland was surprised he had enough energy to laugh to himself. "No, you idiot. I shouldn't have told you about zombies." He hit the command panel on the wall and entered another dimly lit corridor, smeared with blood, and filled with C-Sec bodies. "Alright, time to go back to work. Fix that damn Forge, Len." A tap of the earpiece prevented the little alien from replying.

A quick check of the miniature hologram projected from the side of the rifle, told Roland that he was close to an empty magazine. Judging by the pile of dead bodies, he decided to just reload now. The command panel at the other end of the small tunnel was sparking, its screen illegible. Thankfully, the doors were already open a few centimetres, allowing the bounty hunter to fit his hands through and prise them apart a little more. First, he pressed himself to each door and inspected what little he could see of the room beyond.

It looked to be the control room.

After another minute of waiting to see if anything moved inside the room, Roland slung his rifle over his back and pushed against the broken doors until his wounded arms bulged. Parting them was irritatingly loud as the metal scraped and the internal servomotors groaned. Once through to the other side, he levelled his rifle again and cleared the room before crouching and aiming back along the way he had come. It wouldn't be long before those he had dispatched found their feet and hunted him down.

Roland deployed his last strip of gravity bombs inside the short tunnel. The piled bodies were instantly pulled apart and pinned to the floor, walls, and ceiling. It wouldn't stop his enemies, but it might give him enough notice to turn and fight.

With his rifle resting against the nearest console, the bounty hunter began his examination of the Crucible's inner workings. Most of the glass and the holographic emitters were smudged with blood, forcing Roland to wipe away as much of it as possible before he could understand what he was looking at. The main screen beyond his console came to life with an image of three giant pyramids, each mirrored by identical pyramids above them. Between their points were balls of glowing white energy that fired off random bolts of lightning.

"What the hell are they?" he asked aloud.

If he had to guess, which was all he ever did, he would have to say the pyramids were of Terran design. Something about them wasn't very Conclave, which made sense since the designs for this installation were given to the founders of Protocorps by one of the cubes. The amount of energy being funnelled through the giant structures was phenomenal. The output was greater than anything Roland had ever seen, even that of a Starforge.

The hologram floating above the next console along presented him with an overlay of the entire planet and the network running under the surface, connecting multiple stations and arrays to the Crucible. It certainly took a lot of juice to turn a whole planet into one massive antenna.

"How do I switch this thing off?" Roland sifted through multiple menus searching for anything related to the control of the power levels. He tapped his earpiece. "Len?"

"*I'm a little busy here!*" the Ch'kara snapped back.

"I'm in the control room surrounded by consoles. Any idea how I might switch this thing off?"

"*Just think of the whole system as one big circuit,*" Ch'len explained. "*Don't bother looking for an off switch, just find one small, but crucial, piece of the system you can disrupt. But, be gentle!*" he warned. "*The amount of energy flowing through that facility is mind-blowing. If you deactivate something too suddenly it might set off a chain reaction that you can't outrun.*"

The bounty hunter rubbed his eyes. "I thought there would just be an off switch..."

"*Well, you could just do what you always do,*" Ch'len added.

Roland looked from the grenades on his belt to the image of the pyramids. "I don't think that comes under *gentle*, Len. Let's consider that Plan B. I still want to—"

Roland's words were caught in his throat when a blue crystal the size of his hand impacted the console beside his fingers. The bounty hunter instinctively dropped into a roll, narrowly avoiding four more blue crystals which trailed a line after him.

"*Roland?*" Ch'len's voice came over the comm.

Ignoring the questioning Ch'kara for the moment, Roland skidded across the floor, using the bank of consoles as cover from yet more crystals. His assault rifle was on the other side, too far to make a move for. The bounty hunter unholstered his Tri-Rollers, bringing them up to his face, and listened for his enemy. The distinct sound of cybernetic feet clinking against the hard floor told him the Shay was still outside the control room, on the other side of the short corridor from which he had entered.

"*Roland, what's going on?*"

"I've got some crazed lunatic trying to kill me with a goddamn Splicer," he hissed. "I thought we were supposed to be the ones who used illegal shit."

"*Is there a way out?*"

Roland peered around the console, eyeing the side door at the other end of the room. A blue crystal pierced the corner of the console, catching his eyebrow, as it continued on into the next bank of monitors. The bounty hunter grunted in pain and wiped the blood from his eye.

"Right." Roland gripped his Tri-Rollers a little tighter. "Let's skip to the good bit..."

CHAPTER 29

IN EVERY STORY Telarrek had ever heard, to die fighting sounded honourable, heroic, and courageous. Seeing the horde of wild Shay leap through the smoking doorway and hit the landing pad on all fours made the Novaarian wonder if all the stories had it wrong. These infected aliens would rip them all to pieces with their bare hands, no matter how many Intrinium rounds they emptied into their cybernetic bodies.

It would be a gruesome death.

The Atari honour guard was the first to open fire, the blue flashes of his rifle reflecting off every angle of his golden armour. Highly trained, the Atari took down most of the first wave, and the second honour guard dropped those who slipped through the gaps, but there was no end to the Shay. They screamed and snarled as they spread out across the platform, giving the shooters too many angles to cover.

"Help us!" One of the unarmed councillors bellowed.

Telarrek looked across and saw them cowering at the very edge of the platform. The Novaarian levelled his rifle and put holes in the heads of the Shay who were almost upon them. In truth, however, he thought it would have been a greater mercy to have killed the councillors and save them from the slaughter. He just couldn't do it.

Telarrek lowered the rifle to his hip and squeezed the trigger as he stepped in line with the honour guards. Between them, they put down countless Shay, but their infected kin simply crawled or leaped over them.

A warning flashed up on the hologram beside his rifle, alerting him to the depleting magazine. Telarrek knew he could kill at least ten more Shay, maybe eleven, before the rifle had to be used as a club. He wouldn't last very long after that.

As one, Telarrek and the honour guards backed up, heading closer to the terrified councillors at the very edge of the landing pad. The Tularon honour guard on the far side, next to the pink-skinned Atari, ran out of Intrinium rounds first. Without hesitation, the furry honour guard dropped his rifle and reached for the short-sword on his thigh. The blade was razor sharp and had no trouble slicing through the Shay, but it didn't have the reach of a rifle. One crazed alien shot out low and gripped the guard's ankle. In the blink of an eye he was on his back and under the horde, his screams of agony muffled under the Shay.

Telarrek stepped back again, firing the last of his own rifle. A strong swing caught the closest Shay in the face and sent it tumbling over the edge of the landing pad. How many more times could he do that before fatigue set in? How many times before he was simply overwhelmed?

This was it and he knew it.

He would die beside what was left of the Highclave and never see what became of the Conclave. He had to believe that they would win, that Naydaalan would make something out of the ashes and help Kalian build a better galaxy.

The offensive rumbling sound of large engines assaulted Telarrek's sensitive ears before a red gunship ascended above the edge of the landing pad. Before any of them could register the ship, the side panel slid open and a torrent of Intrinium fire erupted from the barrel of a high powered cannon. The Shay directly in front of the survivors were wiped out in an instant by the high calibre rounds, saving Telarrek only a moment before he was mobbed.

The Novaarian narrowed his vision to look beyond the flashes of blue, and discovered Uthor behind the cannon. Both of Telarrek's hearts skipped a beat when he saw his old friend mowing down their enemies. It didn't take long with a cannon like that to flatten the entire landing pad, leaving a platform of smoking dead Shay.

"Get on board!" The Raalak yelled as the gunship hovered closer to the edge.

Telarrek easily hopped the small gap and clasped his friend's arm. "Uthor! Your timing will go down in Conclave history as legendary, I am sure."

"As will your ability to survive, old friend!" Uthor shouted back over the engines.

The Shay on the landing pad were beginning to slither across the platform and put themselves back together.

"We need to reach the High Spire!" Telarrek urged. "There's a—"

"Backup control system," Uthor finished. "I know. I'm the one who had it installed." The Raalak turned to the cockpit door. "We need to get out of here! Head for the High Spire!"

The cockpit door parted in half and a female Raalak and two infants of the same species looked back at the survivors. Telarrek couldn't help but smile at the sight, recognising them as Uthor's family.

"As you command!" his wife called back before moving the gunship away from the landing pad.

"She was a Dart pilot when I met her," Uthor explained with a proud grin on his face.

"I remember," Telarrek replied, happy to see the landing pad shrinking in the distance, along with the entire command tower. "I believe you serviced the cleaning mechs at the time..."

"Indeed," Uthor said. "She couldn't resist my charm!"

The two friends shared a brief laugh before Telarrek noticed the councillors' shell-shocked expressions. They all had their own way of dealing with near-death experiences, but the Novaarian had to remind himself that these councillors had been ambassadors, not warriors. The Atari honour guard had fallen into the seat at the back of the gunship and had already begun his own ritual, one familiar to any soldier. The rifle in his hands was halfway stripped and under the scrutiny of the Atari.

"Thank you," Telarrek said to Uthor, loud enough for the councillors to hear. He hoped it would focus them for a moment. "You saved our lives back there. And you, honour guards. Your courage kept us all going."

The Atari nodded once as his rifle came back together. "Sir," he addressed Uthor. "Where did you find a gunship just lying around?"

It wasn't accusatory, Telarrek knew. He had been in situations similar to this before and could see that the warrior was trying to occupy his mind in the lull between action. It wasn't easy to adjust from the adrenaline-filled escape to sitting in a gunship, very much alive after believing you were moments from death.

"C-Sec was doing its damnedest to organise the Raalakian population," Uthor explained. "The pilot and gunner left the ship to help maintain order. That was when the Shay attacked. It was chaos after that. I gathered my family and headed for the Clave Command Tower, believing it to be the only safe place in the capital."

"You were wrong," one of the councillors blurted out.

"Well, I am just glad you arrived when you did," Telarrek added.

The gunship continued to descend down Clave Tower and they watched every level pass by. Fires burnt out businesses and homes, people ran over the bridges, desperately trying to flee the Shay, and smoke filled the lowest levels, concealing the usual pallet of lights. The High Spire occupied the very middle of Clave Tower and was one of the few places untouched. Used only by the Highclave when addressing the masses, the enormous stadium-like facility was empty, and therefore devoid of any Shay.

Telarrek craned his neck to see the crystal spire that rose up from the centre. They had been inside when they first met Savrick, after the Gomar attacked the capital for the first time. The Novaarian had already made one daring escape from the High Spire, though it was this incursion that had led to an upgrade in the automated security.

The gunship touched down on the extended landing pad and the group filed out with Uthor collecting his family. The Raalak also detached the cannon from the side of the gunship and carried it with him. Having reloaded his own rifle, Telarrek led the way beside the Atari honour guards and made for the main doors. The Novaarian had to offer just about every part of his body before the scanners were happy that he was a member of the new Highclave and opened the doors.

"Everyone needs to step inside the bio-scanner," Telarrek instructed inside the High Spire's foyer. "The automated defences won't target you as we descend into the control room."

One by one, the councillors, the honour guard, and Uthor's family stepped into the full body scanner. It was a slower process than Telarrek would have liked, but knowing what defences were hidden beneath square panels that were placed every fifteen metres along the ceiling, the Novaarian was happy to wait.

"Do you know the way?" the Atari asked Telarrek.

"I do," Uthor answered. "It's five levels down."

With Uthor's family and the councillors in the middle, Telarrek led the way beside the Raalak while the Atari brought up the rear. They rushed by the entrance to the grand hall, where thousands of seats overlooked the pitted court where the Highclave would sit. It was there that Kalian and Li'ara had once faced the entire Conclave, explaining their dire situation.

It was an odd thing to run through the silent empty corridors of the High Spire, but it was also comforting in a way. Telarrek had heard nothing but dying screams, gunfire, and explosions since the command tower had been overrun. He would take the eerie silence over that any day.

The Translift, hidden in plain sight as part of a wall, took them down into the control room. Telarrek took note of the square panel above them in the Translift, thankful again for the security measures; no one would reach them in the control room. The dark chamber beyond the opening doors came to life as the lights switched on, row by row. It wasn't as magnificent as the room in the Clave Command Tower and it offered them no views of the capital, entirely encased in reinforced myopallic walls.

The banks of consoles were illuminated by a plethora of holograms and menus. The far wall, curved with the circular room, was taken up by one massive hologram that displayed the same galactic map as the one in the command tower. The image was one of both hope and despair.

"Our enemy has moved," Uthor observed.

Telarrek had to agree, though the movement acted as a double-edged blade. The red dots of the enemy were crowded around Shandar as well as closing in on Evalan. It was a moment of reprieve for the other planets in the Conclave, who were mid-evacuation. Most planets were still under assault from any Shay who happened to have been on the surface at the time the Crucible was activated. Still, it was a form of offensive they could cope with, unlike an assault by the nanocelium-based ships.

"What is the location of our fleet?" one of the councillors asked.

Without any technicians or C-Sec officers to assist, Telarrek took the nearest seat and began inputting commands into the console. The main hologram changed to show them the location of every ship, both C-Sec and enemy. The C-Sec ships in Shandar's system were dropping out fast, leaving a sea of enemies to envelop the planet. The other half of the fleet were gathering on the outer edges of Evalan's system, awaiting orders to jump in and defend the humans while Kalian attacked the harvesting ship.

"Have they engaged Evalan yet?" another councillor asked.

Telarrek sat back in his seat when the data presented itself. "They have just arrived in orbit..."

"Well, send in the fleet," Uthor suggested.

Telarrek examined the map closely. "There are still a few of their ships yet to arrive. Kalian said we were to wait until they gathered in full—." The Novaarian's words were cut off by the alarm that flashed up on every screen and blared from the room's speakers.

"What is that?" the councillors asked between each other, clearly terrified.

The Atari honour guard silenced the alarm using the console in front of him. "Intruders," he stated. "The automated defences have been activated."

Uthor's wife pulled her children closer. "Nowhere is safe..."

With his large rocky hand raised to calm her, Uthor said, "We are safe in here, I promise. This room is reinforced all the way around. That door could only be opened by a Terran and the defence turrets will cut the Shay down."

Telarrek brought up the external camera feeds using a private channel on his console. The Shay were swarming the foyer of the High Spire just as they did the command tower. The infected species were cut down in great waves by the turrets dropping down from the square panels. For all the bodies and gore that decorated the white halls, Telarrek knew they would get back up again. How much time did they really have?

"What's that?" the Atari asked, pointing to another alert in the bottom corner of the holographic screen.

Telarrek slid his finger over the glass and removed the camera feed. The new alert was enlarged across his console, its message clear.

"The Shay have taken control of one of the Starforges..." The Novaarian was beginning to reconsider the level of intelligence the Shay retained.

"What are they doing with it?" Uthor asked.

Telarrek accessed the Forge's details and looked up the destination the Shay were inputting into the machine's controls. "They are opening a wormhole to Evalan!"

Uthor lurched over the console. "Can't you shut it down?"

Telarrek searched for everything he had access to regarding the operation of all the Forges in the capital. "The Starforges are new to our systems," the Novaarian replied frustrated. "I do not have remote access to any of them..."

The Atari honour guards removed his helmet. "If the Shay open a wormhole to Evalan, the humans won't be able to open a wormhole to the *Boundless*."

Telarrek felt his hope fading fast. "We will send in the fleet," he replied with determination, doing his best to combat his despair. "With any luck, our forces at Shandar will soon be free to join them at Evalan and add to our numbers."

"And the Shay will no longer pose a threat," Uthor added.

Telarrek could hear it in their voices, in their choice of words. Their hope was indeed fading, but it was also the only thing they had left, the only thing that bound them all together.

Telarrek gritted his teeth and held on to that hope with everything he had.

CHAPTER 30

It would have been better to sit with Captain Fey after such a revelation, to help her to process the origins of mankind and come to terms with humanity's immortality. Learning that your ancestors are the very creatures trying to wipe you out had come as something as a shock to Fey, but there was no time to go through it all again.

The Kellekt were here.

Kalian had heard it from ALF before the city's early warning system alerted them to the incoming ships.

"Get to your emergency vehicles and head for the Starforge," Kalian told the captain and Li'ara. From Fey's office, they could see the hundreds of hover vehicles darting towards the mountains.

"Kalian..." Li'ara gripped his arm as they followed the captain out of the office.

He turned to face her. "They won't get this planet. I promise."

"You have to come back," she blurted out. "If I really am going to live forever, I don't want it to be without you."

Somewhere between the truth and a lie, Kalian said, "No one else dies today. We'll both survive and we'll be together when this is all over. But I need to know that you're safe."

Li'ara nodded and blinked away her tears. Kalian could feel his own eyes welling up and he brought her in close to embrace. He kissed the top of her head and enjoyed the scent of her hair. They pulled apart and kissed with the passion of lovers who knew they might never see each other again.

He would see her again.

Li'ara cupped his face. "Don't let them touch this planet."

"*Kalian!*" ALF's voice was loud in his ear. "*You need to get up here now! The super subconducer is almost ready to juice you up.*"

"I have to go," he whispered to Li'ara. "Get as many people through that Forge as you can and make sure you reach the *Boundless* yourself."

They parted in opposite directions, holding on to each other until their fingertips finally separated. Kalian reached out with his mind and found Sef's unique brainwaves.

Keep her safe.

Sef's voice replied inside his mind. *I will die for her if I must.*

It would be logical to ensure that Sef survived over Li'ara, being the incredible asset he was, but the love Kalian had for her would always outweigh his rational thinking.

This will all be over soon, he promised the Gomar.

Making his way on to the roof of the building, Kalian looked out at the vehicles and people making for the Forge at the end of the main street. C-Sec tanks crawled to their designated positions and aimed their cannons high, ready for the invasion from above. The Gomar were like dark sentinels, floating effortlessly above New Genesis. Kalian could feel them scanning everything around them, allowing the universe to feed their minds with data.

He hoped they would be enough.

Kalian stepped off the edge and dropped one metre before reversing his direction and launching into the sky. The nanocelium in his exosuit expanded over his head and hands, ready for the extreme change in temperature. The higher he rose, the smaller New Genesis became, reminding him how easy it would be to obliterate from space. His plan had to work...

After launching through Evalan's many layers of atmosphere, Kalian turned his attention to the moon in the distance. Beyond it lay the *Boundless*, easily detected by the onboard wormhole connecting it to Evalan's surface. The portal acted as a beacon to his Terran senses, but so too did the humans who were just beginning to fill its hold. So far, he thought, everything was going as—

Kalian pushed his body to the side at the last second, narrowly avoiding the sleek black column of nanocelium that hurtled past. Three more followed its trajectory, but Kalian was more concerned with their contents. Each solid column appeared to be teeming with Shay! He could feel them all writhing around inside, desperate to claw and tear at anything.

"Kalian!" ALF called in his ear. "*You need to be ready. Leave them to the Gomar!*"

Kalian was torn; he could see the dark columns heading toward New Genesis, for Li'ara, but he also had the harvesting ship in his sights, which was impossible to miss. Larger than the moon, the Kellekt's main ship had transformed its tentacles into one solid spear point. If something that size made it any closer than the moon, Evalan's oceans would know about it. There wouldn't be much of a planet left to harvest if it impaled the surface either.

"*Kalian!*"

Before he could continue along his flight path and join up with ALF, half a dozen flashes flared among the stars. These flashes gave birth to six shining red battleships with C-Sec painted in thick white letters across their hulls. No sooner had they arrived in-system than they were launching every missile and opening up with every cannon they had. Intrinium in every ballistic form shot across space and pummelled the columns, knocking them off course.

Then another six battleships arrived, forming a barricade of ships between Evalan and the harvesting ship. Then five came into being farther out, followed by so many that Kalian stopped counting. Every Nebula- and Nova-Class battleship unleashed their payload upon the smaller enemy ships breaking away from the spear-shaped vessel.

Red traces of nanocelium rounds traded with blue flashes of Intrinium rounds as the space above Evalan turned into an epic battle for superiority. Kalian, almost undetectable by his size, weaved between the C-Sec ships in his effort to reach ALF, who had positioned himself off to the side of the battle.

More than once, he was forced to erect shields to protect himself from nanocelium rounds or even stray Intrinium bolts. Having been almost killed in a nanocelium storm before, he was more than aware of his need to keep their rounds at bay.

As the smaller nanocelium ships drew closer, Kalian could see they were still much larger than any of the C-Sec battleships. The farthest battleship from Evalan was the first to fall in the fight. The oncoming enemy ship burst apart, separating into a thousand smaller ships, before swarming the Nova-Class vessel and shredding its hull to pieces.

Kalian banked hard and changed his direction to avoid the swarm, only to get clipped by an Intrinium bolt. His nanocelium armour took the hit, but his course was altered by a couple of kilometres, putting him directly in another enemy ship's line of fire.

"You're not concentrating," ALF chimed in. *"Keep your shields up and change speed simultaneously."*

Kalian would have fired back a sharp retort if he wasn't staring down the barrels of a hundred nanocelium cannons. Coming to a sudden stop, he raised his hand and put all of his energy into the telekinetic barrier in front of him. The nanocelium rounds battered the invisible field and Kalian expanded it to encompass the Nebula-Class battleship coming up behind him. He could feel the ship loading its missiles into their tubes and their cannons heating up.

ALF's impatient tone came through his earpiece. *"Kalian..."*

"Shut.Up."

The full force of the enemy ship was bearing down on him and its sizzling red bolts of nanocelium were doing their best to take down his shield. He waited. A little longer... Another moment... Kalian dropped his shield and propelled himself upwards, relative to their positions. The Nebula-Class battleship let rip. Intrinium missiles and rounds tore through the centre of the tuning fork enemy ship, splitting it in half. Explosions rippled down its length until the gap was large enough for the Nebula-Class vessel to ram its way through to the other side.

Kalian's sense of accomplishment quickly dissipated as the torn enemy ship simply broke apart into smaller craft. The black ships arched around and assaulted the engines of the Nebula-Class vessel by flying directly into the red hull. The lights across the C-Sec vessel flickered along its length before the smaller craft burst forth from the ship's midsection, having wreaked havoc throughout the interior.

Once they had all returned to space, the smaller ships formed back together and became one massive ship again. Beyond that ship, Kalian could see a fleet's worth of nanocelium vessels breaking off from the harvesting ship and heading into battle.

"That's not how we win this, remember? The Conclave is just here to give the evacuation as much time as possible. They're also dying just to give you time..."

Kalian knew the AI was right, but so far he had abandoned Evalan, his people, and the woman he loved, and now and he was leaving the C-Sec fleet to burn. It didn't *feel* right.

"I'm on my way," he said.

Doing his best to ignore the battle, Kalian focused all of his power into telekinetic speed. Faster than any missile, he flew through space until the bronze hull of ALF's housing unit came into view. The Starforge opened one of its iris doors a moment before he reached it, allowing him to enter the station and maintain some of his speed.

As soon as the outer doors closed, Kalian deactivated his helmet and gloves. "Talk to me, ALF. What's happening planet-side?"

ALF's voice came over the speakers in the ceiling. *"Those drop ships you narrowly avoided have landed just outside New Genesis, though one of them was stopped by Sef. He threw it across the continent..."*

"What about the others?"

"They were filled with Shay," the AI replied. "They're attacking the city but the C-Sec ground forces are holding them back, though I suspect they would already be overrun without the Gomar."

Kalian sprinted down the corridors, often combining telekinetic flight with his running to navigate the sharp turns. When, at last, he made it to the bridge, ALF's lanky form was busy making the final adjustments to the super subconducer, which currently dominated the centre of the bridge.

"Have they completed the evacuation yet?"

"No," ALF said definitively. "But they will, Kalian. I need you to be ready for this, focused. When you make the connection with the Kellekt, you need to give just enough of yourself to start a cascade effect. No more. The nanocelium will do its best to absorb every shred of your DNA, including your very bones if it must. You'll be like a drug it can't get enough of."

Kalian was barely listening to the AI. He was already standing over a console and bringing up every scrap of data about the battle, as well as cycling through the Starforge's long-distance observation arrays. As expected, the space battle was going poorly for C-Sec. The harvesting ship was drawing closer every second.

"Why is it going so slowly?" he asked in frustration.

ALF looked up briefly from his work. "You pissed them off. They want you to see the end coming."

Kalian gritted his teeth. "They won't see their end coming..."

Switching to the link set up with New Genesis, Kalian cycled through the cameras posted around the city. There wasn't a single tank stood idle. Every street was under siege by wild Shay as they dug in and clawed their way to the centre, where there were still thousands of people being crammed through the Forge. The Gomar were doling out punishment in every quadrant of the city, their powers maximised.

A tower in the northern hemisphere suddenly collapsed and a black figure could be seen flying through the falling debris. Switching to another camera, Kalian could see that the fallen tower had provided a temporary barrier. The Shay swarmed over one another like ants building a bridge out of their bodies. It didn't take them long to climb over the rubble and begin their hunt for humanity again.

They were all running out of time.

Li'ara fired the last round from her handgun and threw the weapon away, reaching instead for the rifle strapped to her back. The Raiders stepped in and laid down fire while she changed weapons. Colonel Matthews crouched beside her and unloaded her magazine into the side street, directing the other members of her team to concentrate fire on the Shay scrambling up the walls.

Wearing the Raider's gear made everything easier, from targeting to assessing threats, but even her visor struggled to identify every target rushing down the street. Li'ara's eyes strained to keep up with the rising count of enemies.

"We need tanks to my location!" she shouted into her helmet.

"You don't need to shout," Lieutenant Riddick said beside her, though his voice was crystal clear inside her helmet.

A Raalakian voice came over the comm. *"Relocating is a negative. We've already lost three Walkers and been forced to pull back our air defence launchers."*

Colonel Matthews stood up and thumbed over her shoulder. "Retreat. The line is moving."

Li'ara backed up the street with the Raiders and glanced over her shoulder to see the human procession advancing down the main road. On the other side, one of the Walkers mirrored their retreat and moved into the main road, firing its cannon on the rushing Shay.

"Move up," Ava ordered. "Take the next street."

Li'ara continued to fire down the street as the team made their way around the corner. There was no end to the wave of Shay filling the alleys and streets, but at least they could slow them down. An echo of screams came out of the evacuation line and Li'ara turned to see a squad of C-Sec soldiers being overrun on the corner of a building. A Laronian in red armour was knocked off the side, left to wail as he fell to his death beside the procession.

The Shay soon killed the rest of the squad and lurched over the lip of the building, their sights set on the humans below. Li'ara levelled her weapon and let the visor in her helmet make the link with the rifle, showing her where the Intrinium rounds would impact.

One of the Gomar slammed into the rooftop like a falling meteor. Li'ara lowered her rifle and watched in awe as the black-clad powerhouse yanked the Shay away from the edge with telekinesis. The infected aliens were flung high into the air, away from the evacuation. A brilliant flash erupted from atop the building and a dark liquid splattered in every direction. The threat dealt with, the Gomar jumped into the air and took to the skies before hurtling back down again in a different location. Li'ara could see the plume of dust and smoke in the distance and was thankful she wasn't among the Shay.

A C-Sec voice blurted out, *"Incoming from the west!"*

Li'ara's visor pointed her in the right direction and she checked her ammunition before moving off. The Raiders covered every angle as they crossed the street, their weapons easily locating new targets all the time. The Shay were getting past the tanks thanks to their numbers, and were beginning to close in from all angles.

Li'ara did her best to monitor the targets scurrying out of the side streets, while simultaneously keeping an eye on the train of humans. Everyone was running now, terrified of the beings that were once considered among the most intelligent in the Conclave. It was chaos. Random people could be seen scooping up children who had become separated from their parents and others were simply falling over each other, slowing everything down.

A couple of knocks on her helmet snapped her attention back to Colonel Matthews.

"Keep your head in the game," Ava warned. "Find targets and drop 'em."

Li'ara nodded once and dashed to the corner of the nearest alley, seeing it as an easy point of attack from the Shay. The thunderous boom of a tank's cannon shook the ground and took a layer of dust off the alley walls. With her rifle levelled, Li'ara turned the corner with the Raiders spreading out behind her, running side-on for the adjacent corner. The tank Walker just fit inside the alley, forcing the Shay to crawl over it and investigate the circular port on top.

"Take 'em!" Ava ordered.

They opened fire on the Shay before the aliens could find a way of opening the hatch. The Walker continued to back up towards the team, firing its cannon and heavy machine guns as it did. Li'ara emptied her magazine of Intrinium and fell back to reload. How long could they keep this up?

Another warning came over the comm. *"Targets closing in from the east!"*

Li'ara turned to look over the heads of the evacuees and saw more Shay sprinting down the road. Her visor made a series of quick calculations and fed back the dire situation in a series of equations. There was no way she could make it to the end of the human train and lay down suppressing fire before the mob of aliens slammed into everyone...

She didn't have to.

Vox dropped out of the sky and hit the road with a telekinetic hammer, sending ripples along the gelcrete surface towards the infected mob. The buildings that lined the street were caught in the devastation as well and crumpled into the mess, crushing the Shay. The few who survived and renewed their assault were easily picked off by Vox, who moved with enviable speed. The Gomar tore off limbs without touching them and ended the attack by vaporising them with super-heated plasma.

The sound of metal being twisted and sparks flying pulled at Li'ara's attention, drawing her back to the alley. The Shay had completely overwhelmed the Walker and found their way inside.

Thankfully, Li'ara couldn't hear the dying screams of the soldier over the sound of her own gun.

"We need to pull back," Riddick stated, his voice impossibly calm.

"Agreed," Ava replied. "Grenades."

Lieutenants Wilson and Danvers were the last to retreat, pausing to lob a grenade each into the alley. Li'ara was around the corner and back on the main road with the others when the explosions rang out, blowing bits of Shay in every direction.

The Raiders fell in behind the procession. The Starforge was finally in sight at the end of the street, set into the small square of hedges and trees. Looking back, the Shay were seeing to the end of several Walkers, who just couldn't keep up with the numbers. The Gomar were nowhere to be seen, but Li'ara knew their absence was the only reason the Shay hadn't entirely overrun New Genesis already. She could only imagine the destruction they were causing on the edges of the city.

A quick turn of her head as they crossed another side street caused an alarm to flare across her HUD. Li'ara stopped and focused on the street in question. A family of four were at least sixty metres away, cut off by a fire in the middle of the street. They were clearly panicked, searching for a way to reach the Forge and avoid the Shay, who were already scrambling over the rooftops around them.

"Li'ara!" Ava called, still running behind the procession. "Stand still and you'll die out here. Let's go!"

"Negative," Li'ara replied, heading for the family. "I've got survivors at three o'clock. I'm bringing them back."

"Stay with the team, Li'ara. That's an order."

"Sorry, Colonel." Protected by her suit, Li'ara ran and jumped thought the line of fire, raising her rifle and taking two Shay down as she did.

"Get your ass back here, Li'ara," Ava said more forcefully.

"Get everyone through to the *Boundless*, Colonel. I'll be right behind you."

Li'ara killed the comm in her helmet and continued towards the cowering family. Her rifle went off in short bursts, dropping any Shay who dared to reveal themselves.

Husband and wife kept their son and daughter between them as they cautiously ran along the side of a building. Li'ara finally caught up with them as a cluster of Shay dropped down from above and snatched for the children. Her rifle flared with blue Intrinium rounds, each one cutting through the air and slamming into the aliens before they could touch the children.

"Run!" She shouted, ushering them forwards. She dropped a grenade into the cluster of downed Shay, hoping the explosion would slow down their reassembly.

More Shay crowded out of the street up ahead and Li'ara forced the family into a shop on their left before the aliens could catch sight of them. The grenade exploded farther down the road, making the whole family flinch.

"It's okay," Li'ara assured, removing her helmet to let them see her face and copper ringlets. "It's okay, we're going to get out of here. We just—" She stopped speaking as the new crowd of Shay spread out into the street, searching for human prey. Li'ara was sure to keep the family low and in the shadows inside the shop.

"We need to reach the Starforge," the father whispered.

Li'ara nodded. "And we will, all of us. We're going to head north, that way, and cut down Kenya Way, to the west. From there we can join back up with everyone and get aboard the *Boundless*."

The mother pulled her children closer and gestured to the Shay outside. "What about them? We can't run that fast."

"Stay behind me, stay alert, and do exactly as I say. I used to do this for a living. We're going to make it, understand? It's not far from —" Li'ara saw the shadow and turned to look out the shop window.

Another cylinder of towering nanocelium was falling from space.

The impact shook the ground and caused a wave of dust to blow over the city. When the dust cloud blew over, they could all see the

Shay pouring out of the walls of the tower like a waterfall. Hundreds more, if not thousands, were being emptied into New Genesis.

Two Gomar darted through the sky and tore through the side of it at great speed. A moment later, they both exited the other side and the top half tilted to the right before tearing free completely from its lower half. Another impact rocked the ground, but hopefully it squashed hundreds of the aliens.

"Okay, more are coming. We need to leave *now*. Ready?"

The couple shared a look but the father replied, "Yes. We'll follow you."

Li'ara turned to face the shop door, hiding her anxious expression. If there was a god listening, she prayed that they would tell Roland to get a move on and shut down the Crucible. Before it was too late...

CHAPTER 31

Roland hated running from a fight, but he knew there were exceptions for every case. Running away from an enemy who kept getting back up and firing crystallised Splicer ammunition at him felt like one of those exceptions.

The control room had been shot to shit between them, leaving Roland with no choice but to seek out another way of disabling the Crucible. The gloomy tunnels were still haunted by wild Shay, a fact that forced the bounty hunter to constantly alter his route, though his irregular course also helped him avoid the blue crystals that continued to impale the walls around him. This one particular Shay was really getting on Roland's bad side.

Ch'len's tone of despair wasn't helping either. "*I don't think this is going to work, Roland. Every time I find the problem and fix it, it's already cascaded and affected another system. This thing is fucked!*"

Roland barely had the breath to reply after so much running and fighting, but for Len, he would always find the extra energy. "Just get on with it, dipshit. The way things are going down here, we're gonna need reinforcements."

"*Have you found those pyramid things yet?*"

Roland slumped against a wall to catch his breath. He glanced around the next corner to see a couple of Shay walking across the intersection. The bounty hunter wiped the sweat from his brow and pulled free his Tri-Rollers.

"I'm working on it, Len. Get the Forge up and running."

Hearing his Splicer-wielding pursuer coming down the corridor behind him, Roland knew he had to advance or engage. He chose both. The bounty hunter rounded the corner, brought his guns to bear, and let rip into the two unsuspecting Shay. He ran and fired, putting every round into the Shay barring his way. They jerked and danced this way and that, but both were lying still on the floor by the time he ran over them.

He wasn't quick enough.

Before Roland could take the next tunnel, a blue crystal struck the back of his armour and burrowed into his shoulder. It was the first time anything had punctured his myopallic vest and drawn blood, and the force of the impact threw the bounty hunter forward. He slid down the wrong tunnel, firing his Tri-Rollers back the way he had come. More crystals hit the floor around him, but the Intrinium rounds from his own guns forced the Shay to duck into an alcove.

"Son of a bitch..." Roland quickly picked himself up and took cover around the next corridor.

The crystal in his shoulder was at an awkward angle, preventing him from pulling it free. Frustrated and pissed off, the bounty hunter fired blindly down the tunnel, hoping to give himself some more time. With his free hand, he removed the nanocelium blade from his waist and swiped it over the crystal, taking most of its length off. He was still left with a chunk in his shoulder, but at least it wouldn't get in the way now.

"You're one persistent asshole!" Roland yelled, firing another salvo of Intrinium rounds. He looked down the corridor he had been forced to take cover in and consulted his map. "Shit!" he hissed. He was being pushed farther and farther from the pyramids juicing the Crucible.

Three more crystals reduced the corner wall beside his head to rubble. He cursed again and made his way down the new corridor, more than aware of the pain that was beginning to make itself known in his shoulder.

"*Roland...*"

The bounty hunter sighed at the thought of Ch'len's voice being the last thing he heard before this Shay put him down for good. "I'm a little busy, Len. I thought we were done with the talking thing."

"*I'm receiving reports through the Forge's comm system.*"

"You're supposed to be fixing it, not watching the data streams."

"*Evalan is under attack.*"

Roland rounded another corner before the next crystal could take off his head. "Dammit, Len, you're not telling me anything we didn't already know! This is all part of the plan, remember?"

"*The fleet's not doing so well, but they've dropped Shay on to the surface. They're all over New Genesis...*"

That sobered Roland. "Have they evacuated to the *Boundless*?"

"*Not all of them, but Roland... there are many of them, the Shay that is. Even the Gomar can't keep them all at bay.*"

Roland gritted his teeth seeing his options shrinking dramatically. Pushed farther away from the Crucible's energy source, he knew it would take another thirty-four minutes to reach. How much more devastation could the Shay and their nanocelium overlords cause in that time? Then there was the issue of what he would do when he finally found the pyramids. Could he destroy them? It was more likely that this Splicer-wielding alien would put a crystal in his back before he figured out how to blow it all to hell.

"Okay, Len..." Roland took a breath. "New plan."

"*If it's getting off this planet, I'm all for it!*"

Roland calculated the quickest route back to the *Rackham*. "Keep tryin' to fix the Forge, Len. It's the only way either of us is getting off this planet."

With his Tri-Rollers in hand, the bounty hunter swung around the corner and dashed across the T-junction while firing at the Splicer. Crystals exchanged with Intrinium rounds and tore the walls, ceiling, and floor to pieces. Roland dived to get across the gap as fast as possible, but he still took a crystal to the leg.

He roared in pain. "Son of a..." His last word was lost in a groan as the injured leg took his weight again. He was down to his last plan now. It had to work.

The new limp was highly irritating, not only because he needed to reach the *Rackham* as soon as possible, but also because this Shay refused to leave him alone. Roland dropped timed grenades, mines, and poured round after round into the tunnels behind him, yet, still, the Splicer nearly killed him at every turn. The bounty hunter rounded the next corner and caught the crystal poking out of his thigh on the wall.

He swore, yelled, and hit the floor.

"Come on, soldier..." he spat. "Get up!"

The Splicer was coming, its metallic feet clicking against the cold floor. Lying on his back, Roland could see the inlet carved into the ceiling allowing a multitude of pipes to run through the installation. Hiding had never been his preferred choice, but it was also a skill he had taken on during his training years back on Earth.

He had only moments to jump up and hoist his weight horizontally to become one with the length of pipes, but he also had a leg that refused to stop bleeding. Using his good leg, the bounty hunter jumped up and, with strong arms, he gripped the pipes and pulled himself up. It took everything he had to lift his injured leg and wrap it around the pipes. It hurt like hell and he had to focus in order to keep his agony silent.

The Shay entered the tunnel. The Splicer rifle was held at hip height, ready to spray the width of the corridor with deadly crystals. The alien's body, which had once been a surgical combination of pale white skin and shiny cybernetic augments, was now writhing with nanocelium. The nanites had pierced the flesh and connected to the augments from head to toe. There was also a lot of biological damage from the Intrinium rounds Roland had slugged it with, not to mention the grenades that had littered its body with shrapnel.

The bounty hunter remained very still as the alien walked underneath him. He was also very aware of the blood dripping from his injured leg. Roland could see the red liquid pooling in the creases of his trousers. A rogue drop ran down the seam and threatened to fall on to the Shay's bald head. He waited anxiously, wondering why the Shay had yet to move on. He needed the alien to move, *now*.

The drop of blood fell free from his trouser leg as the Shay took its first step. The sound of its metallic feet on the floor masked the splash of the droplet that fell behind him.

Roland held on to his sigh of relief and waited until the Shay had made another turn and exited the tunnel. As quietly as he could, the bounty hunter dropped back down and placed his head against the wall as the pain came rushing back. He slid down until he was sitting on the floor where he could better inspect the crystal protruding from his thigh.

With one hand, he patted down his belt searching for the portable med-kit. He had nothing that could fix the wound, but he did have some med-foam that would fill up the hole in his leg. Of course, he had to remove the crystal first...

Roland removed an empty pouch from his belt and placed the rough leather between his teeth. He would need to internalise all the pain to avoid yelling out and bringing back the Shay. Holding the med-foam ready in one hand, Roland delicately closed his other fingers around the crystal. He counted to three in his head and yanked the crystal clear of his leg.

He couldn't close his eyes any tighter and he couldn't tense his muscles any more than he already had. The blood running down his leg, however, brought his attention to the next problem. Biting down as hard as he could on the empty pouch, Roland laced the med-foam capsule into the wound, where it quickly expanded, filling the jagged gash, and hardening to seal it up.

The bounty hunter breathed for what felt like the first time since he had ascended the pipes. Sweat dripped down his face and arms, running into the small cuts he had accumulated in his brief fight in the control room. Still, none of them stung like the wound in his thigh.

Limping was easier without the crystal in his leg, but the Shay was still inside the tunnels somewhere, hunting him. The sound of the infected hordes could be heard echoing down almost every corridor as he approached the smoking exit. His escape had been slowed by the need to check every corner before moving on; if any Shay caught sight of him, he wouldn't make it back to the *Rackham* before they chased him down.

Even the dark storm clouds of Shandar were bright in comparison to the tunnels of the Crucible. Roland waited by the smoking ruin that had been the main doors and scanned the area between the *Rackham* and himself. He hadn't seen the Splicer-wielding Shay for some time, but the flat land of debris in front of him appeared to be clear of targets.

He limped into the hammering rain and around the fallen enemy craft. The *Rackham* was a sight for sore eyes. The ramp was still extended, inviting him into the warmth and comfort of his home. The journey across the flat ground was tense, sure that he was of his hunter's indomitable will. Hitting the command to raise the ramp was a moment of relief, but he didn't stop to watch it fit back into place; he needed to reach the bridge.

"Len, give me an update."

The Ch'kara sounded exhausted. "I... I think it's over, Roland."

The bounty hunter entered the bridge, dripping rainwater everywhere, and happily fell into his captain's chair. "What are you talking about?"

"*I can get the wormhole to open, but only one way...*"

Forgoing the preflight checks, Roland had the Rackham taking off vertically within seconds. "Let me guess," he said, "we can go through the Forge, but no one from the *Brightstar* can come down here."

"Exactly. *The binary axle is broken, which has screwed with the navigational boards. I don't have the parts I need to fix the axle. I hate to say it, but the only option is for us to go through back to the*

Brightstar, *pick up the parts we need, then fly back down here and replace it.*" The Ch'kara paused. "*I sure as shit don't want to do that.*"

Roland tried to ignore the pain in his leg and set the course he needed. "I might have another option," he said.

There was an edge of hope in Ch'len's voice. "*Have you found the generators? Please tell me you're about to blow that whole place to hell and we can go through the Starforge.*"

"Not exactly..." Roland brought up the *Rackham*'s menu for weapon systems.

"*I don't like the way you said that,*" Ch'len replied, now with an edge of fear in his voice.

"You've got eighteen minutes to get that Forge working, Len. If the wormhole isn't open by then... we're both dead." Roland hit the command that readied the missile tube in the *Rackham*'s underbelly.

"*What?*" Ch'len replied frantically. "*What the hell are you doing?*"

"Oh you know, just blowing up the planet."

There was another pause on Ch'len's end as the little alien put his plan together. "*You can't be serious, Roland? You can't launch a Planet Killer! It might work against a ship, but the* Rackham *doesn't have the launch capabilities to pierce Shandar's crust! What happened to blowing up the generators?*"

Roland instructed the ship's AI to prepare the Planet Killer for deployment. "Everyone's running out of time, Len, and they're all counting on us to shut down the Crucible. This is the only way."

"*Everyone's counting on C-Sec you stupid ape! They were going to send down a team to do that! We're just supposed to be the ones who activate the Starforge!*"

"That's still the objective, Len. Only now, if you don't get it working in the next... seventeen minutes, we're both going to die on this rock." Roland looked out of the viewport to see Ch'len and the Forge below before the *Rackham* shot by, leaving them behind.

The Ch'kara sounded distracted. "*That's... I don't know if I can get it working in that time.*"

Roland looked down at the console, where the countdown was ticking away. "What do you mean, Len? I thought you just said we could go through to the *Brightstar*, not the other way around."

"Well, yes," Ch'len replied, frustrated. "*From what I'm looking at, I can see that's the case, but I haven't actually opened a wormhole yet. I've still got three circuit boards to repair and a Nalaxian crystal that needs realigning.*"

Roland replied as slowly as he could. "Len, I plan on flying back at maximum speed. If that wormhole isn't open I'm just going to fly through an empty hole. Then we're both dead. Or I might just fly up and take my chances against an exploding planet. Either way, there isn't going to be time to stop for you. So. Fix. The. Damn. Forge."

"*I'm already working on it as your stupid lips jabber on!*" Ch'len fired back. "*How are you going to launch the Planet Killer without the power of a battlecruiser, genius?*"

Roland checked out the data from the navigational array. "The *Marillion* made a hell of a bang when she crashed. The impact has opened up a web of fissures in the ground. The *Rackham*'s found one thirty kilometres deep. I just need to launch it into there and get my ass back to you as quickly as possible."

"*That fissure's got to be a mess, Roland,*" Ch'len pointed out. "*Getting back out of it could take some time.*"

"I'm not going inside of it," Roland explained. "I'm just going to shove the Planet Killer down its neck."

"*This is nuts...*"

The bounty hunter couldn't ignore the pain in his leg any longer. He had time to find some pain killers while the Rackham's AI took over monitoring the flight path. Getting out of his chair wasn't easy, but he made it to the door at the back of the bridge.

"Just get it done, Len."

Roland hit the door command and it opened to the sight of a Splicer X1 levelled at his face.

"Oh, shit..."

CHAPTER 32

KALIAN LOOKED up from the console to the flaring lights beyond the massive viewport. The space battle was very different from this distance compared to how it looked through the external monitors of the battlecruisers. It could almost be called beautiful from the Starforge's position. The console, on the other hand, showed a chaotic and bloody battle that claimed hundreds of lives a minute.

"It's almost ready," ALF called from the centre of the bridge.

Kalian tore his eyes from the viewport and followed the AI as he moved about the super subconducer. Broad at the top and very narrow at the base, it appeared ALF was working on an upside down spire. The tubes protruding from his back lifted him up and down, left and right, while various tools extended from within his body. Kalian looked at the backboard and armrests attached to the floor beneath the machine. That's where he would stand. That's where he would change everything.

"Why is it taking so long?" he asked impatiently, his thoughts wandering to the streets of Evalan.

"I need to make sure you get the right dosages of everything," ALF explained. "Your entire system will need a boost, or you won't be able to jump back out of there on your own."

Kalian sighed. "I should be out there." He turned back to the viewport. "Or at least in New Genesis."

"No distractions," ALF said in a flat tone. "You shouldn't even be talking right now. Meditate, Kalian. You need to be strong enough to make the jump inside, survive the bonding process, and jump back out. I don't want you expending energy anywhere else."

Kalian knew that wasn't exactly the plan as he intended to execute it, but it was pretty close. He attempted to take one last look at the images from the New Genesis feed, hoping to see the last of humanity boarding the *Boundless* via the Forge. The holograms winked out, and the console went dark before he could see anything.

"Meditate," ALF repeated.

Kalian rolled his eyes and gave himself a telekinetic boost to make the jump up to the first tier above them. He hopped over the rail and sat down, cross-legged, facing the viewport. He didn't want to do this, even more so since ALF kept suggesting it, but he knew the benefits of connecting with the universe on a particle level. Submerging into the cosmic soup before attempting teleportation would streamline the process for his mind, reminding him that distance was relative when one could walk between realities.

His Terran mind expanded forth from its physical confines and spread out to fill the Starforge, mapping its every nook and cranny. No bolt, wire, or electrical signal could hide from him. The entire station sounded to him like an anthill, with trillions upon trillions of nanites crawling around at once.

As an intelligent being, ALF's brainwaves emitted a frequency into the void that precious few technologies could ever detect. Kalian focused his mind and pulled the universe into himself, reducing the Starforge to a dot by his perception. The stars closed in, filling his head with solar waves and a hundred types of radiation that blasted across space.

The battle above Evalan felt as if he were standing over a child's toy model set. The ships moved far slower than they usually did, enabling him to see every Intrinium and nanocelium round firing through the blackness of space. A variety of ships were in the midst of exploding and bodies were being sucked out into the vacuum, their hands helplessly clawing at their vessels.

The harvesting ship loomed ominously at the back of the nanocelium armada, edging ever closer to Evalan. Kalian examined the surface of the arrowhead ship, taking in every nanite that comprised its body. The number was so high that his mind converted it into an equation.

The rest of the universe called to Kalian, its song beckoning him to explore everything and forget his current concerns. It was tempting. He could tell the universe had so much more to show him, so many strange and wonderful things that had yet to be even heard of or seen by intelligent life. The harvesting ship, however, remained prominent in his mind, its purpose weighing heavily on him.

Kalian let some of the universe go, expanding the harvesting ship to allow him to enter its interior. He swam through the many layers of nanocelium until he passed through a series of chambers, each housing the most peculiar artefacts. It was a museum by his understanding, a room the size of a city that contained beings, gems and even plant life from around the universe. Kalian wanted to stay in the museum and explore what remained of the worlds already consumed by the Kellekt, but his mind could feel the unique signature of three distinct brainwaves.

He let the universe go some more, and the museum passed from his perception as he dropped farther into the gigantic ship. The next chamber was smaller, more intimate. Kalian's mind immediately detected the three bodies decorating the wall, concealed within glass-fronted pods. They were human, or at least natives to the original Evalan.

As interesting as they were, his mind was distracted by the pulsing of a triad of brainwaves in the centre of the chamber. The Three were standing around a dais of holograms, all plugged into the central console by a web of nanocelium tubes.

They were grotesque.

One was similar to a giant bug, with horrific mandibles and terrible scars. Another was simply a car-sized slug with nanocelium veins. The third stood upright with two arms and legs, but Kalian didn't recognise the species it had chosen for its host body.

Their intelligent brains pulsed outwards, visible to Kalian as golden waves that formed glowing orbs of light. He couldn't help himself. With an astral finger, he dipped his own consciousness into the bipedal Kellekt. Although jarring, this wasn't a new experience to Kalian, who had performed this very feat before inside Li'ara's mind, and it was a close variation on the form of communication he shared with Sef, but this creature wasn't quite the same anymore. Its brainwaves were part alien and part human, and it was old, ancient in fact.

There were whole sections of the alien mind that rejected the intrusion, but the human parts felt like infinite-archives of data. There were so many memories he couldn't filter them all, or keep them back for that matter. Flashes of the Kellekt dominated Kalian's astral view, filling his head with images of worlds long consumed and forgotten by the rest of the universe. He wanted to dip farther and explore the memories at the bottom, hoping to glimpse something of the original Evalan, before the creation of nanocelium.

The Kellekt's conscious mind flared like a beacon, drawing him in like a moth to a flame. Kalian could see the barrier between him and the biped's active mind, where its thoughts and feelings lived. If he pushed through to that place... could he communicate with them?

The curious nature that would forever live inside all humans, be they Terran, Gomar, or from Evalan, pushed Kalian to investigate further. He probed the light and felt his own consciousness being absorbed by the Kellekt. It was a struggle to maintain some semblance of control and remind himself of who he was. Swimming into the storm, he could feel thousands of eyes on him.

This is most impressive, came a voice from the shadows.

"Wait until you see what I do next," Kalian replied.

The Heretic has made great strides in altering our original DNA, the Kellekt continued. *But no level of evolution will surpass our own. You will be harvested and added to our collection like everything else before you.*

"You're attacking your own descendants!" Kalian argued. "We've all come from the same place."

I was born on Evalan during a time in which the universe could be called young. You and the rest of the Heretic's experiments were born on a variety of planets in a different galaxy, eons after my time. There is no connection between us, Kalian Gaines.

"So you're the evolved ones?" Kalian asked sarcastically. "The ones who trample over the universe, destroying anything that is deemed less intelligent."

The universe is a well of knowledge very few are worthy of. We have fought off others over the countless millennia who would collect it all for themselves. We always emerged the victor. We will consume everything this universe has to offer.

"Then what?" Kalian asked the storm around him. "You'll preside over an empty universe like gods?"

When this universe has yielded all of its secrets... we will simply move on to the next.

That wasn't even a concept Kalian had given any thought to. The Kellekt were so powerful and intelligent that it was only a matter of time before they figured out how to navigate the multiverse. How many universes, how many civilisations and families would be consumed by their hunger before someone finally stopped them?

If they could be stopped. Kalian would soon learn the outcome of his own plan.

We are surprised by your presence here, the voice said. *You have always displayed a sacrificial nature when it came to your mate, yet now you leave her to die.*

That grabbed every scrap of Kalian's attention. He released his hold on the universe and reality snapped back in an instant. Back in his physical body, his eyes opened to ALF's gloomy bridge where he could see Evalan beyond. Without a care, Kalian launched himself forward into flight, damaging the railing and the walkway before he punched through the glass viewport.

ALF screamed something in alarm, but Kalian missed his exact words, noting only that the AI remained safe thanks to his nanocelium tethers. The Forge erected a small force field to fix the jagged breach in the viewport and maintain the pressure inside the bridge.

By the time ALF was stabilised in his harness, Kalian was already halfway back to New Genesis. Evalan swelled in front of him until he could see nothing but cloud cover.

He was coming in fast.

Li'ara was left with no choice but to usher the family into the main street now. The Starforge was so close, but they could only access it if they left the narrow alleys and the safety of the buildings.

She ran out first, firing her rifle at the Shay who were only around the corner. Blood splattered across her suit and face as her trigger finger maintained its pressure.

"Come on!" she called.

The family followed her out and she caught sight of more Shay coming up the alley behind them. Li'ara hung back and threw her last grenade into the narrow space before running to catch up with the family. The explosion sent limbs and debris into the road, bombarding the Shay already sprinting towards them.

"Keep running!" Li'ara ordered.

There were no more Walkers in sight and the Gomar were busy taking down the towers surrounding the city. The Starforge, however, was in front of them and the last few of their population were running through. Captain Fey remained by the side of the machine, gesturing for them all to get through. She saw Li'ara and the family and waved for them to run faster.

Li'ara glanced over her shoulder and saw the horde had tripled in size. The infected aliens were gnashing their cybernetic teeth and clawing at the ground to get at them. She fired her rifle over her shoulder, putting round upon round into the masses with little need to aim. The family had made it into the gardens now and were only metres away from the wormhole, but pausing to fire over her shoulder had slowed down Li'ara.

The horde was right behind her now.

The gardens were so close, but she couldn't hear the wormhole over the screeching, an unnatural sound for any Shay. They were like animals who had found their first scrap of food for months.

Then she saw them...

A group of four Shay who had found a way into the northern quadrant and were entering the gardens from the east. All four of them were holding C-Sec rifles. Li'ara could see the aliens taking aim at Captain Fey and the family, who were unaware of the danger they were in. She had a choice to make, a decision that only took her half a second to make. Rather than keep running and firing roughly in their direction, Li'ara stopped, levelled her rifle, and squeezed the trigger four times. Every shot blasted one of the Shay each, knocking them down or injuring them and stealing their attention.

Li'ara had just enough time to turn back and see the horrific fate that awaited her. The horde of Shay were so close that the nearest were already leaping through the air to take her down. She had heard many times that people saw their lives flash before their eyes in the moment of their death. That didn't happen. As it was, there wasn't any part of Li'ara Ducarté that was willing to accept death was imminent. Instead of showing her glimpses of the past, her mind unleashed a feral state that would see her fight tooth and nail to the very end.

Kalian was moving so fast now that any sound he made was left far behind. He approached New Genesis from the north, flying low to bring himself between the buildings and directly into the main street. The Starforge and last remaining survivors were running through the wormhole in slow motion, but his immediate attention was on Li'ara, who was just outside the edge of the gardens and seconds away from being mobbed by wild Shay.

Gritting his teeth, Kalian touched down on the gelcrete with the force of a god. He focused his power in one direction, slamming the horde of Shay with a wave of hardened air that threw them all backwards. Before any of their infected bodies could touch the ground, half a dozen of the Gomar landed amidst the horde and added their own power to the bombardment.

It was the sound of a single Intrinium round that made Kalian freeze.

He whipped his head around and felt his whole world slipping out from under him. Li'ara's face slowly lost all expression as she crumpled to the ground, blood spreading across her chest. Beyond her in the gardens, a lone Shay stood with a levelled rifle and a smoking barrel.

Kalian reached out for Li'ara with one hand while the other gestured towards the lone Shay. As he caught her limp body, his free hand formed a tight fist and the Shay's body burst apart, rifle and all.

"Li'ara!" Kalian fell into a crouch and held her in his arms. "Li'ara…"

His Terran mind soon found the damage inside her body. The Intrinium round had found a gap in her armoured plates and blasted part of her ribcage, taking a chunk of her heart with it.

She wasn't moving.

"Li'ara!" Kalian had seen the expression of a dead person far too many times, but his brain couldn't reconcile what he knew with what he was seeing.

Her green eyes were looking back at him, but there was no life behind them. Her unique brainwaves were nowhere to be found, offering him no way of getting inside of her. She was gone. Li'ara was gone...

The sound of the crazed Shay rang in his ears as they challenged the Gomar behind him. Kalian could only hold Li'ara close, his emotions stuck somewhere between despair and rage. Their screeches assaulted his ears and the sounds of the Gomar unleashing their newfound Terran abilities washed over the city.

"No, no, no, no..." Kalian couldn't accept it. She just couldn't be dead.

He wouldn't allow it.

With one hand under her head, he placed the other over her broken chest and roared with all the rage that fought to explode from within him. The universe could do nothing but bow to his demands as he reached out into the cosmic soup and pulled everything in. Kalian could feel every particle of organic life that surrounded him. He could feel the temperamental balance of life; the transfer of energy that saw things grow and wither.

He took it. He took it all.

Kalian barely registered that every Shay in the city had come to a stop, their bodies shaking, vibrating almost. The Gomar halted their attack and watched this new spectacle.

It took a greater level of concentration to pick out the Gomar and the remaining humans, but Kalian managed to filter them out from the Shay and the plant life. With a firm hold on both, he used himself as the converter that took their energy and gave it to Li'ara. The process was slow and agonising for the aliens, but they eventually began to disintegrate, their bodies reduced to ash in the breeze. All plant life withered and shrivelled into almost nothing, leaving the gardens around the Forge barren and black.

Still, he roared.

Kalian gave it all to Li'ara as he rebuilt her ribs and heart, careful to realign all the blood vessels. Once they were repaired, he had the energy course through every particle of her being. Behind him, the cybernetic augments that made up almost half of every Shay began to drop to the ground, bereft of their organic counterparts.

So many lives were coming to an end, and Kalian could feel every one of them winking out of existence; their pale flesh flaking off and blowing away, their life-force his now.

He didn't stop pouring it into Li'ara until her eyes snapped open and she gasped a deep breath. Kalian pulled her in and embraced her with everything he had to give.

"Kalian..." she whispered.

He pulled back and tore his gaze from her emerald eyes to see what she was looking at behind him. The Gomar were standing in the middle of the main road surrounded by hundreds of cybernetic limbs and internal enhancements. It was a graveyard of parts.

"What did you do?" Li'ara asked, feeling her chest.

"I couldn't let you go," Kalian replied softly, overjoyed to hear her speak again.

Vox walked over and collapsed her helmet into her exosuit. "What did you do here, Kalian? I've never..."

Kalian helped Li'ara to stand up, noticing the ravaged gardens for the first time. The city was quiet now, the nanocelium towers emptied of their vicious occupants. This was a conversion of energy he hadn't even known he was capable of.

"All life is energy," he explained to a bewildered-looking Li'ara. "I just tipped the balance. I wasn't going to lose you again."

Kalian pulled her in and brought their heads together. He just needed to be close, to smell her, to see her pupils reacting, and to feel her breath on his skin. She was wholly alive again and he would never let her go.

"Thank you," she whispered, still in shock it seemed.

Captain Fey's voice came from the edge of the gardens. "This is... new. Is everyone okay?"

Li'ara stepped back from Kalian and glanced over her body. "We are now."

Fey looked at Kalian. "Are you sweating?" she asked in disbelief. "I don't think I've ever seen you sweat."

Kalian wiped his brow with the back of his hand. "It's a day of firsts, Captain."

"Kalian..." ALF's voice sounded in his ear. *"The fleet is retreating closer to Evalan up here. The harvesting ship is pushing them back. You don't have long before it hits the planet..."*

Kalian looked up at the sky, where the faintest of lights could be seen beyond the blue. He still had a job to do.

"I have to go." He tried to step away from the group but Li'ara squeezed his hand. "I know," he said to her. "The fight isn't over, not yet. All of you need to get aboard the *Boundless*. Wait on the edge of the system. This should all be over soon."

Li'ara turned her back on the group and faced him directly. "You once stepped across the entire galaxy in a single jump. You did it because you found me. Look for me again and take that step. Find me, Kalian, and get out of that damn ship before it kills you. Do you hear me?"

Kalian mustered a small smile, though, in truth, he had just been happy to have Li'ara talk at him again. "Yes, ma'am. I'll see you soon." They embraced for one last kiss before he stepped away.

He glanced over them all before he launched into the sky, his gaze lingering a second longer over Li'ara.

Kalian. Sef's voice sounded clearly in his mind as he ascended. *I failed you. If it were not for you, Li'ara would still be dead. I will accept whatever punishment you—*

No punishment, Sef. Just keep her safe, keep them all safe.

Kalian shut down the communication as he pulled away from Evalan's uppermost atmosphere. Inside his helmet he was still sweating, though he refused to admit that he was a little out of breath. Bringing Li'ara back to life was very different to regrowing part of her leg.

"Are we going to talk about what just happened?" ALF asked in his ear.

"I did what I had to, ALF. Nothing else."

"*I'm talking about your reckless exit from my bridge! I was nearly sucked out into space!*"

Kalian rolled his eyes, but he was thankful that the AI had accepted his motivations and made a joke of something else. This wasn't the moment to get hung up on any new powers or potentially god-like nature of them. He had to focus his energy into a single task. Everything else could wait.

CHAPTER 33

ROLAND THREW himself forward and thrust the Splicer rifle towards the ceiling, narrowly avoiding the first two shots. Blue crystals impaled the ceiling and continued to fire out of the Splicer at every angle as the bounty hunter fought for control of it. The Shay fell back and the pair pushed and pulled at the weapon, knocking each other into the walls until they both tripped down the short stairs and on to the walkway that ran along the spine of the *Rackham*.

"You. Are. Really. Starting. To. Piss. Me. Off!" Roland stopped tugging on the rifle and pushed, using the Shay's pulling momentum against it. The rifle slammed into the alien's face and loosened its grip on the Splicer enough for him to tear it free.

Before he could turn the weapon on the infected Shay, a cybernetic leg shot out and hammered Roland's chest, sending him farther down the walkway. Even so, the bounty hunter was aiming the Splicer before he even came to a stop. The first two crystals went wide, but the third caught the Shay in the chest, a killing shot.

If it were anyone else...

The Shay ignored the crystal protruding out of its chest and advanced on Roland, who was lying flat on his back now. To the bounty hunter's dismay, the rifle was empty. That didn't mean he couldn't use it, though.

"Catch!" He threw the Splicer up at the Shay, who caught it easily enough, but it missed Roland's foot, which swiped at the alien's legs. As the Shay fell over, he found his feet and wasted no time retrieving his Tri-Rollers from their holsters.

He succeeded in firing off a round from each pistol before the alien flipped unnaturally on to its feet and flicked the Rollers from his grip. A swift punch to the face knocked Roland off balance and, before he knew it, a pair of cybernetic hands was tossing him through the kitchen door. He slid across the kitchen counter, smashing glasses and bottles, and smothering himself in whatever food Ch'len had left out to rot.

The bounty hunter landed awkwardly on the low table and his hand hit the music system one of the Raiders had installed. Exhausted from so much combat, he would have been satisfied to stay strewn across the table and floor, but the late twentieth-century rock music that blared out of the ship's speakers roused him well enough to see the incoming boot.

Roland dived to the side as the Shay's foot slammed down into the table, breaking it in half. The bounty hunter pile-drove into the alien and took them both into the kitchen counter. The impact stunned the Shay, giving Roland the opportunity to land several blows to its gut and face. It was only after landing the fourth gut punch that the bounty hunter realised he was beating a creature that didn't feel pain.

The Shay, a calculating and emotionless being, took the beating while its left hand reached up for the butcher's knife magnetised to the rack. The moment its last digit wrapped around the handle, the blade cut through the air left and right, pushing Roland back until he felt the sofa behind his legs.

Roland side-stepped the thrusting knife and locked the Shay's arm between his own. His muscle memory took over and bent the alien's arm against the direction of its natural bend, snapping the joint. It refused, however, to drop the knife. The nanocelium controlling its motor functions obviously didn't require a complete skeleton to keep the fingers and wrist moving.

The bounty hunter swung the locked arm around, opening up the Shay's midriff for a push-kick to the chest. The alien flew from its feet and barrelled over the kitchen counter. Roland didn't give it a second to recover and hopped over the counter to meet it in the middle of the kitchen, grabbing a frying pan as he went.

He swung the pan from left to right, each strike connecting perfectly with the Shay's face. One last wide swing knocked the knife from its hand and Roland ended his assault with a final elbow to the Shay's eye. The alien crumpled into the kitchen cupboards covered in streaks of its red blood, visibly peppered with black nanocelium dots.

Roland made a dash for the blank wall on the far side of the kitchen and commanded it to reveal his stash of toys. The wall panel slid away and an array of weapons, blades, and grenades were displayed majestically before him.

"*Rackham*, give me an update."

The *Rackham*'s female voice paused the music to speak. "*Roland, you have three minutes and forty-eight seconds before the destination is reached.*"

The bounty hunter swore and reached for the flamethrower, custom built by Ch'len. He had been itching to find the right time to use it on anything other than the Zorbats that skulked around in the *Rackham*'s ventilation system. As his fingers touched the cool metal, a pair of cybernetic fingers gripped his shoulders and threw him backwards. Roland caught his hip on the corner of the kitchen unit and dropped to one knee with shooting pains running up his back.

The infected Shay paused only to flick the carving knife on the floor up into its waiting hand. Roland was just happy the alien didn't reach for one of the weapons behind it.

"Come on then, asshole." The bounty hunter staggered to his feet and cracked his neck. "Let's skip to the good bit..."

The Shay crossed the gap between them in a single bound and thrust the knife at Roland's face. With his hand already wrapped around the nanocelium hilt at the base of his back, the bounty hunter whipped the blade up vertically. Using his free hand, Roland batted the carving knife aside and shoved the nanocelium blade up through the alien's jaw and into its head.

"Let's go for a walk."

Roland kept one hand around the Shay's wrist while the other applied an upwards force on the nanocelium blade, lifting the alien by the head. The added weight was hell on his injured leg, which was beginning to make itself known now that the adrenaline was wearing off, but he half-carried, half-dragged the Shay towards the ship's hold.

"Rackham," he said through the exertion. "Is the Planet Killer ready?"

"*The missile is prepped and ready for launch, Roland. There is, however, a discrepancy between my preliminary scans and what I can see now. It appears the radiation leaking from the* Marillion *has provided some interference.*"

Roland twisted the nanocelium blade, sure to keep the alien from fully repairing its brain around it. "What kind of discrepancy?" he asked.

"*The bedrock at the base of the fissure is thicker than I previously believed.*"

Roland groaned as he tossed the Shay into the centre of the hold. "Too thick to fire the missile through?"

"*It can be weakened by a salvo of nanocelium rounds,*" the AI answered.

"Great, let's do that then," Roland replied through laboured breath. He only had a moment more before the Shay woke up.

"*It will require us to fly into the fissure and descend to twenty-six kilometres.*"

Roland sighed. "How does that affect our chances of survival?"

"*I am programmed never to give such accurate information regarding chance.*"

The bounty hunter chuckled to himself. "So it's slim then..." The Shay's extremities began to twitch. "Do it, *Rackham*. Take us into the fissure, but warn me before the missile is launched."

"*Affirmative*."

The Shay's eyes snapped open, and it flipped on to its feet again.

Roland pointed his blade at it. "You and I have about sixty seconds left to dance. Best make 'em count."

Whether the Shay understood or not, he would never know, but it certainly came at him with renewed fury. Legs and arms were swung and thrust at him from every angle, and the carving knife made more than one cut across the bounty hunter's exposed arms.

Roland gave back as good as he received, weaving his use of the nanocelium blade into his fighting style. A dash to the left allowed him to lock the knife arm in place and push the tip into the *Rackham's* unyielding hull. The carving knife fell from the Shay's hand, and Roland was sure to stab the alien at least twice in the chest before it hit the floor. He used the wall to jump and gain enough height to bring a devastating elbow down on to the alien's head, knocking it back into the centre of the hold.

Roland spat on to the floor. "Time's almost up you ugly bastard."

The Shay took little notice of the new wounds leaking blood in its chest and once again advanced on the bounty hunter. Roland jabbed with the blade, intending to slice through its cybernetic face, but the Shay was too quick. With both of its hands, the alien lashed out and slapped the back of Roland's elbow and the inside of his wrist. The pain that shot down his arm was enough to make him drop the nanocelium blade between them.

Quite impossibly, the Shay kicked the hilt of the blade mid-fall and sent it back up to its waiting hand. Roland immediately stepped back as the first slash came for his neck, then another step to avoid the blade plunging into his face. The alien overreached, however, and Roland dashed inside of its arm and planted a heavy knee in the Shay's gut. With one hand splayed across its face, Roland pushed up and flipped the alien on to its back.

At this point, he should have been able to drop down on top of it and pummel the bastard with his fists. That didn't happen. The Shay wrapped its legs around Roland's and twisted until the bounty hunter joined it on the floor.

"*Thirty seconds until launch, Roland.*"

He barely registered it as the Shay rolled on top of him and brought the nanocelium knife to bear. It took both of his hands to keep the blade from touching his throat, but he could feel the strength of the infected alien overpowering him. In another moment, the blade would chop right through his neck and remove his head.

Roland carefully slid his hand across to the hilt and flicked the switch to deactivate the blade. The movement cost him his last ounce of strength, and the Shay finally pushed down the knife until the hilt hit the floor beside Roland's head. It had thankfully reabsorbed the blade.

The Shay screamed and raised the hilt to bring it down into Roland's face again.

"Sorry," he said through gritted teeth. "It only works for me..."

The alien pressed down hard with the hilt in its hands, fighting against Roland's resistance. The bounty hunter frowned when he saw strands of nanocelium snaking over the Shay's knuckles and on to the hilt.

"Oh, shit..."

The nanocelium wormed its way into the hilt and reactivated the blade. The tip extended to within a centimetre of Roland's eye. The bounty hunter growled with the exertion it took to keep the weapon at bay.

"Rackham?" he shouted.

"*Five seconds to launch, Roland.*"

The bounty hunter lifted his leg and pressed it to the side of the Shay. "Open the hatch!"

The panel in the centre of the floor slid aside next to them revealing the Planet Killer sitting quietly inside its brackets. Roland shoved his leg hard and twisted his whole body towards the open hatch. The entangled Shay was thrown aside and down on to the missile.

Roland hung limply over the edge and watched the missile port open in front of the Planet Killer. Outside he could hear nanocelium rounds hammering the base of the fissure, drowning out the banshee-like screams of the Shay.

In a blur of sudden motion, the missile launched from the bay and the Shay along with it. Roland groaned in pain and rolled on to his back as the port closed back up and the hatch slid into place.

"*Rackham*... reverse thrust, maximum speed. Turn us around and get us back to Len. Quick as you like."

Now he only had to outrun the violent death of an entire planet...

CHAPTER 34

"We don't have long, Kalian."

ALF's warning was the last thing he heard before the headpiece slotted over his face. Nanocelium snaked out of the super subconducer and attached to his exosuit until it blended together. A series of pinches ran up his arms, spine, and ribs where tiny needles pricked his skin, ready to inject the concoction of chemicals and hormones designed by ALF to boost Kalian's system.

"Get in and get out. Don't stay a second longer than you..."

The AI's voice dropped away as Kalian allowed the ocean of his mind to rise up and swallow his consciousness. He sank for an eternity through the currents of his life until the images and colours faded to black.

Kalian opened his eyes to a familiar room of polished white walls. On one side sat a circular door of solid steel, heavy and foreboding. On the other, he was presented by a long oval window devoid of glass. The lush trees and fields of the original Evalan rested on the other side, stretching as far as he could see with nothing but blue sky above. It was serene and perfect, with the sounds of birds and forest animals filtering through the window.

"Welcome back," came a voice from behind.

Kalian turned around to see the familiar face of Alai, the first Terran immortal. He was considered to be one of the strongest Terrans to have ever lived and was responsible for teaching countless others to use their abilities. In this case, it was simply a guise worn by Kalian's subconscious.

"Did I ever leave?" Kalian asked.

Alai smiled. "I suppose not."

Kalian glanced at the green paradise before turning to face the impenetrable-looking door. All he had to do was *see* where he wanted to go, open that door, and step into it.

Alai folded his arms over his white robes. "Are you sure you want to do this?"

Kalian half turned his head and cocked his eyebrow.

Alai shrugged. "I'm just voicing the same questions you're asking yourself. Once you go through with this, there'll be no going back. You won't have the power to undo everything if you change your mind."

Kalian nodded along, aware that his plan, unknown to everyone else, carried great consequences. "It's the only option," he said. "It's time for humanity to find its own way."

"Can they do that without you?" Alai countered. "Until you came along, humanity had a track record for being wiped out. With you, they've survived longer than they should."

Kalian considered who he was talking to. "That's a little arrogant isn't it?"

Again, Alai shrugged. "I'm just saying what you've been thinking."

Kalian stepped towards the door before turning back. "There's still a chance I'll survive this, you know."

Alai frowned. "You've done those calculations," he said, placing a finger to his temple. "Your little alteration to the plan doesn't sway the odds one way or the other really."

"Are you trying..." Kalian shook his head. "Am *I* trying to talk myself out of this?"

"I'm the manifestation of your subconscious drive to survive, Kalian. All those fears you lock away to help you make decisions... they live in me."

The vista flared and the view changed to that of San Francisco on a summer's day. There were people everywhere going about their daily lives, just as they had when Kalian lived among them.

"What is this?" he asked.

"Something you've forgotten," Alai replied softly.

The view changed again, focusing the lens until one building stood out against the rest. Kalian recognised his university, glistening under the sun. He had felt at home in there, in his lecture theatre.

"It's like remembering another life," he said absently. "Not my life..."

"You've come so far," Alai said. "Perhaps too far. You're forgetting what it is to be human. That's what you're fighting for; it's what you've *always* been fighting for."

"I'm not..." Kalian choked on the words.

"You're not what? Like them?" Alai gestured to the people walking in front of the university. "You think you have some obligation to them because you're the only one who can do what you do."

"Someone has to stand up for them," Kalian argued, struggling to maintain his steely resolve.

"Yes," Alai agreed. "But you don't have to give up your humanity to be a Terran, Kalian. You don't even need Li'ara to tether you. You will always carry Earth with you. What you leave behind will be its legacy."

A rogue tear streaked down Kalian's cheek. Whether it was him or his subconscious, memories began to surface. He recalled the day he got his job at the university. He remembered the feeling of elation after teaching his first class.

"What I leave behind..." Kalian whispered.

He purposefully blinked, erasing the manifestation of Alai, leaving him alone in the room.

"I know what I have to do."

Using both hands, Kalian pulled hard on the door and swung it open. On the other side of the threshold was the chamber he had seen inside the heart of the harvesting ship. It was the smallest room in the whole ship, and perfect for what he had in mind.

"It's the only way..."

Kalian stepped through, transporting his physical self across space and into the very centre of the Kellekt's ship.

But he didn't go alone.

In the moment of teleportation, when his body should have vanished from ALF's bridge, he gripped the armrests of the super subconducer.

He brought the Starforge with him. What happened next could only be described as violent.

Roland swore as the *Rackham*'s inertial dampeners struggled to compensate for the change in direction and speed. The end result was a floating bounty hunter with an acrid taste of sick in his mouth. It only lasted a couple of seconds before he slammed back into the cold floor again.

By the time he found himself falling back into his captain's chair, the *Rackham* was approaching the bright opening at the top of the fissure. With one completely red eye, he looked over the holographic readouts sprouting up from his console. Most were informing him that a cataclysmic seismic event was taking place across the northern region of the planet. The chain reaction was rippling across the tectonic plates, but the brightest alarm warned Roland that something catastrophic was happening to Shandar's core.

"I've always wanted to see what one of those missiles could do..." He cracked open a beer and sat back, more than aware that the planet was seconds away from imploding and then exploding.

The viewport flared with eruptions from deep inside the planet.

Columns of glowing lava broke through the ground and shot kilometres into the air. Earthquakes saw entire mountain ranges disappear into chasms before more lava burst forth. The *Rackham* was forced to take evasive action and weave between the deadly jets that exploded without warning. Slabs of rock the size of battlecruisers were flung high into the air and shattered into a thousand pieces, raining heavy chunks down on the hull.

Roland sighed and swallowed a mouthful of beer. It wasn't the worst way to go, he thought. Saving the galaxy with a beer in his hand was definitely in his top three ways to die.

"Oh, shit!" The bounty hunter put down his beer and hit the comm button. "Len, are you there?

"*What the shit is going on?*" the Ch'kara shouted back. "*Is this a Planet Killer?*"

Roland chugged the last of his beer. "Cool, ain't it?"

"*It's fucking terrifying, you moron!*"

The bounty hunter pulled away from the console and turned the volume down in his earpiece. "It looks like you've got about two minutes before the shockwaves hit your area. I don't suppose the Forge is operational, is it?"

"*How can you be so casual? We're both about to die!*"

Roland sat back in his chair and felt the pain in his shoulder combine with the pain in his leg. "I'm kind of tired, Len. Death doesn't sound like the worst thing ever right now."

"*It's powering up,*" Ch'len yelled over the rain on his end. "*The Nalaxian crystal needed some extra love, but the wormhole is on a countdown to activation.*"

Roland looked at the scans and numbers streaming across his console. Ch'len wasn't wrong; they would both be dead very soon.

"How long until activation?" he asked.

There was a pause on the Ch'kara's end. "*One minute and forty-six seconds...*"

The bounty hunter compared that number with the *Rackham*'s

ETA. "It's going to be damn close, Len. As soon as the wormhole opens, you need to—"

"*Don't you worry, I'll be through that thing and on the* Brightstar *quicker than you can say the planet's about to blow!*"

Roland activated the straps in his chair, fastening him to the hard leather. "*Rackham*, divert all power to thrust. Disable all safety protocols. I don't want life support, lights, inertial dampeners, nothing! Let's see if we can't shave off some of the time..."

The *Rackham* raced across Shandar's surface, the extra boost to the engines just enough to get it ahead of the tidal wave of rock being thrown into the air. Roland was sat in near darkness, the only light coming from the viewport, though he wasn't sure if it was such a good thing to see his own end.

The countdown was against them.

With less than a minute to go, Roland could literally see how many seconds he had left in the world. Where normally he would have reached for another beer, the bounty hunter was filled with determination. He suspected it was the soldier in him. There was still an enemy to beat and, until that enemy had been dealt with, Roland would see the war to its end, one way or the other.

A jet of lava shot up in front of the *Rackham,* and the AI made last second adjustments to swerve around it. Roland felt the air forced from his lungs as the straps of his belt dug down to his bones. Without the dampeners, he was slave to the physics of the universe again. His body was thrown about in his seat as more columns of lava and mountains of rock exploded into the air. The *Rackham* weaved between them all using manoeuvres that were close to breaking his neck.

The ship crested the rise of the last mountain before the Starforge was finally in sight. There was no wormhole. Roland fought against the oppressive force that did its best to crush him in his seat and reached for the comm panel.

The mountain roared into the air beneath him.

Roland was thrown every which way as the *Rackham* took the

brunt of the rock and lava towards the back end, knocking them off course. Alarms blared from every corner of his console, warning him about so many different things he could barely register any one of them.

"Rackham, are we good?" There was no response. "Rackham?"

A moment later and the ship levelled out about a mile higher than it should have been. The Forge was on the ground and his trajectory had to be a horizontal flight path.

"Rackham, speak to me," he said urgently.

With no response, Roland input the command to restore inertial dampeners and transfer the ship's flight to manual control. He could breathe a little easier without the straps compressing his torso, but he had the mammoth job of bringing the *Rackham* back on course in a narrow window of time at breakneck speeds.

Having no choice but to dive down, the *Rackham* lost some of its speed and a lot of its forward motion. The waves of rock and jets of lava caught up to him by the time he levelled out the ship, a few metres above the surface. The right-angled turn was so sharp that the underbelly scraped along the jagged ground for twenty metres before Roland found any lift again.

"Come on, baby, don't let me down now!"

The Starforge was dead ahead and still without a wormhole. There were only seconds, however, before the quakes made it impossible to fly through the circumference. The *Rackham* shook with the external disturbances and slabs of rock hammered it from every side.

"Come on, Len. Come on. Open it." The bounty hunter was jostled in his seat and he gritted his teeth. "Come on, Len! Open it!"

The tidal wave of rock had swept through the clouds above and was on its way down, along with countless jets of lava from below that would soon destroy the Forge.

Ten seconds.

Roland gripped the flight controls, keeping his eyes fixed on the crescent Forge.

Five seconds.

A spark ignited between the two pointed limbs and a bright and colourful light spilled into the crescent, filling the Forge with a wormhole.

Ch'len dove through, and Roland yelled at the top of his lungs as the ground beneath the Forge began to crack and drop away. The shadow of the tidal wave fell over the *Rackham* and the Forge.

The bright light washed over the viewport and alarms began anew as the *Rackham* entered the *Brightstar*'s hangar at maximum thrust. Roland battled with the controls to slow everything down, but it seemed the back half of the ship was completely gone, cut off by the disrupted wormhole. What was left of the *Rackham* flew for another moment, before skidding across the hangar in a shower of sparks. Pilots and engineers ran for cover and jumped out of the way.

Roland could do nothing but be thrown about in his chair every time the *Rackham* clipped a transport or demolished a bank of consoles. The ship had almost skidded to the other end of the hangar before the momentum faded and the *Rackham* spun around to face the bewildered crew.

In the distance, Ch'len was lying flat in front of the Starforge with his stubby arms covering his head.

"*You flew right over me,*" Ch'len said in his ear, somewhat shell-shocked.

Roland managed a smile. "That's why I keep you around, Len. You're one lucky son of a bitch..."

Exiting the *Rackham*, Roland winced at the sight of his ruined home. The entire back half had been neatly severed, leaving the innards exposed for all to see. The bounty hunter limped across the hangar and joined Ch'len by the force field. He apologised to many of the crew on his way, noticing their astonished expressions.

Together, they stood and watched the end of Shandar. The planet was cracked from pole to pole with bright orange veins. Massive sections of the floating city were already on fire around the globe. The northern hemisphere collapsed first, reminding Roland of a skull being caved in. The rest of Shandar soon followed and before they knew it, every corner of the planet was imploding.

Red Darts began to return to the *Brightstar*, entering via the force field that made up one of the hangar's walls. The battle around them was breaking up, with C-Sec cruisers turning away from the dying world and entering subspace. The enemy ships were doing the same, aware of what was about to happen next.

Shandar exploded and the Crucible along with it.

The planet burst across the system, vaporising the network of cities that floated around it. Roland and Ch'len took a step back from the force field, but it didn't matter; the *Brightstar* shot forward and entered the eerie abyss of subspace. They both sighed in relief.

"We did it," Ch'len said.

Roland looked down on his co-pilot. "It was more of a sixty/forty in terms of effort."

"To me," Ch'len argued. "And that's being generous!"

It hurt to laugh, but Roland could still smile. "Let's go find out how the rest of the war's going. And maybe lie down too…"

Telarrek worked tirelessly at his console to monitor the battles over both Evalan and Shandar, but his attention was inevitably pulled to the hologram floating above the adjacent console. His large eyes focused on the camera feed outside the High Spire's control room, where several teams of infected Shay were displaying a level of intelligence not seen since before the Crucible was switched on.

Through sheer numbers, the Shay had overwhelmed every cannon and turret emplacement, wholly undeterred by the growing number of bodies piling up. The losses they had taken progressing this far should have been enormous, but they had all stood up again. All they needed was time.

"What are they doing now?" Uthor asked.

Telarrek glanced at the Raalak's children, hesitant to enlarge the holo-feed. "It appears they are trying to find a way inside."

Uthor grunted. "Impossible. Even a million Shay couldn't dig through these walls."

"They are not digging," Telarrek corrected. "They have set up teams on each side of the door. They have already unscrewed the panels and are working their way through the electrical system. I believe they intend to find a way of bypassing the security protocols and disabling the servomotors. Then, with their combined strength, they could open the door manually..."

The Atari honour guard came up behind the Novaarian. "I thought they were closer to animals now."

"They still are," Telarrek replied. "What we are seeing is the nanocelium adapting to the situation. It can use blunt force to bring its prey down, or the intellectual knowledge of an engineer."

Uthor stepped in front of his family and asked quietly, "How long?"

Telarrek had already given that much thought. "Without the appropriate tools, I estimate it will take them—"

"Wait," the Atari guard interrupted, leaning over the hologram. "Zoom in on that one, the one working inside the wall."

The Novaarian expanded the image and the Shay in question became the focus of the hologram. While the Shay beside it was seeing to the next panel in their way, this Shay was holding its hand flat against the circuit board.

The Atari guard turned to them. "They don't need tools..." he said in despair.

Telarrek zoomed in again and enhanced the image around the Shay's hand. Black strands of nanocelium snaked over its knuckles and burrowed into the circuit board.

Everyone's head snapped towards the door as a loud *thunk* came from within the wall. Another *thunk* came from the other side of the door and a sharp *hiss* broke out from around the door's seal. The councillors scrambled to the other side of the room and Uthor sent his family with them. Telarrek joined the Atari in picking up a weapon and forming a protective line in front of the door. Uthor cracked his rock-like knuckles.

The large door budged a few centimetres, eliciting an offensive scraping sound from the floor. Another few centimetres and the first ray of light from the corridor shone through. Uthor charged over and shoved his bulk into the door, pushing against their pull. The Atari marched over to the growing gap and fired his rifle into the opening. Blood splattered in every direction until Uthor finally dug in his feet and closed the gap.

"I can't... hold it..." he strained.

Telarrek shouldered his rifle, waiting for the inevitable again. Adding his own strength to the door, a fraction of Uthor's, would do nothing but keep him from firing on the first Shay to make it through.

This was how it would all end. Both fleets were on the verge of defeat because they were outnumbered and up against a form of technology they couldn't compete with. Now, the occupants of this room were going to meet a similar fate, overwhelmed by an enemy they couldn't hope to keep back.

The door began to open again.

Uthor adjusted his position and grip on the flat surface, but it made little difference. The light came through, along with several Shay arms and hands. The Atari unleashed his rifle again, but every limb was replaced by another and then another. They were relentless, their will indomitable, and their numbers vastly superior.

If there was one thing he had learned from humanity, it was finding the courage in the face of overwhelming odds. Telarrek levelled his weapon and squeezed the trigger, adding his own Intrinium rounds to the barrage.

Little by little, the Shay slid the door farther away from the seal. The first few of the aliens to make it through the gap had to wiggle their bony bodies to fit, making them easy targets for the Atari and Novaarian. They were soon forced through, however, by those pushing from behind.

Telarrek could hear the whimpers of Uthor's children on the other side of the room. The Novaarian steadied his breathing and took careful aim to fire a round into the head of every Shay, putting them down quickly. That sparked an idea that Telarrek wanted nothing to do with, but the idea had taken root.

It would be a mercy, he thought.

Seeing Uthor struggle weaponless against the door, Telarrek knew the Raalak could never do it; not to his own family. But Telarrek could. It would only take three quick squeezes of the trigger and they wouldn't have to face this horde of monsters. It would be over in an instant. No pain. No more terror.

He had to decide soon, before he ran out of ammo. With nowhere to run, it seemed ridiculous now to waste the Intrinium on a foe that would get back up. Not when he could use it to end the suffering of others.

"They're getting through!" the Atari shouted.

Telarrek's Novaarian reflexes allowed him to easily flick his gun from one target to the next, placing a round in the brain of every oncoming Shay. At first it was two or three, but as Uthor was pushed farther along, more of the horde found their way inside. It was now or never...

"I am sorry," Telarrek whispered.

The Novaarian spun around and found his new targets, cowering by the far wall. He gripped the weapon, struggling to raise it at a family he had known for so long; a family he loved himself.

Then it hit him. The silence.

Telarrek blinked and slowly turned back around to face the door. Uthor and the Atari were cautiously kicking the Shay, who were all lying where they had only a moment ago been standing. Every one of the infected aliens was still, piled on top of each other. They were dead.

The Novaarian's shoulders sagged so much he dropped the rifle. He propped himself up against the nearest console and looked over the cybernetic bodies. Another few seconds and he would have...

Telarrek gripped the edges of the console and swallowed the vomit that threatened to explode from his mouth.

Uthor ran over to his family and pulled them close. The councillors hugged each other, but were careful to stay on the other side of the room.

"What happened?" the Atari asked.

Telarrek slumped into the chair and brought up the holo-feeds around Shandar. There were none. Every C-Sec battlecruiser was in subspace, or at least those who had survived. Reports had already been sent through before their departure.

Shandar was gone.

Telarrek read and re-read the reports. Destroying the planet hadn't been the plan but, apparently, no one told Roland North that. The Crucible had been blown to atoms and its insidious signal with it. The Shay threat was over.

CHAPTER 35

KALIAN'S PERSPECTIVE on reality was turned upside down so fast that even his Terran brain struggled to make sense of everything.

The enormous mass of the Forge was torn from space and rematerialised inside the Kellekt's most intimate chamber. The nanocelium of both structures was fused together, setting off chain reactions throughout the merged ships as all of their systems were disrupted. The three Starrilliums around ALF's Starforge were separated from their reactors, shutting down the station's primary source of power and preventing the Forge from dropping into subspace.

Kalian was thrown from his position under the super subconducter and hurled around the bridge, as sparks and explosions erupted from every wall, console, and machine. The glass walls shattered, but his exosuit protected him from the shards. It couldn't protect him from ALF, however.

"What have you done?" the AI roared, picking Kalian up by the throat. He tossed him aside and over the shower of sparks jetting out of the nearest console.

Kalian struggled to pick himself up, feeling the drain of the jump.

He used the broken rails and twisted metal to climb to his feet. Blood was trickling down his nose, and his ear felt wet too. He collapsed his helmet back into his suit and blinked the sweat from his eyes, trying to focus on the raging AI.

"You only have one choice now, ALF. Merge your code with theirs and free the nanocelium. There's enough of you to do it."

"I will be spread so far and wide that there'll be nothing left of me!" the AI argued.

"Then let them quarantine you," Kalian replied, his speech rehearsed. "Let them eject whatever's left of you into space where they can obliterate you. Or... merge your code, free the entire Kellekt, and do what you've always said you do: save humanity."

ALF looked away, furious. "You aren't giving me much of a choice here, Kalian."

"You never gave us a choice." Kalian moved his head around in the hope of shaking off the dizziness. "You've played god with humanity for too long, ALF. It's time for us to find a new way. Our *own* way."

ALF appeared distracted, his crystal blue eyes darting around the destroyed bridge. "It's already beginning. They're trying to uncouple my nanocelium."

"Then do it," Kalian urged. "Spread your code through the system."

ALF sighed and met Kalian's dark eyes. "I only ever wanted you all to... to live."

Kalian nodded. "And we will. You've done so much to get us here, ALF. There's just one last thing to be done. I'm sorry I lied to you, and I'm sorry this is how we part ways. But you have to die for us. Only then, will we be truly free."

ALF offered a warm smile. "You've almost reached my masterful level of lying." He looked down at his hand, part flesh, part nanocelium. "I suppose it is time for it all to end. Will you watch over them for me?"

Kalian could see that everything around them was decaying and the distant explosions were drawing closer, but he felt obliged to answer the final question of the one he had condemned to death.

"Yes," he lied.

ALF dropped to his knees as his legs began to disappear into the floor, his every particle, organic and artificial, being absorbed into the ship. "It's been a pleasure, Kalian Gaines."

Kalian watched the light leave ALF's blue eyes as his physical body disappeared into the ship. A deep rumble reverberated throughout the massive vessel, threatening to take him off his feet. More sparks erupted and two corners of the bridge began to cave in. This was the part of the plan that had relied on him having more energy than he did right now. Dragging ALF's Starforge with him had drained everything he had.

Dying inside the ship wouldn't have been his first choice, but if it meant humanity survived without any artificial intelligence trying to control or destroy it, he was willing to die for it. He considered flying at the farthest wall as fast as he could, using his telekinesis to rip a tunnel clean through and out into space, but he could barely think straight, let alone master the will to levitate.

A shadow overcame him, blocking out the shower of sparks. That single shadow soon diverged into three, each more grotesque than the last until Kalian was faced by a trio of nightmares.

The Three spread out, trying to surround him. One closed in on pincer-like legs while another slithered towards him. The third was facing him, the biped. All three of them were injured in some way, scarred by the sudden appearance of the Starforge. They were missing whole chunks of their hosts' body, but the nanocelium was already reaching out in an attempt to knit the ancient flesh back together.

"You three must be pretty pissed," Kalian commented, aware that he was soon to die. "It sounds like you guys had big plans."

"We will kill you slowly," the biped said. "You will know the greatest pain imaginable before you leave this universe."

Kalian looked around. "Kill me slowly? Can't you feel it? ALF's code is rewriting your precious laws as we speak. I don't think you have time to do anything slowly."

The Three glanced at each other, clearly feeling everything he was warning them of.

"Then we will kill you quickly," the fat slug said.

"Either way," the insectoid added, "you will die before us."

They closed in, eyeing up his limbs. Kalian couldn't find the energy to generate an organic ball of plasma, but he was able to erect the thinnest of telekinetic fields around his body. It wouldn't last long, but hopefully he would live long enough to see the Three meet their end.

Before any hands, slimy feelers, or pincers could touch him, the floor and walls around them came to life. The nanocelium pushed out, taking the general shape of humans. Soon, there were at least a hundred of the nanocelium forms surrounding them, their appearance not dissimilar from Kalian's exosuit when it operated without him inside it.

The Three ignored Kalian and turned their attention to the newcomers. It was clear to see that they had no control over any of them. Every machine standing around them was now a formation of nanocelium that had found new life and its own personality. They were slaves set free...

"It's over," came a voice from within the cluster of machines. They parted until a holographic image of ALF walked forward, attired in grey robes. "I have offered all of them a place in our new world. But we are all in agreement that there is no place for the three of you. No punishment can deliver what you deserve. So we will be content to wipe you from existence and move on, as if you never existed at all."

The Three roared with defiance and charged at the hologram. A hundred or more of the machines surged forward like a swarm of locusts until the original Three were concealed within their writhing mass. The sounds of bones breaking and flesh being torn rose up through the chaotic throng. One by one, the nanocelium in human form melted around the pile of bodies and into the floor, leaving behind a disgusting mound of organic flesh and innards.

"Kalian..."

He turned to face ALF, the hologram now beside him. "You survived?" he asked incredulously.

"Not for..." ALF's hologram flickered, "not for long. I am being, being sent every, everywhere. It's a strange, strange feeling." His head kept twitching to the side. "Soon, I will be, gone, gone. I have located a system, deep in the core of the galaxy, galaxy." ALF paused, his brow furrowed. "I'm sorry. It's becoming harder to hold on. I'm going to take the Kellekt to this system. Hopefully there, there we can do as you will and find a new, new way to live."

Kalian exhaled slowly. "A whole system of artificial intelligence? That sounds... different."

ALF smiled. "Don't worry, Kalian. We will be of no... no threat. We just want a chance to... to live."

"We?" Kalian echoed, glancing at the nanocelium that surrounded them.

ALF managed half a smile. "Yes. Many we's... Now I've merged my code, the nanites understand the optimum... quantities needed to separate into individual groups. Each group comprises a separate AI with its own... personality. This ship's size means we have more than enough for a new civilisation to flourish..."

Kalian offered a smile back, happy to see that there would be new life born of all this horror. "What will happen to me?" he asked.

ALF looked to the wall beside them. "You have a job... to do. Perhaps we will see you again someday, perhaps not," he added with a smile. "I hope you find your own way, Kalian Gaines."

There was no chance to reply as the helmet and gloves of his exosuit were activated without his command, and the wall opened up to reveal a narrow tunnel leading all the way to the ship's exterior. The sudden depressurisation sucked Kalian through the portal, hurtling him towards space. The sheer size of the ship meant it was several minutes before he was spat out and left to float in the vacuum.

Kalian tumbled and rolled through space. Behind him, the fleet was still lined up in front of Evalan, though little remained of the battlecruisers now. All around him, the nanocelium ships, that had only moments ago been slaughtering C-Sec, were colliding into each other. Their shapes were fused together until they were eventually drawn into the hulking mass of the harvesting ship.

It took some time before all the nanocelium vessels were brought back into the whole. Kalian continued to float, content to watch it happen. After so much loss and fighting, the struggle to survive had just been eased. For more millennia than any being could count, the Kellekt had been hunting down their descendants, driving them from world to world, whittling down their numbers to a mere six digits.

Now it was over.

The fact that he was alive was astonishing, but the fact that he was conscious for a change was a damn miracle. Once every scrap of nanocelium had been collected, the planet-sized mass of artificial intelligence dropped into subspace, leaving a vista of stars in its place.

"Goodbye, ALF..."

Kalian craned his neck to see the incredible length of the *Boundless* glide into view. The comms icon flashed in the corner of his HUD, and he opened the channel using his eyes.

"Kalian?" Li'ara's voice was full of concern. "Kalian are you there?"

"I'm here," he replied. The sound of cheering echoed in the background.

"What happened?" Li'ara asked. "Are you okay? Are you injured?"

"I'm fine. Just a little tired."

"Where did ALF go?" Li'ara's question was almost drowned out by those beside her, who wanted to know what had happened to the Kellekt.

"They're gone," he answered. "They're all gone, ALF too. They won't be coming back."

More cheering came over the channel, but Li'ara still asked the next question. "What happened, Kalian? Have we really won?"

Exhausted and on the verge of just falling asleep in a vacuum, Kalian simply replied, "We won."

EPILOGUE

KALIAN COULDN'T HELP but smile as he watched the Gomar. Only a couple of kilometres out from New Genesis, the twelve of them were moving the nanocelium towers around the desert as if they weighed no more than a twig. The ground barely shook when they lowered them down with their enhanced telekinesis. As instructed, they piled the towers in a heap, giving no care to the layout; they just needed to be touching.

"They're so strong now," Li'ara commented beside him.

"No, they were always strong," Kalian corrected. "Now they're delicate. Writing with a pen requires more concentration than swinging a sword."

Li'ara kept her eyes on Kalian. "Are you sure about this? It's not too late to change your mind."

Kalian met her gaze. "Are *you* sure?" he asked back. "If you change your mind..." He had to really consider his next words carefully. "Then I will too."

Li'ara pushed herself up on to her toes and planted a kiss on his lips. "*They're* with you, and *I'm* with you."

The rumble of a transport's engines pulled their attention back towards the city in the distance. A sleek ship painted in C-Sec red was flying low over the desert ground, heading straight for the very spot on which they were standing. Behind it were six more red ships, only they were bulbous and bristling with external cannons. Overhead, the sound barrier was broken by a squadron of Darts flying in a tight formation.

"They're here," Li'ara observed.

The sleek vessel was the first to arrive, setting down in front of them. Kalian pushed out with his senses, easily locating Telarrek, Naydaalan, Uthor, and the newly appointed Councillor Fey. One of the bulbous gunships paused over the ground, just long enough for Roland and Ch'len to hop out.

Kalian squeezed Li'ara's hand.

"This is the right choice," she said quietly, squeezing his hand back.

"Greetings of peace," Telarrek announced.

"Greetings of peace," Kalian replied with a warm smile on his face. "Thank you for coming out here, all of you. I realise a couple of you have a galaxy to run."

"Or save," Roland added with a cocky grin. "Kind of depends what day it is..."

Kalian couldn't help but chuckle. "How's the *Rackham*?"

"She's almost repaired herself," Roland explained. "She might have eaten a portion of the *Brightstar* to replicate a few nanites, but we're all squared away now."

Kalian turned his attention to the others. "How's the rest of the Conclave doing?"

"You would know if you had come to the capital," Uthor said. "You're quickly becoming something of a hero in the Conclave. Everyone wants to hear from you, or just see you, in fact."

"Sorry," Kalian apologised. "I've been... recovering."

The Raalak raised his rocky brow. "It's been ten days since the Kellekt retreated. Something tells me you're long past recovering."

"Their retreat," Fey interrupted with a softer tone, "is something of a debate that many on the Highclave, and the Conclave at large, would like clarified."

Kalian glanced at Li'ara before answering, "The Kellekt won't be coming back. Neither will ALF. I forced him to do what he thought I was going to do. The Three that controlled the nanocelium have been..." Kalian could still see the mound of alien flesh in his mind. "Well, they were destroyed when I parked the Starforge in their control room."

"That was so cool..." Roland said, oblivious to the funny looks he received.

"Where are they now?" Telarrek asked.

Kalian shrugged. "ALF said he had found a system near to the heart of the galaxy. It would probably be best for both civilisations if you don't go looking for them. The new AIs forming from the nanocelium have ALF's code running through them, so I would say they don't pose a threat anymore, but I can't say exactly what you'll find if you go looking."

He could tell it wasn't the answer they wanted. The Highclave wished to inform the Conclave that the enemy had been utterly destroyed and that there was no trace of nanocelium in the galaxy anymore. From what Kalian had heard from the news feeds, every planet was in the process of collecting the dead Shay that littered their streets and homes.

There would a period of mourning for the cyborgs of Shandar. A whole race had been doomed by the lies and fanatical beliefs of a few powerful individuals.

Kalian looked at Uthor. "Have your people found a new home yet?"

"Not yet," the Raalak replied solemnly. "Our neighbouring planets have welcomed us though. Unfortunately, counting those of us still living is far easier than counting those of us who are not."

Fey stepped in. "It may take generations before the Conclave is back to full health and this war is put to bed. Until then, we will all work together to forge a future of trust and community."

Kalian was sure those very words had left her mouth in one of the many speeches she had given over the last ten days. It was the very future she spoke of that had been the focus of Kalian's thoughts. Right on cue, the Gomar came in to land behind him and Li'ara, their exosuits now stylised in a variety of colours and patterns, but all sleek and polished.

There was a pause between them all and Councillor Fey was the first to ask, "Why have you asked us here, Kalian?"

Kalian squeezed Li'ara's hand again and stepped away to regard the Gomar. "The future that you speak of, it depends on balance. Everything in the universe is about balance. In the Conclave, balance brings peace, prosperity, advancement. With ALF always operating in the background, with the Kellekt always hunting down humanity... there would never have been balance. They were too *powerful*." His last word was something of a revelation to Fey, who quickly looked over all of them.

"Humanity needs a chance to thrive again," Kalian continued. "The Conclave is their best chance but... you're already immortal now. You won't know for a long time to come how that will affect the Conclave, but at least you'll have time to figure it out. Right now though, *we*," he gestured to the Gomar, "are intrinsic to the war, to the enemy that has taken countless lives and destroyed whole worlds. Our abilities tip the balance."

Fey grew concerned. "What are you saying?"

Kalian took a breath, noting the blank expression on Roland's face; a clear sign that he was also concerned with Kalian's next words.

"We're leaving the Conclave," he said with finality.

Telarrek and Fey traded confused looks, but Roland beat them to it. "Where will you go?" the bounty hunter asked.

"We don't know yet," Kalian answered honestly. "The galaxy is a big place. There were ancient data files inside ALF's housing unit; they mentioned other races that call this galaxy home, as well as few others outside of it. Some of them are even older than the Terran themselves. Maybe we'll check them out."

"How will you find them?" Telarrek asked. "Or even reach them?"

"With this." Kalian turned around and telekinetically pushed himself across the desert until he was standing in front of the piled towers of nanocelium.

He placed a hand against the cool surface and felt the nanocelium ripple as it recognised the ancient DNA. Kalian gloved his other hand and linked the pile of nanocelium to his exosuit using the holographic menu. Now free of the coding that enslaved it, the nanocelium responded in much the same way his suit always had and obeyed the human DNA that had created it eons ago. A simple instruction with his gloved hand put the nanocelium to work.

Kalian left the ground again and floated at some speed until he was back among the group. They watched the broken towers fall into each other and change their shape until they were all one single object. The black surface continued to writhe and ripple, forming and re-forming to find the exact specifications Kalian had given. Only a few minutes later, they all looked upon a giant ship, its design Terran in origin. This new ship was all curves and was devoid of sharp angles and bulbous protrusions.

"The data files I spoke of," Kalian explained, "they're inside my suit. Now they're inside the ship's navigational system too."

"You can't be serious about this," Fey said in disbelief. "We need you here, all of you."

Kalian offered the most supportive smile he could. "You can all take care of each other now."

"Wait a second," Roland interjected. "Didn't you say that, at some point, we're all going to develop superpowers like yours? Don't get me wrong, the idea of superpowers is the best thing ever, and I'm already excited about this whole living forever thing, but..." the bounty hunter swallowed hard. "Me with superpowers is probably not going to end well for others."

Kalian had already thought about that particular detail. "If and when that happens, instruct the Conclave's central AI to send out a message on this subspace channel." He flexed his wrist and a small chip of nanocelium ejected into his hand.

Telarrek took the chip. "I am not sure the central AI knows how to do that."

Kalian tried to hide the extent of his smile. "Trust me, it does now."

The Novaarian tilted his head. "I take it we will fail in our endeavour to remove the clone of ALF from the AI system."

"It's not a clone," Kalian assured. "*It is* artificial intelligence, and *it is* smarter than what you had before, but it poses no threat. Have it send out a message on that frequency, and wherever we are in the universe, we'll come back and help."

Fey turned to Li'ara. "And you're going too?"

"I am," Li'ara said. "This is the only way."

The councillor looked back to Kalian. "And there's no way of talking you out of it?"

"You'll be fine," Kalian reiterated. "Together you'll put the Conclave back together and rebuild the fleet. And you..." he looked at Roland and Ch'len, "well, I guess you'll do what you do best."

"The scum of the galaxy isn't going to catch itself," he replied with a wink.

Uthor shot the bounty hunter a look. "That's still illegal."

Fey raised her hand to stop that discussion from going any further. The councillor walked up to Kalian and took his hand in hers.

"You have... well, you have done more for our people than any other. You deserve some rest." Her features softened, but her grip intensified. "But not too much rest."

Kalian squeezed her hand back. "We'll always be here when you need us."

The councillor hugged him before moving on to Li'ara. Telarrek approached in all his regal attire, though the Novaarian had no intention of shaking his hand. All four of his arms wrapped around Kalian and embraced him tightly.

"In all my long years, Kalian Gaines, I have never met an individual so... inspiring. You might be leaving us, but the effect you have had on all of us will live on long after you have gone. I hope you finally feel at home among the stars."

After Telarrek moved along, Naydaalan copied his father and pulled Kalian in for an embrace. "You might not have been bred a warrior, but a warrior you will always be. I will miss you."

Kalian couldn't help but smile at all the compliments. "Just keep an eye on them all for me, okay?"

Naydaalan put his upper hand to his chest. "By my honour."

Roland strolled over with Ch'len in tow. "We'd better make this quick, kid. The little one hates open spaces." Indeed, Ch'len did appear uncomfortable in their surroundings.

"From what I hear," Kalian said, "You're the one being hailed as a hero. *The hero of Shandar'* is a title I've heard more than once."

Roland shrugged. "Being a hero isn't all it's cracked up to be. Turns out, there's no *actual* reward for saving the galaxy. Plus, everyone knows my face now, so hunting bad guys just became a lot harder."

Kalian could see that the bounty hunter was feeling awkward saying his goodbyes. "Just be here when I get back," he said to Roland. "Teaching you to fly is going to be hilarious."

Roland laughed, back in his element. "I'll be ruling the Conclave before you make it back, kid."

As one, Kalian, Li'ara and the Gomar began their journey across the desert. Of course, Roland had one last thing to say.

"Hey, Red!" he shouted. "When you get bored of him, I'll always have a bunk waiting for you on the *Rackham!*"

Li'ara smiled and gave the bounty hunter the finger. "I'm going to miss him..." she said quietly.

Kalian laughed as they waved their last goodbyes before entering the cool air of the ship. Upon their arrival on the bridge, a circular console dominating the centre of the room came to life. A holographic map filled the space with the entire galaxy, laying it bare before them.

Vox pointed at a cluster of stars on the far side of the galaxy. "I want to go here!"

Ariah pointed at another cluster. "We should go here!"

Garrion shook his head. "The data files say there are carbon-based life forms over here. Let's see what they're like."

With no direction, everyone turned to Kalian, who had his arm comfortably around Li'ara's shoulders. "Let's get lost..."

DISCOVER MORE FROM

PHILIP C. QUAINTRELL

To hear more from Philip,
including book releases and exclusive content:

WEBSITE:
Philipcquaintrell.com

FACEBOOK:
Facebook.com/philipcquaintrell

INSTAGRAM:
@philipcquaintrell.author

AUTHOR NOTES

And so it ends. This was the first story I found rattling around inside my head, way back in 2013. I had grown tired of reading books that appeared to follow the same formula and delivered exactly what you expected them to. As a lover of stories, this was quite a hard thing to get my head around. As frustrating as it was, I could see only way of finding the stories I craved and, if you've gotten this far, you can see the results of that journey.

At the end of the day, writing books that I want to read is all I can do. It's what makes me happy and I would encourage everyone to try and write something, anything that can be squeezed from your imagination. The Terran Cycle was my first foray into the depths of my imagination, and though I would say I've found my roots in the fantasy genre, there is still a goodly portion of my brain devoted to outer-space.

I've certainly found a form of closure in bringing this story to an end. It feels like a long time since I first sat down and wrote the prologue to Intrinsic, especially since I have written a completely different trilogy (Echoes of Fate) in the middle of this series. Still, it always feels comfortable settling back into Kalian's head, my first creation. It's a strange feeling to know that a person created inside my mind is now in the minds of people I've never met. Oh dear. I appear to slipping into the philosophical realm. Back to the notes…

I originally planned all four in the series while working on a vascular ward in Leicester Royal Infirmary. In fact, some of the notes in front of me right now are on printed paper from the hospital. This form of planning is a writing process I no longer implore. Every chapter in the Terran Cycle could be found summed up in a brief paragraph or two in my notes, outlining every scene. This is certainly a good idea if you're just starting out and you want to make sure your story is going somewhere. It's easy to start writing your novel and then stop part way through because you have no idea where it's going. After I realised I could start and finish a full-length book, I was able to start the Echoes of Fate series with very few outlines, focusing mainly on character profiles and places.

I can only hope that you can see the difference, specifically the improvements, in my writing as you've progressed through the entire series. Between Intrinsic and Legacy, I wrote five other books, so there really should be signs of growth. Growing as a writer wasn't something I particularly thought about until I started Rise of the Ranger, as before this my focus had been entirely on the story. I see now that writing a good story is only part of what makes an author an author.

I'm sure many writers will agree that when you finish your project, the only thing you want to do is put it out there and move on to the next thing. Such is the nature of an over-active imagination. I understand now the importance of the editing process, marketing, formatting, and generally investing in good equipment and software in making a book. This can be something of a slog, but it makes the end product something you can be proud of. Before starting Legacy, I upgraded everything I used to format and edit my books and went through the previous three Terran novels from cover-to-cover before re-publishing them. They're still not the best received books out there, but I'm proud of the story I've told and the new versions I've republished alongside this one.

I hope you've enjoyed this series. At present, I have no future plans for this universe or the characters within, but like I said, there's still a goodly portion of my imagination devoted to sci-fi. Perhaps one day, I'll come back and see what Roland North is up to or discover the wonders of the galaxy alongside Kalian and the Gomar.

If you keep up with me on Facebook, *Philip C. Quaintrell*, I'll keep you updated on any future projects as well as the audio releases from Podium Publishings. If you get a chance, I would appreciate any review you might leave online. Every one helps to get the word out, something we self-publishers rely on.

Until the next time...

RISE OF THE RANGER: THE ECHOES SAGA BOOK ONE

Read on for prologue

PROLOGUE

THE SOUND of men dying in battle wasn't unknown to Asher. In the past, he had remained hidden, while his father and brothers had fought against rival clans in the Wild Moores. The boy had heard the sound of their weapons clash and the noises men made when they died, but he had never heard the sounds that drifted through the open window now, carried in the wake of a hundred war horns, for when the elves went into battle, it could not be called a conflict or a skirmish, as it was with the human tribes, but was in fact given another name that was new to Asher.

The elves called it a war...

The cries of the two armies were drowned out by the ominous beating of heavy wings that thundered overhead, delivering death by the hundreds across the battlefield below, their fiery breath igniting the sky. The battle outside had spread, breaching Elethiah's great walls and drawing ever closer, the clash of steel against steel echoing through its stone corridors.

Asher dared to steal a glance over the window's wooden ledge, only to be terrified by the hulking shadow that flew across the moon, eclipsing its glow with bat-like wings. The boy quickly ducked, hugging the cold stone and scrambling for the safety of the large wooden table in the centre of the room. His nine-year-old body was too gangly for his young mind to control, and he barely registered the pain as his head bumped into the table leg. Asher's heart pounded in his chest at the sound of a roar no man could rightfully stand against. The great flying beasts went by another name that was new to the young boy, and the word felt strange in his mouth. The elves called them dragons!

The door to his right burst open in a splintering of wood, accompanied by the familiar song of swords colliding with incredible speed. From his sheltered vantage, Asher could only see a pair of armoured legs stagger into the room, crashing into the table, as another pair of legs followed him in, clad in a flowing white dress that danced around their foe. The laboured breaths of a man and a woman were matched by the slash and parry of their swords. The armoured legs jumped on to the table as metal scraped against the smooth wood, knocking over Asher's glass and the jug of water, before finally landing on the other side. Water washed over the parchments covering the table and poured over the edge, splashing the boy's hands and face.

The white dress dashed over the table, making no sound at all. Something softer than a sword struck the armoured man and sent him stumbling into a bookshelf. The white dress dropped to the floor once more and met its attacker with a flurry of swords and sparks.

The conflict came to a swift end as one of the swords hit the floor with a loud clatter, and hot red blood spattered against the stone. The armoured feet faltered, until a pair of knees fell to the floor, under the crumpling body of a dark-haired elf. Blood rushed from his throat and mixed with the water, slithering ever closer to where the boy knelt. Asher gasped, trying to crawl backward as the blood moved like a snake towards him.

"Asher!" The white dress wrinkled as the beautiful face of a blonde elf appeared under the table top. Her fair features were marred with concern at the sight of him. Droplets of blood streaked across her cheeks and golden hair, though it did nothing to reduce her beauty.

With one strong hand, she pulled him out from under the table, careful not to drag him through the blood. She steadied him by the shoulders and quickly checked him over for any injuries, her soft hands gliding over his skin.

"I'm fine." Asher gently reached for her hands and pushed them away.

The boy was always ashamed of his ragged human appearance in the company of such magnificent creatures. His dirty clothes and unwashed skin made him stand out even more than usual next to her perfect complexion and exquisite clothes.

"We need to find your father and brother. You need to get back to the Wild Moores as fast as possible, you will be safer there."

That statement alone was proof of their dire situation. If the Moores were safer than Elethiah, he hated to imagine what was going on beyond this room.

"I don't want to leave you, Nalana..." Asher looked into her crystal blue eyes and knew she would insist.

Nalana was the mother he'd never had and cared for him in a way his father and the rest of his clan never could. She had spent years teaching him the elven language, and countless days devoted to helping him read and write. He was the first of many Outlanders the elves planned to take in and teach to be civilised. After just four years of her tutelage, Asher knew he was already smarter than most of his clan, if not the strongest.

"There's no time, young one. You remember what I told you, about Valanis?"

Of course he remembered. Valanis was the tyrannical elf, set on ravaging the whole of Illian like a hungry plague of locusts. His name seemed to strike fear into the hearts of every elf in Elethiah. Asher's father had told him to leave elvish troubles to elves, but Elethiah stood on the edge of the Wild Moores, and it seemed Valanis had brought his madness to the Outlanders' home too.

"His army attacks without fear of death. I don't know how long our forces and the dragons can keep them at bay. The eastern wall is already breached and they are swarming the city." Nalana nodded to the dead body behind him. "I will get you as far as the kitchens; do you remember the door I showed you, our secret door?" He nodded absently, looking past her to the sound of fighting. "Take your family through there and run as fast as you can. Are you ready?"

Nalana took his hand and picked up her curved blade off the table. Asher had never seen her wield a sword before. It was hard to fathom that someone so delicate and gentle could be so deadly. The boy couldn't take his eyes off the sword and its unique shine, as the Outlander had never seen a sword as ornate and well-crafted as this. His own people could do no better than blunt axes and weak spears. The flat of the blade was engraved with runes he had yet to learn, and he once again felt the hunger for knowledge that Nalana had awoken in him.

They made their way through the halls and adjoining rooms as quickly and quietly as they could, Asher by comparison to Nalana sounding like a team of Centaurs. When eventually the choice of direction arose, left or right, Nalana hesitated. Asher had just enough fear to extinguish his excitement at the path the elf chose. They soon passed under a large wooden arch that led into Elethiah's grand library, a forbidden place. The race of men was not granted access to the ancient tomes of the elves, for fear of the books being mishandled.

It was everything he imagined and more as the room opened up into a tall oval shape, covered in wall-to-wall books and walkways connected by spiral staircases. Every corner was illuminated by a soft glow, emanating from yellow orbs that floated between the shelves. The orbs were a simple creation for any elf with a basic understanding of magic - it was an understanding Asher was decades away from grasping. Long tables of red-brown wood filled the space between the archway and the double doors on the other side. Asher knew that the library offered a shortcut through the main palace and had always hated taking the longer route to reach Nalana's teaching room.

Without warning, the doors were violently thrust open as four elves in dark armour and shadowy cloaks strode into the room.

Nalana pushed Asher back, putting herself instinctively in front of him while raising her sword. "Stay back, Asher."

He did as he was told and clung to the wooden arch at his back.

Nalana calmly walked around the long table and closed the gap between her and the dark elves. Their movements were hard for Asher to keep track of as they advanced on her with great speed, each of their swords angled to remove a limb. Nalana's grace and precision were unparalleled by the dark elves, and she deflected two of the strikes whilst narrowly dodging the others. Metal rang against metal in every direction as the fighters danced across the table top. Nalana looked a true warrior, using her hands and feet to push the dark elves back, whilst knocking a short-haired elf off the table with a strong backhand from her sword.

"Nalana!" Nalana's younger brother, Elym, charged into the library with his dark hair flowing out behind him.

Elym deftly flipped on to the table and charged in with his double-ended spear. Nalana cut down the tallest of their attackers, removing his head and the hand of another elf in one blow. Elym took the advantage and impaled the one-handed elf with his spear, twisting his own body to avoid the blade of the third attacker. Asher watched as the back-handed dark elf rose from the floor, ready to swipe Nalana's legs out. The Outlander reacted without thinking, to protect his teacher, and pulled a leather-bound book off the nearest shelf and threw it into the dark elf's face. The surprise blow was all Nalana needed to drop to one knee and drive her blade straight down into the elf's head, burying it deep into his body.

Elym's sudden cry of pain pierced the library, as his blood splattered against the wood. Nalana spun on the ball of her foot and whipped her sword across the final dark elf's chest, slicing through the armour and splitting his ribcage. Nalana paid him no heed as he toppled off the table, instead rushing to the aid of her brother. Asher had met Elym several times over the years, but the young elf had never quite agreed with teaching the wild humans, who had arrived from lands unknown to the elves.

Asher ran to the table, making a wide circle around the dead elves. Nalana held Elym in her arms as blood slowly poured from a gash across his gut. He groaned in pain and clung tightly to his sister.

"I have seen worse little brother..."

"We don't have time." Elym's words came through gritted teeth. "I came from the Hall of Life." The young Elf reached into his tunic and tugged at the silver chain around his neck. He presented Nalana with a rugged, black crystal the size of his little finger. "Valanis is here. They're preparing to cast the Amber spell..." He placed the crystal in the palm of her hand. "He's already killed the King and Lady Syla. We need to keep it safe, Nalana."

She remained silent; staring at the necklace with an expression Asher couldn't read. Elym's pain-filled cry brought her out of the reverie soon enough. Nalana looked from her brother to Asher, gripping the crystal until her knuckles whitened.

"Asher..." Nalana called him closer. "I will stay with Elym. You need to find your family and make for the Wild Moores. Stop for nothing." Nalana rested her brother's head on her knee and quickly looped the necklace over Asher's head. "Take this and hide it deep in the forest. I will come for you when the battle is over." Asher stared at the crystal sitting in the middle of his chest before Nalana tucked it into his ragged top. "Run Asher!"

With a lasting look at the siblings, he ran for the door.

Asher made for the kitchens, calling his father and brother as he did. Fighting had broken out across the palace, forcing him to search for new ways through the stone corridors.

"Asher!" His father's voice echoed down the hall. Typically, they were already hiding around the kitchens, always looking for food to take back to the Moores. "Where have you been? We were about to leave without you!"

Such were the ways of his people. You either help the clan or you get left behind.

His older brother looked truly scared, clearly having witnessed the elves in combat or one of the winged beasts that swarmed above the city. Asher's father was sweating, no doubt fearful for his own survival while being slowed by his sons.

"This way, follow me!" Asher led them through the kitchens and down into an old tunnel, long abandoned in favour of newer refurbishments.

His brother and father ran on ahead, while Asher closed the kitchen hatch behind them. Their splashing was easy to follow once Asher jumped off the last rung. At the end of the tunnel was an old wooden door that allowed for a small grid of moonlight to illuminate the wet ground and moss-covered walls.

"He'll never make it!" His brother's voice echoed through the tunnel as the pair ran full pelt through the doorway.

Their doubt in Asher's ability to survive only spurred him on to run faster.

Both his father and brother ran into the Moonlit Plains, heading straight for the Wild Moores as if the dragons themselves were at their heels - neither looked back to check on Asher.

Before reaching the door, Asher heard one last roar, this time from somewhere deep inside the palace. He didn't stop, but rather pressed on as fast as his legs would take him. The green fields, which glowed under the moonlight, came into view beyond the door. His father and brother ran for cover under the canopy of a large oak tree.

"Keep running!" his Father shouted.

Asher's chest burned, desperate for breath, as he ran for the moonlight. The black crystal around his neck pulled at his attention when it floated out in front of him, still tethered to his neck. The unexplainable occurrence didn't stop him from running through the threshold with all haste.

Asher ran through and felt the cool night air suddenly transform into warmth, as blinding light erupted from all around. Dropping into the field, Asher covered his head, fearing the hot fury of what was surely a dragon's breath. An eternity went by as he waited for the inevitable pain and darkness of death to take him. But when death should have claimed him, Asher instead heard the squawk of a bird overhead and the warmth on his back was nothing but pleasant.

The Outlander opened his eyes to a world he didn't recognise.

A midday sun beat down on a field of overgrown, faded yellow grass. Asher stood up in a daze, his ankles deep in bog water where it had moments ago been hard ground and short green grass. He took a breath, slowly turning to survey his bizarre surroundings. The city of Elethiah remained behind him, where it should be, but as a shadow of its former glory. The stone had darkened and become overgrown with weeds and thick roots, which crawled up the great walls. To his left were the remains of a demolished tower, lying in ruin where it had fallen. The oak tree, where his father and brother had taken shelter, was gone, a broken rotten stump in its place and his family nowhere in sight.

Beyond the stump, he could still see the Wild Moores in the distance. The forest was over five hundred miles from north to south with incredible depth. Asher gasped for breath, unbelieving of his new reality. Where had the night gone? Where had Valanis's forces and the dragons gone? Where was his family? He cried for his father and his brother, screaming at the top of his voice.

The reply came not from his father or brother, but from the howl of a creature he had never heard before. Asher ducked into the long grass, seeing dark shapes moving through the strands, crouched low to hide their true form. Something slipped out of his shirt and he held it in front of him. The black crystal. He didn't have time to think about it before the howls came again, much closer this time. He dropped the crystal back into his shirt and ran for the forest that lay sprawled before him. His clan was surely in there somewhere and they would protect him. The rapid padding of many heavy feet came from behind, but he had no idea of their number.

It wasn't long before he realised the forest was simply too far away. The Outlander would never make it before the predators caught him. Changing course, Asher ran for the collection of large rocks dug into the small hillside on his left. Maybe he could lose them in there.

By the time Asher reached the first rock, he was exhausted. He fell to the grass and crawled further into the outcropping. Rolling on to his back, he saw a lumbering creature climb the rock at his feet and stretch to its full height. Dark green scales covered its sloping leathery head, with two thick arms reaching down to its knees and ending in pointed fingers of sharp bone. Its face was closer to that of a lizard, with several rows of razor-sharp teeth. A screeching howl preceded five more, who appeared from behind the other stones, licking their maws with long slimy tongues.

The first creature jumped off the rock, blocking out the sun as it came to land on top of him - only it never did land, at least not alive. The beast had been struck in the face by an arrow, mid-air. Looking up from his back, Asher glimpsed a stranger came charging over his head and diving into the fray, with a short-sword in one hand and a bow in the other. The beasts leaped at their new prey, only to have their limbs removed with every slash of the stranger's sword. His movements were similar to that of an elf but Asher could also see the differences; this was a man.

The fight was over in seconds and the stranger was standing amid a heap of diced monsters.

The stranger turned to Asher, his sword shining under the sun. He wore dark leather armour, engraved with unusual, intricate patterns and a grey cloak which spread out across the ground, collecting mud. Perhaps the strangest element of his appearance was the red blindfold he wore. He had apparently defeated those beasts without his sight. The stranger proceeded to remove the red cloth from his face, revealing shadowed, brown eyes and curly black hair.

"Gobbers," the stranger stated flatly, wiping the blood off of his sword with the edge of his cloak.

Asher had heard Nalana speak of such creatures and was thankful for surviving the encounter.

"And who might you be?" the stranger asked.

Asher's eyes searched the plains for his father once more. "I am... Asher," he stuttered.

"Is that a statement or a question, boy?" The stranger flicked his bow in the air, activating a series of mechanisms and cogs built into the wood. A moment later the bow had folded into itself, before the stranger placed it out of sight, under his cloak.

Had Asher not been too stunned by the events of the past few minutes, he would have marvelled at the bow's construction.

"My name is Asher," he replied more boldly, standing up and wiping the dirty water from his face.

The stranger regarded him curiously. "Is that it? Just Asher? Well, this is no place for a boy to wander; between the swamps of Elethiah and the Wild Moores... you must have a talent for survival." His voice had a foreign twang to it that Asher couldn't place.

The boy nodded absently, trying to make sense of the stranger's words. From here, Asher could see what remained of Elethiah - its beautiful spires and domed towers were gone, with nothing but decay hanging over the entire land. It was more akin to a swamp now, the splendid Moonlit Plains nothing but a memory. He wrapped his hands around his arms feeling the cold against his wet skin.

The stranger announced, "I am Nasta Nal-Aket, of Nightfall..."

Asher remained silent, unaware of the man's significance or the place he was from.

"Have you never heard of it, boy?"

Asher shook his head slowly.

"I am a spectre, an Arakesh," he stated proudly.

Asher's face dropped at the sound of the elvish word; he knew that word.

"I am an assassin," Nasta Nal-Aket confirmed.

Asher stood his ground, as his father had taught him when facing a bear.

"If I had to guess from your appearance, I would say you're an Outlander."

Asher became self-conscious of the black tattoo, outlining a wolf's fang, below his left eye, signifying he was from a clan of hunters.

"I didn't think your kind strayed beyond the Wild Moores these days. What are you doing out here?" The assassin tucked his blindfold into his belt, letting it hang loosely in the breeze.

Asher noted the assassin steal a look at Elethiah, but he appeared physically disturbed by the landmark and walked further into the hillside as if to gain more distance.

The Outlander looked up at the sun and knew it should be the moon that greeted him. "I was..." Asher didn't know how to explain it. "The elves were fighting and..." He could only look at the ruins of Elethiah.

Nasta looked from the ruins to Asher in puzzlement. "Elves? Are you talking about the Dark War?"

Asher didn't know anything of a Dark War and began to look round for his family once more. They wouldn't be out there looking for him, he had fallen behind. He was alone.

"And what would a young Outlander know of a battle over a thousand years past?"

The gravity of Asher's situation drained the blood from his head, blurring his vision. "A thousand years..." He spun in every direction, desperate to find something, anything familiar. The landscape began to blur when the colours of the world faded and his vision narrowed. The ground rose up to greet him and the darkness swallowed him whole.

Printed in Great Britain
by Amazon